wilde and deadly

WILDE SECURITY WORLDWIDE
BOOK 1

TONYA BURROWS

author's note

It's been ten years since I wrote the original five *Wilde Security* books, but the Wilde brothers have never let me go. Serious Greer, uptight Reece, daredevil twins Cam and Vaughn, and troublemaker Jude still hold my heart, and I've long wanted to return to their world. I toyed with different ideas—long-lost cousins, a secret brother, even an alternate reality—but in the end, the best way to revisit them was through the next generation.

With this book, I'm launching *Wilde Security Worldwide*, a brand-new series featuring the children of the Wilde brothers... and a few other familiar faces!

Buckle up. It's going to be another Wilde ride!

-Tonya

The Wilde Family Tree

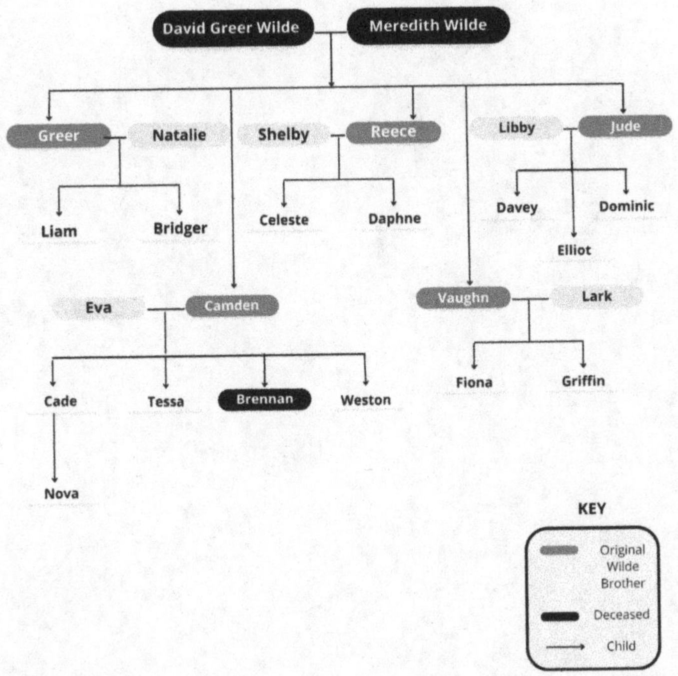

one

SEVEN DAYS.

Seven long fucking days.

Davey Wilde groaned and leaned back in his office chair. His first official week as the head of Wilde Security Worldwide was a goddamn disaster.

It started with him being tied to his bed on Christmas Eve and having his dog stolen by a woman he couldn't decide if he hated or was helplessly, irrationally attracted to. Rowan fucking Bristow—danger wrapped in temptation, a beautiful weapon he'd never learned how to resist. Sleek and lethal, all sun-warmed skin over wiry muscle, straight dark hair spilling down her back like ink, and those damned golden eyes that saw straight through him. Every smirk, every sharp-edged taunt was a calculated strike, designed to burrow under his skin, to make him forget what was at stake.

He'd chased her across three states, following every scrap of intel, every whisper, every hint she might've left behind, only to find himself one step behind each time. The woman was an expert at disappearing, and every dead end stoked his frustration to dangerous new heights.

But Rowan wasn't his only problem.

Half his cousins were considering mutiny—led by Cade, the smug asshole—and two major clients were threatening to pull their contracts unless certain vague "security concerns" were addressed immediately. He'd barely had time to breathe, much less sleep, caught in a constant battle between managing the company and tracking down the one woman who'd always had the power to tear his carefully controlled life to pieces.

He still couldn't believe she'd gotten the drop on him like that. Tied to his bed with his own fucking Christmas lights—could she have chosen anything more humiliating?—while she calmly made off with Luka.

His dog, for Christ's sake.

It was a low blow, even for her.

And the worst part? He still wanted her. Even now, his pulse raced at the thought of her, at the memory of her body pressed against his, her lips brushing his ear as she whispered tauntingly, teasingly. He should have known better—*did* know better—and still, he'd let himself fall into her carefully laid trap.

He scrubbed a hand over his face, fingertips

rasping against days-old stubble. Sleep had become a distant luxury. Every time he closed his eyes, Rowan's face—sharp angles softened by full lips, tiger eyes gleaming with mischief and challenge—was right there.

Haunting him.

Daring him to chase her down again.

And, dammit, he knew he would.

And not only because her father had hired him to find her.

The weight of responsibility settled heavily on his shoulders, but he refused to let it crush him. He was a Wilde, dammit, and Wildes didn't buckle under pressure. They thrived on it.

As he sat in his new office, poring over the latest report from his cousin Daphne about a cyberattack on their network, his cell phone buzzed against his uncle's—no, *his*. It was *his* mahogany desk now. Solid, heavy, imposing. The kind of desk meant for a man who commanded a room with a single look and made decisions that shaped empires.

Would he ever get used to sitting here, making the decisions that used to be Uncle Greer's to make?

Jesus.

He needed to get his shit together. Fast.

His phone vibrated again. Elliot, his middle brother. He started to pick it up—

The door burst open.

A tall, blond man strode in without knocking,

moving with the easy arrogance of someone who had never once hesitated before inserting himself into a situation. He was all effortless charm and careless confidence, dressed in a crisp, open-collared button-down and dark slacks that should have looked polished but somehow gave the impression he'd just rolled out of bed wearing them. His golden hair was too long, a little too artfully tousled, as if he'd spent the morning tangled in silk sheets—or wanted people to think he had.

Jean-Sabin Cavalier was the kind of man who made bad decisions look like a good time.

Davey dragged a hand down his face again, inhaled deeply, and exhaled even slower.

Of course.

Because the universe wasn't content with just testing him this week—it wanted to see exactly how close he was to snapping.

He steeled himself, locking down his patience before lifting his gaze to meet Sabin's smug grin. "Whatever it is, the answer is no."

Sabin threw his long body down in one of the worn leather chairs and hooked a leg over the arm. He never sat like a normal person.

"Ever heard of this crazy new invention called an orgasm?" His voice was thick with bayou heat, a slow Cajun drawl that made every sentence sound just a little bit like trouble. "Best stress relief there is, for real."

Davey pinched the bridge of his nose. As irritating as Sabin could be, the man was a genius when it came to intelligence gathering—and he was one of the very few people Davey trusted implicitly. Even if that trust came at the expense of his sanity.

"What do you want, Sabin?"

Sabin's grin widened, white teeth flashing against his tanned face. "To win the office bettin' pool on when you'll finally snap and attack your computer with a baseball bat. I know you a stubborn bastard so I said you wouldn't, but it been a week and you done nothing but *boudee*. I'm seeing cracks in the armor, *mon ami*. Gotta shore 'em up, or you're gonna lose me some serious cash."

A growl rumbled deep in Davey's chest, even though amusement threaded reluctantly through his irritation. Sabin had a gift for cutting tension—often by making Davey want to strangle him. "Your concern for my mental health is touching." His phone vibrated again, and he reached for it. "Unless you've got anything useful—"

Sabin leaned forward, eyes crinkling mischievously. "Actually, I do got somethin'." He reached into his back pocket and withdrew a crumpled piece of paper, smoothing it carefully on the polished wood.

Davey eyed it with suspicion. It looked like Sabin had fished it straight from the trash. Still, he picked it up, scanning the printout of a map dotted with red marks. "What's this?"

"That is a list of places upstate where Rowan might be hiding out. My contacts came through with some intel."

By "contacts," he almost certainly meant his old man. Jean-Luc Cavalier, retired mercenary and former right-hand man to Gabe Bristow before he retired to spend his days fishing on Lake Pontchartrain. "Tell me you didn't mention that I lost Bristow's daughter while she's supposed to be under my protection."

Sabin grinned. "*Mon père* can keep a secret better than anyone—*mais*, no, I didn't tell him. He's outta the game now and likes it that way. This came from some old buddies from my less-than-legal days before I got respectable-ish. They still got fingers in them pies that are a bit too hot for regular hands."

Davey exhaled slowly, his frustration ebbing as he studied the map. He needed something—anything— to go on. "All right, what's the catch?"

Sabin's smile dimmed just a fraction. "These ain't the usual hidin' spots. They're places folks don't ask questions 'cause they're too scared of the answers. If Rowan's there, gettin' her out won't be a simple extraction."

Davey nodded, scenarios already clicking into place. He'd known Rowan wouldn't hide somewhere safe and predictable—not her style. "And what do you get out of this?"

Sabin spread his hands wide, a shrug lifting his shoulders slightly. "Just doin' my part for Wilde Security Worldwide. Hopin' to keep my boss from spiralin' into sleepless nights and unshaved mornin's. Nobody wants to see that." His grin returned. "If you find Rowan, we all look good, yeah?"

"You're protecting your bet in the pool, aren't you?"

Sabin laughed, a big, boisterous sound that filled the office. "Guilty as charged." He stood, rolling smoothly out of the chair. "Consider this part community service, part self-preservation."

"I appreciate the intel." Davey also rose, folding the map and tucking it into his jacket pocket. "Seriously, Sabin. I owe you one."

Sabin paused at the door, glancing back with a familiar, mischievous gleam. "Put in a good word with your cousin, and we'll call it even."

"Which cousin? I have nine." Only four were female, but he wouldn't put it past Sabin to try his luck with any one of them.

Sabin's grin turned wicked, blue eyes sparking with mischief. "The lovely Fiona, of course. That woman tougher than gator hide, but I think I'm wearin' her down. Yesterday, she almost smiled at me —*mais*, I felt that one straight in my bones."

"What makes you think I have any sway with her?"

"Come on, Davey. Fiona respects you more than

most. A little nudge from you? Might just tip them scales in my favor."

"She thinks you're trouble, Sabin. And she's not wrong."

"Pshh." He waved that off with a lazy flick of his wrist. "What's life without a little trouble? You tell her I ain't near as bad as the stories say. Maybe even throw in a lil' somethin' about my legendary charm and devastatin' good looks."

"How about you just focus on keeping yourself out of the kind of trouble that ends with more paperwork for me?"

Sabin's rich laugh echoed down the hallway as he left. He was definitely *not* going to stay out of trouble.

Davey turned back to his desk with a sigh. He'd talk to Fiona later—not that he could change her mind about Sabin, but at least he could warn her before she got tangled too deep with the incorrigible ex-thief.

As silence reclaimed the office, his thoughts drifted back to Rowan. He unfolded the map again, fingertip tracing the red marks Sabin had made. Each dot was a possibility, a place Rowan might be hiding—or trapped. His gut clenched at the thought. She was dangerous, infuriating, and completely unpredictable, yet somehow, he couldn't stop himself from worrying about her.

He'd underestimated her once. Thought she was just another job: protect the daughter of a fellow ex-SEAL. Easy.

Except Rowan was anything but easy.

She was a firecracker, a deadly mix of danger and allure that mesmerized and exploded through his life, leaving nothing behind but sparks, smoke, and an unfamiliar ache in his chest.

Davey shoved the map into his jacket pocket and stood. It didn't matter how far she ran or how much hell he had to wade through. He was going to find Rowan Bristow—and when he did, they'd settle this thing between them. For good.

two

THE CRACKED motel mirror reflected a face she barely recognized—her father's sharp angles and hazel eyes staring back, shadowed with exhaustion. She didn't remember the lines around her mouth being quite so deep, but maybe that's what running did to a person. Maybe that was what hiding cost.

God, she was tired.

At the foot of the bed, Luka shifted, letting out a sleepy sigh as he nestled his head against her knee. Rowan stroked his velvety ears, anchoring herself in the dog's calm presence. She'd dragged Davey's dog halfway across the country, justifying it in every way except the one that mattered.

She wanted him to come for her.

Every choice she had made, every step she had taken, had brought her here. A dingy motel room miles away from home. Miles away from family. The kind of place where guilt and regret crept under the door like the draft of cold January air.

Her phone buzzed on the bedside table, and Rowan's pulse jumped, a traitorous flicker of hope flaring before she could crush it. Davey? Her stomach tightened, dread replacing hope as quickly as it had surfaced.

It wasn't Davey.

It was Rue.

She nearly ignored the call—but Rue never called just to chat. In Rowan's experience, her younger sister only reached out when she was neck-deep in trouble and needed rescuing—again. Rue was mayhem incarnate, always diving headfirst into chaos and expecting Rowan to pull her out before she drowned.

But what if this call was about Dad? Fear tightened in her chest, sharp and sudden. Ignoring Rue wasn't an option—not when their father was still recovering from surgery.

Five minutes. She could spare at least five minutes. The line was encrypted, and she was safe.

She tapped the screen. "All right, Rue. What trouble are you in this time?"

Rue's face filled the screen, her expression immediately morphing into a mixture of relief, irritation, and concern. With her honey-blonde hair, scattering of freckles, and ridiculously dainty features, Rue was so much like their mother that it sometimes stole Rowan's breath.

"What trouble am *I* in?" Rue scoffed. "You can't be serious! You're the one who's been MIA for months. Where the hell are you?"

Rowan sighed, running a hand through her tangled hair. "Are you okay? Are Mom and Dad?"

"Well, Mom's worried sick about you, and Dad..." Rue trailed off, and her expression softened.

"Dad, what?" Rowan asked, her heart rate quickening. "Is he okay?"

Rue's eyes narrowed again, that softness evaporating like it had never been there. "Oh, now you care?"

"That's not fair. I've always cared. You know that."

"Running away in the middle of the night after he had major surgery without so much as a goodbye doesn't exactly scream '*I care.*'"

Guilt twisted sharply in Rowan's gut, heavy and bitter. Rue wasn't wrong—but Rowan couldn't tell her the truth, either. It would only endanger her sister further. "I had my reasons," she finally managed, knowing the words were hollow even as she said them.

"Oh, I'm sure you did." Rue's tone was biting. "Let me guess— it has something to do with that Wilde guy you're so obsessed with. You know Dad hired him to find you?"

Heat crept up Rowan's neck. "I am not obsessed with Davey."

At the sound of Davey's name, Luka lifted his head

from her knee. The dog's brown eyes were steady, warm with a loyalty Rowan knew she didn't deserve. She swallowed hard, guilt and longing colliding inside her, painful and sharp.

"Right," Rue said. "That's why you stole his dog."

"I didn't steal him. I... borrowed him." Even as she said the words, she realized how dumb they sounded.

"Borrowed?" Rue's eyes bugged out almost comically. "You can't borrow a living creature!"

"I'm going to give him back."

"You'd better. Elliot says Davey's been tearing the country apart looking for you two."

"Wait. Since when do you and Elliot talk?"

Rue's cheeks flushed a soft pink, and for the first time in weeks, a real smile tugged at Rowan's mouth.

"You like him."

"Of course I like him. He's a nice guy."

"No, you *like him*, like him."

"That's not—" Rue sputtered, her cheeks flushing a deeper shade of pink. "This isn't about me. It's about *you stealing Davey's dog*. I thought you were trying to avoid him, but you might as well have sent him an engraved invitation to come after you by taking Luka. What were you thinking?"

Rowan looked at Luka, who was still watching her with almost human-like focus. She stroked his ear and realized she had no answer, so she stayed quiet.

Rue nodded. "You want him to find you. I see it all over your face."

"No." The denial was automatic.

"Oh, come on. You've had a crush on Davey since we were kids."

"And apparently, you've had a crush on Elliot?"

"Rowan. Deflecting won't work on me."

"No, I don't have a crush on him." That would be simple. Manageable. What she felt was worse—messier, tangled, impossible. But she wasn't going to tell Rue that. "I don't like him, and he hates me."

"Which is why you've been fucking each other's brains out every chance you get, right?"

"Jesus, Rue." Her sister may look sweet and innocent, but she'd been raised by badasses, too, and had the mouth to match.

"I'm just saying. Elliot mentioned how he and Dom found Davey naked and tied to his bed on Christmas morning. But I'm sure you know *nothing* about that, right?"

"Elliot needs to keep his mouth shut." Rowan's whole body lit up like a sparkler at the memory of all of that powerful muscle and stubborn man tied up under her, at her mercy, helpless and wanting. She shook her head, trying to clear the image. "And that was... I needed to get away, and he wasn't going to let me go."

Rue snickered. "You left him there for *hours*!"

"He deserved it," Rowan muttered, but even she could hear the lack of conviction in her voice. "He was being an ass that night." While simultaneously giving her multiple shattering orgasms. But, still. An ass.

"Uh-huh," Rue said.

"Seriously, Rue, it's not what you think."

"Oh really? Because I think you two have more chemistry than a meth lab, and you've been dancing around each other for years, pretending to hate each other while secretly pining away."

"We're not pining," Rowan snapped. "It's not like that with us."

"Then what's it like?"

She exhaled in a rush. "I don't get your sudden interest in my sex life, but we... made an agreement. We don't like each other, so there is no chance of ever becoming more than fuck buddies. It works for both of us."

"Uh-huh," Rue said again, doubt heavy in her voice. Then she sighed, and she suddenly looked exhausted, which was more than a little worrying. Rue was caffeine personified, constantly bouncing around the globe from one adventure to the next, thriving off thrills and spontaneity. But right now, she just looked tired and sad.

"Rue, is everything okay with you?"

Her smile fell flat. "Of course. I just... I'd like to see my big sister—"

"You're seeing me now."

"*In person,*" Rue stressed. "Before I go on my next trip."

Something about the way she said the word "trip" made the little hairs prickle at the back of Rowan's neck. "Where are you going?"

"Just taking some scientists to Antarctica. No big deal."

Rowan's eyes narrowed. "Antarctica? In January? That sounds dangerous."

Rue waved a dismissive hand. "It's fine. January is summer down there, and I've done plenty of cold-weather expeditions before."

"Yeah, but... what kind of scientists? What are they studying?"

"Just some climatologists and geologists. Boring stuff." Rue's eyes slid away from the camera. "Look, can we not talk about my work?"

The abrupt change of subject set off alarm bells in Rowan's head. "Rue, what aren't you telling me?"

"Probably about as much as you're not telling me," she shot back. "You share, I share."

"No."

"Then, also, no." Rue sighed, her shoulders slumping. "I just miss you, okay? Mom and Dad miss you. Why don't you come home?"

A lump formed in Rowan's throat. "Is Dad losing his mind?"

"You know he is. Mom practically had to tie him down to keep him from coming after you."

"Is he okay?"

"He's grumpy."

"He's always grumpy. But he's healing well?"

After decades of dealing with a busted-up foot from a car accident that happened before they were born, Gabe Bristow had finally been forced to have the limb amputated below his knee late last summer. Rowan had waited until he'd made it safely through surgery, then took off, figuring she'd have a good head start with him in the hospital for two weeks. Of course she'd expected Dad to send one of his guys after her—probably Jackson Quinn or Wyatt Warrick, since they were poised to take over the team when Dad finally decided to retire. What she hadn't expected was for him to hire the job out to Wilde Security Worldwide—to Davey, the one person she needed to avoid at all costs, the one person who was like gravity, constantly pulling her back into his orbit.

Did Dad know how she felt about Davey?

Maybe.

Probably.

And, as usual, Dad had out-maneuvered her.

"Yes, he's healing," Rue said in answer to her question. "He's started using the prosthetic, but he can't move as quickly as he'd like. And that pisses him off. He hates the walker more than he hated his old cane."

Rowan smiled at the image of her big, tough father using a walker. He *would* hate that. He'd barely tolerated the cane, using it only when absolutely necessary.

Unlike Audrey Bristow, who had embraced aging by letting her hair go steel gray—according to her, she was in her "witchy era"—Gabe steadfastly refused to admit he was getting older. He had a workout regimen that most men half his age wouldn't be able to keep up with, and at the rate he was going, he would live to be one hundred and fifty.

Unless something happened to him.

Unless Rowan's enemies went after him to get to her.

And he was vulnerable right now, healing from a major surgery, learning to use his prosthetic.

Her smile faded at the thought. "I can't come home. I'll put everyone in danger."

Rue rolled her eyes. "Uh, hello? Remember who we live with. Our 'uncles' are as scary as our father. I think they can handle a bit of danger."

The "uncles" were not blood-related but Dad's brothers-in-arms. They could handle themselves, but they were all mostly retired now.

"It's not just a bit of danger," Rowan said, frustration seeping into her tone. "It's not something they can handle with an old rifle and a couple of hand grenades."

Rue's golden-brown eyes narrowed. "So what's your plan, then? Run away and hide forever?"

Rowan glanced down at Luka again, his warm body comforting against her leg. She had no intention of hiding, but she wasn't about to tell Rue that. "If that's what it takes."

Her sister sighed heavily and ran a hand through

her honey-colored hair in a gesture that was so reminiscent of their father that it made Rowan's heart clench. "That's not what Dad would want."

"Dad can't dictate my life forever."

"No," Rue said quietly. "Of course not. But he loves you, and he wants you safe."

But I'm not safe. Nobody I love is safe.

Silence stretched between them for several seconds before Rue finally spoke again. "Mom wants to talk to you."

A lump formed in Rowan's throat. She hadn't spoken to her mother since she'd disappeared from home months ago. As much as she wanted to hear her mother's voice, she also dreaded the conversation that would follow. Audrey Bristow wasn't a woman who minced words.

"She'd be pissed if I said no, wouldn't she?"

"Oh, furious."

And in Rowan's opinion, their easy-going mom's fury was much more frightening than their dad's. She glanced at the clock in the corner of her screen. More than five minutes had passed, but she could spare a few more. "Okay, give her the phone. But *not* Dad."

The screen was blank for a second, and then came the familiar face of her mother. Audrey Bristow was undeniably beautiful even in her sixties, with her gray hair styled in loose waves around her face. She'd streaked in some color since Rowan had last seen her—purples and teals. Her amber eyes sparkled with a warmth that Rowan wanted to wrap herself up in.

"Rowan Kendra Bristow," Audrey chided gently, her tone laced with exasperated affection. "You're every bit as stubborn as your father."

Tears burned suddenly in Rowan's eyes, catching her off guard. She felt like she was five again, trapped in a nightmare, desperately wanting her mother's arms around her. "Hi, Mom."

"There's my fierce girl," Audrey murmured. "You've been missed."

Silence fell between them. What could she say? That she had missed them too? That she wished things were different?

"I'm sorry," she finally managed to choke out.

"Honey, I know," Audrey said softly. "And although I don't understand your reasons for leaving, I trust you have them. But you need to come home. Whatever trouble you're in... you don't have to face it alone. We're your family, remember? Your dad—your uncles —they can protect you. Let us help."

As much as Rowan longed to heed her mother's advice, she knew the danger she was in—and she knew she could not risk bringing it home to those she loved. And part of her was afraid that once they found out why she was running, once her dad found out, they wouldn't be nearly so understanding. What she'd done... what she'd agreed to do...

How could they ever forgive her?

How could Davey ever forgive her?

She was just tired. So tired. And alone. And scared.

Rowan swallowed hard, fighting back the tears that threatened to spill over. She couldn't break down in front of her mother. If she did, Audrey would move heaven and earth to get her home.

"I... I can't explain everything right now. But please trust me when I say it's safer for everyone if I stay away."

Audrey's eyes softened with understanding and a hint of sadness. "Oh, sweetheart. You didn't just get your father's stubbornness. You got his heart, too. Always trying to protect everyone, even at your own expense."

But that wasn't true. Gabe Bristow was a hero, a man who'd spent his life rushing into danger to save others. Rowan was none of those things.

"Mom, I..." she began, but the words trailed off, caught in the knot of emotions tightening in her throat. "I'm sorry. I have to go."

She hung up before her mother could respond and stared at the blank phone screen, half-expecting it to start ringing again immediately.

It didn't.

She turned it off to make sure, then exhaled in a rush and flopped back on the bed. Luka crawled up to lay beside her, his head resting in the crook of her arm.

You got his heart, too.

No. She wasn't selfless like her father. She hadn't

stolen Davey's dog to protect anyone. She'd taken Luka because she couldn't stand to leave behind the last connection she had to Davey. And, okay, yes, Rue was right— she'd done it so he'd be forced to come after her. Which painted a giant target on his back and defeated the whole point of... well, everything she was trying to accomplish.

Stupid. Reckless. Dangerous.

She needed to get her head out of her ass and fix this.

Rowan sat up abruptly, and Luka lifted his head, staring at her with concern. She stroked his ear reassuringly.

"I can't keep you, boy. As much as I want to."

He whined softly, and her heart clenched. She'd grown attached to the dog in the short time they'd been together. His steady presence had been a comfort during her lonely nights on the run. But she couldn't keep endangering Davey like this. If she returned his dog and somehow convinced Dad to release Davey from the assignment, he'd have no reason to chase her and put himself at risk.

She gathered her meager belongings, shoving them haphazardly into her backpack. Her fingers brushed the burner phone she'd purchased, and she hesitated.

Should she call Davey? Let him know she was bringing Luka back?

No. That would only complicate things.

He'd try to convince her to stay, to let him help. Or, worse, he'd alert her father, who would tell him to bring her home.

She zipped up her backpack with a decisive tug. She couldn't risk calling Davey or anyone else. She'd just sneak into his place, drop the dog off, and disappear again.

"Come on, Luka," she said softly. "Time to go home."

His ears perked up at her words, his tail wagging slightly, and guilt gnawed at her belly. Luka clearly missed Davey as much as she—

No. She wouldn't let herself finish that thought.

She walked to the door but then hesitated with her hand on the knob. Beyond it lay danger, uncertainty, and Davey Wilde.

The man she'd turned her life upside down for. The man she was trying to protect, though he didn't know it. The man she—

Nope. Again, she wasn't going to finish that thought, even inside her own head. So she sucked in a fortifying breath, opened the door...

And there he stood, as if she'd summoned him with her thoughts—Davey Wilde, dangerous and impossible, waiting right outside her door.

three

SHE LOOKS TIRED.

It was Davey's first thought when the door swung open just as he raised his hand to knock.

Her hazel eyes widened in shock, and her lips parted slightly as she took him in. They both stood frozen, the air between them charged with tension.

Luka's excited bark broke the spell. The dog bounded forward, nearly knocking Davey over in his enthusiasm. He dropped to one knee, burying his face in Luka's fur as the dog licked and whined happily.

"Hey, buddy. I missed you too."

When he looked up, Rowan was still standing in the doorway, emotions battling across her face. Shock. Worry. Anger. Fear.

It was the fear that hit him like a gut punch. The Rowan Bristow he knew was fearless, but now she looked like a frightened deer trapped in headlights, ready to bolt at any second.

"Don't even think about running," he said, rising to his feet. "We have this place surrounded."

"We?" Her gaze swung to the mostly empty parking lot behind him. "What'd you do, bring an army of squirrels?"

"Deadly squirrels," he corrected, deadpan. "They've been trained in advanced reconnaissance. Highly coordinated."

Her lips twitched, but she quickly schooled her features. "Sure they have. Bet you even taught them how to do synchronized nut juggling."

"Don't mock the squirrels," he shot back. "They've got tiny earpieces and everything. Very professional."

"Right." Her gaze narrowed, and Davey felt his half-baked lie crumble under her scrutiny. "It's just you, isn't it?"

Damn it. She saw right through him.

"Okay, you got me," he admitted, throwing his hands up. "But I've been tracking you for weeks, Rowan. You're not getting rid of me that easily."

Her lips parted, but she said nothing. He thought she might close the door in his face. Then she glanced down at Luka, who was wagging his tail like nothing was wrong.

"You shouldn't have come here," she said finally. "It's not safe."

"Not safe for who?" Davey stepped closer, crowding her space. "You? Or me?"

Her gaze darted back to the parking lot, her body taut like a coiled spring. "You need to leave."

"That's not happening," he said firmly. "What's going on?"

"None of your business."

"You made it my business when you took Luka."

The dog wiggled happily at the sound of his name, but as much as he wanted to hug his boy again, he didn't dare take his eyes off Rowan.

Her fingers tightened on the doorframe. "How did you find me?"

"I'm good at what I do. Though, if it makes you feel any better, you didn't make it easy. What were you thinking taking off like that? With my dog, no less?"

A ghost of a smile twisted her lips before disappearing. "Your dog came willingly." She reached into her pocket, and he tensed, but she only pulled out a jerky treat, which Luka hungrily snatched. The dog gulped it down, then leaned against her leg and stared up at her with adoring eyes.

"Traitor," Davey accused, crossing his arms. "We survived war together, and this is the thanks I get?"

Luka looked completely unrepentant, his tongue lolling from his mouth in a happy grin.

Rowan stroked his ear. "He knows who has the better treats."

"So you stooped to bribing my dog. Why? Why take him and leave me tied up in bed?"

Rowan's eyes flashed. Lots of guilt there, but it was smothered under her trademark defiance. "I didn't have a choice, Davey. You wouldn't have let me go otherwise."

"Damn right, I wouldn't have," he growled, taking another step closer. "You're in trouble, Rowan. I can help you, but you need to trust me."

Something vulnerable flickered in her eyes, but it was quickly replaced by steely resolve. She shook her head, her long dark hair swaying with the motion. "I don't want your help."

"But you need it. You've got that look, Rowan. The one that says you're about to do something reckless and probably illegal."

Her lips curved. "Reckless, maybe. Illegal? That depends on your definition."

"I'm not sure I want to know," he said, stepping closer. "But I do know you're not running from me again."

Her gaze darted past him to the parking lot, and he felt her muscles tense like she was a second away from bolting. His hand shot out, resting against the door-frame, caging her in. Not quite touching, but close enough that the heat between them felt like a live wire.

"Am I your prisoner now?" she asked, her voice light but her eyes dark with challenge.

"Are you planning to make a break for it?"

Rowan tilted her head, her hair brushing against his arm. "And if I do? Are you going to tackle me to the ground? Or does this mysterious squirrel army of yours handle the dirty work?"

Her voice was little more than a purr that sent shivers down Davey's spine.

He leaned in closer, trapping her against the doorframe. "I think we both know I prefer to handle you myself."

"You could try." She pushed up to her tiptoes and brushed her lips against his ear. "But we both know how that would end."

Images flashed through Davey's mind— tangled limbs, heated skin, breathy moans. He gritted his teeth, forcing himself to focus. "Don't start something you can't finish, Bristow."

"Who says I can't finish it?" Her fingers trailed down his chest, igniting sparks beneath his skin.

His pulse hammered as her fingers skimmed over his chest, deliberate and teasing. Every instinct told him to grab her, flip her onto the couch, and remind her exactly who she was playing with. Except that's what she wanted. A distraction. A carefully laid trap. And if he let himself get pulled into it, she'd slip right through his fingers—again.

He caught her wrist before she could trail her fingers further south. "Not this time. We need to talk."

Her lips curved, wicked and knowing. "Careful,

Davey," she murmured, her voice dropping into a sultry whisper that sent heat curling low in his gut. "You're in my space now."

Jesus Christ.

The way she said his name, low and taunting, like she was daring him to lose focus—it did things to him. He should've known better. Hell, he did know better, but knowing and resisting were two different things when it came to Rowan Bristow.

His grin turned sharp, and he leaned in just enough for her breath to hitch. "And what happens when I'm in your space, Rowan?"

She arched a brow, daring him. "You find out exactly how dangerous that can be."

Oh, he already knew. Had known from the moment she walked back into his life like a hurricane, leaving chaos and frustration in her wake. And still, here he was, standing in the middle of the storm.

"I've never shied away from danger." He dragged the words out slowly, giving her a fraction of a second to react before flipping the script. "Last chance," he murmured, his lips a breath away from hers. "Come with me willingly, or I'll have to use these."

He pulled the cuffs from his back pocket, the metal catching the dim light.

Rowan stilled. Her pupils flared. But not with fear.

Her tongue flicked out, wetting her lips, and God help him, his self-control was hanging on by a thread.

"You wouldn't dare."

He smirked. "Try me."

For a long moment, they stood frozen in a silent battle of wills. This was always how it went with them. A game. A fight. A dance with no clear end.

Then, to his absolute shock, Rowan's shoulders sagged. "Fine. You win. I'll come quietly."

Wait. What?

Davey blinked, thrown off guard by her sudden capitulation. His brain scrambled to process it, to read between the lines. This was too easy.

She was up to something.

But she stood still, wrists extended, waiting. Daring him to believe her.

"Don't make me change my mind," she said softly.

His jaw flexed. He was missing something. He knew it. But if this was the game she wanted to play, fine.

He clicked the cuffs into place, the metal cool against her skin.

Then, the shift. A glint in her eyes. A slow, knowing smile.

Predatory. Calculated.

Oh, fuck.

Realization came a second too late.

She moved before he could react, her leg hooking behind his knee, striking fast and hard. He tried to block, but she knew exactly where to hit—his bad leg. She used his momentum against him, a perfect take-down executed with infuriating ease.

A heartbeat later, he was flat on his back, staring at the night sky. The air whooshed out of his lungs.

Son of a bitch.

She'd played him. Again.

And despite himself, despite the fact that he should be pissed as hell—he couldn't decide if he wanted to strangle her or kiss her senseless for it.

His body was still reeling from the fall, his lungs burning from the impact, but the sharp thrill running through his veins had nothing to do with pain.

Yeah, apparently, he was a goddamn masochist because part of him loved every second of sparring with her.

Rowan straddled his chest, her cuffed hands pressed lightly against his throat. Not choking, but a warning. A clear, undeniable threat.

He stilled. Not because he was afraid—no, not even close. But because she wanted him to react, wanted him to try and throw her off balance. And Rowan never made a move without already knowing how it would end.

She eased the pressure on his neck and dragged her hands down his chest until she found the hem of his shirt. Lifting it, she dragged her nails back up his chest, tracing along his ribs, making him tense, then squirm.

That little brat. She knew exactly what she was doing.

"Rule number one," she purred, her voice all sugar and steel. "Never underestimate your opponent."

He knew better than to let his guard down around her for even a second. Rowan had always been unpredictable, a force of nature that couldn't be contained. She was wild and dangerous, and yet here he was, letting himself enjoy this when he should be hauling her ass out of here.

She grinned like she'd won something.

Davey's jaw tightened. Oh, hell no.

"Rule number two," he growled, his hands clamping onto her hips. "Don't get cocky."

With a quick twist, he flipped their positions, pinning her beneath him.

Her eyes widened in surprise—briefly—before narrowing with determination. Yeah, that was more like it.

She bucked against him, trying to throw him off, but he sank his weight, holding her in place.

And holy hell, that was a mistake.

Her body pressed against his, warm and strong and so goddamn tempting, and for the first time in his life, he cursed every ounce of training that told him how to stay in control.

It was torture. Each upward thrust of her body rubbed against him in all the right ways, sending white-hot sparks licking through his veins. His pulse kicked up, fueled by the push and pull of this fight, this game they were always playing. He wanted to snake a hand around the back of her neck and fasten his lips over hers. Wanted to feel the heat of her skin, taste the challenge on her tongue.

But, again, that was precisely what she wanted him to want.

She wanted him horny and distracted so he'd make a mistake.

His breath was heavy, his restraint slipping—and she knew it.

Her lips curved into a wicked, knowing smirk. And then she surged upward, capturing his mouth in a searing kiss.

His brain short-circuited.

Heat exploded between them, wiping out all logic, all reason. Rowan kissed like she fought, all teeth, heat, and sheer, reckless determination to win.

For a moment, he forgot everything—the mission, the danger, even his own damn name.

There was only Rowan, soft and pliant beneath him, her body molding to his as if she were meant to be there.

The kiss was all heat and desperation, weeks of pent-up tension and unresolved feelings slamming together in a collision they both should've seen coming.

His hands roamed down her back, pulling her impossibly closer, gripping her like he had the right to keep her.

She moaned into his mouth, and that was it. That was his breaking point.

A small, rational part of his brain screamed at him to stop, to remember why he was here.

But Rowan's soft, needy little sound drowned out that voice, replacing it with a primal, gut-wrenching need to take her, claim her, own every beautiful, infuriating inch of her.

He didn't even realize he was moving until he hauled her off the ground, her legs wrapping around his waist as he carried her toward the bed, his hands mapping the curve of her thighs, the dip of her spine.

He kicked the door shut behind them and barely registered the low, confused whine.

Rowan broke the kiss just enough to murmur, breathless, "Let him in."

Wait, what?

It took him a full five seconds to process what she meant.

Luka. He'd shut the dog out of the room.

Davey hesitated, torn between his instincts as Luka's handler and the burning, all-consuming need to keep Rowan exactly where she was—pressed against him, her body arching, her fingers tangled in his hair.

With a frustrated groan, he set her down and yanked open the door. Luka bounded inside, tail wagging happily.

"Stay," he commanded, pointing to a worn armchair in the corner.

The dog trotted over, obedient as ever, but his sharp, knowing gaze never left them.

Davey dragged a hand through his hair, his pulse still thrumming, his body still wired, still wanting as he turned to face Rowan again.

She stood in the middle of the room, chest heaving, lips swollen from their kiss. Her eyes blazed with a mixture of desire and defiance that made his blood sing. And that smug little look on her face told him she knew exactly what she was doing to him.

Jesus Christ.

He was in so much trouble.

And he didn't care.

"Now," he growled, advancing on her. "Where were we?"

Rowan's smile turned wicked. Dangerous. "I believe you were about to make a very big mistake."

He barely caught the glint of metal before she brought her hands up, the cuffs dangling loosely from her finger.

Fucking hell.

Of course. Of course she'd gotten out of the damn cuffs.

Goddamn it. He wasn't even mad.

Annoyed? Sure. Turned on? Absolutely.

She was infuriating. Reckless. Uncontrollable. And he enjoyed the hell out of every second of it.

He let out a slow exhale, rolling his shoulders, readying for the next round. "I should've known."

"You really should have. Rule number three," she said, voice low and husky. "Always have an escape plan." She threw the cuffs at his chest and darted past him, making a break for the door.

He lunged and managed to snag her arm just as she reached the handle. He spun her around, pinning her against the wall with his body.

"Nice try," he said, his breath coming fast. "But you're not getting away from me that easily."

She laughed, and the sound rolled through him like a tidal wave of fire as she speared her hands into his hair. "Who says I'm trying to get away? This is just foreplay."

And she captured his lips in another searing kiss. His body responded instantly, pressing her harder against the wall as his hands tangled in her hair.

In the back of his mind, a warning bell sounded. This was a mistake. He needed answers, not another night of passion that would leave him with more questions than ever. But as Rowan's nails raked down his back, coherent thought fled.

She nipped at his bottom lip, drawing a low groan from his throat.

"Rowan," he breathed against her mouth. "We're not doing this—"

"Shut up," she murmured, her fingers working at the buttons of his shirt. "Just... shut up."

His resolve crumbled. With a growl, he hoisted her up, and her legs wrapped around his waist as he carried her to the bed. He threw her onto the mattress and froze. All he could do was drink her in—hair mussed, lips swollen, those golden cat eyes burning with challenge and want. Wild. Untouchable. Every bit the force of nature that had been wrecking his life since the day they met.

When it came to this woman, he was utterly, help-lessly doomed.

A slow, unraveling kind of doom—one he had no interest in escaping.

"Davey," she breathed, reaching for him.

He caught her hand, pressing a lingering kiss to her palm before pinning it above her head. Her breath hitched as he hovered over her, their bodies barely touching, the heat between them crackling like a live wire.

"Tell me why you ran," he murmured against her neck, his lips grazing the delicate skin just above her pulse. He felt the way it fluttered beneath his mouth, fast and unsteady.

She arched beneath him, her breath coming in shallow, uneven gasps. "Davey, please..."

"Tell me," he insisted, trailing his lips lower, his teeth grazing her collarbone. His free hand slid under her shirt, fingertips skating over the smooth expanse of her stomach, feeling the tremor in her muscles.

She wasn't faking it. She couldn't fake the way her

body reacted to him—the sharp inhale, the trail of goosebumps, the way her nipple tightened under his thumb.

She wanted him. Just as much as he wanted her.

But it wasn't just want.

It was more. It had always been more.

"I can't," she whispered.

The words sent a chill through him.

He pulled back slightly, searching her face. The hunger in her eyes was still there, but it was buried under something else. Something raw and unsettled.

Regret.

Fear.

And that sliver of desperation that always seemed to lurk below her surface.

Fuck.

She had him right where she wanted him.

Again.

In a fluid motion, she flipped their positions, straddling his hips, her thighs clamping tight around him. His back hit the mattress, and his wrists were pinned above his head. He stared up at her, dazed from the heat of her body against his, from the phantom press of her lips.

She was breathing hard, her chest rising and falling against his as she held him pinned. The wicked gleam in her eyes should have sent heat racing through his veins—but this time, it was different.

This time, something was wrong.

Finally, his lust-addled brain caught up. His muscles tensed beneath her grip, and every instinct roared to life.

"Rowan," he warned. "Don't."

She leaned down, lips brushing his ear. "I'm so sorry, Davey."

A sharp sting at his neck.

His body betrayed him instantly. An unnatural cold slithered through his veins, blooming outward from the puncture like ink spilling into water. His pulse staggered, sluggish and uneven, as if his blood had thickened to something syrupy, too heavy to move. A deep, insidious numbness crept into his chest, his limbs, taking over until his body was no longer his own.

Panic clawed through him, sharp and jagged.

What the hell did she give me?

He tried to shove her away, to fight, to do *anything*—but the paralysis took hold too fast. His nerves stopped responding, his arms refused to lift, his hands curled uselessly at his sides. The room wavered, tilting at the edges.

No. No, no, no.

"What... whatdidya..." His tongue felt clumsy and foreign, his words slurring before they could fully form.

"Just a sedative," she murmured, brushing her fingers gently through his hair. "Relax and let it take you. You'll be fine in a few hours."

Davey fought like hell to stay awake, but the darkness wasn't just creeping in. It was crashing over him like a wave, dragging him under.

He was sinking.

"Rowan..." His voice barely made it past his lips. "Don't..."

She bent down, pressing a gentle, lingering kiss to his lips.

Soft. Like she cared.

"I wish things could be different between us, Wilde. I really do."

So did he.

And then she was gone.

Slipping through his fingers again... just as he slipped into the abyss.

four

SHE'D CROSSED A LINE. Again.

The pounding rhythm of the bus wheels against the cracked highway throbbed in time with Rowan's growing headache. The lush forests of the Catskills had long since given way to the suburban sprawl of downstate New York as the bus hurtled toward the city. She slumped against the window, staring blankly at the changing scenery.

Her lips still tingled from kissing Davey, the taste of him burned into her memory. Reckless. Stupid. A moment of weakness she couldn't afford. But God help her, she'd never been able to resist him. That man ignited fires in her that no amount of distance could smother.

Distance. Right.

That had been the whole point of drugging him and leaving him and his dog in the motel room.

Her chest tightened as she thought about the job —the deal that had dragged her into this mess. She'd accepted it with ruthless precision: no emotions, no attachments. Just business. Easy.

Until it wasn't.

When she failed the first time last summer, the threats against her family had sent her running. She'd promised herself she'd stay away from Davey until she figured out how to fix it. But then Christmas Eve happened, and once again, she'd ended up in his bed, right back where she'd sworn never to be again.

But then Davey had... well, been Davey. Infuriating, loyal, stubborn, sexy Davey Wilde.

Rowan closed her eyes, her pulse quickening as the memories rushed back—the way his intense blue gaze burned into hers, hungry and possessive. The way his strong hands had gripped her waist, pulling her flush against him like he couldn't get her close enough. How he'd pinned her down, mouth hot and demanding, teeth scraping gently along her throat, his breath ragged against her skin. The way she'd shuddered beneath his touch, coming apart for him, helplessly tangled in the sheets and his arms.

She exhaled sharply, frustration and longing twisting into an aching knot deep in her chest.

Enough.

She sat up straighter, rubbing the gritty exhaustion from her eyes, forcing herself back into the cold reality of the moment. Her focus needed to stay locked on what came next.

Ahead of her, the city loomed, a concrete jungle teeming with possibilities and hidden dangers. Her contact wouldn't wait forever, and the information he held could change everything.

The bus lurched to a stop in the grimy Port Authority terminal, and Rowan hefted her backpack, slipping silently into the crowd. The cacophony of the city engulfed her— horns blaring, people shouting, the constant hum of energy from the city that never sleeps. Perfect for losing herself, for becoming just another face in the throng.

The seedy bar where she was to meet her contact was tucked away in a less savory part of town, the kind of place where questions weren't asked, and discretion was guaranteed for the right price.

Rowan pushed open the heavy wooden door, the stench of stale beer and cigarettes curling around her like an unwelcome embrace. The bar was the kind of place where people kept their heads down, their business to themselves—exactly the type of place Benji preferred.

Her gaze swept the room, past the hunched figures nursing their drinks at the bar, past the murmured conversations drifting from shadowy booths. Then she spotted him in the farthest corner, half-hidden in the dim light, hunched over his ever-present laptop bag like a dragon guarding its hoard. His wire-rimmed glasses sat crooked on his nose, and his knee bounced under the table in a telltale nervous rhythm.

She forced a smile as she approached. "Hello, Benji."

He startled, nearly knocking over his beer. "Jesus. Would it kill you to make a little noise when you walk? You move like a damn ghost."

She slid into the seat across from him, ignoring his dramatics. "You have what I need?"

Benji licked his lips, his fingers drumming against the sticky tabletop. "Yeah, yeah, I got it. But listen, this is—this is big, all right? Bigger than I thought. And, uh..." He hesitated, shifting in his seat like an over-caffeinated squirrel. "The price went up."

Rowan leveled him with a flat stare. "Benji."

"It's not greed!" he yelped, holding up his hands. "It's hazard pay! You don't even know the kind of digital footprints I had to cover, the firewalls I had to dodge, the—"

She leaned forward, lowering her voice to a dangerous whisper. "Benji, you change the deal on me again, and the only hazard you'll have to worry about is whether I let you keep those twitchy little fingers."

Benji swallowed hard, his eyes darting to the knife she'd casually drawn and rested on the table. "Okay, okay, no need to get all stabby," he muttered, fishing a flash drive from his pocket. "Here. Just, you know, try not to get me murdered with it."

Rowan reached for the drive—

Crash.

The bar door slammed open, cutting through the low hum of conversation. Every muscle in her body tensed as her instincts screamed danger—

Then she saw the broad silhouette framed in the doorway, shoulders squared, stance radiating controlled fury. He filled the space, his powerful frame accentuated by the dark tactical shirt molded to every hard line of his chest, the sleeves hugging his muscular arms like a second skin. His jaw was tight, eyes blazing a stormy blue, utterly focused on her. The slight limp in his stride only heightened his intensity, a visible reminder that he'd survived worse than anything this bar could throw at him.

He moved forward with a predator's ease, each deliberate step brimming with lethal potential. Power and determination rippled off him, palpable enough to silence the room around them.

Davey. Fucking. Wilde.

And right now, he looked ready to tear apart anything—or anyone—that stood between him and what he'd come for.

Benji made a strangled noise, snatched the drive back, and shoved it deep into his hoodie pocket. "You brought a tail."

She glared at Davey. "Not intentionally."

Benji was already sliding out of the booth. "Uh, well...this seems like a great time for me to, uh, not be here."

"Benji—"

"Nope. No, no. That guy looks like he eats people who piss him off, and I like my insides... uh, inside." He shot her a panicked look. "You should really stop making enemies this big, Rowan."

"Relax. He's a..." She hesitated, jaw tightening. Friend wasn't exactly the word she'd use for Davey—not after tying him up and stealing his dog, and definitely not after drugging him. But *enemy* wasn't quite right either when they'd blurred so many lines they barely knew where they stood anymore. He was something far more complicated, more dangerous—a mistake she kept making, a lover she couldn't quit, and the one man who could blow her entire world apart with a single look.

"Friend?" Benji suggested with a hopeful note in his voice.

"Complication," she finished tightly.

"Well, your complication doesn't look all that friendly."

"He's harmless," she lied.

Benji didn't look convinced, but at least he didn't bolt immediately.

"Look, just sit tight. I'll handle him." Rowan rose from the booth, moving quickly to intercept Davey before he completely scared off her lead. She was acutely aware of the room's sudden attention, the way conversations stilled as heads turned toward them.

"You put a tracker on me?" she hissed as he

reached her. It was the only possible way he'd found her so quickly. The sedative she'd slipped him would've knocked him out for a few hours, so even if he'd used all of WSW's vast resources when he woke up, there was no way he could've tracked her down this fast without some kind of device.

"You're surprised I had a contingency plan?" He laughed, but it was not a happy sound. He grabbed her arm, his grip just shy of bruising. "We need to talk. Now."

"I'm busy," she shot back, glancing toward Benji. But the weasel was already slinking away.

"Fuck," she muttered, watching her only lead disappear into the crowd. Panic clawed up her throat, sharp and desperate. She'd been so close, and now it was all slipping through her fingers. Her gaze whipped back to Davey, fury blazing alongside something deeper—fear. Fear for herself, fear for him. "Do you have any idea what you've just done?"

His grip on her arm tightened, his expression granite-hard. "What *I've* done? That's rich coming from you. You drugged me and left me in a goddamn motel room."

Guilt twisted sharply beneath her ribs. Drugging him hadn't been personal, hadn't been about hurting him—but telling him that now would only make this mess worse. "At least I left your dog this time."

"Yeah, thanks for that. He's the one who woke me up."

"Dammit." Of course it had been Luka. She should've known Davey's dog would never let him stay down long. She cursed herself silently—another miscalculation she couldn't afford.

"Why'd you do it, Ro?" His voice softened just a fraction, and it cut her deeper than his anger ever could. He was looking for answers, something she could never fully give him.

"I had my reasons." Reasons she wanted desperately to share, even if just to see that wounded look vanish from his eyes—but she couldn't. It wasn't safe. Not for either of them.

"Oh, I'm sure you did." His voice sharpened again, the brief vulnerability buried beneath bitterness. "Care to share them with the class?"

She swallowed hard, the tension between them crackling like lightning. Too many eyes were watching now, the bar's other patrons leaning closer, drawn to the drama unfolding between them.

Attention was dangerous.

Attention got people killed.

"Not here."

"Yes, here." He stepped even closer, the heat of his body practically searing hers through the thin shield of her clothing. "You're out of time, Rowan. Whatever game you're playing, it ends now. I'm taking you home to your father. Let him deal with you."

Panic spiked again, bitter and icy in her chest. The idea of facing her father, admitting all she'd done, all the ways she'd failed, was unbearable—but worse was the thought of Davey caught in the crossfire. She met his gaze, and her breath hitched painfully. The anger there she could handle. But the hurt—the raw, aching hurt lingering beneath it—shredded her from the inside out. She had done this to him, had pulled him into her tangled web of half-truths and desperate gambles. He didn't deserve this, any of it.

"Walk away, Davey." Her voice cracked, betraying the weakness she tried so hard to hide. "Please. Before you get hurt."

Before I get you hurt. Before I have to watch the light drain from your eyes because of me.

But she knew he wouldn't listen. He never had.

A storm gathered in those beautiful blue eyes, dark and dangerous. "Not a fucking chance."

Dammit. Why did the man have to be so stubborn?

She opened her mouth to retort, but the words died on her lips as she caught movement in her peripheral vision. A hulking figure had just entered the bar, his hand reaching inside his jacket in a way that set off alarm bells in her mind.

"We need to move. Now."

He must have sensed the shift in her demeanor because his grip on her arm loosened slightly. "What is it?"

"Trouble," she hissed, already maneuvering them toward the back of the bar. "Big, angry-looking trouble with a gun."

Davey's eyes widened as he glanced over his shoulder just as two more goons filed in. "Shit. Friends of yours?"

"Not exactly."

This was bad.

Very bad.

She'd hoped to have more time before they caught up with her.

"How about we find an exit?"

The hulking man's eyes locked on them, and his face twisted into a snarl. He pulled a gun from under his coat.

"Down!" Rowan yelled, shoving Davey to the floor as gunshots erupted.

Chaos exploded in the bar. Patrons screamed and dove for cover. Glass shattered as bullets tore through bottles behind the bar.

Rowan army crawled toward a nearby table. Davey was right behind her. He flipped the table over to use as a shield, then grabbed his gun from its holster, checking his ammo situation before thumbing off the safety.

"Care to fill me in yet?"

"Answer's still no." She checked her weapon and then assessed their options. The back exit was blocked by one of the goons, and the front door was a death trap. She cursed under her breath.

"Christ, Ro. What have you gotten yourself into?"

Before she could answer, the table splintered

above them. She rolled, coming up in a crouch with her weapon drawn. She fired two quick shots, satisfaction flaring as one of the goons went down, clutching his shoulder.

"Less talking, more shooting."

Davey complied, his aim as deadly accurate as ever. "I can do both. Any brilliant ideas on how to get out of here?"

"Working on it." She scanned the bar, her gaze landing on the picture window in front. It wasn't bulletproof. A bullet had already cracked through the glass, and it wouldn't take much to break the rest out.

"There," she said, nodding toward it. "We can make it if we time it right."

Davey looked at the window and then back at her like she was crazy.

"You got another plan, hot shot?"

He exhaled in a rush. "No. On three?"

She nodded, tensing her muscles, readying to spring to her feet and run. "One... two..."

Before she could say "three," Davey surged up, firing off several rapid shots. One attacker went down with a cry of pain, but more flooded in.

God. They were like rats streaming out of a sewer during a flood—relentless, impossible to contain. Her pulse spiked, adrenaline surging as the reality of how screwed they were sank in.

"Go!" Davey shouted.

He didn't have to tell her twice.

Rowan sprinted for the window, crashing through it shoulder-first. Glass exploded around her, glittering like deadly confetti, slicing into her skin as she fell. Her backpack absorbed most of the impact, but pain still rippled sharply through her shoulder and ribs, stealing her breath. She forced herself to roll with it, gritting her teeth as she landed in a crouch on the sidewalk.

Her muscles screamed, but there was no time to register the hurt. She spun around, gun raised, finger hovering on the trigger, pulse roaring in her ears. She braced herself, scanning wildly for Davey, heart in her throat.

He burst through the shattered window a heartbeat later, landing heavily, his leg nearly buckling beneath him.

"I didn't say three yet," she snapped, fear bleeding into frustration. She grabbed his hand and hauled him upright.

"You were taking too damn long." He winced as he put weight on his bad leg, but it didn't slow him down. His grip tightened on her hand as they shoved through the startled pedestrians. Furious shouts echoed behind them, footsteps closing in.

Too close.

Way too fucking close.

"This way." He yanked her down a narrow alley that stunk of garbage.

Rowan's heart pounded relentlessly. How had she

let it get this far? How had she dragged Davey into something she should've handled alone? Guilt, sharp and nauseating, coiled through her as they burst from the alley onto another crowded street.

She'd lost control of the situation.

And now Davey was in the crosshairs. Right where she hadn't wanted him to be.

He flagged down a cab, practically shoving her inside before sliding in after her and slamming the door shut.

"550 West 34th Street," he said to the driver like they hadn't just run for their lives.

The cab pulled smoothly from the curb just as their pursuers burst into view, their angry faces receding into the distance. Rowan twisted in her seat, watching them vanish, heart still racing wildly.

"You okay?" Davey asked, not so subtly scanning her for injuries.

"I'm fine." She winced as she plucked a shard of glass from her arm. "You?"

"Still breathing." He shifted his bad leg as if testing it and hissed out a breath. "What the fuck was that?"

She slumped into the seat, her adrenaline fading into bone-deep exhaustion. Her entire plan—carefully crafted, meticulously arranged—had blown apart like a grenade in her face. "That's why I told you to walk away."

"Not a chance in hell." Davey's eyes darkened, and his voice had gone dangerously soft. "You're in deep shit, Ro. Way deeper than I thought. It's time to come clean."

Only then did she register the address he'd give the driver. 550 West 34th was the location of Summit One, the sleek, asymmetrical glass and steel skyscraper that housed Wilde Security Worldwide.

No.

Oh, hell, no.

If he got her to Summit One, she'd be trapped under the watchful eyes of WSW, with no chance to slip away unnoticed. Panic surged through her veins like liquid fire, and she reached for the door.

Davey's fingers wrapped around her wrist. "Relax," he murmured. "You're safe now."

Safe.

If only that were true.

She shifted slightly in her seat, her gaze darting to the cab driver. The man was oblivious, humming along to a tinny pop song on the radio. She needed a distraction—something to give her a chance to bolt. Her hand crept toward the strap of her backpack.

Davey's eyes narrowed. "Don't even think about it."

"Think about what?" she asked, aiming for casual innocence.

"Whatever reckless stunt you're planning. I can see the wheels turning in that devious mind of yours."

"You're paranoid, Wilde. I'm just sitting here being perfectly good."

He scoffed, dark amusement flickering briefly. "Bullshit. You've never been a 'good girl' a day in your life."

The words triggered memories she'd buried deep—the heat of last summer at his parents' Fourth of July barbecue, when he'd held her trapped between his body and the wall of the shed, impaled on his cock, as he told her to be a good girl and not make a sound...

His gaze dropped briefly to her lips, then lower still, tracing the shape of her body with undisguised hunger, his grip on her wrist tightening. His thumb brushed over her pulse as if remembering the feel of her heartbeat beneath his mouth and the desperate way she'd gasped his name.

Yeah. He was definitely thinking about it, too.

Which was exactly the distraction she needed.

With a sudden lurch, Rowan slammed herself against the door, all her weight behind it. It flew open, the cab swerving violently as she tumbled gracelessly onto the pavement. Pain shot through her shoulder, but adrenaline overrode everything. She pushed herself to her feet, running on pure instinct and fear.

"Rowan! Dammit, stop!"

She didn't dare look back, didn't dare slow down. The crowded sidewalk swallowed her as she ducked between pedestrians, fear driving her forward. Her heart twisted with guilt and regret, but the need to keep him safe outweighed everything else.

She turned sharply, disappearing into a subway

station. The press of bodies swallowed her, offering the anonymity she desperately needed. By the time Davey reached the entrance, she was already lost in the rush-hour chaos, but she suddenly knew two things with startingly clarity:

Every step she took away from Davey only made him more determined to capture her.

And she was running out of places to hide.

five

DAVEY STEPPED off the elevator into the sleek, glass-walled command center of Wilde Security Worldwide, each step sending a sharp ache radiating up from his leg. The adrenaline rush of the chase had faded, leaving only a bitter cocktail of frustration and exhaustion in its wake. He ran a rough hand over his face, suddenly feeling every hour of lost sleep, every dead-end lead, and every maddening encounter with Rowan Bristow.

Damn that woman.

WSW's top-floor operations room buzzed with activity, agents and analysts exchanging rapid-fire information beneath the cool glow of dozens of screens—satellite imagery, live security feeds, and encrypted data streams. It was cutting-edge tech, the best money could buy, but even all their resources couldn't pin down one stubbornly evasive woman.

He caught the quick, sideways glances from the team. Sympathy mixed with curiosity. The unspoken question lingered heavy in the air: *How the hell had she managed to slip away again?*

Luka, waiting near Elliot's desk, lifted his head at the change in Davey's scent. As soon as he spotted him, the Malinois rose gracefully to his feet, padding over and pressing his warm, solid weight against Davey's leg. He let out a low huff, as if sensing his frustration. Davey gave his head a quick rub, grateful for the grounding presence.

"Hey!" Dominic's too-bright voice sliced through the tense hum, instantly grating on Davey's frayed nerves. Dom bounded toward him, all restless energy, a coffee mug sloshing precariously in one hand. His dark hair was a tousled mess, and he flashed a grin wide enough to make Davey's eye twitch.

Luka's ears perked up, tracking Dom's movement like he wasn't sure whether to expect a fight or another game. The dog had long since learned that Dominic's energy was unpredictable at best.

"Look who's back from another round of hide-and-seek. You look terrible, big brother."

Davey gave him a flat, withering look. "Not. Now."

Dom didn't miss a beat, practically bouncing alongside him like an overgrown golden retriever. "What happened this time? Rowan drug you again? Steal your dog? Your manhood?"

"Dom, he's about two seconds from throttling you." Across the room, Elliot didn't even glance up from his workstation. "Stop pushing your luck."

"Aw, c'mon. We all know I'm his favorite brother."

"Maybe his favorite pain-in-the-ass," Elliot said.

Dom scowled over at him. "Don't you have some spreadsheets to cuddle or something?"

Elliot finally looked up, his sharp blue eyes narrowing thoughtfully behind his glasses. He was dressed casually today in a dark crewneck sweater, his sleeves precisely folded back to his forearms. "As annoying as he is, Dom's right. You look like hell. You okay?"

"I'm fine," Davey grumbled.

"Uh-huh." Elliot's brow furrowed, concern hidden behind his typically calm expression. "It might be worth handing this one off—at least temporarily—to someone... a little less emotionally invested."

Heat crawled up Davey's neck. "I'm not emotionally invested."

Luka let out a small, almost skeptical huff.

Davey scowled down at his dog. *Traitor.*

Dominic snorted loudly. "Denial isn't just a river, and even your dog knows it."

Elliot held up a placating hand. "I just mean, a fresh perspective might help. Rowan knows exactly how to push your buttons, Davey. You can't deny that."

"Yeah, face it," Dom chimed in. "She's your kryptonite."

"Both of you," Davey warned darkly, his jaw aching from how tightly he'd clenched it, "back off."

Jean-Sabin Cavalier, lounging at his workstation nearby, tilted his head back and laughed. "*Mais* ya, your brothers got a point. That woman more slippery than a catfish in the bayou. You sure you ain't lettin' her go on purpose? I think you like the chase."

Davey shot him a glare. "Remind me why I hired you again?"

"You didn't. Your uncle did."

"Then remind me why I haven't fired you?"

Sabin's blue eyes twinkled mischievously as he flashed an easy Cajun grin. "My charmin' personality and stunnin' good looks, of course. Plus, I keep you humble, *mon ami*."

Brody O'Connell swiveled lazily in his chair at the workstation next to Elliot. "Send me after her. I'll have her back here within the hour."

"She'd eat you alive," Davey muttered.

Brody's grin widened. "You say that like it's a bad thing."

Davey narrowed his eyes, annoyance bleeding into every word. "Don't you have somewhere else to be, O'Connell? Like guarding a witness?"

He waved an unconcerned hand. "I needed a break, so Sully stepped in for a few hours."

"Yeah, well, break's over. Get back to the safe house and do your job."

Brody heaved an exaggerated sigh and levered out of his seat. "Fine, I'll go babysit," he said, giving a mock salute. "But when you strike out again, my offer still stands."

Davey glared at Brody's retreating back as he sauntered to the elevator, whistling cheerfully enough to set his teeth on edge. He closed his eyes for just a second, inhaling long and slow, forcing down the hot sting of annoyance and the dull, persistent ache radiating from his leg. The last thing he needed was to let his team see just how deeply Rowan Bristow had gotten under his skin.

It was time to refocus. He exhaled deliberately, feeling the tension ease from his jaw, his shoulders, his spine, as he wrestled his frustration into submission and locked it down tight. When he opened his eyes again, he was back in command—focused, calm, unshakeable.

Rowan was still out there, alone and in danger. Whatever had happened between them personally, whatever tangled web of emotions and mistakes lay behind him, the team needed clear-headed leadership right now—not a hot-tempered, lovesick fool distracted by his own wounded pride.

He straightened, and the lingering chatter in the ops center immediately quieted, every gaze snapping to attention. The teasing was over. He had a job to do.

"Listen up," he said, voice clear and steady, every word infused with authority. "Rowan's in deeper trouble than we realized. The guys after her tonight meant business—heavy hitters, well-armed, and clearly desperate to silence her."

The words settled over the room, leaving a charged silence in their wake. He could practically hear the gears turning in his team's heads, processing the seriousness of the threat. He opened his mouth to continue—to outline their next steps, lay out the plan—but before he could speak again, the elevator doors slid open, drawing everyone's attention.

Cade strode into the room, and instantly, tension thickened like a storm about to break. Everyone knew Cade's resentment simmered beneath the surface. After years preparing to lead Wilde Security, their uncles had handed the reins to Davey instead, and Cade had punched him at Christmas when he found out.

"Failed again?" Cade's voice was cold, each word deliberate. "How many more resources are you going to waste before you admit you're not up to this task?"

Davey crossed his arms. "Didn't ask for your opinion, Cade."

"You don't need to ask. This is family business, and your incompetence affects all of us."

"You want to talk about incompetence?" Davey's voice was low, dangerous. "Then let's revisit Belgrade."

Cade took a step closer, and his fists balled at his sides as if he were considering throwing another punch. "That has nothing to do with your inability to bring in one woman."

Luka stiffened, ears pricking forward, eyes locked on Cade like he was assessing a threat.

Davey felt the tension ripple through the dog's body and reached down, brushing his fingers over the Malinois's collar in a silent command to stand down.

Luka relaxed but still kept his eyes glued to Cade.

"She's not just 'one woman,' and you know it. Rowan's been trained by the best. She knows our tactics, our tech. She's—"

"Special?" Cade interrupted, his voice dripping with sarcasm. "Yes, we've all heard how 'special' she is. But the fact remains, she's a threat to our reputation if you don't bring her in. Time to hand her off to someone who isn't constantly sidetracked by a nice ass."

The words hit with all the cold calculation of a sniper's bullet. Davey could feel the eyes of everyone in the room boring into him. This wasn't just a verbal sparring match; this was Cade laying down the gauntlet, a public challenge to his leadership. His pulse thudded in his ears, a mix of anger and the crushing weight of responsibility. Cade's words cut deep because they echoed his own insecurities—the nagging fear that maybe he wasn't enough, that maybe Cade was right. But he couldn't let those doubts show. Any show of weakness would only bolster Cade's twisted sense of superiority. The guy had been waiting for this moment—waiting for him to fail so he could swoop in and claim what he thought was rightfully his.

"What, someone like you?"

Cade's eyes narrowed, a muscle twitching in his jaw. "Face it. She's got you wrapped around her little finger. Every time you get close, she bats those pretty eyes, and you falter. It's pathetic."

"You want to talk pathetic? How about spending years sulking because you never get Daddy's approval? You're forever living in the shadow of your hero younger brother." As soon as the words left his tongue, he knew he'd gone too far.

Brennan's death was not something the family spoke about.

Ever.

Silence fell like a bomb...

Until Sabin let out a low whistle and kicked back in his chair, planting his boots on the corner of his desk. "Ooh, this is gettin' spicy."

"Sabin, how about you don't fan the flames?" Elliot muttered.

Cade ignored them. His expression was a mask of fury, his jaw clenched so tight a muscle ticked near his temple. He jabbed a finger at Davey's chest. "Don't you dare bring Brennan into this."

Shame burned through him. He'd be furious, too, if their roles were reversed, but he couldn't back down now. Letting Cade win this confrontation would only set him up for more challenges in the future. "Then don't question my ability to do my job. I'll bring Rowan in. My way."

He turned away, intending to end the argument, but Cade's next words stopped him mid-step.

"Careful, Davey. Just because you run WSW now doesn't mean you're untouchable."

He swung back. "Is that a threat?"

"A warning. Your failures reflect on all of us. If you can't handle this, step aside."

Davey stepped into Cade's space. Cade was bigger, more muscular, but Davey was taller by a couple inches. He used the slight height difference to his advantage, crowding Cade until he was forced to take a step backward.

"Let me make something crystal clear. This is my op. My responsibility. My *company*. So unless you want to take it up with the uncles, back the fuck off."

Cade's lips curled into a sneer. "You didn't earn this position. It was handed to you."

"And maybe that's because you can't get through a single mission without burning bridges. Ever wonder if that's why they picked me over you?"

Direct hit. Davey saw it instantly—the flicker of pain in Cade's eyes, the tightening at the corners of his mouth. For half a heartbeat, the arrogant mask slipped, revealing raw bitterness beneath.

Davey almost felt bad.

Almost.

Then Cade's expression hardened again, sharper and colder than before. "At least I don't let my emotions cloud my judgment."

"Because the only emotion you've mastered is being pissed off," Davey shot back.

"You want to see me pissed off? Keep pushing. See what happens."

"Okay, that's enough," Elliot cut in, stepping between them. He pressed a hand to Davey's shoulder and Cade's chest, giving them both a hard shove. "This isn't productive."

"Aw, let 'em whip their dicks out," Sabin chimed in and reached into his desk drawer, withdrawing a ruler. "We can measure. Course, I ain't participatin'. Don't wanna embarrass y'all too bad."

Davey shot Sabin a scorching glare, but it only made the Cajun's grin widen. But it was enough of a distraction, allowing common sense to prevail. He couldn't let Cade goad him into a fight, not here in front of everyone. It would only further undermine his authority, which was precisely what Cade wanted.

He backed up a step. "I don't have time for this."

Cade's face flushed red, his eyes flashing with barely contained rage. Davey thought he might actually take a swing at him like he had at Christmas. Part of him almost wanted it—an excuse to let loose some of the frustration and anger boiling inside him.

But he couldn't.

He was the leader now, and leaders didn't lose control like that.

He took a deep breath, forcing his fists to unclench. "This conversation is over. I've got work to do."

He turned his back on Cade, a deliberate dismissal that he knew would sting. As he strode toward his office, he heard Cade's parting shot:

"You're going to regret this."

A warm weight pressed against his leg. Luka. Silent, steady, and unwavering. The Malinois nudged his thigh, then sat at his feet, his presence grounding in a way nothing else was.

Davey exhaled slowly, his fingers threading through Luka's thick fur as he let the worst of his frustration drain away.

"Well, that was entertainin'," Sabin drawled from behind him. "You two should charge admission next time."

"Shut it, Cavalier," he growled, but there was no real heat behind it. He straightened to find them all gathered in the doorway—Sabin, his brothers. "Show's over. Back to work. Pull up Rowan's tracker. Let's figure out where she's headed."

Sabin patted his shoulder. "Don't you worry, *mon ami*. We'll find your femme fatale before she drives you completely *fou*."

Davey shook his head, exasperated but grateful beneath it all. "Too late, Sabin. Way too fucking late."

Sabin obediently—for once—returned to his station, but Dominic approached, his earlier teasing replaced by genuine concern. "You good?"

Davey ran a hand through his hair. The confrontation had left him drained, the ache in his leg more pronounced than ever. "I'm fine. Cade can go to hell."

"You know he's not going to let this go, right?" Elliot said quietly, shutting the door and leaning back against it.

Davey sighed, sinking into the big leather chair behind his desk. "I know, but I can't worry about him right now. We need to focus on Rowan."

Dom perched on the edge of the desk. "About that... maybe everyone has a point, and you're not the right person for this."

Davey's gaze snapped up, frustration flaring again. "Jesus, not you, too."

"Hey, I'm just saying," Dom said, lifting his hands in surrender. "Would it really hurt to let someone else take point? She did tie you up with Christmas lights last time you were alone."

Christmas lights. Davey nearly laughed, a bitter sound he swallowed down. Dominic had no idea that Christmas wasn't the last time he'd tangled with Rowan, and the memory of the motel room flooded back—her body warm and supple beneath his hands, her breath hitching softly against his mouth. She'd been so close, so perfectly within reach—and he'd let her slip away. Again.

He forced the memory down, clenching his jaw. "I'm not handing this off to anyone. Uncle Greer trusted me with this, and I'm going to finish it."

Dominic shot Elliot a helpless glance. Elliot's steady, thoughtful expression didn't waver as he pushed off the door, adjusting his glasses. "Your closeness to Rowan cuts both ways, Davey. It gives you insight, sure, but it also makes you vulnerable. She knows you too well, and she's proven she's willing to exploit that."

Davey felt the words sink like stones into his gut. Elliot wasn't taking shots to hurt him—he was telling the uncomfortable truth, voicing concerns Davey had privately admitted to himself more times than he cared to count.

"Who says I'm trying to get away? This is just foreplay."

He flexed his hands and swore he could still feel the heat of her skin under his palms. His brothers weren't wrong. He was too close, too involved... but admitting that felt too much like admitting defeat.

But before Davey could respond—before he could find a way to dismiss Elliot's point without admitting he was right—Sabin threw open the door, narrowly missing Elliot, who stumbled back with a muttered curse.

Elliot shot him an exasperated glare, adjusting his glasses as he stepped aside. "Seriously, Sabin?"

Sabin ignored him. "Bossman, we got trouble—Rowan's tracker just went dark. Looks like your femme fatale done pulled another vanishin' act."

Davey's stomach dropped. *Son of a bitch.* Of course she had.

six

IT STARTED RAINING.

Because, of course, it did.

Rowan darted around a corner, her breath sharp, heart thundering in her chest as her boots splashed through a puddle. The crowded streets of New York City swirled with noise and movement, but all she could focus on was the gnawing feeling that Davey was right behind her.

She checked over her shoulder, half sure she'd see him charging through the crowd.

But there was nothing.

Just a sea of strangers, oblivious to her panic.

Davey wasn't chasing her. Not yet. But it wouldn't take long for him to catch up—not if he still had that damn tracker on her.

She slowed to a walk and scanned the street, her gaze landing on a valet stand in front of an upscale restaurant. A sleek black sedan idled as the young valet stood by the open driver's side door, chatting with one of his coworkers.

Perfect.

She slid into the passenger side and scooted over into the driver's seat.

The valet didn't notice something was amiss until she pulled the door shut from under his hand. His shocked face appeared at the window.

"Hey! You can't—"

She didn't wait for him to finish. The tires screeched on the wet pavement as she peeled away from the curb, weaving between cars and sending up a cacophony of angry honks.

She needed distance.

The farther, the better.

The city blurred around her as she sped toward the West Side Highway. Her knuckles turned white as she gripped the steering wheel, her gaze darting between the road and the rearview mirror. No sign of pursuit yet, but she still couldn't shake the feeling of being watched.

The river came into view, a dark ribbon cutting through the city, reflecting the glow of the skyline. She pulled the car into an empty stretch of parking lot along the riverbank, her breathing still uneven as she killed the engine. She sat there for a long moment, still gripping the wheel until the tremble in her hands subsided.

The tracker.

That nagging feeling wasn't just paranoia. Davey had put a tracker on her, and if she didn't find it now, he'd catch up to her before she had a chance to disappear again.

She tugged at the zipper of her jacket, peeling it off and tossing it into the backseat. Next came her boots, her shirt, and her jeans. She stripped down to her bra and underwear, methodically running her hands over every inch of fabric.

Nothing.

"Dammit," she muttered, tossing her jeans onto the passenger seat.

She moved to her body next, skimming her hands along her arms, legs, torso… and then between her legs because Davey's hand had been there just hours ago.

And there it was.

A tiny patch clung to her skin at the crease of her inner thigh.

She remembered his hand sliding down the front of her pants, stroking her through the thin fabric of her panties, driving her insane with need. At the time, she'd been too consumed by the heat of his touch to realize his true intention.

"Son of a bitch," she hissed and peeled the tracker off, the adhesive tugging at her skin. She held it up, the device nearly invisible between her fingers. Of course, Davey would have the audacity to put it *there* in the most intimate of places.

She stared at the tracker for a long moment, fury, shame, and something dangerously close to hurt roiling inside her.

Jesus, why was she hurt?

Trust had never existed between them and the rest...

Well, she just had to lock down the rest of her messy emotions. She couldn't afford to feel anything when it came to Davey Wilde.

She crushed the device between her fingers like a bug, then rolled down the window and flung the tracker as far as she could into the murky waters of the Hudson.

Good riddance.

She shouldn't have let her guard down. Davey was too smart and too focused, and she... dammit, she was slipping. Letting all those messy emotions make her sloppy.

No more.

She dumped the clothes she'd been wearing out the window—she wasn't going to trust anything she'd worn around Davey—and grabbed a fresh set from her backpack. She dressed fast, her mind already on her next moves. She had to get out of the city. But she also still wanted to know whatever intel Benji had dug up for her. She'd have to reach out to him again and convince him another meeting was in his best interest. Which meant she'd have to up the price.

The thought made her groan. She wasn't low on

funds, but she also couldn't keep this up indefinitely. Eventually, she'd have to take another job. If anyone would offer her one.

A worry for another time.

Right now, her focus had to be on keeping her family safe and Davey alive.

Just as she pulled on her favorite leather jacket—thank God she hadn't been wearing that earlier; she'd have been pissed to lose it—the sound of tires screeching shattered the quiet.

No. No way.

Her pulse spiked. He couldn't have caught up already.

Rowan's head snapped up, instincts screaming danger. The air felt different now—thick, electric, the way it did right before a storm hit. Headlights bore down on her, too fast, too direct. A black SUV, its engine snarling like a predator closing in.

Not Davey.

And that SUV wasn't going to stop.

She leaped aside a half second before metal crashed into metal. The impact was deafening. The sedan jolted violently, skidding across the pavement with a tortured screech of steel. If she'd hesitated for even half a second—

Shit.

She hit the asphalt hard, rolling to absorb the impact, but pain lanced through her shoulder. No time to dwell on it. Adrenaline drowned out the sting as she sprang to her feet. Her eyes flicked to the SUV. The doors swung open in near-perfect sync. Two men, dressed in black, masked. No hesitation in their movements. No wasted energy.

Mercenaries. Trained. Armed. And here for her.

Fan-fucking-tastic. Exactly how she wanted to spend her evening after getting shot at.

Her fingers twitched, aching for a weapon. Anything. But she'd have to make do with the one advantage she still had—momentum.

The first man lunged. Fast. A blade flashed in the dim streetlight, aiming straight for her ribs.

Rowan pivoted, twisting away from the strike. A fraction too slow—she felt the whisper of steel against her jacket, a near miss. She grabbed his wrist, twisting hard. The sharp, wet pop of bone snapping under pressure sent a sick thrill down her spine. The knife clattered to the pavement.

"Bitch!" he snarled and swung at her with his other hand—angry, sloppy, desperate.

She ducked it easily. Drove her elbow into his solar plexus, her entire body weight behind it. He folded with a choked wheeze.

The knife.

She dropped low, snatching it up in one fluid motion. Because what was a good street fight without a little upgrade?

The second attacker was already on her. Bigger. Faster. No hesitation. His fist connected with her jaw before she could block. Pain detonated behind her eyes, white-hot and blinding. Her skull snapped sideways, and her vision went dark for half a second—long enough to know she was in trouble.

No.

Focus.

She staggered but refused to go down. Instinct kept her moving. She tightened her grip on the knife, the hilt slick in her sweaty palm.

Blood pooled in her mouth. She spat it out, the sharp tang of copper coating her tongue, and tracked the bastard in front of her.

Her gaze locked onto the bastard in front of her. Big, broad, and overconfident. He easily outweighed her by a hundred pounds, but size wasn't everything.

"Come on, sweetheart," he taunted, circling her like a predator. "Don't make this harder than it needs to be."

Sweetheart? Cute.

She rolled her shoulders, resetting her stance. Every inch of her body ached, but pain meant she was still alive.

She didn't waste breath on a reply. Instead, she feinted left. His weight shifted. Got you.

She ducked right, pivoting on the balls of her feet, and slashed upward. The blade sliced clean across his forearm. Not deep enough to cripple him, but enough to piss him off.

He let out a sharp hiss, jerking back. "You'll pay for

that," he growled, his voice dropping into something meaner. His good hand went for his waistband.

Shit.

Rowan's stomach dropped as the gun came into view.

She was good, but she wasn't that good.

Behind her, the first guy groaned, struggling to his feet, his broken wrist cradled against his chest. "Just shoot the bitch!" he snarled.

Time slowed.

The gunman's finger tightened on the trigger.

Move.

Rowan dropped, rolling hard, feeling the rush of air as the bullet passed just inches from her skull. The crack of the gunshot ricocheted off the nearby buildings, so loud it made her ears ring. Someone had to have heard that.

She came up behind the sedan, shoving her back against the cool metal, sucking in a breath. Another shot pinged off the car, sending sparks flying.

"You can't hide forever!"

No, but she could make him regret thinking she would.

Her grip on the knife tightened. She took a steadying breath and threw it, aiming for the center mass. She didn't wait to see if it hit.

Instead, she vaulted over the hood of the car, launching herself at him.

The suddenness of her attack caught him off

guard. Her shoulder slammed into his ribs, knocking the gun from his grip. It hit the ground with a metallic clatter. They went down hard, his weight crushing her for half a second before she twisted, fighting for leverage.

They grappled, rolling over pavement, trading blows. His fist rammed into her ribs, and something inside her cracked. The pain was instant, sharp enough to steal her breath.

Ignore it.

She drove her knee up, fast and vicious. It landed squarely between his legs.

He let out a strangled sound, body seizing up. She didn't give him time to recover. Snatching a fistful of his shirt, she yanked him forward and slammed his face against her knee. The cartilage in his face crumpled under the blow, and he went limp.

Panting, she scrambled back from his body, only to spot the first guy fumbling for the fallen gun.

Yeah, that was not happening.

She lunged, and her fingers closed around the grip just before his. She rolled to her feet, gun aimed at his chest. "Don't."

Her voice was low, dangerous. No breathless panic. Just promise.

He froze, fury and fear warring in his eyes.

"Who sent you?" she demanded.

He spat at her feet. "Fuck you."

Wrong answer.

She stepped closer, pressing the barrel of the gun to his forehead. Her finger tightened on the trigger, just enough to make him sweat. "I won't ask again."

For a moment, she thought he might crack. His Adam's apple bobbed. Then his eyes hardened. "You're dead anyway," he sneered. "They'll keep coming. They won't stop until—"

Yeah. Enough of this.

She pulled the trigger.

His body hit the ground with a dull thud.

Rowan exhaled. One down.

A roar of rage tore through the night.

The second man was back on his feet, blood streaming down his face, the knife in his hand.

She pivoted, but not fast enough. He charged, wild with fury, and drove the blade deep into her side.

Pain.

Blinding, searing pain.

She gasped, the breath ripped from her lungs as fire bloomed in her ribs. Her legs wanted to buckle, but if she went down, she was as good as dead. She forced herself to stay upright, one hand clamped over the wound.

At least the bastard wasn't functioning at one hundred percent, either. He stumbled, dazed from his head injury, and braced himself against the SUV.

She had seconds before he came at her again. Seconds before the pain dragged her under.

Her fingers tightened around the gun.

She raised it.

Fired twice.

The shots rang out like thunder.

The man jerked, his body spasming before it hit the pavement.

Silence.

For a long moment, all she could hear was her own ragged breathing. The distant lap of the river. The dull roar of blood in her ears.

She took a step. Wobbled. The world swayed violently.

Shit.

The world tilted sideways. Rowan threw a hand out, catching herself against the hood. She could feel the blood pooling in her boot now. Not good. She lifted her fingers from the wound. Dark red gleamed in the streetlights, soaking into her jacket.

"Fuck," she hissed through clenched teeth.

The knife was still in her. She knew better than to pull it out, but damn, everything in her screamed to do something.

Her vision blurred as she yanked open the badly dented car door, and the interior swam in and out of focus.

"Come on," she growled at herself. "Move."

She slid behind the wheel, each movement a new level of agony. Her hands trembled as she slammed the start button. The engine thankfully roared to life.

The SUV, the bodies, the bloodstained pavement—

they all disappeared in the rearview mirror as she peeled out, tires squealing.

She merged onto the highway, her bloody hands slipping on the wheel.

God, that was a lot of blood. Too much.

A wave of dizziness crashed over her, and the road tilted like a ship in a storm. She gritted her teeth and tightened her hands on the wheel until the leather creaked under her palms, and her knuckles went white.

Stay awake. Stay upright. Don't pass out.

Her body screamed. Her vision pulsed at the edges.

But none of that mattered.

They'd found her. Which meant nowhere was safe. Which meant Davey wasn't safe.

Her stomach twisted, not from pain but from the realization that settled like lead in her gut.

She had no choice.

As much as she hated to admit it, she couldn't patch this up on her own.

She needed help.

She needed *Davey.*

seven

DAVEY WAS bone-tired as he parked his car in his reserved space in front of the stately brownstone on the Upper West Side. His parents had bought the place when WSW moved its headquarters to New York City from Washington, D.C., eventually turning the huge house into apartments for him and his brothers. He had the first two floors, Elliot had the next two, and Dom the two above that. The seventh floor and rooftop terrace were common spaces they all shared. Usually, he liked having his brothers close by, but tonight, he was glad to see neither Elliot's BMW nor Dom's Camaro in their spaces, even though he'd left work long after they had.

For once, the house would be quiet, and he needed that.

The day had been brutal, his body aching from the chase, his leg reminding him with every damn step

83

that he wasn't invincible. He turned off the car and sat there for a long time, listening to the engine of the vintage Ford Mustang tick as it cooled. His brothers made fun of him for driving such an ancient vehicle.

"It's older than Dad!" Dom liked to remind him every time the car acted up.

But Davey had always loved all things vintage. Maps, watches, cars, weapons. Mom always said he was an old soul, born about a century too late. Maybe she was right. There was just something about old things—the craftsmanship, the history, the stories buried in their bones—that felt more solid, more real than anything new.

He loved the way the old car growled when he hit the gas and enjoyed the smooth leather of the steering wheel beneath his hands. He was half-tempted to drive out of the city and find a deserted road where he could really open her up, let the power of the engine drown out his thoughts. But his leg was throbbing now, and the idea of a hot shower and a half-decent night's sleep won out.

A soft whine from the passenger seat pulled him from his thoughts. Luka's golden eyes stared at him, his tail wagging slowly, thumping against the door.

"You and me both, buddy," Davey muttered, scratching behind the dog's ears. "Come on. Let's get inside."

He climbed out of the car, Luka bounding ahead toward the entrance. Davey grabbed his bag, his mind already shifting to tomorrow's plan. He had to figure out another way to find Rowan now that she'd destroyed the tracker. He couldn't let this slip turn into a full-blown failure. It'd just give Cade more ammunition against him.

Luka's sharp bark sliced through his thoughts. Not a playful bark. A warning.

Davey's head snapped up, his entire body going still, instincts kicking in hard and fast. His fingers skimmed the grip of his gun, ready to draw. Luka never barked like that unless something was wrong.

The dog stood rigid at the edge of the building's landscaping, pawing frantically at the bushes. His ears were flat, tail stiff—every sign of distress Davey had learned to recognize over years of training and fieldwork.

Something was there.

Someone.

A shot of adrenaline burned through his veins as he stepped closer. "Luka, heel."

Luka didn't listen. Instead, he let out a low whine and shoved his nose deeper into the greenery.

Davey's pulse quickened. Luka was disciplined and sharp as hell—he only ignored commands when the situation was critical. "What's wrong? What is it?"

Then he saw her.

Rowan.

The breath punched out of his lungs.

She lay crumpled among the bushes, her dark hair

tangled with leaves, her jacket soaked with blood. The moonlight cast her face in shades of gray, her skin too pale, lips parted in shallow, uneven breaths.

Luka nudged her arm, whimpering low in his throat, pressing closer like he could keep her here just by sheer force of will.

Davey forced himself to move. He dropped to his knees beside her, fingers searching for a pulse, for a sign that she wasn't slipping away from him.

There.

Weak, but steady.

Relief slammed into him, violent and overwhelming, stealing his breath. His vision tunneled for half a second, body caught between the sharp edge of panic and the crushing weight of that relief. His pulse hammered so hard it felt like each heartbeat rattled his ribs. His whole damn chest ached like he'd taken a hit straight to the sternum, like something inside him had been wound too tight and just snapped loose all at once.

Jesus.

His throat closed up. He exhaled hard through his nose, a sound that was half-growl, half-shudder, and forced himself to breathe. To move.

She wasn't gone.

Not yet.

But she could have been.

Would have been if Luka hadn't found her.

Davey swallowed hard, his gaze flicking to the dog.

Luka stood guard, his body tense, ears flat, eyes locked on Rowan. Still watching her. Still protecting her.

He reached out, running a quick hand over his dog's head in silent thanks.

Luka had saved her.

Now, it was up to Davey to keep her alive.

His focus snapped back to Rowan, to the knife still embedded in her side, to the too-shallow breaths barely moving her chest.

"Rowan." His voice was sharp, cutting through the night. No softness, no hesitation. He needed her awake. Needed her fighting.

He gave her shoulder a firm shake. "Rowan, can you hear me?"

Her eyelids fluttered, barely. A faint moan slipped past her lips, pained and distant, but her body barely stirred.

Not good.

"Fuck." His throat was tight, his brain calculating, assessing. Knife wound. Blood loss. Exposure. If she'd passed out outside, in this condition, she hadn't been in control of how long she was bleeding out.

He needed to get her inside. Now.

But the knife—if he moved her wrong, if it nicked something vital...

He was already pulling out his phone before his thoughts fully caught up. One-handed, practiced, automatic. His fingers flew over the screen as he dialed.

The call connected on the second ring.

"Tess, I need you at my apartment. Now."

"What's going on?" his cousin asked, instantly alert.

"It's Rowan. She's hurt—bad. Looks like she got into a fight. Bring your med kit."

"I'm on my way," Tessa said without hesitation.

He hung up, tucking the phone away and turning his attention back to Rowan. Her skin was clammy, her breathing shallow. Shock was setting in.

"Stay with me, Ro." His voice was low, urgent. A demand, not a request. He pulled off his jacket and laid it over her, but it felt useless against the bone-deep chill radiating off her skin. "Help's coming."

Luka whined again, nudging Rowan's hand with his nose.

"Good boy," Davey said absently, gaze scanning the area for any signs of threat. Whoever had done this could still be nearby.

But then he spotted the car parked haphazardly on the curb with the crumpled driver's side door hanging open. He drew his gun and left her side long enough to do a quick check of the vehicle. It was still running. Her blood had pooled in the seat and streaked the steering wheel and the door.

So, whatever happened, Rowan had gotten herself here.

And, somehow, he knew this wasn't her personal car. Most likely, she stole it.

He reached in and hit the ignition button, shutting it off. Then he shut the door and grabbed his phone again, texting Sullivan O'Connell.

Black car in front of my place, dented driver's side, blood in the seat. NJ plates. It needs to be wiped and dumped.

The reply came back in seconds:

On it, boss.

Davey exhaled sharply, shoving his phone back into his pocket. He cast one last glance at the car before turning on his heel and striding back to Rowan.

She hadn't moved.

His stomach twisted at how damn still she was, her face too pale, her body unnervingly limp. Luka whined softly, still pressing close to her, his nose nudging at her shoulder.

"Yeah," Davey murmured, crouching beside her again, running his hand over her hair without thinking. "I'm worried about her, too, buddy."

The minutes crawled by like hours until he finally heard the screech of tires.

A sleek black car skidded to a stop, and Tessa Wilde leaped out, medical bag in hand, her dark hair spilling over her shoulders in loose waves. She moved with sharp, no-nonsense efficiency, her dark eyes already assessing the situation before she even reached them. The amber glow of the streetlights softened the warm caramel of her skin, but there was nothing soft about her expression.

"Jesus Christ," she breathed as she knelt beside them. "What happened?"

"I don't know. Found her like this. Knife's still in her."

Tessa's hands were already moving, checking Rowan's vitals. "We need to get her inside. Can you carry her?"

Davey nodded, sliding his arms carefully under Rowan's limp body. He lifted her as gently as he could, gritting his teeth against the twinge in his bad leg.

They made their way quickly to Davey's apartment, Tessa clearing a space on the dining table. "Put her here," she directed, already pulling supplies from her bag.

Davey laid Rowan down, but he couldn't make himself let her go right away. His hand lingered on her cheek. "Don't you dare die on me, Bristow. You hear me? You don't get to check out like this."

Tessa shouldered him out of the way. "I need space to work, Davey. Go make yourself useful and boil some water."

He nodded, forcing himself to step back. As he moved to the stove, his gaze never left Rowan's pale face. Whatever had happened, whoever had done this to her, they were going to pay. He'd make damn sure of that.

His hands shook as he filled a pot with water and set it on the burner. *Shook.* His hands never did that. He clenched his jaw, forcing his grip steady, but the tremor wouldn't stop. His fingers felt numb, foreign, like they belonged to someone else.

Boil water. Like this was any other night. Like Rowan wasn't bleeding out on his kitchen table. Domestic normalcy clashing violently with the fucking nightmare unfolding behind him.

He braced his hands on the counter, gripping the edge so hard his knuckles went white. His lungs felt too tight.

Breathe, he reminded himself. In. Out. Again.

Behind him, the soft snick of scissors slicing through fabric made his stomach drop.

"Shit," Tessa muttered. "This is bad, Davey. The knife's in deep."

He turned, dreading what he'd see—but unable to look away.

Blood. So much of it.

His gut twisted violently at the sight of her torso, skin streaked red, her shirt ruined, her body unnervingly still. He had seen wounds like this before—on the battlefield, on mission recoveries—but never on her. Never on Rowan.

And that was different. That was worse.

His voice came out rough, gritted between his teeth. "Can you get it out?"

Tessa's face was grim. "I have to. But there's a risk of further internal damage. We really should get her to a hospital."

No.

His breath locked in his chest, muscles coiling like a live wire. A hospital meant exposure. A hospital meant more eyes, more risk, more people knowing she was alive when someone had just tried to make damn sure she wasn't.

His voice came out sharper than he intended. "No. No hospitals. If someone's after her, that's the first place they'll look. You know that."

When Tessa met his gaze, her expression shifted—frustration, uncertainty, maybe even pity. He hated it.

"Davey, she could die."

His stomach bottomed out.

She could die.

Something snapped inside him, something feral and instinctive, something that wouldn't—couldn't—accept that possibility.

"Then you'd better make sure she doesn't," he growled.

Tessa's jaw tightened, but she nodded. "I'll do my best. But I need your help. This is going to be messy."

Davey moved on autopilot. He'd done this before—field medicine, trauma care, triage. He could patch a bullet wound in the dark, keep a dying man alive with duct tape and grit. But this was different. This was Rowan.

Her face was ashen, her breathing shallow and ragged. He placed a hand on her forehead, alarmed at how cold and clammy her skin felt.

"Stay with me, Ro," he murmured.

She didn't react. Didn't even stir.

Fuck.

Tessa worked fast, clearing the blood away from the wound with steady, clinical efficiency. "Okay, I'm going to remove the knife. Be ready to apply pressure the moment it's out."

Luka whined softly from his spot by the table, eyes locked on Rowan's still form. The dog knew. Knew she was bad. Knew how close this was.

"It's okay, boy," Davey murmured and positioned his hands where Tessa indicated. "She's tough. She'll pull through."

He wasn't sure if he was trying to convince Luka or himself.

eight

"ON THREE," Tessa said. "One...two...three."

She pulled the knife out in one swift motion.

For a split second, there was nothing. Just the slick sound of metal sliding free, the tense beat of silence before the inevitable.

Then—blood.

It gushed from the wound, dark and endless, pooling over her skin, soaking into the gauze, spilling between his fingers. Too much.

Pressure built in his chest, sharp and unbearable, like his ribs were trying to crush his heart. His stomach twisted violently as he pressed down, harder than he should have, trying to stop the impossible.

"Fuck." His voice came out strangled, more breath than sound, because—Jesus Christ, that was too much blood.

His hands were slick with it, hot, sticky, a stain he

couldn't wash off. He'd seen this before. Too many times. On battlefields, in dark alleyways, in places where men didn't always make it back alive.

But this wasn't some faceless soldier.

This was Rowan.

And she was dying right in front of him.

A shuddering breath left his lungs. He forced himself to steady his grip, to keep the pressure even, but every instinct in his body was screaming, panic clawing at his ribs, at his throat.

This wasn't supposed to happen. Not to her—the woman who had outmaneuvered him three damn times.

Once by sexing him stupid, tying him to his own bed with Christmas lights, and disappearing with his dog before he even woke up.

Once by jabbing him in the neck with a sedative—one he still fucking felt—and slipping into the night, leaving him groggy, furious, and cursing her name.

Once by jumping out of a moving cab like a goddamn lunatic while he was still swearing at the driver to stop.

She always got away.

Always had a way out.

But now she wasn't that warrior. She wasn't untouchable. She was silent, still as death, and bleeding out in his arms.

And he couldn't lose her.

He *wouldn't*.

"Tessa—" His voice cracked, his grip tightening as he felt her breath hitch beneath his hands, too shallow, too weak.

"I know," she said quickly, already moving. "Just keep that pressure steady. I've got her, but you need to hold her together."

Hold her together.

Jesus.

He was holding her together, quite literally, and yet it still felt like she was slipping through his fingers.

Tessa's hands were steady, working fast, her voice low and even. "Davey, look at me."

He couldn't. He couldn't take his eyes off Rowan.

"Davey." This time, her voice was sharper. "She's still breathing. That means she's still fighting. And if she's fighting, we fight for her."

His fingers flexed against the gauze, his jaw clenching.

Fighting.

That was Rowan. That had always been Rowan.

So, yeah.

He'd fight for her.

Minutes ticked by, the silence broken only by Rowan's labored breathing and Tessa's terse instructions.

She worked fast, methodical, efficient, moving with the kind of confidence that only came from experience. Surgical scissors glinted under the kitchen lights as she cut away more of Rowan's ruined shirt, exposing bruised skin and raw edges of the wound.

She grabbed a syringe from her kit, popped the cap off with her teeth, and injected something near the wound. A local anesthetic, probably. Then came the antiseptic—a sharp, biting scent that cut through the thick metallic stink of blood.

Davey barely moved. He just kept pressing down, kept feeling the slow, sticky warmth seeping through the gauze.

Tessa didn't flinch. She threaded a curved needle through Rowan's torn skin, her hands steady, precise, closing the wound stitch by stitch.

"Come on, Ro," Davey muttered under his breath, voice low and strained. "Don't make this a one-sided fight."

Tessa didn't look up, didn't comment. She just kept working, her brow furrowed in concentration, a slight crease between her eyes. The look she always got when she was too focused to let herself feel.

She reached for the gauze, layering clean bandages over the stitched wound and taping them down with quick, practiced movements. Then, she pressed two fingers to Rowan's pulse, watching the slow, unsteady rise and fall of her chest.

A beat.

Then another.

Finally, Tessa stepped back, removing her bloody gloves and wiping sweat from her brow.

"I've got the bleeding under control," she said. "But she's lost a lot of blood. She needs fluids, antibiotics, and close monitoring."

He nodded, his gaze never leaving Rowan's face. "What can I do for her?"

"For now, just keep her comfortable. Keep an eye on her vitals." Tessa crouched and rifled through her kit, pulling out a saline bag and other stuff for an IV. When she straightened again and took in her patient, pale and quiet on the table, and Davey hovering, her expression softened. "What the hell is going on? Who did this to her?"

Frustration surged through him, thick and acidic. His fingers flexed involuntarily at his sides. He could still feel the warmth of her blood seeping through them. "I don't know. She won't tell me."

Tessa's eyes narrowed as she pulled open the sterile packaging around the IV line. "Won't tell you or can't tell you?"

"Both, probably," It came out gritted, full of an exhaustion that had nothing to do with his body and everything to do with Rowan's stubbornness, the walls she always kept between herself and everyone who gave a damn about her. "She's so fucking stubborn."

Tessa huffed a quiet laugh, shaking her head as she fitted the IV tubing together. "Sounds like someone else I know. Actually..." She paused and tilted her head, considering. "Sounds like every one of my family members with a Y chromosome."

Davey ignored the jab, his focus locking back onto Rowan. Her breathing was too shallow, her chest barely moving beneath the fresh bandages. Her eyelids fluttered, a soft moan escaping before she settled again.

"She's in pain."

The words came out hoarse, barely more than a breath. Like saying them made them more real.

Tessa paused, looking up from where she was priming the IV line, before sighing and tossing her used gloves into the trash. She didn't argue. Didn't tell him it was fine, that Rowan would be okay.

Instead, she reached for a fresh pair of gloves, stuffing them in her pocket, and grabbed the saline bag. "All right. Let's move her somewhere more comfortable before I set up the IV."

"My bed." He scooped his arms under Rowan, but Tessa put a hand on his arm, stopping him.

"Are you sure you're okay to carry her?"

He couldn't stop the growl of annoyance. Ever since his injury, his family talked to him like he might shatter—little pauses in their voices, too-casual offers to 'help' that felt more like doubts. Like they were waiting for the moment he proved them right. "I'm not a fucking egg. I'm not going to break."

"I know you think you're Superman," Tessa said gently but dropped her hand from his arm and backed up. "But I see you favoring that leg. Let's get her settled, then I want to take a look at you."

"I'm fine," he muttered, carefully lifting Rowan into his arms. He gritted his teeth against the twinge in his leg as he carried her upstairs to his room, with both Tessa and Luka following close behind.

Jesus. She felt so small and fragile, nothing like the fierce, dangerous woman he knew her to be. As he laid her gently on the bed, a strand of her dark hair fell across her face. Without thinking, he brushed it back, his fingers lingering on her cheek.

"Davey," Tessa said softly from behind him.

He jerked his hand back as if burned. He cleared his throat, stepping aside to give Tessa room to work. "What's next?"

Tessa gave him a knowing look but mercifully didn't comment. "I'll set up the IV and start her on antibiotics. Can you grab some extra pillows? We need to keep her elevated."

He found a stack of pillows in the closet and positioned Rowan more comfortably, then stood helplessly back and let Tessa do her thing. She started the IV and checked Rowan's vitals again.

"Her pulse is steadier, but she's still not out of the woods. We need to watch for signs of infection or internal bleeding. I don't think the blade hit anything vital, but I could be wrong. And if I am—"

"How often are you wrong?"

Tessa's lips curved into a faint smile that looked a

hell of a lot like her brother's when Cade actually bothered to smile. "Never, but there's always a first time."

"I trust your work, but I'll keep an eye on her."

Tessa double-checked the line of stitches, then covered them with a bandage and turned to face him, her expression stern. She pointed toward the door. "All right, downstairs. It's your turn now. Let me see that leg."

When he hesitated, she made a shooing motion. He reluctantly followed her into the living room, his eyes lingering on Rowan's still form as he left the bedroom. Luka jumped up on the bed and nuzzled into Rowan's side.

Good boy.

Downstairs, Tessa pointed to the couch. "Sit."

Davey sank to the cushions with a grimace he couldn't quite hide. Now that the adrenaline was fading, the ache in his leg was impossible to ignore.

"All right, tough guy, drop the pants. Let's see the damage."

He choked on his own spit. "No."

Tessa stood in front of him, hands on her hips, eyebrow raised. "What's wrong? You going commando?"

When he didn't answer, she rolled her eyes. "Oh, please. You think I haven't seen a dick before?"

Davey made a strangled noise in the back of his throat and shot her a horrified look. He did *not* want to think about his baby cousin seeing a man's dick. Ever. "Christ, Tessa."

She snorted. "You think my medical training came with a 'no cocks allowed' policy? Believe me, yours is nothing special. Drop 'em, Davey."

Muttering a string of curses under his breath, he unbuckled his belt, grateful that—for once—he'd actually put on underwear this morning. He usually went without, and if he'd been commando right now, he would've had to move out of the country just to avoid ever speaking to Tessa again.

Still, a fresh wave of discomfort hit as he shoved his jeans down, exposing the scarred flesh and metal of his reconstructed thigh. He wasn't self-conscious about it—he'd made his peace with the damage a long time ago—but having his cousin poke at his leg like he was some lab experiment wasn't exactly on his bucket list.

Tessa's hands were gentle but firm as she probed the area, her brow furrowed in concentration. "How bad is the pain, scale of one to ten?"

"Four."

She raised an eyebrow. "So, seven then. You always underreport."

"It's fine, Tess. I've had worse."

"That's not the point, and you know it." She sighed, sitting back on her heels. "It's inflamed. Have you been overdoing it again?"

"Define 'overdoing it.'"

She shot him a withering look. "You know exactly what I mean. Running around the city, getting into fights, carrying wounded women up flights of stairs..."

"It's fine," he insisted again, even as a twinge of pain shot through his leg. "I can handle it."

Tessa's expression softened. "I know you can handle it, dumbass. That's not the problem. The problem is that you shouldn't have to."

He looked away, his jaw locking. He wasn't in the mood for this conversation.

Tessa let out a slow breath. "You need to ice it regularly—not just when it starts hurting, but before. Twenty minutes, twice a day. You still doing the stretches Dr. Patel gave you?"

"Sometimes."

Tessa rolled her eyes. "Which means no." She pointed at him. "Start doing them. Every morning, every night. And take the damn anti-inflammatories before it gets this bad, not after."

He grumbled under his breath, but she ignored it, already rummaging in her bag. "I'll wrap it for you now, but if it's still this bad tomorrow, you're taking a rest day."

Davey scoffed. "I don't have time for a rest day."

"Yes, you do," she shot back, yanking out a compression wrap. "You'll be sitting here with Rowan anyway. She'll be out of it for a while, so take it easy, or I'll tell Aunt Libby you're being reckless with your health."

His scowl deepened. "You wouldn't."

She smirked. "Try me."

Davey muttered another curse but let her work, even as irritation burned in his chest. It wasn't her fault. She was right, and they both knew it.

Tessa finished wrapping his leg, then sat back, studying him. "You're not invincible, Davey."

The words hit harder than they should have.

Images of the explosion that killed several of his men and ripped his leg to shreds flashed across his mind, but he shoved them away, locking them back inside that vault where they belonged. He tugged his pants back up. "Well fucking aware."

Tessa's eyes held something softer now—concern, understanding, something too close to pity for his liking. "I know you are. But you need to take care of yourself too—not just everyone else."

He nodded, knowing it was easier to agree than argue. "Thanks for coming. I owe you one."

"You owe me several," she corrected with a wry smile.

Unable to stop himself, he looked toward the stairs. The urge to get back to Rowan was overpowering. He needed to make sure she was still breathing.

Tessa followed his gaze. "She'll be okay."

He nodded, his jaw locked tight. "She has to be."

His cousin studied him with her dark, all-too-knowing eyes. "You care about her, don't you?"

He didn't answer, but he didn't need to. His silence spoke volumes.

"Yeah, I thought so." Tessa let out a quiet breath as if she'd just confirmed a suspicion, then sat beside him and reached for his hand. "You okay?"

He scowled. "You just looked at my leg. I'm fine."

"I wasn't talking about your leg." She squeezed his hand. "Your jaw's clenched so tight it looks like it might snap, and you've been walking around with a storm cloud over your head since Christmas. Is it Cade? I heard you two got into it again at the office."

He sighed and pulled his hand from hers, scrubbing it over his face. His eyelids felt coated in sandpaper. "He's been a pain in my ass since I took over."

Tessa's lips compressed into a thin line. "Cade's... complicated."

"That's putting it mildly." He glanced at her. "You're his sister. You've got to see it, too. The guy's got a chip on his shoulder the size of the Hudson."

She didn't deny it. "I don't think it's just about the company, Davey. You know how he is. He keeps everything bottled up until the pressure builds and builds, and then he explodes. He was already under so much pressure trying to prove himself to Dad and the uncles, and then he found out he was going to be a dad. Then Nova was born, and he lost Emma. And then Brennan —" She paused, swallowing hard. "He doesn't talk about it, but I think losing Brennan was the last straw. It broke something in him that was already cracking, and now all that pressure is releasing, and we're getting that explosion."

Davey leaned back, feeling like shit all over again for his comment about Brennan earlier. Brennan's death had fractured their family. Where they'd once been a tight-knit unit, now cracks and fissures ran through all of their relationships.

And the uncles had trusted him to somehow heal the wounds. It should've been Elliot, with his mind for strategy, or Bridger, with his cool head and talent for diplomacy, or even Tessa. She was the healer in the family.

But no, they handed the reins to him, expecting him to hold the family together when he could barely do it for himself.

"I get that," he said finally. "Cade's been through hell. But it doesn't give him the right to take it out on me. I didn't ask for this job. I didn't want it, but you try telling the uncles no when they corner you with the paperwork all ready to go."

He hadn't even had a chance to breathe before the decision was made. No discussion, no time to think. Just signed, sealed, and shoved onto his shoulders like a goddamn boulder.

Tessa's eyes softened. "I know. And I think, deep down, Cade knows, too. But he's always felt like he had to prove himself—especially after Brennan. And now, seeing you in the position he thought he was working toward..." She hesitated, choosing her words carefully. "It's a reminder of all the ways he feels like he's failed."

Davey exhaled sharply. "I'm not his enemy, Tess."

"I know you're not," she said quietly. "But Cade doesn't see it that way right now. He has a lot of anger, and he doesn't know what to do with it."

"Well, I'm not his damn punching bag." The words lacked the heat he'd been going for. He was just... fucking tired. Tired of the fights, tired of the tension, tired of walking into a room and seeing Cade's barely concealed resentment burning behind his eyes. Like Davey had stolen something from him.

"I'm not saying you should be," she replied gently. "But maybe... just try talking to him. Not about work, not about WSW." She paused. "Have you ever even met his daughter?"

The question made him blink. Had he?

"I saw her briefly at Christmas." It had been a blur of a night—booze, tension, their uncles watching every move like he and Cade might come to blows over the mashed potatoes. But he remembered Nova. The baby had been cute, with chubby little cheeks and spiky black hair tied up in pigtails.

And Cade...

Cade had been different with her. He wasn't the cold, calculating bastard everyone else knew him as. He was softer, gentler—like the edges of him had been sanded down just enough to let some light in.

"He's a different guy around her. I'll give him that."

Davey sighed. "I guess I haven't really made an effort there. It's just... every time I see Cade, he's got this look in his eye like he's contemplating my murder."

Tessa's lips quirked into a small, sad smile. "That's just his resting face these days. But I think if you made the effort, he might surprise you. He needs to hear you're on his side, even if he's not ready to admit it yet."

Davey let the words settle, but doubt twisted in his gut. How was he supposed to be on Cade's side when Cade wasn't on his? Every time they spoke, it felt like another battle. Like Cade was waiting for him to fail so he could say, 'I told you so.'

"I don't know. I'm not sure he even wants to fix things."

"Maybe not right now," she admitted. "But he's not a lost cause, Davey. He's just... hurting. You might be the only person who can get through to him. You two used to be so close, and I hate seeing you at each other's throats like this. Just talk to him. Please?"

Davey swallowed against the knot forming in his throat. Once, Cade had been his best friend. Back before everything had gone to hell.

But things weren't like that anymore. They hadn't been for a long time.

"Yeah," he said finally. "I'll think about it."

Tessa offered him a small, reassuring smile. "That's all I'm asking." She stood, slinging her med kit higher on her shoulder, and nodded toward the bedroom on the second floor. "Take care of her, okay? And yourself. I'll check back in tomorrow, but call me if you need anything before then."

Davey nodded. "Thanks, Tess."

She hesitated in the doorway, her dark eyes lingering on him. "Don't wait too long to talk to Cade, Davey. You both deserve better than this."

With that, she left.

He leaned back in his chair, her parting words echoing in his mind. And whether he liked it or not, he was going to have to find a way to fix this thing with Cade—for the sake of the family and for WSW.

nine

ROWAN WOKE GASPING, her breath sharp, her pulse a frantic drumbeat against her ribs. Instinct had her scanning the room even before her brain came fully online.

A dark gray comforter, heavy over her legs. A sturdy bed, built like it wasn't meant to move. Soft blue walls with a framed world map hanging over the headboard. The scent of cedar and leather wrapped around her, grounding her before she could remember why she shouldn't feel grounded at all.

She knew that smell.

She knew this room.

Soft light bled through the blackout curtains, edging the two floor-to-ceiling windows. The city's ever-present hum barely reached inside, as if this space—*his* space—existed in a world apart.

She swallowed hard, her gaze landing on the

nightstand. A digital clock's glowing numbers, a book with a worn spine, and a framed photo of Jude and Libby Wilde, smiling, with Elliot and Dominic beside them.

And—

Davey.

Flashes of memory slashed through the haze. Blood slick on her hands. The wheel slipping under her grip. The tilt of the world as she stumbled out, breath ragged, vision swimming.

Luka's anxious whine.

Davey's face—concern carved deep into his expression.

And then—nothing.

Her stomach twisted, nausea rising fast.

God, why had she come here? The whole point of running was to keep Davey safe. Yet here she was in his fucking bed.

No.

She needed to leave.

Now.

She pushed herself up, her muscles screaming in protest, her ribs tightening like a vise. She clenched her jaw against the sharp ache flaring in her side. Lifting the oversized US Navy T-shirt—*his* shirt—she traced the edge of the square bandage. Beneath it, stitches pulled against her skin. Not deep, or he would've taken her to a hospital.

She exhaled. Okay. Good.

She swung her legs over the side of the bed. The moment her bare feet hit the cool hardwood, the room tilted, and the floor lurched.

Shit.

She gripped the mattress, sucking in a slow breath, waiting for the dizziness to pass. How much blood had she lost?

Her bloodstained shirt lay in tatters over the chair in the corner.

Rowan stared at it, her stomach tightening.

Someone had cut it off her.

The thought sent a sharp ripple of unease through her. She hadn't taken it off. She hadn't felt it being removed.

Which meant—

Her fingers curled into the hem of the oversized T-shirt hanging loose on her frame. A dull pulse of heat crept up her neck, not from embarrassment but from the stark reminder that she'd been out. Useless. Vulnerable.

They'd had to cut her free.

She swallowed against the bitter taste in her throat. She should've been able to get out of her own damn clothes. Should've been awake enough to at least be aware of what was happening to her.

But she hadn't been.

And now she was here.

Her jeans were missing too. Probably trashed. Probably soaked in blood.

She sucked in a breath, exhaled slow. Didn't matter.

What mattered was getting out.

Move.

She wasn't staying.

Not here.

Not with him.

Her breaths came shallow and uneven, but she forced herself to focus and put one foot in front of the other. She pushed open the bedroom door and found Luka curled up in the hallway. The dog lifted his head, his golden eyes locking onto hers. His tail wagged once, hesitant, as if unsure whether to alert Davey or let her pass.

"Shh," she murmured, crouching to stroke Luka's ear. "I'm fine, buddy. Just need some air."

Luka whined softly but didn't bark. Good boy.

She straightened and continued shuffling forward. The apartment's layout was ingrained in her memory. His bedroom door led to a mezzanine overlooking the lower floor. There was another bedroom and bathroom straight back, and she could only hope he was asleep in there as she picked her way downstairs to the living room.

The space had always felt like Davey to her: solid, dependable, and utilitarian. A place where everything had its purpose, everything was under control.

It felt safe.

She didn't belong here. She didn't belong in a

space like this, in a life like his. Her chaos had no place in this order.

Another large, very old framed world map decorated the brick wall over the low leather couch. She'd always wanted to ask him about his fascination with vintage maps because he also had one in his bedroom. But every other time she'd been in his apartment, they were too busy doing more interesting things with their mouths to talk.

And she sure as hell wasn't about to wake him up now to ask.

Except—he wasn't in the second bedroom upstairs.

He was on the couch.

Asleep.

Christ.

One arm was draped over his eyes, his broad chest rising and falling in the slow rhythm of deep sleep. The thin blanket barely covered his lower half, leaving way too much of him exposed.

The three intricate swirls of ink along his ribs caught her attention—a tattoo she'd always wanted to ask him about but never had. It seemed out of character for him, for a man who never made unnecessary statements, never sought attention.

But it wasn't just the ink that had her breath hitching.

It was all of him.

The harsh edges of his muscular frame softened in sleep, golden-brown hair a tousled mess, as if he'd spent hours dragging his fingers through it. Stubble shadowed his sharp jaw, dusting his skin in rough gold, making him look less like the dangerously in-control leader she knew and more like—

A man she wanted to curl into.

A pang of longing hit her so hard she nearly staggered. She locked her knees, forcing herself not to move toward him.

Because that's what she wanted. What she always wanted.

To slip under that blanket, press herself against all that heat and strength, let his arm curl around her, solid and steady, unshakable as the man himself.

To breathe him in and let the world disappear.

This was exactly why she needed to leave.

She dragged in a shaky breath, tearing her gaze away, forcing herself to focus. Backpack. Clothes. Out.

She hesitated at the bottom of the steps. The front door was right there, across the foyer. Freedom.

But she couldn't go out there in nothing but his T-shirt.

She peeked over the banister toward the back of the apartment. His kitchen was all dark wood and industrial steel, striking an impossible balance between harshly masculine and warmly inviting.

And right there, on the kitchen island—

Her backpack.

Her clothes, her weapons, her emergency cash. Everything she needed.

She just had to make it across the room without waking Davey.

Rowan took a deep breath and started moving, each step careful, measured. The hardwood floor creaked beneath her feet.

Her heart slammed against her ribs as she whipped her head toward the couch. Davey stirred, mumbling something unintelligible, but he didn't wake.

She let out the breath she'd been holding in a slow, controlled exhale and continued forward. She was halfway to the kitchen when a low woof behind her stopped her in her tracks.

Luka.

He'd followed her downstairs and now stood between her and the front door, ears pricked forward, his intelligent eyes locked on her with quiet intensity.

"Shh, Luka," she whispered, lifting a hand. "It's okay. I'm just—"

"Going somewhere?" Davey's sleep-roughened voice cut through the silence like a knife.

Fuck.

When he sat up, the blanket pooled around his hips, leaving far too much golden skin and hard muscle on display. He dragged his hands over his face and yawned, stretching, the shift of his abs pulling her gaze like a magnet.

Unfair. The man had no right to look that good while exhausted.

"I was just... getting some water," she lied. Weakly. Pathetically. He was going to see right through it.

His eyes narrowed. "Try again."

Her first instinct was to fight back, to push him away before he got too close. She lifted her chin. "So what if I was sneaking out?"

Davey exhaled through his nose, but she couldn't tell if he was out of frustration or amusement. Probably both.

"You really think walking out of here half-dressed, with a stitched-up hole in your side, is a good idea?" His voice was rough with sleep, but his eyes were sharp now, cutting straight through her. "That smart survival instinct of yours take the day off?"

She bristled. Damn him. He knew exactly how to needle her, how to get under her skin in ways no one else ever could. "I'm not being reckless. I'm trying to keep you safe."

His expression hardened. "Keep *me* safe? Ro, *you* are the one who showed up at my door bleeding and unconscious."

She flinched.

Unconscious.

She hated that word. Hated the helplessness of it.

Davey pushed himself up from the couch, wincing slightly as he put weight on his bad leg.

Her eyes betrayed her before she could stop them, tracking the hard planes of his stomach down to where his sweatpants sat dangerously low on his hips. The cut of muscle, the defined V—

She forced her gaze back to his face before she did something stupid. Like drool.

"You're in no condition to go anywhere," he said, his voice rough with something she didn't want to name. Something she wasn't ready for. "Christ, Ro, you were half-dead two nights ago. You really think I'll just let you disappear again?"

Two days. She'd lost two whole fucking days.

Her chest went tight.

"I don't need your permission," she snapped. "I'm not your responsibility, Davey."

He took a step closer. Too close.

Her body locked up, her instincts screaming move, but she couldn't. Not when he was looking at her like that—like she was something breakable, something worth keeping.

"You made it my responsibility when you came to me." He took another step toward her, crowding her. "You trusted me enough to come here when you were hurt and vulnerable."

Vulnerable.

She hated that word even more than unconscious.

"I made a mistake," she forced out, hating the way her voice wavered, hating that he heard it too.

He didn't respond, but a muscle in his jaw ticked. He was grinding his teeth.

"I shouldn't have come here," she added. "I put you at risk."

"What kind of trouble are you in?" he asked finally. "Who's after you?"

She shook her head. "The less you know, the safer you'll be."

His expression darkened. His next breath came slow, measured—controlled only because he was forcing it to be.

"Don't do that," he said, voice rough. "Don't stand there with a hole in your side and tell me to stay out of it."

"Well, I am. This isn't your fight. You don't need to be involved."

"I was involved the moment they hurt you."

A sharp twist of emotion punched through her.

No.

She wouldn't let this touch him. Wouldn't let her wrecking-ball life crash into his. "I can handle it on my own."

He barked out a humorless laugh. "Yeah, you were handling it real well when you were bleeding all over the sidewalk out front."

Her breath caught at a sudden sliver of memory—

his hands on her, pressing against the wound, the fear in his eyes before the darkness swallowed her whole.

She hated that he'd seen her like that. Hated that she'd let herself get that weak.

"That won't happen again," she said, willing her voice to stay steady. "I'll be more careful."

Davey's eyes flashed. "More careful? You nearly *died*, Rowan. If you hadn't made it here…" He trailed off, dragging a hand through his hair, making it stand up in an endearing cowlick. His throat worked as he swallowed. "Just… stay. Let me help you."

The earnestness in his voice made her chest ache. For a moment—a single, splintering second—she wanted to say yes. Wanted to sink into his warmth, let him wrap his arms around her, just for a little while.

"I can't," she whispered. "I'm sorry, Davey, but I have to go."

She turned toward the kitchen, forcing her feet to move, forcing herself not to look back.

Just grab the backpack.

Get out.

But Davey was faster.

In two quick strides, he was between her and the island, his broad frame blocking her path.

"Move," she growled, glaring up at him.

"No." He crowded her until her back hit the wall, until all she could see, all she could breathe, was him. "Not until you tell me what's going on."

Her patience snapped.

She shoved at his chest, but he didn't budge.

"Dammit, Wilde! Why can't you just let me go?"

Her voice cracked.

She hated that.

Hated that he was too damn steady, too damn stubborn, too damn *him*.

"Why do you even care?"

ten

WHY DID HE CARE?

She *didn't* just ask him that.

Was she really that naive? Or was she just refusing to see it?

Christ. He was so fucked.

He could've answered a thousand different ways.

That she'd crashed into his life years ago and never really left.

That she was the only woman who could drive him insane and still make him want to drag her closer.

That no matter how hard he tried, he couldn't stop watching her, wanting her, worrying about her.

Instead, he braced his hand against the wall beside her head, crowding her, forcing her to see what she refused to acknowledge. He watched her breath catch and her eyes widen. Her lips parted slightly, and he fought the urge to close the distance, to claim her mouth with his.

"You haunt me, Ro." His voice came out rougher than he intended. Raw. "Every time I close my eyes, you're there. Every time I let my guard down, you slip through the cracks. And I fucking let you."

He hadn't wanted to. Had tried not to.

But he'd been sitting beside her bed, watching her fight something he couldn't see, couldn't stop. He'd listened to her whimper for help in her sleep, and it had wrecked him.

"For two days, I've been watching you fight an enemy I couldn't help you with. And now you want to go back out there alone? I can't just stand by and watch you throw yourself back into danger."

She swallowed hard, her gaze flicking to his lips before meeting his eyes again.

There. Right there. That hesitation told him she felt it, too—the tension crackling between them like a live wire.

"Davey," she whispered. "You don't understand. I'm not running from danger. I *am* the danger."

His stomach twisted. Not with fear, this time, but with rage. She wanted him to believe that? That she was some untouchable force, like she wasn't standing right here in fornt of him, barely stitched together, barely fucking breathing?

He shook his head. "Bullshit. You're running

scared, Ro. I've seen you in action. You don't scare easy."

Her eyes flashed with anger. "You think you know me? You have no idea what I'm capable of."

"Then enlighten me," he challenged, his face inches from hers.

She shoved against his chest, but he didn't budge. "Who is after you?"

She remained stubbornly silent.

"Who did you piss off?"

Still, nothing.

"I can't help you if you don't tell me."

He felt the sharp press of steel against the front of his sweatpants and looked down.

A fucking paring knife.

He sighed. He'd faced down insurgents, IEDs, and the kind of hellfire most people wouldn't walk away from. He wasn't about to lose sleep over a five-foot-four spitfire and a damn kitchen knife.

"Where the hell did you find that?"

Her gaze flicked to the magnetic knife rack on the wall right next to them. Sure enough, the paring knife was missing. He hadn't even seen her take it.

"Back off, or I'll cut off your favorite appendage."

"You won't," he said and smiled. "You like that part of me too much."

She hissed like a pissed-off hell cat, but the pressure of the blade eased. "I hate you."

"So you've said. Many times."

"I don't need your help. I can handle this on my own."

He let out a humorless laugh. "Right, because you've done such a bang-up job of it so far." He leaned in closer, his nose nearly brushing hers. "In case you haven't noticed, you're bleeding all over my shirt."

She looked down at the spreading stain on the borrowed shirt and swore.

"Yeah. So cut the tough girl act and just tell me what the hell is going on."

She shoved at his chest again, but he still didn't budge. "You shouldn't care about me or my safety. We fuck, Wilde. We use each other to scratch that itch. That's it. No emotions. We don't even like each other!"

No emotions?

He would've laughed if it didn't feel like she'd just taken that damn knife and twisted it straight into his gut.

No emotions.

Like they were nothing.

Like she didn't know damn well what this was.

Like she hadn't just looked at him like he was the only thing keeping her standing.

His grip on her flexed. His breathing slowed, rough, uneven.

The smart thing would be to let go of her. To back away and let her go on pretending all they had between them was sex.

But, fuck, he didn't want to be smart. He wanted to

fight her on this. Wanted to make her say it first. Wanted to shove her against the wall and kiss every goddamn lie out of her mouth.

He was tired of pretending.

And before he could stop himself, those dangerous words clawed up his throat, words he couldn't take back once said.

"You're right. I don't like you." His voice dropped, rough, unsteady, scraping his throat raw, betraying him. "I fucking love you."

Her eyes flared wide. Yeah, he'd caught her off guard with that one. Hell, he'd caught himself off guard. He hadn't meant to say it. Not like that. But now that the truth was out, he couldn't take it back.

Didn't want to.

He'd spent most of the last year trying to bury this.

Telling himself it wasn't real.

That it was habit, frustration, just good sex.

But he'd been lying to himself.

Because after two days of watching her bleed, watching her break, watching her fight something too big for her to handle alone—

He couldn't keep up the lie any longer.

Rowan's face paled, and she looked more terrified than he'd ever seen her. The knife trembled slightly in her grip.

"What?" She laughed, but the sound was too high and brittle. "Uh, no. You're wrong. You're confused. You're—"

He cupped her face in one hand and brushed his thumb over her lips, silencing her. "You don't get to decide how I feel, Hellcat."

They stood frozen in a silent battle of wills.

Rowan's eyes blazed with a mix of anger and something else—fear, maybe, or longing. She jerked her head away from his touch. "You can't love me," she said, her voice cracking. "You don't know me."

Jesus, this woman. She was infuriating and stubborn and impossible. She was probably going to be the death of him. And, still, he wanted her more than his next breath.

"I know you're stubborn as hell and too damn proud for your own good. I know you're fiercely loyal to those you care about. And I think you care about me more than you want to admit, which is why you've been keeping me at arm's length." Slowly, he moved his other hand down to grasp her wrist. "Put the knife down, Ro. Let me in."

She pressed her lips together in a tight line, refusing to give an inch. But he could see the weariness under the shadows in her eyes, the tension coiled in her muscles. She was running on fumes and stubbornness.

"Why won't you let me help you?"

"Because I don't want you hurt," she said almost inaudibly.

He smirked at that. "You're holding a knife to my balls."

Her lips twitched, almost forming a smile before she caught herself. "That's different. I know you can handle me."

"Can I?" His voice dipped lower, teasing, dangerous.

The air between them charged with something new. Something inevitable.

She swallowed hard, her eyes darting to his lips. "You're the only one who can." Her grip on the knife loosened, and it clattered to the floor.

In an instant, he had her wrists pinned above her head with one hand, his body pressing her against the wall.

"Can you handle me, Ro?" he murmured, his lips a breath away from hers.

She tried to glare at him, but her eyes were dark with desire. "Fuck you, Wilde."

"Is that a request?" He nipped at her earlobe, drawing a soft gasp from her.

"I hate you," she whispered, but there was no venom in her words.

"No, you don't." His free hand slid under her shirt, caressing the soft skin of her waist. "Tell me the truth now. Who are you running from? Who hurt you?"

And, like that, her resolve crumbled. She sagged against him, burying her face in his chest. "It's bad, Davey. Really bad."

"Talk to me."

"I was hired to do a job, and I didn't do it." She

inhaled deeply as if the words had been keeping her from taking a full breath, and a knot of dread tightened in his gut.

"What kind of job?"

She simply lifted her head and stared at him with those golden cat eyes. She didn't have to speak. She'd finally raised her shutters enough that he saw the truth all over her face.

And he didn't like what he saw.

"Oh, Jesus." He backed away and paced a few steps, dragging a hand through his hair. "Fuck me, Rowan."

"Maybe later," she said with a faint smile.

He whirled back to face her. "You were supposed to kill someone."

Her chin lifted. "Yes."

"For money?"

Rowan's eyes flashed with defiance. "It's what I do. It's what I've always done. I'm good at death."

His stomach twisted. How many times had she walked into this apartment, dropped her bag by the door, stripped him down, and fucked him like it was the only thing tethering her to reality—only to walk right back out into a world where she ended lives for money?

And he'd never had a goddamn clue.

How long had she been living like this?

Who had she killed?

The thought made his blood go cold.

"Who was your target?"

She hesitated. Not a flicker, not a beat— a full hesitation. Long enough to make something in his chest lock up.

"It doesn't matter."

His breath hissed between his teeth. "The hell it doesn't. If someone's after you because you didn't complete a hit, I need to know who and why."

She stayed silent. Jaw tight. Shoulders squared. Refusing to give an inch.

His patience snapped, and he grabbed her by the shoulders, giving her a hard shake. "Dammit, Rowan!" His grip tightened, his voice rough, raw, breaking open. "Who was the fucking target?"

Her eyes blazed, but it wasn't just defiance he saw in the golden depths. Not just fury. There was desperation. Maybe even fear.

"Rowan, tell me."

"You. Okay? It was you." She shoved his hands away. "So still think you love me?"

eleven

ROWAN WATCHED the shock hit like a blow, rippling across his face, freezing him in place. His blue eyes widened—not just in disbelief, but with something worse.

Oh, God.

He hated her.

For a long, suffocating moment, he didn't move. Didn't even breathe.

Then his jaw clenched. His hands curled into fists at his sides, and he took a step back.

Away from her.

"Me," he said, his voice flat, emotionless in a way that made her stomach knot. "You were hired to kill me."

She nodded, her throat tight. "Yes."

"So when you came here at Christmas…"

She remembered that night so clearly, the last

night they'd spent together. The way he'd felt beneath her hands, the taste of his skin, the sound of his ragged breathing. He'd been so surly after returning from his family's party, his lip split from Cade punching him, and he'd taken his bad mood out on her in all the best possible ways. And, yes, she'd shamelessly used sex as a distraction because that was also the night her father hired WSW to find her, and she'd been so afraid he'd take her back to Dad's compound in Wyoming. She'd tied him to his bed with Christmas lights and slipped out while he shouted at her to come back.

"I was supposed to do it that night," she admitted quietly. "It was my second chance."

His eyes almost bugged out of his head. "*Second*? What was the first?"

Her gaze dropped to the floor, unable to meet his eyes as shame burned up the back of her neck. "Your parents' Fourth of July barbecue last summer."

"You've been planning to kill me for *six months*?"

"No." She winced as she pushed off the wall. The adrenaline was wearing off, and the pain from her injuries was setting in again. "I mean, yes, technically, I was supposed to be planning it. I was supposed to do it before you took control of Wilde Security. But I already knew I wouldn't. Both times."

Davey's expression was unreadable. "So instead of killing me, you fucked me. Both times."

She flinched at his harsh tone. "It wasn't like that."

"Then what was it like?" he demanded, his voice

rising. "A couple nights of mind-blowing sex and suddenly you decided to grow a conscience and not to kill me? How romantic."

"It wasn't just the sex," Rowan snapped, the frustration spiking into something dangerously close to heartbreak. "It was you, you idiot."

God, why couldn't he see it?

"The way you look at me, like I'm more than just a body to warm your bed."

Like I matter. Like I'm worth something.

"The way you hold me after, like you never want to let go." Her breath hitched, but she refused to let the words die in her throat. "It's never been just sex between us, and you know it. That's why I took the job in the first place. I never planned to kill you. I took it to protect you. And now, because I didn't do it, they're coming after me and threatening my family."

His laugh wasn't really a laugh. It was sharp, jagged, more like a broken edge of glass.

Her stomach twisted. She had expected the anger, the betrayal. But this? This cold, distant, hollow sound—this was worse.

"*Protect* me?" His voice was softer now but all the more dangerous for it. "By accepting a hit on me? That's some twisted logic, Ro."

"I knew if I didn't take the job, they'd just hire someone else. Someone who wouldn't hesitate to put a bullet in your head. At least with me, I could control the situation, buy some time to figure out who was behind it and why."

"You don't know who hired you?"

"No. The job came through an intermediary." She raised a hand to touch him, but he knocked it away and put the length of the room between them.

"Don't. You're gonna have to give me a minute here because I'm having a hard time wrapping my head around the fact that the woman I love was hired to kill me. I mean... fuck!"

She stayed back and watched him pace, noting his limp was more pronounced than usual.

Finally, he stopped moving and let out a humorless laugh. "Jesus Christ, Ro. You really know how to fuck things up, don't you?"

"Excuse me?" She stepped into his space and jabbed a finger at his chest. "You should be thanking me."

Davey's eyes flashed dangerously. "Thanking you? For what, exactly? For not killing me? For lying to me for months?"

Rowan's finger curled into a fist against his chest. "For saving your life, you ungrateful bastard. If I hadn't taken that contract, you'd be dead right now."

"You should have told me."

She scoffed. "Oh, sure, that would have gone over well. 'Hey Davey, just so you know, someone wants you dead and hired me to do it. But don't worry, I'm not going to follow through. Want to grab dinner and fuck?'"

Davey ran a hand through his hair, frustration evident in every tense line of his body. "At least I would have known there was a threat. I could have protected myself. Instead, I've been walking around with a target on my back for months, completely oblivious."

"And what would you have done if I had? Gone charging in like some alphahole to save the day? You would have gotten yourself killed, and then all of this would have been for nothing."

He grabbed her wrist, pulling her hand away from his chest. "That wasn't your call to make. I had a right to know someone wants me dead."

"And now you know," she shot back. "Happy?"

"Ecstatic," he growled. His eyes blazed, his fingers flexing at his sides. His breathing was rough, uneven, like he was fighting something inside himself.

Then, all at once, he stopped fighting.

His grip on her wrist tightened, hard enough to steal her breath, and he yanked her against him. Before she could react, his mouth crashed down on hers in a bruising kiss. Rowan gasped in surprise but quickly melted into him, her free hand fisting in his shirt as she kissed him back with equal fervor.

The kiss was all teeth and tongues, a clash of anger and passion. Davey's hands roamed her body roughly, pulling her impossibly closer as if he could erase the lies and betrayal with the force of his touch.

She slid her hands up his chest and around his neck, fingers tangling in his hair as she pressed herself against him. The pain from her injuries faded to a dull throb, overwhelmed by the heat of Davey's touch. She bit his lower lip, drawing a growl from deep in his throat.

Suddenly, Davey broke the kiss and spun her around, pinning her against the wall with his body. He delved a hand under the oversized t-shirt and stroked between her legs.

"You're going to tell me everything, Ro." His breath was hot against her ear, his voice low and dangerous. "Every detail about this contract, who might be behind it, and why they want me dead."

"I don't know much," she gasped, arching against him as he teased her clit. "The job came through an anonymous broker. All I know is that someone powerful wants you out of the picture before you can fully take control of Wilde Security."

He shoved a finger into her as if punishing her, and then another, and a third until she was stretched and her knees nearly gave out from the intense mix of pleasure and pain. His fingers curled inside her, finding that spot that made her see stars.

"Not good enough," he growled. "I need names, Rowan. Who's the broker?"

She gasped, struggling to form coherent thoughts as he worked her mercilessly. "I don't...I can't..."

He stilled his hand, denying her the friction she craved. "Try harder."

Frustrated tears pricked her eyes. "Dammit, Davey. I don't know names. That's the whole point of using brokers."

His thumb circled her clit, sending jolts of pleasure through her core. "Then give me something I can use. Anything."

She racked her brain, desperate for information that might satisfy him. "The money...it came through a shell company. Kryos Solutions."

His fingers resumed their torturous rhythm, drawing a moan from her lips.

"Kryos Solutions," he repeated, his voice a low rumble against her ear. "That's a start. What else?"

She tried to focus through the haze of pleasure and pain. "The... the contract. It specified you had to die before the end of last year. Before you officially took over Wilde Security."

His hand stilled again, and Rowan bit back a frustrated groan.

"Why?" he demanded. "What changes when I take over?"

"I don't know," she gasped. "But it must be significant if someone's willing to pay this much to prevent it."

Davey's free hand came up to grip her chin, forcing her to meet his gaze over her shoulder. His blue eyes were dark with a mix of lust and anger, and she could feel the hard ridge of his cock against her ass. "What else?"

She shook her head, barely able to form words. "Nothing... that's all I know. Please, Davey..."

He nipped at her earlobe. "Please, what?"

"Let me come," she gasped and reached down between her legs, desperate to finish the job herself. "God, please let me come."

He slapped her hand away, and his eyes bored into hers, searching for any hint of deception. "How much?"

"Two million. Half up front, half when the job was done."

His jaw worked soundlessly. "Jesus. Christ. Where's the money they already paid?"

"I donated it to a women's shelter. I never wanted it."

"Why?"

"I told you." Her voice came out husky with need. "It was never just sex."

Something flickered in Davey's eyes— a softening, a hint of the tenderness she'd seen before. But it was quickly replaced by steely determination.

"We're not done here," he said, his voice low and dangerous. He kicked her legs apart, and she heard the rasp of his zipper. "But right now, I need to fuck you."

She didn't protest. She was aching for him. She

constantly ached for him, and that was part of the problem, but now wasn't the time for analyzing her feelings. He thrust into her hard, burying himself to the hilt in one smooth stroke. She cried out, her body stretching to accommodate him.

He set a punishing pace, each thrust driving her harder against the wall. His fingers dug into her hips, sure to leave bruises, and her side ached, and she didn't care. She pushed back against him, meeting him thrust for thrust, desperate for more.

"Is this what you wanted?" Davey growled in her ear. "To fuck the man you were supposed to kill?"

"No," she gasped. "I wanted you. Just you."

Davey's rhythm faltered for a moment, then resumed even harder than before. One hand slid around to rub her clit in tight circles.

A shockwave of pleasure went through her, and her legs trembled, threatening to collapse under her. She had to brace herself against the wall to stay upright.

His clever fingers worked her clit, building her pleasure higher and higher. She could feel her orgasm approaching, a tidal wave ready to crash over her.

"Davey," she gasped, "I'm close."

He nipped at her earlobe. "Not yet. You don't get to come until I say so."

She whimpered in frustration but nodded. She knew this game well— the exquisite torture of being held on the edge. His thrusts became more erratic, his breathing ragged against her neck.

"Tell me again," he demanded. "Why did you really take the contract?"

"To protect you," she panted. "Because I couldn't bear the thought of someone else hurting you."

His grip tightened on her hip, his thrusts becoming more forceful. "And why is that? Why do you care if I live or die?"

The truth clawed its way up her throat, ripping past every wall she'd spent years reinforcing.

No. She couldn't—she wasn't ready.

But with Davey buried deep inside her, his hands gripping her like she belonged to him, like she was his, she wasn't strong enough to hold it back anymore.

She had never been strong enough when it came to him.

"You know why," she whispered.

"Say it." His fingers increased their pressure on her clit. "I want to hear you say it."

"Because..." she gasped, her body trembling right on the razor's edge of release. "Because I love you, too, you stubborn asshole."

Davey went still.

Completely. Utterly. Still.

His grip on her hip tightened, not rough, not punishing—just firm, anchoring, like he was afraid she'd vanish if he let go. For a long, agonizing second, he didn't move.

Oh God. Had she said too much? Had she just—

Then his body snapped back into motion. Harder. Deeper. More desperate than before.

"Say it again."

"I love you," she repeated, the words coming easier now. "I love you, Davey Wilde. I've loved you for so long, I can't remember a time when I didn't."

His fingers rubbed her clit harder, faster, sending her hurtling towards the edge. "That's it, Hellcat," he rasped. "Come for me. Let me feel you."

Her world shattered, white-hot pleasure exploding through her as her orgasm finally crashed over her in wave after wave of ecstasy. Her knees buckled, but Davey's strong arm around her waist held her up, and he followed her over the edge, spilling himself inside her with a hoarse shout of her name.

For several long moments, they stayed frozen in place, panting heavily, their sweat-slicked bodies still joined. Davey's forehead rested against the back of her neck, his breath hot on her skin. Then, slowly, almost reluctantly, he withdrew and tucked himself back into his sweatpants, leaving her feeling suddenly empty and bereft. He turned her to face him and cupped her cheeks in his big hands as his eyes searched hers. Anger no longer blazed in those beautiful blue irises. Instead, there was a mix of confusion, hurt, and something else, something soft— longing, maybe.

"Did you mean it?" he asked quietly.

She nodded, unable to look away from his intense gaze. "Every word."

Davey's thumbs stroked over her cheekbones, his touch gentle now in contrast to the rough passion of moments before. "I want to believe you, Ro. Jesus, I want to believe you so badly. But..."

"But you don't trust me," she finished for him. "I get it. I wouldn't trust me either, after everything I've done."

He closed his eyes briefly as if in pain. When he opened them again, they were filled with a deep sadness that made her heart ache.

"It's not that simple," he said roughly. "I do trust you. At least, I trust that you wouldn't hurt me, not physically. Even when you're holding a knife to my balls, threatening to castrate me." A faint smile flickered across his mouth but was gone in a blink. "But emotionally? You have the power to destroy me, and that's fucking terrifying."

The vulnerability in his eyes, the raw honesty of his admission, it was almost too much to bear. She reached up to cover his hands with her own, her thumbs stroking over his knuckles. "I will never intentionally hurt you, Davey. Not in any way. I want to be the person you can trust, the one who stands by your side no matter what comes our way."

He leaned his forehead against hers, his eyes closing briefly. "You lied to me, Ro."

The words weren't a slap.

They weren't even angry.

They were just quiet. Final. True.

She winced anyway.

"For months." His breath was slow, measured. "You let me walk around with a target on my back."

Guilt sliced through her, sharp and merciless.

"So now we've got a hell of a mess to sort through before we can even think about what comes next for us."

For us.

Her heart clenched hard.

Even now, after everything, he was still talking about them as an "us."

But she knew—trust wasn't a switch you could flip. It was something rebuilt brick by painstaking brick.

Davey exhaled and stepped back. The loss of his warmth made her feel colder than it should have. "I need to call my brothers." His gaze flicked downward, catching on the small stain of blood on her borrowed shirt. "And Tessa. Have her come look at those stitches."

"I'm fine."

His jaw tightened. "I wasn't gentle."

"I didn't want you to be."

For the barest second, his eyes darkened, the heat from earlier sparking again. A hint of a smirk tugged at the corner of his mouth, but it disappeared just as quickly.

His walls were back up.

Guarded. Controlled.

She hated it.

"I washed all the clothes in your backpack. They're in the dryer upstairs. Go clean up," he said, his voice cooler now, more practical. "Then we're going to have a very long talk about all of this."

Rowan nodded, knowing there was no avoiding it. She'd confessed her darkest secret. She'd told him she loved him, but that didn't erase the lies. The months of deception. The ways she'd broken his trust.

She had to earn that back.

Brick by fucking brick.

Davey turned and grabbed his phone from the coffee table before heading for the stairs. He paused at the bottom step, his back to her. "And, Ro?"

She lifted her head, heart slamming into her ribs. "What?"

Slowly, he turned. His blue eyes locked onto hers. Unreadable. Intense.

A beat.

Two.

"The answer's yes."

Rowan stopped breathing. "What?"

His lips curved—not a smirk, not quite a smile. Something softer. Something only meant for her.

"Yes," he said quietly, like it wasn't even a question. "I still love you."

Her breath rushed out of her in an explosive

exhale, and tears blurred her vision. She blinked hard to hold them back. She would not cry in front of him, dammit.

"Even if I'm pissed as hell right now, that hasn't changed." He shook his head and let out a low, self-deprecating laugh. "I don't know what it says about me, but I'm starting to think there's nothing you could do, nothing you could confess, that would change how I feel."

Then, before she could even think of a response, he was gone—disappearing up the stairs and leaving her standing there, chest tight, hands shaking, wondering what the hell she was supposed to do with that.

twelve

HIS BROTHERS ARRIVED within minutes of his call, which meant neither had left for work yet.

Elliot strode in first, his polished dress shoes clicking against the hardwood floor, and Luka trotted over to meet him, tail wagging as if this were a casual family visit instead of a crisis. Elliot took a moment to give the dog the attention he deserved before straightening and pushing his sliding glasses up his nose.

"What's going on? You sounded tense on the phone." His gaze flicked to Rowan as she descended the stairs dressed in a tight black crop top and black tactical pants, her hair hanging loose and damp over her shoulders.

His brow furrowed. "You found her."

"More like she found me."

Dominic burst through the door behind Elliot. Despite it being nearly eleven a.m., he was still dressed in flannel pajama pants and a New York Rangers T-shirt, his hair sleep-tousled. His boyish grin faded as he sensed the tension in the room.

"Shit, is this a family meeting or a standoff? Because it's feeling like a standoff, and I haven't had coffee yet." He yawned and shouldered by Elliot, headed toward the espresso machine in the kitchen.

Luka followed, nudging his leg for attention or, more likely, treats. Dom was always feeding Luka table scraps behind Davey's back. He patted the dog's head once and yawned again. "Hey, buddy. Not now. Uncle Dom needs caffeine before pets."

"Whose bed did you wake up in today?" Elliot asked dryly.

"My own, thank you very much."

"Yeah, who with?"

"I never kiss and tell." He grinned over his shoulder at Davey and Rowan. "But it smells like sex in here, so I can guess who big bro woke up with."

Rowan's face flushed. Davey opened his mouth to tell Dominic to go to hell, but the espresso machine screeched, drowning out his words and Dom's laugh.

He pinched the bridge of his nose, fighting the urge to smack his little brother upside the head. "Can we focus here? We've got a situation."

"Right, right," Dom said and pulled himself up to sit on the island, sipping his espresso. "Family meeting. Okay, I'm here. I'm sort of awake. Shoot."

Elliot's eyes narrowed behind his glasses as he studied Rowan. "What kind of situation?"

Rowan crossed her arms, her stance defensive. "The kind where someone wants Davey dead."

Dom's head snapped up. "Wait, what?"

And here came the hard part.

Davey exhaled slowly, steeling himself against the storm about to hit. Luka, who had curled up on the couch when Dom didn't feed him, lifted his head at the shift in the room, ears pricking up.

Yeah. Davey wasn't the only one bracing for impact.

His fingers flexed at his sides before he met his brothers' gazes, something in his chest twisting at the concern already shadowing their expressions. "Someone put out a hit on me last summer. Rowan was hired to do the job."

The room went deathly silent.

Dom's espresso cup clattered against the countertop as he set it down hard. "Holy... fuck."

Elliot pulled off his glasses and rubbed the bridge of his nose like he needed a second to process what he had just heard. He was the most easy-going of them, but that didn't mean he didn't have a temper, and that temper now simmered in his eyes as he slid his glasses back into place. "Why the hell is she still breathing?"

"Hey!" Davey's body moved before his brain caught up, stepping into Elliot's path, his palm slamming flat against his brother's chest. Luka startled at the sudden motion, scrambling up from his spot on the couch and giving a sharp bark.

"It's okay," he told his dog, then focused on Elliot again. "Back off, El."

"Back off?" "Back off?" Elliot shoved his glasses up the bridge of his nose, his expression twisting, disbelief warring with fury. "She was *hired to kill you*, and you're *defending her*?"

Dominic jumped down from the counter, his usual cheerful demeanor replaced by a hard glint in his blue eyes. "You tried to kill our brother?"

"No," Davey said, keeping his tone sharp and authoritative, hoping to curtain all arguments. "She was hired, but she never intended to go through with it."

Rowan remained silent, her face impassive, but Davey felt the waves of tension radiating from her. Like a coiled spring, ready to snap. He hated that. Hated that she was prepared to fight his family if she had to. That she expected to.

"Have you lost your mind?" Elliot demanded, running a hand through his hair in frustration. "She's an assassin, Davey. She can't be trusted."

"I trust her."

"Are you fucking serious?" Dom said.

"I am. Rowan could have killed me a hundred times over if she wanted to. She didn't. She came to me instead and told me the truth." Of course he'd had to fuck the truth out of her, but he hadn't minded that part.

And given the faint stain of a blush coloring her skin, Rowan was remembering it, too. But that wasn't something he was about to share with his brothers.

"Jesus Christ," Dom muttered, running his hands through his messy hair. "This is way above my pay grade for this time of morning."

"It's almost noon," Elliot reminded.

"But it's not yet, so it's still morning. You know I don't do mornings."

Patience, Davey reminded himself, was a much-needed quality when dealing with Dom, but his supply was running low. He gave himself a moment to rein in his irritation. "Look, I know this is a lot to take in, but Rowan's on our side. She's in danger, too, and she's going to help us figure out who's behind this."

Elliot scoffed and crossed his arms. "And we're supposed to believe that? For all we know, this could be part of her plan."

Rowan snorted. "If it were, it would be a very stupid and convoluted plan. I could've just walked up to him at any point, shot him through the head, and walked away, and none of you would've been the wiser. But I didn't because I don't want him dead any more than you do."

Jesus, her tone was frighteningly cold.

Davey couldn't quite reconcile that with the

woman he knew who ran so fucking hot when she was in his arms.

"Appreciate that," he muttered. He also appreciated her restraint. If she felt so inclined, she could wipe the floor with his brothers, and he wasn't in the mood to clean up more blood.

She gave him a saccharine smile and took his hand, squeezing his fingers. "You're welcome." Her attention shifted back to his brothers. "I don't expect you to trust me, but I'm not here to harm him. I never was. I only took the job to buy some time and figure out who's behind the contract."

Both of his brothers stared down at their entwined fingers for an awkward beat.

Dom let out a disbelieving laugh, picked up his espresso, and threw it back like a shot of liquor.

Elliot just shook his head, something like disappointment in his eyes. "Damn, Davey. You're the last guy I'd expect to think with his dick instead of his brain."

Heat burned up the back of his neck. Embarrassment or anger? He couldn't really tell at this point. "It's not like that."

"Oh, wait, so you're not still fucking her?" Sarcasm dripped from Dom's every word. "Wow, that's a relief because I seem to remember..." He pulled his phone from his pocket, found what he was looking for, and held it out.

Davey's gut clenched as he caught a glimpse of

himself on the screen—naked, tangled in sheets, hands tied to the headboard of his bed with Christmas lights.

Dom wiggled the phone for emphasis. "Last time, she fucked you in more ways than one."

Beside him, Rowan gave a very unladylike snort. Her shoulders shook, lips pressing together as she fought to keep the laugh in. She failed. Miserably.

He scowled over at her. "It's not funny."

"Yes, it is," she said, completely unrepentant.

Dom pointed at her. "That we can agree on."

He turned his glare on his youngest brother and tried to snatch the phone, but the little shit was too fast. "How much do you want to delete that photo?"

"Oh, big brother, there is not enough money on planet Earth. This is going to come out every time we argue until one of us kicks the bucket."

"Which could be soon, from the sounds of it," Elliot said, his glare still firmly locked on Rowan.

Davey's patience snapped. "Enough!" His voice rang out with the authority that had once commanded troops in battle. "Dad and our uncles trusted me with this company, and I don't intend to let them down. But I can't do that if we're too busy tearing each other apart to focus on the real threat. Someone inside Wilde Security wants me dead, and that's where our attention needs to be. Not on bickering like damn children."

The room fell silent.

Elliot's anger seemed to deflate, and in its place came the worry. "You think it's someone inside the company?"

"Yes," Rowan said without a shred of doubt in her voice. "One of the stipulations on the contract was it had to be completed before Davey took control."

"I mean..." After a moment's thought, Dom nodded. "Makes sense. Cade has a damn good reason to want him dead."

"Cade wouldn't..." Elliot trailed off and didn't finish the thought. Because the truth was, they all knew Cade was capable of it.

A chill scraped down Davey's spine at the mention of their cousin. Cade had always been volatile, but murder? He couldn't quite wrap his head around it. But neither could he discount it.

"We can't rule anyone out at this point. Not even family."

More silence filled the space between them until it was like a living, breathing thing sucking up all the oxygen in the room.

"Look," Davey said finally. "You have to trust me. Rowan's not the enemy here."

Dom snorted. "Right. Because assassins make such great allies."

"Ex-assassin," Rowan corrected quietly. "And I understand your skepticism. But I'm here to help, whether you believe it or not. Someone wants Davey dead, and I intend to find out who and why."

Elliot squeezed his eyes shut and pinched the bridge of his nose. "All right, let's say we believe you. What's the plan?"

Davey exchanged a glance with Rowan before answering. "We need to investigate quietly. If it is someone inside Wilde Security, we can't risk tipping them off."

"I've always wanted a reason to build a super-secret spy team," Dominic said.

He was probably only half-joking, given his James Bond obsession as a kid.

"We need people we can trust implicitly," Elliot said, the gears already turning in that sharp mind of his. "A small team. The fewer people who know, the better."

"Sabin," Davey said. If there was one person in WSW he trusted more than his brothers, it was Jean-Sabin Cavalier. "We might need someone who can get in and out of places undetected and access secure systems."

"Oh, sure." Dom rolled his eyes. "We already have a former assassin on the team, so why not invite the former thief?"

"Sabin's a pain in the ass, but he's a solid choice. He'd never betray Davey," Elliot said. "And what about Sullivan O'Connell? He's got contacts all over the place, and he's loyal to a fault. He'd never betray us. I've saved his brother's ass too many times."

"Good call. He can be scary as fuck," Dom said. "What about Weston?"

Davey shook his head. "No. West's loyalties will always be with his brother first, and if Cade's involved..." He didn't finish the thought.

"Right," Dom said on an exhale. "Well, should probably at least add Daphne to the list. She's a tech whiz, and we know we can trust her."

Davey considered it, then shook his head. "Not unless we need her. We keep this tight. No one else."

"Liam," Rowan said quietly. All eyes turned to her, and she shrugged. "He's not afraid to get his hands dirty if needed."

Elliot raised an eyebrow. "You seem awfully comfortable making assumptions about our family."

"I'm not making assumptions. I'm stating facts based on intel I've gathered over the years. Liam Wilde is better with a weapon than anyone in this room, and he's fiercely loyal to your company. Those aren't assumptions. They're tactical advantages we'd be foolish to ignore."

Sharp. Confident. Unapologetic. She met Elliot's glare head-on, her shoulders squared like she was daring him to challenge her again.

That's my girl.

Davey smothered a smile. "She's right about Liam. He's in. Let's get him on board."

Dom let out a low whistle. "Well, shit. I guess we're really doing this, huh? Assembling our own little

Avengers team to take down whoever's gunning for you."

"This isn't a game, Dom," Elliot said, heavy on the exasperation.

"You think I don't know that?" Dominic shot back, the usual spark of mischief in his eyes hardening into something steely. "Someone's trying to kill our brother. Trust me, I'm taking this plenty seriously."

Davey studied him for a beat. Gone was the easy grin, the lazy slouch. Dom stood rigid, his jaw clenched, fingers curling and uncurling at his sides like he was holding back the urge to hit something—or someone. His usual sharp retort didn't follow. No deflection, no joke to lighten the mood. Just pure, unshakable resolve.

Davey felt something tighten in his chest. Dom might be the wildcard, the one who laughed in the face of danger—but when it mattered, he stood firm.

He reached out, clasping the back of Dom's neck in a firm squeeze before letting go.

"I know you are, and I appreciate it," he said quietly, then slipped into command mode. "Elliot, reach out to Sullivan. Dom, you contact Sabin. I'll call Liam. We'll meet tonight..." He glanced over at Rowan, who shook her head.

"Not here. We have to assume they know where you live. Do you have a safe house?"

"The apartment on West 82nd," Elliot supplied.

"Wasn't Brody O'Connell running security for a witness there?" Davey asked.

Elliot shook his head. "The witness testified today, and WITSEC swept them up right after they left the courthouse. The apartment's open." He frowned in thought. "If we're bringing Sullivan into this, we should probably bring Brody in, too. You know how they are."

Actually, Davey didn't. He hadn't spent enough time around the O'Connell twins—or any of his employees, for that matter—to know them all that well. It was something he needed to remedy.

"Okay," Davey agreed. "Get Sullivan and Brody looped in. We're meeting at the West 82nd apartment, twenty hundred. Keep it under the radar."

Elliot nodded, pulling out his phone to start making calls. Dominic was already tapping away on his, presumably texting Sabin.

Davey turned to Rowan. "You good with this plan?"

She inhaled sharply, let the breath go in a rush, then nodded. "It's a start. But we need to move fast. Whoever's behind this won't wait forever to make another attempt."

A comforting thought.

His gaze traced down her body. As much as he appreciated the way the tight top clung to her breasts, he was worried. He let his hand brush the strip of bare skin at her back and leaned in, lowering his voice. "Are you okay? Did we pop any stitches?"

Rowan shook her head, a small smile playing at her lips. "I'm fine. Bled a little, but your stitching held up well."

"It wasn't my handiwork. It was my cousin's."

Her eyes narrowed. "Which cousin? You have, like, a gazillion."

"I only have nine."

Used to be ten, until Brennan...

He shut down that line of thought before it put the familiar lump of grief in his throat and added, "It was Tessa."

"Only nine," she scoffed. "Know how many I have? Three."

"Sounds peaceful."

"Oh, it is." She wrinkled her nose. "Unless you start counting the kids of all my honorary uncles. Then... not so much."

Davey chuckled softly, his thumb tracing small circles on her lower back. The tension in her muscles eased under his touch. He wanted to pull her close, to shield her from whatever was coming, but he knew she'd bristle at the overprotectiveness.

"All right, lovebirds," Dominic called out, breaking the moment. "Sabin's in. If we're done here, I'm gonna head home and sleep before tonight's super-secret spy meeting."

"You're the only man I know who can down a

double shot of espresso and then go to sleep," Elliot said, not looking up from his phone.

"What can I say? It's a gift." Dom shrugged and headed toward the door. He paused at the threshold and glanced back. It seemed he was going to say something more, but he just shook his head slightly and left without uttering a sound.

Elliot pocketed his phone. "Brody and Sullivan are in. They'll meet us there." His gaze lingered on Rowan, still wary, but he didn't voice his concern. "I have to go into the office for a few hours. I assume you're working from home today?"

Davey nodded, grateful for Elliot's restraint. He was too tired to go another round with him right now. "Yeah. We'll see you tonight."

As Elliot turned to go, Davey hesitated, then called after him. "Wait. Can you drop Luka off at Mom and Dad's on your way to the office? They're not going back to Virginia until the end of the month, right? I don't know how long this is gonna take, and I don't want him here if this place isn't safe."

Elliot sighed, adjusting his glasses before glancing at the dog curled up on the couch. Luka's ears twitched, but he didn't lift his head.

"Yeah, I'll take him. C'mon, Luka. Let's go for a ride." He whistled softly, and the dog hopped off the couch, stretching indulgently before padding over to bump his head against Davey's leg.

"Sorry, I can't go, buddy." Davey crouched, rubbing

behind his ears before kissing the black spot on his forehead. "Be good. I'll come get you as soon as I can."

Luka gave a short wag of his tail.

Elliot picked up the leash hanging by the door, then shot Davey a look. "You owe me for this. Mom's already mad enough you don't visit. If I show up with your dog but not you, I'm dealing with that fallout."

"Add it to my tab."

Elliot just shook his head and, with Luka at his side, headed for the door. As he left, closing it behind him, Davey felt some of the tension drain from his shoulders.

At least Luka would be safe.

He turned to Rowan, who was watching him with those sharp hazel eyes.

"Well, that went about as well as could be expected," she said dryly.

He snorted. "Yeah, considering I thought Elliot might actually try to strangle you for a minute there."

"Please. I'd like to see him try."

His lips twitched. "I wouldn't. I'm not in the mood to patch up either of you." He stepped closer, his hand finding its way back to that strip of bare skin at her waist. "So, we've got all day until the meeting..."

"You don't have to work?"

"I'm the boss. I say when I work."

She arched an eyebrow, a smirk playing at her lips. "Abusing your power already? I'm impressed."

"I prefer to think of it as prioritizing." His fingers

trailed along her spine, liking the way it made her shiver. "And right now, keeping you safe is my top priority."

"Is that what we're calling it?" Her hands came up to rest on his chest, but she didn't push him away. Instead, her fingers curled into the fabric of his shirt, pulling him closer.

"We shouldn't," she murmured, even as she tilted her head, exposing the curve of her neck to him.

"Probably not," he agreed, brushing his lips against her soft skin. He loved the breathy little noise she made when he opened his mouth on her neck and sucked.

Her fingers tightened in his shirt as his mouth worked its way up her neck. Her breath hitched when he nipped at her earlobe.

"We have a lot of work to do," she breathed, even as she arched into him.

He dragged in a slow, uneven breath, trying—really trying—to remember why this was a bad idea.

"You're right," he murmured, his hands sliding down her waist instead of away like they should. "We need to focus. Go over everything that's happened in the past year... piece together connections... find leads..." His mouth brushed along her jaw between each word, derailing his own train of thought.

Rowan hummed in agreement, though she clearly wasn't paying attention to the words coming out of his mouth—just the way his lips moved against her skin.

"We should stop," he muttered, though he was already tilting her head back for better access.

"Mm, yes." She threaded her fingers into his hair and deliberately scraped her nails against his scalp, knowing damn well what it did to him. "But if we're going over everything, I can think of one very memorable event we should... examine closely."

A needy sound rumbled from his throat before he could stop it. *Fuck.* "Christmas?"

"Mm," she hummed in agreement and tugged on his lower lip with her teeth. "I think we need to recreate that night. For investigative purposes, of course. We need to examine every...single...detail."

"You're not tying me up again, Rowan."

"We'll see about that."

Heat blazed through him as her tongue swept past his lips, teasing and exploring, and his restraint snapped like a frayed wire. He gripped her hips, pulling her flush against him as he deepened the kiss and backed her against the nearest wall.

When they finally broke apart, both breathing heavily, Rowan's eyes glittered with mischief and desire. "Now, about those Christmas lights..."

He groaned, his resolve crumbling. "Fuck, Ro..."

Her lips curved in a wicked smile. "That's the idea."

thirteen

HE DIDN'T LET her tie him up again. Which was a shame. She'd liked having him under her and at her complete mercy...

But she also liked him over her, pounding into her, with her legs locked around his hips as he growled dirty things in her ear. And behind her, drilling so deep that she saw stars with every thrust.

She never got tired of it, tired of him.

When they first started sleeping together last summer, she'd foolishly thought she'd fuck him right out of her system and go back to hating him. But every time they were together, the line between love and hate blurred until she couldn't tell where one ended and the other began.

It was maddening and addictive all at once.

Now she lay sprawled across his chest, both of them panting and slick with sweat. His heart thundered beneath her cheek, matching the frantic rhythm of her own. She should move, should put some distance between them before the vulnerability of the moment consumed her. But his arms were locked around her waist, holding her close, and she found herself sinking deeper into his embrace.

"Fuck," he breathed. "That was…"

"Yeah," she agreed, unable to form a more coherent response. Her body hummed with the lingering pleasure of orgasm number… she didn't even know.

She felt his fingers tracing idle patterns along her spine, and a shiver ran through her. It was too tender, too intimate.

And, God help her, she loved it.

She loved him so much it hurt.

And she was so fucking afraid of losing him.

Her throat closed up, and she squeezed her eyes shut against the sudden sting of tears as she tightened her arms around him.

"Hey," Davey murmured, his hand coming up to cup the back of her head. "You okay? I didn't hurt you, did I?"

She shook her head against his chest, not trusting her voice. His fingers tangled in her hair, gently massaging her scalp, and she had to bite back a whimper. Why did he have to be so damn gentle with her?

"Rowan." His voice was soft, concerned. "Talk to me. What's going on in that head of yours?"

She took a shaky breath, trying to steady herself. "Nothing. I'm fine."

His hand stilled in her hair. "You're trembling."

Rowan cursed inwardly. Of course he'd notice. Davey noticed everything about her, always had. It was part of what made him so infuriatingly irresistible.

"I'm just... overwhelmed," she admitted, the words barely above a whisper.

Davey shifted, rolling them onto their sides so he could look into her eyes. His piercing blue gaze searched her face, and she felt exposed in a way that had nothing to do with their nakedness.

His thumb brushed lightly back and forth over the curve of her cheekbone. "Overwhelmed by what?"

"You." She caught his hand and pressed it to her cheek. "This. Us... loving each other like a real couple."

Davey's eyes softened, a mix of understanding and tenderness that made Rowan's chest ache. "Hey," he said softly, "we are a real couple. Pretty sure we have been from the beginning."

"No." The denial was automatic, and his lips twitched into a smirk.

"Well, I haven't seen any other women since we got together last summer."

She scowled at him. "You better not have. I'll go get that knife from the kitchen and finish what I started earlier." To emphasize her point, she dropped a hand between his legs and cupped his balls, giving them a squeeze she knew would border on painful.

Davey's breath hitched, but his smirk only widened. "Easy there, killer. I'm rather attached to those." He rolled suddenly, pinning her underneath him as his cock hardened against her hand. "And so are you."

"Oh my God, you can't possibly be ready for round four."

"Wanna bet?"

He captured her lips in a searing kiss, stealing her breath and any remaining coherent thoughts. His tongue swept into her mouth, demanding and possessive, as his hips ground against hers. Rowan moaned, arching into him, her body responding instantly despite her exhaustion.

"Fuck," she gasped when he finally released her lips to trail hot, open-mouthed kisses down her neck. "You're insatiable."

"Only for you." He nipped at her collarbone.

His words sent a shiver of pleasure through her, but also a pang of fear. This was exactly what she'd been afraid of—getting in too deep, becoming too dependent on him. And yet, she couldn't bring herself to push him away.

His hand slid between her thighs, fingers finding her still-slick folds. She arched into his touch, her body oversensitive but craving more. He teased just enough to have her panting, but then pulled back.

"Have you been with any other men since we got together?"

Rowan's breath caught in her throat. She knew the answer, but admitting it felt like surrendering the last shred of her defenses. Still, she couldn't bring herself to lie to him.

"No," she whispered, averting her gaze. "There's been no one else."

Relief and triumph flashed in his eyes before he claimed her mouth in another searing kiss. His fingers resumed their teasing strokes between her thighs as he ground his hardening length against her hip.

"Good," he growled against her lips. "Because you're mine, Hellcat. All mine."

A shiver ran through her at his possessive tone. Part of her wanted to bristle at being claimed, to assert her independence. But a larger part thrilled at belonging to him, at having him belong to her in return.

"And you're mine," Rowan breathed, surprising herself with the fierce possessiveness in her voice. She tangled her fingers in his hair, pulling him closer as she nipped at his lower lip. "All mine."

"Damn right I am." He shifted, positioning himself between her thighs, the thick head of his cock pressing against her entrance.

Her breath caught in anticipation, her body already aching for him again.

But then he paused, his gaze softening as he

looked down at her. "I love you, Rowan. I've never said that to another woman. So, this?" He sank into her, making them both groan, but then withdrew until they were barely connected. "Us?" Again, he thrust and withdrew. "It's as fucking real as it gets."

She swallowed hard, fighting against the surge of emotion threatening to overwhelm her. "Is it? Because I don't know how to do this, Davey. I don't know how to be... normal."

He chuckled, the sound low and warm as he continued that torturously slow pace. "Normal? Hellcat, we're anything but normal. And that's okay. We don't have to fit anyone else's definition of a couple. We just have to figure out what works for us."

She wanted to believe him, to trust that they could make this work. But fear lingered, a dark shadow at the edges of her mind.

"And what if we can't figure it out?" she whispered, hating how vulnerable she sounded. "What if we're too broken, too fucked up?"

Davey's eyes blazed with intensity as he gazed down at her. "Then we'll be fucked up together. I'm not letting you go, Rowan. Not now, not ever."

He punctuated his words with a deep, slow thrust that made her gasp. Her body arched into his, craving more.

"Davey," she breathed, her voice catching. She wrapped her legs around his waist, urging him closer. "Please."

He understood without her having to elaborate. With a low groan, he buried himself inside her, filling her completely. She gasped, arching beneath him as pleasure ricocheted through her oversensitive body.

Their movements were slower this time, more deliberate. Each thrust felt like a promise, each caress an unspoken vow. Davey's eyes never left hers, and the intensity of his gaze made her feel simultaneously exposed and cherished.

Her fingers dug into his shoulders as he rocked into her, her body trembling with each deep thrust. The slow, deliberate pace was exquisite torture, building her pleasure gradually but inexorably. She could feel every inch of him, every ridge and vein of his cock as it slid in and out of her slick heat.

"Davey," she gasped, his name a plea and a prayer on her lips. "I love you. God, I love you so much."

The words tumbled out, raw and unfiltered, stripped of her usual defenses. In this moment, with him buried deep inside her, she couldn't hold them back any longer. Didn't want to.

Davey's breath hitched, his hips stuttering briefly before resuming their steady pace. "I know, Hellcat." His voice was rough with emotion. "I love you too. More than anything."

He sealed his declaration with a deep, passionate kiss that stole her breath and made her toes curl. His tongue swept into her mouth, tangling with hers in a sensual dance that mirrored the rhythm of their joined bodies.

Rowan clung to him, losing herself in the heat and strength of him, in the overwhelming rightness of being in his arms.

The world narrowed until there was only this—the slick slide of their bodies, the mingled sound of their gasps and moans, the overwhelming sensation of being so wholly possessed by him. Nothing else mattered in this moment - not the dangers that awaited them outside this room, not the uncertainties of their future together. There was only Davey, the man she loved with every fiber of her being, the man she would fight for, kill for, die for if necessary.

"That's it, Hellcat," Davey growled, his pace increasing until the mattress creaked under them. "Take what you need. I've got you."

And she did, letting herself get lost in the rhythm of their lovemaking, in the electrifying pleasure building with each drive of his hips. Higher and higher, until she was teetering on the edge, her body wound tight and desperate for release.

Her nails raked down Davey's back as the coil of tension inside her wound tighter and tighter. She was so close, her body trembling on the precipice of ecstasy.

"Davey, please," she gasped, arching into him. "I need..."

"I know what you need," he growled, his thrusts

becoming harder, more urgent. "Come for me, Rowan. Let go."

As if on command, her orgasm crashed over her, a tidal wave of pleasure that had her crying out his name. Her inner muscles clenched around him, gripping him like a vise as spasms of bliss rocked through her.

Davey groaned, his rhythm faltering as her climax triggered his own. She felt him swell inside her, felt the hot pulse of his release as he spilled himself deep.

They stayed like that for long moments, wrapped around each other, hearts pounding in sync as the aftershocks slowly subsided. Rowan kept her eyes closed, savoring the feeling of him still buried deep within her, the comforting weight of his body pressed against hers.

She didn't remember falling asleep, but sometime later, she woke with the uneasy feeling of being watched. Years of training had sharpened her instincts, and even half-asleep, she knew something was off. She cracked one eye open to find Davey leaning on one elbow, studying her like she was some kind of puzzle he couldn't quite figure out.

"What?" she murmured, her voice shockingly husky. She cleared her throat and tried again, "What?"

His beautiful blue eyes softened, but his brow remained furrowed. "Just waiting for you to bolt again."

"Relax, Wilde." She rolled onto her back, stretching

languidly. Everything hurt, but mostly in a good way. "If I were going to run, I'd have done it earlier, while you were snoring like a freight train."

He scowled. "I don't snore."

She patted his chest. "Keep telling yourself that, big guy."

Davey's scowl deepened, but there was a hint of amusement in his eyes. "You're one to talk. You kick like a mule in your sleep."

Rowan snorted. "At least I don't hog all the blankets."

"No, you just steal them completely."

She glanced down, realizing he was right. She had the blankets wrapped around her like a cocoon. With a grin, she unwound herself and tossed half the covers over him, leaving her bare to his gaze. "There. Happy now?"

She didn't miss the way his eyes flicked down to the bandage on her ribs, no doubt checking for more spots of blood on the fresh white gauze. His gaze lingered there for a moment before traveling back up to meet hers.

"I'll be happy when you're healed up and we've dealt with whoever put that hole in your side."

"I already dealt with them. They won't be coming after me again."

He reached out, tracing the curve of her hip with a gentleness that never failed to surprise her. "But others will."

"It's an occupational hazard."

"And that doesn't bother you? The constant danger, always looking over your shoulder?"

"Did it bother you as a SEAL?"

"Sometimes," he admitted softly. "It wears on you after a while. If I hadn't been blown up, I probably would've gotten out sooner rather than later."

She shrugged, but the casual gesture felt forced. "It's the life I chose. The only one I know."

"But why?" He propped himself up on his elbow, his gaze intense as he studied her face. "What made you go down that path? You could've worked with your father. Joined the military. Hell, WSW would've snapped you up and offered a fat paycheck for your skills. Why choose a life as an assassin?"

Rowan's throat tightened. It was a question she'd asked herself countless times over the years, usually in the dark hours of the night when sleep eluded her and the ghosts of her past crept in to haunt her. She'd never been able to come up with a satisfactory answer, at least not one she was willing to share. But with Davey looking at her like that, his eyes soft and searching, she found herself wanting to try.

She rolled onto her side, mirroring Davey's position so they were face to face. "I guess I just wanted to be in control for once. To call the shots instead of following orders."

His brow furrowed. "And you couldn't do that working for your father or the government?"

"It's different." She struggled to find the right words. "When you're a soldier or working for a PMC, you're part of a system. There are rules, protocols. Doing what I do, I make my own rules. I choose my jobs, my targets. It's…"

"Liberating?" he suggested when she trailed off.

"Yeah, you get it." She searched his eyes, seeing only patience and understanding. No judgment, no condemnation. Just a desire to know her, to understand what made her tick.

"My entire life, I watched my dad and his men fight against the evil in this world. And even when they won, they didn't. Not really. Because there were always more evil people to take the places of the ones they eliminated. I guess I just got tired of feeling like we're on a hamster wheel, you know? Running and running but never actually getting anywhere. At least as an assassin, I can make a tangible difference. I can target the worst of the worst and know that when I take them out, the world is a little bit safer."

Davey was quiet, his brow still furrowed in thought. Then he reached out, tucking a strand of hair behind her ear with a tenderness that made her heart ache. "I do get it. I can't say I've never thought that myself. But the system and rules are in place for a reason. What happens when there are no rules at all? When the lines between right and wrong get blurred, and it's hard to tell the good guys from the bad?"

She leaned into his touch, her eyes fluttering

closed briefly. "I'm not saying my way is right. It's just... it's the only way I know how to cope with all the shit I've seen. All the evil I've witnessed." She opened her eyes, meeting his gaze head-on. "Does that make me a monster?"

"No," he said firmly and cupped her cheek in his palm. "It makes you human. We all have our ways of dealing with the darkness we face. I can't judge you for yours any more than you can judge me for mine."

She covered his hand with her own, turning her face to press a kiss to his palm. "And what's your way of coping, Davey Wilde?"

A wry smile tugged at his lips. "Apparently, it's falling in love with a beautiful, deadly woman who frustrates me and challenges me in every way possible."

Rowan's heart stuttered in her chest at his words, a warmth spreading through her that had nothing to do with the heated tangle of their bodies. "Careful, Wilde. Keep saying things like that, and a girl might start to think you're going soft."

His smile widened into a grin. "Oh, I assure you, Hellcat, there's nothing soft about me right now."

As if to prove his point, he rolled his hips, pressing his unmistakably hard length against her thigh. Rowan bit back a moan, her body instantly responding to the promise in his touch.

"Again? Seriously?"

"What can I say?" He dipped his head, nuzzling the

sensitive spot just below her ear. "You bring out the insatiable beast in me."

She laughed and rolled onto her back, pulling him with her until he settled in the cradle of her thighs. "Then, by all means, let the beast out to play."

Davey grinned wolfishly down at her before capturing her lips in a heated kiss that stole her breath. His hands roamed her body, his touch alternately gentle and demanding, stoking the embers of desire within her into a blazing inferno. She arched into him, her fingers tangling in his hair as she lost herself in the sensations he evoked.

A loud chirp from her phone on the nightstand jolted them both out of the moment. Davey groaned against her neck. "Was that mine or yours?"

"I think it was mine."

"Ignore it." He cupped her breast in his big palm and swirled his tongue around her nipple. "We still have time before the meeting."

Oh, how she wanted to. But the phone buzzed again. And again. With an aggravated sigh, she stretched out an arm and snatched it up, glancing at the screen.

"Shit." She shoved at Davey's shoulder until he let her sit up. "It's Benji."

"Who's Benji?"

She sent him a dry look. "My informant that *you* scared away."

He grunted. "The assholes with the guns scared him away, not me."

Rowan rolled her eyes but didn't argue the point as she opened the text messages. "Either way, he still wants to meet."

She swung her legs over the side of the bed, wincing slightly as her stitches pulled.

Davey's hand on her arm stopped her. "Is he reliable?"

"As much as any informant looking to save his own ass can be." She shook off his grip and stood, gathering her clothes from the floor. "But he's never wasted my time before. I asked him to dig around for the name behind Kryos Solutions, and if he's this eager to meet, it's worth checking out."

"Kryos Solutions. The broker that hired you to kill me?"

She winced. "Yeah. Sorry."

"I've mostly forgiven you."

She glanced back at him over her shoulder as she scooped up her pants from the floor. "Only mostly?"

He propped himself up on one elbow, the sheet riding low on his hips. "Well, you did take the job initially. That's not something a man easily forgets from just a few rounds of good sex."

"I took it to save you." She stepped into her cargo pants and glowered at him as she fastened the button. "And what do you mean by *good* sex? That should've ruined you for all other women."

Davey's eyes glinted with mischief as he stood. He was shamelessly, comfortably naked, his cock still half-hard. She couldn't help but look her fill as he prowled towards her, all lean muscle and tanned skin. He stopped just short of touching her, leaning in close enough that she could feel the heat radiating off him.

"I mean, yeah, it was good, but not quite enough to make me forget you agreed to kill me at one point. You'll have to try harder next time."

Rowan narrowed her eyes at him, but the slight twitch of her lips ruined the effect. "You're an ass."

"Yeah, I am." He pulled her against him and his hands slid down to cup her ass, giving it a firm squeeze. "But you love me anyway."

Rowan rolled her eyes but didn't resist, letting her hands come to rest on his chest. "I love parts of you. The jury is still out on the whole package."

"I think the jury came back with a pretty definitive verdict today," he murmured, dipping his head to nuzzle her neck. "Several times, in fact."

Her heart did a little flip at his words, even as she tried to maintain her unaffected facade. Damn him for making her feel things, for making her want things she had no business wanting. Like a future. With him.

She allowed herself a moment to savor his embrace, the solid strength of his body against hers, before regretfully pulling away. "As much as I'd love to stay here and stroke your ego—among other things—I really do need to meet with Benji."

Davey sighed but released her. "I know. But I'm coming with you."

She caught his arm. "Like hell you are."

He shook her off and opened his dresser, pulling out a fresh pair of tactical pants. "I'm not letting you go alone, Rowan."

"I think I can handle myself against a computer nerd with more drugs in his system than blood."

"Need I remind you, you were just stabbed?"

"Not by Benji."

Davey paused with his pants halfway up his thighs, fixing her with a stern look. "That's not the point, and you know it. Until we find out who's behind Kryos and why they want us both dead, you're not going anywhere alone. End of discussion."

Rowan glared at him, hating that he was right. She was used to working solo, relying only on herself. Having someone else watching her back, caring about her safety, was foreign and unsettling. But also, if she was honest with herself, kind of nice.

"Fine," she bit out. "But you follow my lead."

fourteen

THE LAUNDROMAT SMELLED of detergent and fabric softener, the air thick with humidity from the industrial dryers churning in the back. Rowan adjusted the strap of her holster beneath her jacket as she scanned the space. The fluorescent lights overhead buzzed, flickering slightly, casting an artificial glow over the rows of humming machines. The place was mostly empty—just an elderly woman folding towels in the corner and a guy in a hoodie pretending to scroll on his phone.

Davey stood a few paces behind her, arms crossed over his chest. "You sure this isn't a trap?"

Rowan shot him a look. "No."

He huffed. "Reassuring."

She ignored him, stepping further into the laundromat. Benji had picked the spot—neutral ground, public enough to deter immediate violence but with enough noise and cover to have a private conversation. Still, her fingers itched to pull her gun, instincts screaming at her from too many double-crosses.

A rustling noise came from behind a row of machines, and she tensed. A moment later, Benji stumbled into view, shoving his wire-rimmed glasses up his nose with one hand and clutching a battered laptop case with the other. His shirt was three sizes too big, his jeans also baggy, and his sneakers were scuffed and untied.

"Got any quarters?"

Davey shifted beside her. "That him?"

Rowan nodded. "That's Benji." She sighed and turned toward the guy. "I'm not giving you money until I get the flash drive."

"Oh, c'mon!" He gestured toward a rattling dryer beside him, the display flashing 00:01. "These ancient-ass machines run on change and I miscalculated. My favorite hoodie's still wet, and I need another cycle."

Rowan arched a brow. "You called me here for a laundry crisis?"

"Well, I still got the intel you want, don't I?" Benji shrugged. "Multitasking. Got any quarters or what?"

Davey fished in his pocket and tossed him a couple. Rowan sent him a sidelong glance as Benji fed the quarters into the machine.

"What?" Davey said. "Easier to just give him the damn quarters than argue about it."

"You brought your tail again." Benji straightened, his gaze flicking to Davey, then back to her. "He's got that 'kill-you-and-hide-the-body' look."

"Benji, Davey Wilde," Rowan introduced, nodding between them. "And he's here for my protection."

Benji snorted. "Oh, so *I'm* dangerous now? I mean, sure, I know things, but—" He paused, looking at Davey again. "Wait. Wilde? As in the guy you were supposed to kill?"

Rowan sighed. "Yes."

Benji's eyes widened. "And now you're working with him? That's either really badass or really stupid. Maybe both." He whistled. "Damn, girl. You don't do anything halfway, do you?"

Davey gave him a flat look. "You got information or not?"

Benji's gaze flicked to Davey, then back to her. "Okay, okay, but before we start, let's talk protection. And payment. I want both."

Rowan let out a dry laugh. "You're still trying to bargain? With what leverage?"

Benji straightened, pushing his glasses up his nose. "With information you *want*. And I know you're gonna want it bad. But my last little data expedition put a target on my back, and I'd like to stay very much alive, thank you." He tapped his temple. "I'm smart, but I'm not 'dodge-a-hit-squad' smart. That's where *he* comes in."

He nodded toward Davey.

Davey exhaled sharply. "You want protection from *Wilde Security*?"

Benji smirked. "Oh, don't act so shocked. I know how this works. I spill my secrets, and you two disappear into the night while I get a bullet in the back of my head two days later. Not a fan of that outcome."

Rowan folded her arms. "You're assuming we'll find your intel worth the trouble."

Benji grinned. "Oh, you will. But I want cash and coverage. Non-negotiable."

Davey considered him for a long moment before nodding. "Fine. But if what you've got is worthless, you're on your own."

Benji clapped his hands together. "See? *That's* a deal I can work with." He pulled out his laptop and slid into the plastic chair beside the change machine. "Now, onto the good stuff."

The screen lit up with a mess of files, diagrams, and transaction logs. "Kryos Solutions is a brokerage firm," Benji said. "They connect people who need dirty work done with the ones willing to do it."

Rowan tapped her fingers against her arm. "We already know that, Benji."

He wiggled his fingers over the trackpad. "Yeah, yeah, hold your horses. The part you *don't* know? Who's pulling the strings. Because I followed the money, and it led right to someone you're *definitely* gonna want to pay attention to."

Davey's posture stiffened. "Who?"

Benji licked his lips. "Atlas Frost."

Rowan's stomach dropped.

Davey let out a slow breath, his expression darkening. "You're sure?"

Benji turned the laptop toward them. A network of accounts linked to offshore banks sprawled across the screen, the highlighted name at the center: Frost International.

"I triple-checked," Benji said. "Everything leads back to him. He owns Kryos."

Rowan's pulse kicked up. Atlas Frost wasn't just a name in the criminal underworld—he *was* the underworld. Smuggler. Broker. Black-market financier. He had his hands in everything from corporate espionage to weapons deals. And while his businesses weren't always legal, they weren't always *illegal* either.

Wilde Security had even used him in the past.

Hell, for that matter, so had her father.

She turned to Davey. "So is Frost trying to destabilize WSW to move into the security sector?"

Davey rubbed a hand along his jaw. "That's not his style. He only deals in information and money. He's a computer nerd—"

"Hey," Benji said, offended. "We nerds can be plenty dangerous."

They both ignored him.

"He doesn't like getting his hands dirty," Davey finished.

Rowan frowned. "Then why would he put out a contract on you?"

Davey's mouth pressed into a thin line. "I don't know. But I intend to find out." He looked at Benji. "You're sure about this?"

Benji held up his hands. "Hey, I just follow the money. And it all leads back to Frost. What he wants with you two, how should I know? I'm just a computer nerd. But if you want to pay me a bit more... let's say... $500? I can tell you where he's gonna be tomorrow night."

"Nice try," Davey said, pulling out his phone. "But I already know."

Rowan arched an eyebrow. "You do?"

Davey nodded, tapping at his phone screen. "The Arctic Preservation & Climate Resilience Gala. It's being held at the Plaza tomorrow night. Frost never misses a charity event. He likes to rub elbows with New York's elite."

Benji huffed, snapping his laptop closed. "Well, there goes my leverage."

Davey glanced up from his phone, a slight smirk on his lips. "Looks like you'll have to settle for the original deal, Benji-boy."

Benji grumbled something under his breath as he shoved his laptop into its case.

Rowan ignored him and looked up the event on her phone. "It's black tie, invite-only. We'll need a way in."

"Luckily, I have an aunt who loves a party and a rich uncle who loves her enough to indulge her. If Uncle Reece doesn't already have tickets, he can get them for us." Davey lifted his phone to his ear, his expression unreadable as he waited for his uncle to pick up. After a moment, his face shifted into an easy smile. "Uncle Reece? It's Davey. Listen, I need a favor..."

As he walked a few paces away from the loud dryers, Rowan turned back to Benji, who was now shoving his laptop into a ratty backpack with unnecessary force. She reached into her pocket and pulled out the cash she owed him.

"Hey," she said, catching his attention. "You did good, Benji. This is the lead we needed."

He paused, then snatched the envelope with a slightly mollified expression. "Yeah, well, just remember our deal. I want that protection detail set up ASAP."

"We got tickets," Davey said as he came back. "If you want protection, you need to come with us now."

Benji glanced at the still-rumbling dryer. "But my hoodie..."

"Forget the damn hoodie," Davey snapped, his patience clearly wearing thin. "Unless you want to be wearing it in your casket."

Benji's eyes widened behind his glasses. He swallowed hard, then nodded. "Right. Okay. Let me just..."

He fumbled for the dryer door, yanking it open and grabbing his damp hoodie.

Rowan rolled her eyes. "Really?"

Benji clutched the hoodie to his chest. "What? It's my lucky hoodie."

"For fuck's sake." Davey pinched the bridge of his nose. "Just move your ass."

They hustled Benji out of the laundromat and into the backseat of Davey's vintage Mustang.

"Ohh, this is nice," Benji said, rubbing the leather seat with both palms.

Rowan twisted in the passenger seat to glare at him. "Touch anything, and I'll break your fingers."

Benji snatched his hands back, holding them up in surrender. "Message received, scary assassin lady. I'll keep my paws to myself." When the car rumbled to life, he cackled with delight. "A combustion engine? Not electric! Damn, I didn't think anyone still drove these things."

Davey glanced at him in the rearview mirror. "It's a classic. Now shut up and keep your head down until we get to the safe house."

Benji mimed zipping his lips, but his eyes still gleamed with excitement as he hunched down in the backseat, hugging his hoodie.

Davey pulled the Mustang smoothly into traffic, the powerful engine purring as they wove through the midday crush of taxis and self-driving cars. The gleaming spires of Manhattan rose around them, the sleek glass and steel of the skyscrapers reflecting the watery winter sunlight.

The ride across town was tense and mostly silent, broken only by Benji's occasional nervous tapping against his laptop case.

Rowan stared out the window, her mind churning.

Atlas Frost.

What was his play here?

And how deep did this go?

They arrived at a quiet luxury high-rise on West 82nd, its sleek facade elegant but unobtrusive— the kind of place where high-profile residents valued privacy over flash.

"This is your safe house?" Benji asked, peering out the window. "Looks pretty swanky for a bunch of mercenaries."

"It's an investment property," Davey said shortly, steering the Mustang into the underground parking garage. He parked in a corner spot near the elevator and killed the engine. "Easier to secure than a hotel. Now move."

They hustled Benji into the private elevator, with Rowan keeping a wary eye on the garage until the doors whispered closed. The ride up was tense, Benji shifting from foot to foot, still clutching his damp hoodie like it was a shield.

The elevator doors slid open on the 15th floor, revealing a spacious apartment with floor-to-ceiling windows and a sweeping city view. Minimalist furniture in muted tones and abstract art pieces gave the space a modern, curated sophistication—sleek, expensive, and impersonal. Everything was deliberate. Nothing personal. Nothing traceable.

Davey ushered Benji and Rowan inside, and her gaze swept the room out of habit. The rest of the team was already there, gathered around the large dining table between the kitchen and the living area.

"You're late." Elliot looked up from his tablet, his eyes narrowing slightly behind his glasses as he took in Benji's disheveled appearance. "Who the hell's that?"

fifteen

"THIS IS BENJI," Davey said. "He's one of Rowan's informants. He's offered us intel in exchange for protection."

Benji shifted nervously from foot to foot, his eyes darting to each man in the room. Elliot sat at the end of the table doing something on a tablet. He had his glasses on, so he was deep in work mode. Dominic paced the length of the room, radiating restless energy, his need to *do something* palpable. Meanwhile, Sabin lounged in a nearby chair, one leg thrown over the arm, perfectly relaxed. Too often, he reminded Davey of a big cat, seemingly lazy but always ready to pounce at a moment's notice.

Sullivan and Brody O'Connell sat at the opposite end of the table from Elliot, a forgotten card game splayed between them. The twins were identical—same dark hair, same intense gray eyes—but the scar slicing down the side of Sullivan's face set them apart. While Brody was all polished charm, Sullivan had a rough edge that made people think twice before messing with him. But according to Elliot, Sully was a good guy. Loyal, reliable, steady. His twin was a little more reckless and carefree but no less loyal.

And, finally, rounding out the group, there was Liam, leaning against the wall, his arms crossed, his head tilted back, eyes closed. Liam had been born deaf, but had a cochlear implant that he usually turned off in busy environments. Whether or not he had it turned off now was anyone's guess. Either way, he was about as deadly as men came and could shoot any weapon you put in his hands with almost preternatural accuracy.

Benji swallowed audibly, his fingers tightening around the edge of his hoodie like it was the only thing keeping him grounded. His eyes darted to the table, then to the door, then he turned like he wanted to bolt.

Rowan stepped in front of the door, blocking his path. "Where do you think you're going?"

"Yeah, I-I don't know about this, man. I just want to stay alive, all right? I didn't sign up for some James Bond spy shit."

Rowan rolled her eyes and spun him around so he was facing the room again. "Relax, Benji. No one's asking you to play secret agent. You wanted protection..." She motioned to the men. "Meet the best in the business."

Elliot frowned and took off his glasses, folding them on top of his tablet. "What kind of intel?"

Since Benji didn't seem inclined to answer, Davey did. He crossed to the fridge and tapped the door to see what they had stocked. "I assume you've briefed everyone on the situation?"

"Yeah, someone put a goddamn hit on you," Brody said, his hand tightening into a fist on the table.

Beside him, Sullivan shook his head in disbelief. "It's a ballsy move."

"That's one word for it." Davey wanted a beer, but settled for a water. He turned and offered one to Rowan, tossing it to her when she nodded. Then he grabbed one for himself and shut the fridge.

"The contract on Davey came through a brokerage firm," Rowan explained to the room. "Kryos Solutions. I've done work for them before, but I didn't know until recently Atlas Frost owns Kryos."

Dominic sat back in his seat and blew out a breath. "Well. Fuck."

Sullivan frowned. "Isn't Frost an ally?"

"Wouldn't go that far," Davey said. "He's a... necessary evil."

Benji let out a humorless laugh. "Yeah, a necessary evil who's gonna bury us all if we don't play our cards right." He glanced at Rowan, then back at Davey. "Look, I got access to some of Frost's financial records. And I'm talking deep, dark, off-the-books transactions. The kind that'd make even a crooked Fed blush.

The kind that gets guys like you killed and guys like me chopped into bitty pieces and thrown into the East River."

Davey took a long swig of water, his mind racing. "And you think those transactions connect to the contract on me?"

"I'd bet my last bitcoin on it," Benji said.

Elliot groaned softly and pinched the bridge of his nose like he had a headache. "Frost has been playing both sides for years, but it's doubtful he put out the hit himself. He's just the middleman."

"So who's pulling his strings?" Brody asked the room.

A beat of silence.

Finally, Benji lifted a shoulder. "Hard to say. Money comes in, and Frost hands it out for all sorts of shady shit. Mercenaries, weapons, tech that's not even on the market yet. And he has a big chunk of change coming in from a company called Praetorian Holdings."

Elliot straightened and grabbed his tablet. "Praetorian? Why does that sound familiar?"

"Because we've run into them before," Liam said, finally opening his eyes and pushing away from the wall. "They're mercenaries. They were involved in that clusterfuck in Kyrgyzstan."

He didn't have to specify which op. They all already knew exactly which he was talking about: the one that killed Brennan.

Silence settled over the room like a heavy fog. No one moved. No one spoke. Brennan's absence was a wound that had never fully healed, a scar that still ached when pressed.

Davey exhaled slowly, the sound sharp in the stillness.

Dom shifted on his feet, restless energy vibrating the air around him. The guy hated silence. Usually, he'd crack a joke, flash that easy grin, or do something to shake off the tension. But not this time. Instead, he wore the doleful expression of a dog who didn't understand why his favorite person wasn't coming home.

Elliot sat unnaturally still, fingers curled against the edge of his tablet like he wanted to break it in half.

Liam just stood there, arms crossed, expression unreadable. He didn't move, didn't speak, but the tension rolling off him said enough. He felt it, same as the rest of them. He just wouldn't let it show.

Even Sabin, who could joke his way out of anything, just stared at the floor, jaw locked tight.

Brennan should be here.

He'd be pacing, already three steps ahead of the problem, flipping through possibilities in that sharp, calculating way of his. He'd crack some dry remark just to break the tension, maybe nudge Davey's shoulder and say, *"We'll handle it."*

But he wasn't here.

All they had was the hollow space where he should

be and the questions about his death that never stopped haunting them.

Davey set his water bottle down on the counter with a thud. "So, what are you saying? That Praetorian put out the hit on me?"

Benji shrugged. "I'm just telling you what I know, man. Frost and Praetorian are in bed together. Praetorian doesn't like you, and someone wants you dead." He started pacing, clutching his hoodie like it might somehow shield him from all the wrong choices that had landed him here. "You do the math."

Elliot finally spoke, his voice level but edged with something sharp. "Then we need to talk to Frost."

Dom blew out a breath. "Well, that sounds like fun."

Liam didn't react, which was reaction enough.

Benji stopped mid-step, blinking. "Are we sure this is the best plan? I mean, Frost is a guy who makes people disappear. And me? I'd rather stay not disappeared." His gaze darted to the door, then to the laptop sitting on the table.

Davey inhaled slowly, forcing himself to stay measured, controlled, even though the kid's twitchy anxiety was wearing on his patience. "Don't do it." If Benji ran, they'd lose their only tech advantage, and the poor bastard would be dead before sunrise. "We'll keep you safe. But you need to trust me, Benji."

Sabin watched the whole exchange with lazy

amusement. "*Oui*, relax, *mon ami*. Nobody's disappearing tonight."

Benji hesitated. Then exhaled sharply and muttered, "Yeah. Okay." But his grip on his hoodie didn't loosen, and he still looked like he'd jump out of his skin at the first unexpected sound.

"All right, let's get back on track," Elliot said, drawing everyone's attention back to the mission briefing. "First things first—we can't talk to Frost unless we find him."

"We already know where he'll be," Rowan said. "The charity gala at the Plaza Hotel tomorrow night."

Elliot glanced over at her, a flash of irritation in his eyes. Yeah, he still hadn't forgiven her for taking the contract. The man could hold grudges like nobody else. "The gala is VIP-only. Security's tight. Biometric scanning at the doors, plainclothes security inside. Nobody's getting in without a ticket."

Sabin grinned, always the fucking showman. "Careful. I'm might take that as a personal challenge."

"We have tickets," Davey said before Sabin decided to plan a heist. As all eyes turned to him, he leaned against the counter and crossed his arms over his chest. "I talked to Uncle Reece and he got us two tickets, so Rowan and I are going in as guests."

Elliot let out a low whistle. "Well, damn. Didn't expect you to pull the family connection card."

"Wasn't my first choice," Davey admitted. "But it's

the safest. No fake IDs, no biometrics to worry about. Just two legit invitations."

Dominic groaned. "So, you two get to wine and dine with New York's elite while we do the grunt work?"

Davey rolled his eyes. "Yeah, because babysitting Rowan in a room full of potential enemies sounds like a damn vacation."

Rowan shot him a glare. "Oh, please. If anything, *I'll* be keeping *you* out of trouble."

He scoffed. "Do I really need to remind you which of us was stabbed recently?"

She smiled in a way that looked sweet but was all venom underneath. "Keep it up, and I'll give you a hole to match."

"Yikes," someone—probably Dom—muttered, but Davey didn't look away from Rowan to see who it was.

Her hazel eyes flashed with defiance, daring him to push back. And damn if a part of him didn't want to rise to that challenge, to see just how far they could take this clash of wills.

He took a step closer, invading her personal space. Rowan didn't back down, tilting her chin up to maintain eye contact. His fingers itched to reach out and touch her, to take a fistful of her long dark hair and pull her flush against him.

Mine, something primal whispered.

She'd used his soap in the shower earlier, and the scent of it on her skin short-circuited all higher logic.

It was a stupid thing to fixate on—she'd needed a damn shower, it wasn't a claim—but fuck if his body cared about the distinction. He suddenly wanted every man in this room to know she was his. He wanted to close his mouth over hers and stake his claim.

Sabin gave a low whistle. "You two gonna kiss or kill each other?"

"Undetermined," Rowan said, still glaring up at him with heat in her eyes.

"*Mais*, either way, I'm here for it. All this sexual tension. It's better than porn."

"Jesus," Elliot muttered and pressed his fingertips to his eyelids like he was trying to rid himself of a mental image.

Dom smacked the back of Sabin's head. "I never want my brother and porn to be in the same thought bubble ever again. Just... no."

Shit. He needed to get control. He forced himself to step back before he did something reckless. "All right, people. Let's focus up."

"You're the one losing focus, *mon ami*, and gettin' the rest of us all hot and bothered."

Elliot pushed up from his seat. "Cavalier, I swear to fucking God—"

"Y'all prudes." Sabin shrugged but levered up out of his chair to get out of Elliot's reach. He crossed to Rowan and tilted his head, giving her a slow, considering once-over that had every caveman instinct in Davey roaring. In a heartbeat, without even consciously making the decision to move, he was between them, shoving a hand against Sabin's chest.

"Touch her, and I'll break your fucking fingers."

Sabin held up his hands in mock surrender, but his eyes danced with amusement. "Easy. I was just going to offer my expertise on formal wear. Our little warrior princess could use a lil' polish, *non*?"

Rowan blinked. "Excuse me?"

Sabin arched a brow, giving her a slow, considering once-over. "You ain't exactly Met Gala-ready in that jacket and them combat boots."

Rowan narrowed her eyes. "I'm sorry, are you critiquing my wardrobe?"

Davey sighed. "Jesus Christ, Sabin—"

Sabin ignored him, tilting his head like he was appraising a painting in a gallery. "Ain't nothin' personal, *bébé*. Black tie means black tie. Unless you got a designer gown stuffed in that duffel, you're gonna stick out like a gator at a garden party."

Rowan groaned. "I don't have a damn dress, all right? Been a little busy dodging assassination attempts."

Sabin grinned like she'd walked straight into a trap. "Lucky for you, I know just the person who can fix that."

He let the words hang just long enough to make them all look at him.

Then, with a smirk and a lazy tip of an imaginary hat: "*Ma p'tite sœur*, Vivianna."

Davey frowned. "Your sister?"

Rowan crossed her arms. "The fashion designer?"

"The very one," Sabin said smoothly. "And lucky for you, she owes me a favor."

Davey narrowed his eyes. "Why do I get the feeling that favor stems from something illegal?"

Sabin pressed a hand to his chest, looking deeply offended. "Davey, *mon ami*, you wound me. I am merely a man with excellent connections and impeccable taste."

"Yeah, how did you get those connections?"

He waved his hand. "A story for another day."

"Uh-huh."

He gave an exaggerated sigh. "Why do y'all always assume the worst of me?" A beat. Then he grinned. "Wait, don't answer that. But Vivi is all legitimate and above board..." Another beat. Another quicksilver grin. "Now."

Rowan folded her arms. "You think your sister will help me on such short notice?"

Sabin's expression turned downright indulgent. "Oh, cher, she lives for this kind of thing. Dressing a woman with your—" he waved a hand vaguely in her direction "—particular aesthetic? She'll consider it a challenge."

Rowan's eyes narrowed dangerously. "That sounded an awful lot like an insult."

Sabin didn't bother denying it. He just tilted his

head, eyes gleaming with mischief. "That's 'cause it was, *bébé*."

A choked sound came from Dominic's direction. "Vivianna?"

Davey glanced over at his brother, who had suddenly gone tense.

"Coming here?" Dom asked, his voice carefully neutral.

Sabin's smirk turned wicked. "Ahhh," he drawled, eyes lighting with amusement. "So you do remember my sister."

Dominic's jaw tightened.

Brody, sensing something, leaned forward with a shit-eating grin. "Wait. Are we glossing over something juicy here?"

Sullivan elbowed him. "Not our business."

"*Oui*, let's not get distracted." Sabin stretched, looking far too pleased with himself. "We got a mission to run, yeah?"

Dominic muttered something under his breath and scrubbed a hand over his face, but his ears? Red as hell. It was gone in an instant—the muttered curse, the tension in his jaw—but Davey clocked it.

Vivi.

Fucking hell.

Of all the people Sabin could pull into this mess, it had to be *her*?

Davey didn't know what happened between the two of them since he'd still been with the SEALs and was gone more often than not, but he knew it had ended messily. Messy enough that Dom avoided even hearing her name. Messy enough that Vivi had looked right through him the last time they'd crossed paths.

But Sabin was right. Rowan did need a dress, and Vivi was the most discreet option.

"All right," he said, bringing the focus back. "We have a plan. Rowan gets a dress. We go in as guests. We'll sneak Sabin, Dom, and Liam in as catering staff."

"What about us?" Brody gestured between himself and Sullivan.

Davey considered. "Brody, work the crowd as they come into the lobby and hotel bar. Find an excuse to get near Frost's people and listen."

Brody smirked. "So, be my usual charming self?"

"Yeah," Elliot said dryly. "Just this time, don't flirt your way into a gunfight."

Brody sighed. "One time."

Davey turned to Sullivan. "You're security. Quiet, armed, and watching our backs."

Sullivan nodded once. "Got it."

"And Elliot will run point from here and make sure our guest"—he pinned Benji with a cold stare—"doesn't do anything stupid."

Elliot exhaled, rubbing a hand over his face before picking up his glasses. "Babysitting duty. Fantastic." He slid his glasses on and shot Benji a flat look. "Anything else you'd like me to do? Fold his laundry? Tuck him in?"

Benji shrank under their combined stares, his fingers tightening around his hoodie. He looked like he wanted to disappear, shoulders curling inward like that might somehow make him less of a target. His gaze darted toward the door again.

Davey had seen plenty of fear before—men in combat, civilians in warzones, people with a price on their heads. Benji wasn't a fighter. He was just a guy who knew too much, standing in a room full of people he didn't trust.

And that made him a liability. But it also made him Davey's responsibility. If someone wanted Benji dead, they'd have to work a hell of a lot harder for it because nobody was putting the kid in the ground on his watch.

Davey turned to Sabin. "Call your sister."

Sabin pulled out his phone with a theatrical flourish. As he dialed and raised the phone to his ear, he eyed Dominic. "Oh, Vivi's gonna love this."

Dominic cursed under his breath.

Davey scrubbed a hand down his face. This mission was already giving him a migraine—and he had a feeling it was only getting worse from here on out.

sixteen

ROWAN HAD SURVIVED GUNFIGHTS, explosions, and more assassination attempts than she cared to count. But nothing—absolutely *nothing*—had prepared her for Vivianna Cavalier sweeping into the hotel suite like a goddamn fashion hurricane.

Of course, she knew the Cavaliers. She had grown up with both Sabin and Vivi. Their dad had been one of her father's men until he retired and was, honestly, one of her favorite honorary uncles. But she hadn't seen Vivi since they were teenagers and hadn't known what to expect.

"Where is she?" Vivi's accent reminded Rowan of sweet tea and slow Southern summers. It had the same lyrical lilt as Sabin's, but where his accent danced on the sharper edges of their Cajun roots, Vivi's was smoother, softer—refined by years of high society, but still carrying the unmistakable rhythm of the bayou.

Sabin, leaning lazily against the kitchen counter, barely glanced up from his coffee. "Now, *ma petite*, you wound me. Not even a hello first for your big brother?"

Vivi shot him an unimpressed look as she breezed inside, a stack of garment bags slung over one arm, a pile of boxes balanced effortlessly in the other. Her golden hair was styled in a sleek twist, her makeup flawless, her entire aura screaming high fashion.

"Oh, please," she drawled. "You don't need a hello. You need a swift kick in the ass." Her eyes narrowed. "And a haircut. You're looking a bit scruffy, *mon frère*."

"You ever gonna admit I'm the better-looking sibling?"

"Oh, sweetie. Confidence is adorable on you. Delusion, less so."

Sabin smirked. "Love you, too."

Vivi's gaze swung to Rowan, and she unleashed a noise high enough to make a dog wince. "Ro! Oh my God, look at you! You're even more gorgeous than I remember." She dropped everything unceremoniously on the nearest surface and pulled Rowan into a tight hug. "It's been way too long."

Rowan tensed, instincts flaring at the sudden contact. But then Vivi's familiar scent wrapped around her—warm vanilla and jasmine, the same kind of perfume Vivi loved as a teenager—and the tension melted away. Memories rushed in, unbidden. Long summer days on horseback, racing each other through the fields. Climbing the rocky trails around the HORNET compound, their laughter echoing off the mountains. Sneaking out for midnight swims in freezing alpine lakes. Whispered conversations and giggles as they drooled over the elite warriors training around them. Two girls finding solidarity in a world dominated by testosterone.

They had been inseparable once.

Rowan hadn't realized how much she'd missed this—*missed Vivi*—until now.

Why the hell had she let that slip away?

She relaxed, allowing herself a brief moment of genuine warmth as she returned the embrace.

"Jesus, Vivi," she said as they pulled apart. She eyed the garment bags and boxes. "Did you rob a boutique on your way here?"

Vivi's laugh was musical and carefree. "Please, darling. Like my brother, my thieving days are long behind me. These looks are one hundred percent Vivianna Cavalier originals. Now, let me look at you." She circled Rowan like a predator, then tsked. "You look like you're going to a funeral, not a gala."

Rowan glanced down at her all-black ensemble and shrugged. "What? It's practical."

"Practical isn't going to cut it tonight, honey. We're going for drop-dead gorgeous."

"I prefer my targets drop-dead, period," Rowan muttered, eyeing the dresses warily.

Vivi laughed, a rich, warm sound that filled the room. "Oh, I've missed your dark humor." She circled again, then tilted her head, tapping a manicured nail against her chin. "Strong build. Good posture. Great shoulders." She gave a smile so much like her brother's Rowan blinked in surprise and clapped her hands together. "Oh, this is going to be fun!"

Rowan glanced at the mountain of silk, lace, and beaded fabric Vivi had brought. "That's debatable. You sure you packed for the right person?"

"Oh, yes. You have power, *cherie*. And you're sexy as hell. We need to lean into that."

She glanced down at herself. Sexy. Right. She'd always looked at her body as a weapon and had never felt particularly sexy. Well, except in Davey's arms.

She shifted uncomfortably, fighting the urge to cross her arms over her chest. If Vivi noticed her unease, she didn't comment.

"Okay, let's get you out of those combat boots and into something that'll make Davey's jaw hit the floor."

Rowan snorted. "I'm not trying to impress Davey."

"Sure, sugar." Vivi turned to her brother, motioning to all the dresses she'd dropped. "Sabin, be a sweetheart and help me get all this into the bedroom?"

Sabin opened his mouth to say something no doubt sarcastic, but there was a knock on the door, stopping him. He set down his coffee and moved fast, casually drawing his gun as he checked the camera.

For never having been a soldier, he sure moved like one.

Or, no. An assassin. Quick, quiet, deadly.

"It's Dom." His posture relaxed and he re-holstered the weapon, then pulled open the door. "We all good, yeah?"

"Yeah, Davey just sent me to—" Dominic froze for a second when he spotted Vivi. Then he exhaled through his nose, his mouth pulling into something that was *almost* a smirk as he stepped into the room. "Vivianna. Didn't know you'd be here already."

Vivi lifted her chin, her expression unreadable. "Surprise."

Sabin made a low, long-suffering noise and shut the door, leaning against it. He dragged a hand over his face. "*Mais*, really? We gotta do this again?"

Rowan glanced back and forth from Dom to Vivi and could all but see the tension like lightning crackling in the air between them. Oh, yeah, there was a story there, and it didn't seem to have ended happily. Dom's jaw was tight, teeth grinding like he was chewing glass, while Vivi's eyes burned with the kind of heat that could set the whole room on fire.

Finally, Rowan took pity and stepped between them. She waved a hand in front of Dom's face, breaking their staring contest. "Davey sent you to...?"

He blinked, shaking his head slightly as if to clear it. "Right. Uh, he sent me to make sure everything's set for tonight. Security details, comms, all that Elliot-type stuff since Elliot's still at the safe house guarding your friend."

"Benji's not really a friend. More like a necessary but annoying pest."

His grin appeared briefly, and he pulled out his tablet, tapping the screen. "We've got a three-hour window to—"

"Excuse me," Vivi said sweetly, flipping her hair over one shoulder and plastering on a too-bright smile. "Rowan is busy right now."

Dom's grin evaporated, leaving behind an expression of frustration and a hint of fatigue. "We have to go over this stuff, Viv."

"Then you're welcome to wait. She's mine for at least the next hour." With that, she turned her back on him and ushered Rowan toward the bedroom. "All right, darling, let's get to work."

"Wait, *hour*?" If she weren't so horrified, she'd be embarrassed by the squeak of panic in her voice.

"Oh, at least."

Rowan eyed the array of dresses with a mix of trepidation and curiosity as Sabin brought them into the bedroom and Vivi hung them up, creating a colorful parade of fabric along the closet rod.

She sighed, accepting her fate. "Fine. Do your worst."

"Oh, honey, I plan to do my best." Vivi worked fast, throwing gowns at her with the expertise of someone who had dressed models, celebrities, and royalty.

Rowan found herself stepping into silk, lace, satin—turning, assessing, rejecting.

The first dress was too stiff, too glittering. The second clung in all the wrong places. The third was too revealing; the fourth made her feel like a Victorian ghost.

Vivi was ruthless in her assessments, tossing rejected dresses aside as Rowan tried them on.

And then, as Rowan zipped up the fifth dress, Vivi's voice turned sly.

"So, *chérie,* Sabin told me you and Davey..."

Rowan stilled. She turned slowly, eyes narrowing. "Sabin told you *what* exactly?"

"Oh, just that you two have been dancing around each other for months. That there's enough sexual tension between you to power a small city. And that you finally gave in to it."

Rowan shot a glare toward the closed bedroom door and called, "My love life is not your personal soap opera, Sabin!"

"Ah, *cher,* but it's so much fun!" he called back.

"Stop gossiping about me, or the next time you wake up, it'll be to the sound of me sharpening my knives very close to a body part you value."

He poked his head into the room and grinned, unfazed by her threat. "Sounds kinky. I'll try anything once, but does Davey know you're into that?"

"Want me to demonstrate my considerable knife

skills now? I can take one ball, two, or the whole package. Your choice."

He winced. "You'd really deprive womankind of my talents? That would be a crime against humanity, *cher*."

Vivi rolled her eyes and pointed. "Out."

He studied the midnight-blue dress. "That's not the one."

"I know. Now, shoo, you menace, so she can change."

He retreated, chuckling, and Vivi turned back to Rowan with a gleam in her eye. "So, it's true then? You and Davey?"

"Keep poking and I'll start asking about you and Dom."

Vivi's eyes flashed, but she quickly masked it with a breezy laugh. "Touché. Let's focus on dressing you to kill instead, shall we?" She unzipped another garment bag, revealing a deep red gown. "Try this one. I have a feeling."

Rowan slipped into the dress, the silk sliding against her skin. As Vivi zipped it up, she caught sight of herself in the mirror and froze.

She barely recognized herself.

The deep, blood-red silk was smooth and liquid-like against her skin. It clung just enough to be dangerous, the fabric pooling elegantly at her feet. The neckline dipped, but not too much, the cut sleek and devastating in its simplicity. A daring slit ran up her right thigh, revealing just enough leg to be tantalizing without compromising her ability to move—or fight, if necessary.

Vivi's smile was knowing. "*There* she is."

"Holy shit." Rowan exhaled, smoothing her hands over the fabric. "Not bad."

Vivi laughed and once again walked a circle around her. "*Not bad?* Darling, Davey's tongue is going to roll straight out of his mouth."

Rowan scoffed, but heat crept up her neck. "I highly doubt that."

Vivi smirked and motioned to the bedroom door. "Go show Sabin. See what he thinks."

Rowan hesitated, suddenly self-conscious. She wasn't used to being on display like this. Give her a sniper rifle and a target any day over parading around in a fancy dress.

But Vivi was already opening the bedroom door, calling out, "Gentlemen, prepare yourselves!"

Okay, she could do this. She squared her shoulders and strode out of the bedroom, chin held high. She refused to let a dress intimidate her.

The conversation in the living room cut off abruptly as she entered. Sabin's eyebrows shot up, a low whistle escaping his lips. Even Dom looked impressed, his usual smirk softening into something more genuine.

"Well, well," Sabin drawled. "Look who clean up real nice."

Rowan rolled her eyes but couldn't entirely hide her pleased smile. "You sound surprised."

"*Non*, not surprised," he corrected. "Just... damn, *cher*. Davey's not gonna know what hit him."

From the couch, Dominic nodded in agreement. "That dress is a weapon."

Vivi, hovering by the bedroom doorway and admiring her handiwork, turned toward him sharply. Her nose wrinkled in distaste. "Like *you* would know?"

Dominic's gaze flicked to her, and his smile returned, but it wasn't a nice one. "You used to wear weapons just like it, baby. I peeled you out of enough of them to know."

Sabin buried his face in his hands. "*Mon Dieu.*"

Rowan watched, slightly horrified, slightly intrigued, as Vivi's entire demeanor shifted again. Something icy and dangerous slid into place behind her eyes. And, holy shit, speaking of weapons, the smile she aimed in his direction was sharp enough to draw blood.

"You lost the right to call me 'baby' a long time ago, Dominic." Compared to all of Vivi's sugary *darlings* and *honeys*, the way she said his name was downright glacial.

Rowan shifted on her feet. Was this how others felt when she and Davey fought? Uncomfortably and slightly voyeuristically dirty?

Dom's jaw tightened, a muscle ticking. "Viv—"

"Don't," Vivi cut him off. "Just don't."

Sabin cleared his throat loudly. "Okay, let's take it down a notch, yeah?"

Rowan turned toward him and swung her arm toward the pair, who were still glaring daggers at each other. "Do I even want to know the history here?"

Sabin groaned. "Absolutely not."

Vivi sniffed. "It's ancient history."

Dominic let out a quiet chuckle. "Sure. Keep telling yourself that."

Yeah, Rowan did not have the bandwidth to deal with whatever the hell this was. She turned back toward the bedroom and caught a glimpse of herself in the floor-length mirror through the open door. She paused, studying her reflection. She did look damn good. "So, we're settled, then. This is the dress."

Vivi gave a self-satisfied smile. "Oh, for sure, *it's the dress*."

Davey had spent the entire day knee-deep in WSW business, running logistics for an upcoming high-profile client while also juggling the fallout from an op overseas that went sideways. It had been one thing after another—securing intel, double-checking security protocols, putting out fires before they could spark into infernos. By the time he made it back to the hotel suite to pick up Rowan, his patience was wearing thin.

At least, that was until he opened the door and saw her.

The room barely registered. He didn't notice Sabin and Vivi bantering, didn't clock Dominic's sour mood. His world had shrunk down to one thing.

Rowan.

And *fuck*, he wasn't ready for this.

He had seen Rowan Bristow in a hundred different ways.

He'd seen her in the field, dirt-streaked and bloodied, moving like a predator through enemy lines with lethal precision. He'd seen her bare and breathless beneath him, her body slick with sweat, her nails carving into his skin as she came apart in his arms. He'd seen her stripped down to her rawest edges, on the nights when the weight of their lives pressed too damn hard, when she let him close enough to see the fractures beneath the steel.

But he had never—*never*—seen her like this.

And it hit him like a fucking freight train.

He stepped into the suite, fully prepared to bark out orders about the night ahead, but the words died in his throat. His mind short-circuited.

Rowan stood across the room, wrapped in a dress the color of blood and sin, her body encased in silk that clung to every lethal inch of her like it had been *painted on*. The slit rode high, giving him a glimpse of toned, battle-hardened thighs that he'd watched snap men's necks. The neckline skimmed the dangerous edge of indecent, dipping just enough to tease but not enough to satisfy, and *fuck*, wasn't that just the cruelest part?

She was temptation wrapped in a goddamn weapon, and for the first time in his life, Davey Wilde forgot how to breathe.

Rowan caught his stare, arching a brow. "Jesus, Wilde. Say something before I start thinking you had a stroke."

His voice was rough when he found it. "*What the fuck are you wearing?*"

Vivi made a dramatic sound of exasperation. "Oh, don't be a caveman, Davey." She flicked a hand toward Rowan like she was presenting a masterpiece. "This is pure *art*, mon cher. I told you she had it in her."

"*Jesus Christ*," Davey muttered, dragging a hand down his face, because this was *not* the time for his brain to be short-circuiting.

Vivi smirked. "I take it that means the dress is a success?"

Rowan rolled her eyes. "He looks like he's about to combust. So, yeah, let's call that a win."

Davey forced himself to move, stepping closer before he could think better of it. His gaze swept over her again, tracking every criminally perfect detail.

"This was a bad idea," he said, voice low.

Rowan scoffed. "Oh, come on, Wilde, it's just a dress."

"No," he murmured, his fingers twitching at his sides. "No, *it's not.*"

He'd seen her naked. He knew every inch of the body beneath that silk—knew how she tasted, how she moaned, how she unraveled when he pushed her past her limits. But this was *different.*

This wasn't Rowan Bristow, the soldier, the mercenary, the deadly thing with a gun in her hands and a sharp tongue that cut just as deep.

This was Rowan Bristow as a weapon of another kind. One built to *destroy* him.

And *fuck*, she knew it.

Her lips curled at the corner, wicked and knowing, as she tilted her head. "You gonna survive the night, *boss*?"

His jaw flexed. His restraint was *hanging by a thread.* "You planning on making that difficult?"

Her grin widened. "Depends. Do you plan on being difficult?"

"Always."

Her eyes flickered with something dark and electric, something he *felt* in his goddamn spine.

He needed distance. Space. *Something* to get his head on straight before he forgot how to *not* touch her.

Instead, he stepped in closer, crowding into her space. His fingers ghosted along the fabric at her waist, and his pulse hammered at how *fucking soft* it was.

How soft *she* was.

He lowered his head just enough that his breath brushed the shell of her ear. "You do this on purpose?"

Her own breath hitched—so quick, so *subtle*, but he caught it.

"Do what?"

His lips nearly grazed her skin. "Make it impossible to think about anything but peeling this off you?"

She swallowed, her pulse jumping against his jaw. "*I don't know, Davey.*" Her voice was light, teasing, but threaded with something unsteady. "Sounds like a *you* problem."

His grip flexed on her waist before he wrenched himself back.

Because if he didn't, there wouldn't be a gala to get to.

His eyes dragged over her one more time, like he was committing her to memory.

Then he exhaled sharply, shaking his head. "Get your clutch, Bristow."

She smirked, a slow, taunting thing as she turned toward the counter. The slit in her dress parted, offering one last devastating glimpse of thigh.

Davey ground his teeth.

It was going to be a *long fucking night.*

seventeen

AS ROWAN DRAGGED her sister toward the bathroom, Atlas Frost watched them go with the same expression a grandmaster might give a pawn—already predicting every move, already seeing the checkmate.

Davey had spent years dealing with men like Frost. The kind who never raised their voices, never lost their tempers, never needed to make threats outright—because their mere presence was enough. Men who always had an angle. Men who made you feel like you were already two moves behind.

But Davey had spent years learning how to read the board, too.

He knew how to spot the tells, hear the unsaid, watch the way power shifted beneath the surface.

He knew how to play Frost's game.

Frost took a sip of his champagne, his smirk barely hidden behind the glass. "Well, that was dramatic."

A calculated opening move. A test.

Frost wanted a reaction. Wanted him to bristle, to bite. Wanted to test the strength of his position, to see where Davey's pieces were placed.

So Davey did the opposite of what Frost wanted, letting an indulgent smile creep onto his face. "Everything with Rowan is."

Frost's smirk froze—just for a fraction of a second. A moment of recalibration, like a player realizing his opponent was a better player than he'd expected.

Then, smoothly—almost too smoothly—he let out a low chuckle. "Yes, I imagine so." He took another sip of his champagne, his movements measured now, more deliberate. "She's fascinating, isn't she? The way she moves, the way she thinks... It's no wonder someone like you took an interest."

Davey let the words sit for a second, weighing them like a potential sacrifice.

That "someone like him" was not complimentary.

It was a calculated maneuver. A probe. Another attempt to test the board.

He let his smile sharpen at the edges. "Flattering, the way you're so invested in my personal life."

Polite. Crisp. Empty of anything real, forcing Frost to decide whether to press or pivot.

Frost pivoted. His gaze flicked toward the bathroom doors before settling back on Davey. A new move. A shift in strategy.

"I must admit, I didn't expect to find both Bristow sisters here tonight."

A lie. A feint.

He'd expected Rowan to be here. That was probably why he'd invited Rue. Davey had seen the flicker of satisfaction, the way Frost's smirk deepened when he spotted her in the crowd.

At that moment, he'd seen the whole board laid out before him.

A perfect path to checkmate.

But then he'd spotted Davey.

And the game changed.

That was why Frost kept pressing for a reaction. He was trying to map out the new terrain, trying to see what Davey's presence meant for his strategy.

But Davey refused to give him anything. "Didn't expect to find Rue on your arm, either."

Frost let out a small, satisfied hum, as if a pawn had moved right where he wanted it. "Did that surprise you?"

Davey exhaled slowly. This game was exhausting —he much preferred men like Sabin or Dom, who spoke exactly what was on their mind. But rushing the next move would give Frost the advantage. Play it clean, careful. "Just didn't think she's your speed."

Frost's next move was immediate. A knight sliding into position.

"I've always had a taste for fast things—cars, deals, women." He sipped his drink, watching over the rim, waiting to see if the play had forced a mistake. "And I have an eye for potential. Your Miss Bristow? She's full of it."

And, fuck if that move didn't land. Just a little.

A crack in the defense.

Disgust curled through Davey's gut, and for the first time, his mask of polite indifference slipped. He hated the way Frost said, "*Your Miss Bristow*." Hated the slick, possessiveness of his voice, the way he spoke about Rue like she was something to be traded.

Like she was an asset. A commodity. A well-placed pawn on the board.

Davey forced his expression back into neutrality, but his jaw was still clenched, and his next words came out too tight. "Is that what this is? A patronage?"

Frost sighed as if genuinely regretful. "You wound me, Wilde. You act as if I'm something sinister, when, really, all I do is provide opportunities for people with potential."

"Yeah, you're a real humanitarian."

A waiter approached, moving with easy grace, the silver tray of fresh champagne balanced effortlessly in one hand.

Sabin.

He must have sensed the tension.

He barely spared Frost a glance as he held out the tray, but Davey caught the question in his eyes. *Need me to step in?*

Davey gave the barest shake of his head. *It's fine. I got this.*

Sabin gave the tray a slight tilt, offering the champagne with his usual lazy charm. "Drink, gentlemen?"

Damn, he was good. There was no hint of his Cajun drawl in his voice. He sounded like a born-and-bred New Yorker.

Frost exchanged his empty glass for a fresh one without so much as a glance at Sabin.

That was his weakness.

He looked through people he deemed below him.

Davey also took a glass—even though he didn't plan to drink any of it—and the moment Frost's attention locked back on him, Sabin slipped away, melting back into the crowd.

Frost swirled his champagne, smirking. "How are you enjoying the evening? This isn't your usual scene, but I must say you wear a tux well. Though I imagine you still prefer combat boots to Italian leather."

Another fucking move. Still trying to get that rise.

Davey didn't bite. "I don't hate it," he said mildly, scanning the room.

Was Rowan still in the bathroom?

She'd been in there too long. Or maybe it just felt that way. His gut told him to check, to move, to do something—

But he forced himself to stay still. Forced himself to hold the line, and returned his attention to Frost.

"Good drinks, decent music. Shame about the company."

Frost laughed, and it was the first genuine thing he'd done all night. "I like you, David. We could be good friends, you know."

He took a sip of champagne—not because he wanted it, but because it forced a pause, forced Frost to wait. Then, smoothly, he set the glass down. "Given the circumstances, probably not."

Frost raised an eyebrow. "And what circumstances would those be?"

Enough.

Davey turned to face him fully, his voice flat. "Someone put a contract out on my head. I followed the money straight to you."

For the first time, Frost's expression faltered. It was quick. So quick that if Davey hadn't been watching for it, he might've missed it.

But he had been watching.

And that one flicker, that tiny misstep, told him everything.

Frost recovered fast. He took a slow sip of champagne, the very picture of amused indifference. "Now, see, that's interesting. Because if I wanted you dead, Wilde, you wouldn't be here enjoying these good drinks, decent music, and questionable company." Then, with casual precision, he turned, surveying the glittering guests.

His gaze zeroed in.

Right on Sabin.

"Your men are hovering."

Fuck.

A slow, tight coil of tension locked into Davey's spine.

He'd been careful. Sabin had been careful. But somehow, Frost had known. Had been playing along. Letting Davey think he was steering this conversation when, in reality, he'd already mapped the board.

Davey's pulse kicked up, but he forced himself to stay still. To stay in control. "They're worried you'll try to kill me."

"With what? A cocktail fork?"

"It can be done."

"Messy." Frost scoffed. "Give me a little credit. Poison is much more economical in these situations."

Instinct won. Before he could stop himself, his gaze flicked—just a fraction of a second, just a breath —to the champagne glass he'd set down on the table.

He caught himself, but it was too late.

Frost's wicked smile widened. "Tell me, David. How much do you really trust them? How loyal are they?"

Davey wanted to hit him. Just to wipe that smug fucking smile off his face.

He'd been so goddamn sure that Frost's weakness was his arrogance. That he looked straight past the people who weren't important to him.

But that was the thing about grandmasters.

They always saw every piece on the board.

"See, loyalty's such a fragile thing," Frost mused. "So easily bought, so easily broken. And sometimes, it's simply... misplaced." He let that sit for a beat, then smiled like he'd just let Davey in on a private joke. "The threat, my friend, isn't coming from *me*."

Davey's jaw clenched.

Frost swirled his champagne lazily. He was enjoying the hell out of this. "As I said, I like you. Any contract that may or may not have come through my company?" He shrugged. "Just business."

Casually—*too fucking casually*—his gaze slid back toward Sabin. "If you want to find the real threat, I'd start looking inward if I were you."

Davey's stomach went ice cold.

This was the real move. The real play.

Frost had been toying with him up until now. Testing him, waiting.

But this?

This was the moment he tipped the king.

The threat was coming from inside Wilde Security.

Someone in *his house*.

His jaw locked down hard. His breath came a little too sharp. He gritted his teeth, fought to keep his voice steady. "You really expect me to believe that?"

"Believe whatever you want," Frost said dismissively and checked his cufflinks, adjusting them with careful precision. Then, finally, he met Davey's gaze one last time and smiled.

Checkmate.

"But not everyone you love is safe tonight."

Every nerve in Davey's body went tight. A spike of heat shot through his limbs, then something colder—something that sank deep, coiled tight in his ribs. Adrenaline surged, his body tensing before his brain could catch up.

His jaw clenched so hard it ached. His hands itched for a weapon that wasn't there.

His throat felt too tight, his breath just a little too sharp.

Rowan. Rue.

His gaze snapped to the hallway and there they were—Rue stepping back into the ballroom, Rowan stalking after her, anger in every line of her body.

Davey exhaled, forcing his pulse to slow.

But his stomach hadn't unclenched. His hands hadn't stopped itching.

"Ah, here we go. My date's returned." Frost smiled again, knowing, taunting. "Enjoy the gala, David."

He offered Rue his arm when she reached them. She shot Davey only the faintest of worried looks before accepting the offered arm.

They walked away, disappearing seamlessly into the crowd, leaving Davey standing there as a wrongness settled in his bones. Not the kind you could quantify, but the kind years of war had hardwired into him. The kind that meant the difference between walking out of a mission or getting sent home in a bag.

"Comm check," he said under his breath.

"Sullivan, check."

"Liam, check."

"Yo," Dom said, sounding bored. Knowing him, he was probably only half paying attention.

"If I go dark," Sabin drawled, all lazy amusement, "it won't be foul play—it'll be foreplay. There some *real* pretty ladies here."

Brody groaned. "Yeah, yeah, we get it, Sabin. You got game, and the rest of us are just background noise."

The easy rhythm of the check-in stalled. The beat stretched too long.

Where was Elliot's dry comeback?

"Elliot?" Dom said, suddenly alert. "Where are you?"

No answer.

Davey's heart rate spiked. "Elliot, report."

Nothing.

"Elliot, goddammit, respond!" His voice sharpened, drawing a few curious glances from nearby partygoers, but the silence stretched, each second feeling like an eternity as Frost's warning curled through his thoughts like smoke.

Not everyone you love is safe tonight.

"Fuck," he growled, scanning the room. His gaze locked on Rowan, who was fuming as she stormed after her sister.

He didn't have time for this.

He intercepted her, grabbed her arm, and steered her toward the exit. "We're leaving."

"What the hell?" she hissed, trying to yank her arm free. "I have to stop Rue—"

"We've got a situation."

She must have heard the panic in his voice because she stopped struggling and fell into step beside him. "What's going on?"

Instead of answering, he tapped his comm again, harder this time. "Elliot, respond."

Still nothing.

A cold knot twisted in his gut.

The first few times? A miss. A distraction. A bathroom break.

But now the silence wasn't just an absence. It was a fucking void. A dead space where Elliot should have been.

"Shit," Rowan breathed, catching on. "Did he go dark?"

"Yeah," he said, and his voice came out tight, clipped—barely his. "And Frost just gave me a pretty fucking clear warning that someone I care about is in danger."

Because control was slipping.

His mind raced through the possibilities, each one worse than the last. Elliot, bleeding out. Elliot, taken. Elliot, already— No. No. He slammed the door on that thought before it could take shape.

Not again. He wasn't losing another teammate on his watch. He wasn't losing his brother.

The past clawed at the edges of his mind, ugly and familiar. The fraction of a second between normal and devastation, when the world held its breath. When he'd held his breath.

His pulse hammered against his ribs, adrenaline surging too fast, too sharp. He needed facts. He needed a target. But all he had was nothing.

Nothing except Frost's smirk. His fucking voice. His certainty.

Davey swallowed the burn rising in his throat and forced himself to focus as they burst out of the hotel and into the crisp night air. He scanned the street for a cab and, spotting one, quickened his pace, pulling Rowan along.

"Team, rendezvous at the safehouse immediately," he ordered into his comm. "Elliot's gone dark. This is not a drill."

A chorus of affirmatives crackled through the line as they reached the car. Davey yanked open the door, practically shoving Rowan inside before sliding in after her.

"Drive," he barked at the driver. "Fast."

<h1 style="text-align:center">eighteen</h1>

THE SAFE HOUSE was too quiet without his brothers and teammates filling the space.

Elliot sat at the wide dining table, fingers drumming against the surface as he scanned the monitors in front of him. If he didn't think it'd distract too much, he'd turn on some music—something loud and fast to match the adrenaline thrumming through his veins.

But he needed to stay sharp. Needed to catch every whisper, every rustle coming through their comms.

Everything was running smoothly.

For now.

Across the room, Benji was twitching like a junkie two days into withdrawal. The guy had been fidgety since everyone else left yesterday, but tonight, it was worse. His knee bounced. His fingers tapped out an erratic rhythm on the arm of the couch. His eyes kept darting toward the door like he was expecting someone to bust in at any moment.

It was *grating*.

Thank fuck his shift was almost over. After the gala, the kid would be Dom's problem for the next twenty-four hours.

"Hey, man," Elliot called out, trying to keep his tone light. "You need to chill. You're making me nervous just looking at you."

Benji huffed. "I'm making you nervous? Dude, you've been staring at those screens for, like, an hour without moving. It's weird. Like—do you even blink?"

Elliot groaned. He shouldn't have opened the door to conversation because now Benji wasn't going to stop.

"Swear to God, you're just sitting there like some... I dunno, creepy robot. Or, like, one of those snipers in a movie that never talks until the last five minutes. It's unsettling." He shifted, wincing. "And another thing— who the hell designed these safe houses? Because this couch is a war crime. I swear, I've sat on cinder blocks that were softer."

Elliot sent him a flat look. "Unless you've got something useful to say, shut the fuck up and let me work."

Benji rolled his eyes and flopped back against the cushions, but his knee kept bouncing. He shot another glance at the door.

Then—a chime.

"The hell?" Elliot was on his feet instantly, gun drawn before the second chime sounded. His pulse didn't spike—he was too well-trained for that—but his muscles tensed as he signaled for Benji to stay put as he moved to check the door cam.

No one was supposed to know this place existed.

Benji, however, had the audacity to look *sheepish*. "Uh... okay, so, before you, like... freak out... I may have ordered a pizza."

"You *what?*"

He winced. "Look, man, I was hungry. And *you* sure as hell weren't offering to cook me a five-star meal. Figured I'd make myself comfortable. Or as comfortable as I can on this couch."

Elliot stared at him for a full five seconds, then he exhaled through his nose to quell the urge to throttle the guy.

"You dumb motherfucker," he muttered before stalking toward the door.

He checked the cam. Sure enough, a teenager in a red uniform and a visor stood at the elevator, balancing a pizza box in one hand while scrolling through his phone with the other. No visible weapons. Nothing suspicious.

Still. Elliot wasn't taking chances. He pointed at Benji. "Don't fucking move." Then he jabbed the elevator call button. The doors whispered open, and he stepped inside, keeping the gun down by his leg but visible.

When the doors opened in front of the delivery guy, the kid's eyes went wide. He held out the pizza box. "Uh... p-pizza for Benji?"

Elliot scanned him and found nothing overtly threatening. Just a regular teenage kid. He grabbed the box and hit the door close button. He fumed the entire ride back up to the apartment.

"Eat your goddamn pizza," he snapped, tossing the box onto Benji's lap.

Benji grinned. "You know, you should really work on your hospitality."

Elliot ignored him, settling back into his chair as Benji flipped the box open and inhaled deeply.

"Jesus," he moaned, lifting a slice like it was a religious experience. "This is what I needed."

Elliot shook his head and returned to his spot at the table, setting his gun down beside the monitors. His focus zeroed in on the screens, back on the mission—until Benji, mouth full, shoved the pizza box under his nose.

"Want a slice?"

He was about to refuse—he didn't eat on duty, and he sure as hell didn't trust anything Benji ordered—but the smell of melted cheese and garlic hit his nose, and his stomach made a low, traitorous sound. Shit, he couldn't remember the last time he ate something. And now that the thought had taken root, he couldn't shake it.

"One," he muttered, snatching a slice.

Benji smirked like he'd won something, but Elliot ignored it. He took a bite and—yeah, okay, it was good. He returned his attention to the screens.

That was when everything went to hell.

"*The fuck?*" Dom's voice muttered over the comms.

Excitement rippled through the gala's guests, and his stomach dropped like he'd just crested a roller coaster. Because there, standing in the middle of the gala, right beside that bastard Frost—

Was Rue Bristow.

For a heartbeat, everything froze.

His chest locked up. Breath caught, stuck somewhere between a gasp and a curse.

His brain lagged behind, refusing to accept what his eyes were telling him.

Rue.

In the middle of the gala. Standing beside Frost.

The pieces didn't fit. Couldn't. Shouldn't.

Then—

Terror. Fury. A sharp, brutal mix that shot through him like an electric pulse.

"Rue?!" His chair clattered back as he stood, heart hammering. "What the fuck is she doing there?!"

No one answered him. He barely heard anything beyond the blood rushing in his ears. He reached for his gun, ready to move—ready to go—

Something was wrong.

His vision blurred, then snapped back too sharp. A moment of clarity, then—wrong again. The room lurched, a half-second delay between what he saw and what his body felt. His pulse slammed too hard, too fast, like he'd run a sprint, except he hadn't moved.

A creeping, foreign sensation crawled under his skin, burrowing deep.

Move! His brain screamed the command, but his limbs weren't listening.

Breath hitched. Too shallow.

Fingers tingled. His hands wouldn't grip.

His skin burned, then went icy cold.

His first thought was *Benji*.

That slimy little shit—it had to be him.

Some kind of set-up. Some kind of betrayal. Some—

But—

Benji was seizing.

His back arched violently, his entire body convulsing as foam bubbled from his lips. The pizza box slid from his limp fingers.

Not Benji.

It was the goddamn pizza.

Fuck.

He tried to reach for his phone, for his comms, but his muscles weren't cooperating.

His knees buckled.

His stomach wrenched, twisting violently—painful, raw.

He gagged, choked—couldn't stop it, didn't try. He had to get it out.

But his lungs—his fucking lungs—

They weren't working.

His world blurred.

The last thing he saw before everything went black was Benji's body jerking violently beside him, his own heartbeat slowing in his ears.

nineteen

THE STEADY BEEP of the heart monitor was the only sound in the room.

It should have been reassuring. Proof that Elliot was alive. Breathing. Recovering.

But to Davey, it was a taunt.

A reminder that for the past eight hours, his little brother had been teetering on the goddamn edge.

Davey sat in the stiff hospital chair beside Elliot's bed, elbows braced on his knees, hands clasped together so he wouldn't be tempted to punch something. Or someone. His jaw ached from how tightly he'd been clenching it, and his temples throbbed with the weight of too many sleepless hours.

Elliot looked small in that bed, pale against the white sheets, an IV taped to his arm, monitors tracking his vitals like he was still one wrong move from flatlining.

Davey had seen him injured before. Had seen him walk away from wreckage, bloodied but still smirking. Had watched him take a bullet in the shoulder and crack a joke about ruining a perfectly good shirt.

But this?

This was different.

Poison.

Someone had poisoned his brother.

Someone had gotten that close, slipped something inside their walls, inside their goddamn safe house, and nearly killed him.

If he'd eaten any more than a bite of that pizza...

Fuck.

A muscle in Davey's jaw ticked. His fingers curled into fists.

Whoever had done this was already dead.

They just didn't know it yet.

The door behind him creaked open, but he didn't look up. Soft footsteps approached, and a strong hand settled on his shoulder. "Davey," his father's voice was steady, low. "Come eat."

"I'm not hungry," he muttered. He wasn't leaving Elliot's side for anything until his brother opened his eyes.

"That's not the point," Jude said.

His mother sighed as she stepped up beside him. "You can't help him if you collapse from exhaustion."

Davey exhaled sharply but knew better than to

argue with his mom. She was a former prosecutor and won any argument he'd try to start.

Still, he couldn't bring himself to move.

"Five more minutes," he said instead.

Libby's hand was gentle when she smoothed his hair back, the touch so achingly familiar that for a moment, he was seventeen again, sitting on the floor of a hospital waiting room while doctors worked on his father after a mission had gone sideways.

Jesus, they'd always lived like this, hadn't they? One disaster to the next, one hospital visit after another.

And he was so fucking tired.

"Elliot's stable," his mom murmured. "The doctor said—"

"I know what the doctor said. The words came out harsher than he meant. "I just—" He swallowed the rest.

He just needed to see Elliot wake up. The steady rise and fall of his chest wasn't enough. He needed to see those eyes open, hear that smartass voice crack another joke.

Libby exchanged a look with Jude, then pulled up a chair beside him. "I remember the first time you held him," she said, voice soft. "You were three, and you were so serious about it, like you understood right then that he was yours to protect."

Davey squeezed his eyes shut. "I should have done a better job."

"David Greer Elliot Wilde." His mother rarely used his full name, but when she did, it hit like a hammer. "You did not do this to him."

"No, but it happened on my watch."

Jude crouched in front of him, steel in his blue eyes. "Then do what you do best. Get up. Get even. But don't sit here beating yourself up for something you couldn't have seen coming."

Davey let out a breath, tension coiled so tight in his chest it ached.

"Just eat something," Dom said from the doorway, his usual easygoing demeanor absent. "Then go hunt down the bastard who did this."

Davey huffed. "Thought you were supposed to be the nice one."

"I am," Dom said. "But I draw the line at someone poisoning my brother."

Before Davey could respond, a soft groan from the bed cut through the room.

He shot to his feet, heart slamming against his ribs as the heart monitor spiked.

Elliot shifted, his brow furrowing. His eyes fluttered open, bleary and unfocused, before landing on Davey.

For a long second, he just blinked.

Then his lips parted, his voice rough as hell. "Shit. Am I dead?"

Libby made a choked sound—a half-laugh, half-sob—as she pressed a trembling hand over her mouth.

The relief in her eyes was stark, glassy with unshed tears.

Jude exhaled sharply, tension draining from his body so fast he had to grip the back of Davey's chair to steady himself. His fingers flexed against the worn fabric, knuckles white, but his voice, when it came, was even. Firm. "Not yet."

Dom let out a breath and scrubbed both hands over his face. "Jesus, El." His voice was thin, unsteady. "Had to make an entrance, huh?"

Elliot's lips twitched—just a flicker of his usual smirk—but then he winced.

Davey picked up the cup of water the nurse left and held it to Elliot's lips. "Easy. Small sips."

Elliot obeyed, taking a few careful swallows before leaning back against the pillows like that little bit of movement had exhausted him. "Ugh. Feels like someone used my stomach as a basketball."

"Because they pumped it," Davey said. "Maybe don't eat poison next time, dumbass."

Elliot's eyes flickered to his mother, then back to Davey. The haze of confusion was clearing, replaced by a sharpness that belied his weakened state. "Right. Poison. And here I thought it was just bad pizza."

A sharp inhale from Libby. She crossed to the bed in a rush, smoothing Elliot's sweat-damp hair back with shaking fingers. "God, baby, you scared the hell out of us."

"Sorry, Mom," Elliot mumbled, his eyes closing as

he leaned into her touch. When he opened them again, his gaze swept the room, taking in the tense faces of his family. "How long was I out?"

"Eight hours, fourteen minutes," Davey said, his voice clipped.

Elliot's eyebrows rose. "You weren't keeping count of seconds, too, big brother?"

"Twenty-six seconds. Happy now?"

A flicker of understanding passed between them. Elliot's expression softened. "I'm okay, Davey."

"You almost weren't."

Jude's jaw flexed. He didn't speak, but the weight of his fury settled over the room like a tangible thing. Dom stood rigid beside him, his usual happy-go-lucky energy replaced with something colder, more focused.

Elliot shifted, wincing as he tried to sit up straighter. "What about Benji?"

Davey hesitated. Then shook his head. "Didn't make it. He was already gone by the time we got there, and you were blue—" His voice broke, and he couldn't finish the sentence.

"Fuck." Elliot exhaled sharply, scrubbing a shaky hand over his face. "Fuck!"

"Yeah," Davey muttered, dropping back into the chair. "Fuck."

Silence stretched between them.

Elliot's jaw clenched, a muscle ticking in his cheek. "Who did this?"

"We don't know yet," Jude said. "But we will."

"And when we do," Dom added, his usual cheerful tone replaced by something cold and sharp, "they're going to wish they'd never been born."

Elliot nodded, his eyes hardening. "Good. I want in on that."

"No," Libby said sharply. "You're staying right here until the doctors clear you, and then you're going home and resting."

Elliot groaned. "Mom, I'm fine. If anyone should rest, it should be Davey." His gaze slid toward Davey. "You look like hell."

Davey huffed. "Yeah, well. You tried to die on me, asshole."

Elliot's eyes softened. "Sorry about that. Didn't mean to scare you."

"You didn't scare me. You pissed me off."

Elliot gave a weak chuckle but winced. "Liar. You were terrified."

Davey's jaw flexed. The humor was vintage Elliot, but his voice was thin. Tired. He hated this—being weak, being stuck in a hospital bed, being the one who needed looking after.

Davey hated it more.

The memory of finding Elliot convulsing on the floor, foam at his lips as he turned blue—it slammed into Davey like a physical blow. His hands clenched into fists, nails biting into his palms.

"Yeah," he said roughly. "I was fucking terrified."

Elliot's eyes widened slightly at the raw admission. He reached out, gripping Davey's forearm with surprising strength, given his weakened state. "Hey. I'm okay. Really."

Davey nodded, not trusting himself to speak. The room felt too small suddenly, the walls closing in. He needed air. Needed to move. To do something.

He stood abruptly, his chair scraping against the linoleum floor. "I'm gonna... go touch base with the team, come up with a plan. I'll be back in a bit."

"Dav—" Elliot started, but he was already striding toward the door. He couldn't stay in that room with his worried parents and angry brothers for a moment longer.

The new safe house wasn't as nice as the last one. Just a forgettable apartment in a forgettable building, tucked away in a part of the city where no one would ask questions. The furniture was basic, the lighting dim, and the air held the lingering scent of fresh paint, like the place had been renovated just enough to look *lived in* without actually being *home* to anyone.

But it would do.

For now.

Rowan sat on the arm of the couch, rubbing at the tension in her temples as the others moved around her, voices overlapping—low, urgent. They had regrouped, pulled what was left of the team together after Elliot had been stabilized. The poisoning had shaken all of them, but Davey?

Davey was *furious*.

And he was gone.

Not in the sense that he'd left—no, he was here, somewhere in this apartment. But she knew that *look* he'd had when they arrived. The way his jaw had been clenched so tight it could've cracked. The way his shoulders had been coiled with too much tension. The way he'd barely said a word before slipping away, needing space before he detonated.

She exhaled, pushing off the couch. She scanned the apartment, searching for any sign of Davey, but he wasn't in the main living area or either of the bedrooms. The tension in her chest tightened.

Across the room, Dominic leaned against the kitchen counter, arms crossed, expression uncharacteristically serious as he listened to something Liam was saying. He caught her looking and tipped his chin toward her. "Looking for our fearless leader?"

She stopped, hesitating for a beat before nodding.

Dom sighed. "He's stewing. Bad."

"I'll talk to him."

He studied her for a second, then shook his head. "I already tried, but you know how he gets all broody and shit. And after today..." He trailed off, running a hand through his hair.

"Where is he?"

"Where do all the comic book heroes go to brood?"

Rowan rolled her eyes. "Just tell me, Dom."

His smirk was faint, but it disappeared just as fast. "Roof. He's got that stormy, 'I'm about to break something' energy, so..." He winced. "Tread carefully."

Rowan huffed a laugh. "Yeah, I don't do careful."

His expression softened. "I know. That's why you're a good match for him." He pushed off the counter and clapped her shoulder lightly as she passed. "Good luck."

She didn't need luck.

She needed Davey to pull his head out of his ass.

With a quiet sigh, she made her way up the stairs, slipping through the rooftop access door.

And there he was.

Davey stood at the edge of the roof, silhouetted against the night sky, hands braced on the ledge as he stared out over the city. His broad shoulders were rigid, his stance tense like he was barely holding himself together.

He looked like a man standing at the edge of a battlefield, right before the first shot was fired.

She approached quietly, her footsteps barely audible on the concrete. She knew he'd heard her anyway—Davey's situational awareness was second to none. Still, he didn't turn, didn't acknowledge her presence.

"Didn't take you for the brooding rooftop type, Wilde."

Davey didn't flinch, didn't turn. "Not in the mood, Bristow."

Rowan scoffed, moving to stand beside him at the ledge. "When are you ever in the mood?"

His jaw clenched, a muscle ticking. "I'm serious. I need to think."

"And you think better when you're alone, freezing your ass off on a rooftop?" She leaned her hip against the ledge, studying his profile. The harsh lines of anger, the barely contained fury simmering beneath the surface. "Talk to me, Davey."

His jaw flexed, but he didn't answer.

Rowan sighed and moved beside him, leaning her forearms on the ledge. The city stretched out before them, neon lights flickering, people moving below like nothing had changed.

Like Elliot hadn't nearly *died* today.

She glanced at Davey, watching the way his fingers curled into fists. "You're blaming yourself."

He exhaled sharply, finally turning to face her. His blue eyes were stormy, filled with a mixture of rage and fear that made her heart clench. "He is *my* responsibility."

"You really think Elliot would let you put that on yourself?"

Davey let out a bitter chuckle, shaking his head. "Elliot can think whatever the hell he wants. It doesn't change the facts."

Rowan studied him, then nudged his shoulder with hers. "You're right."

That got his attention. His head turned slightly, blue eyes flicking to her in suspicion. "I am?"

"Yeah." She nodded. "It *was* your responsibility."

His gaze narrowed.

She smirked. "And you handled it. You got to him in time. You *saved* him."

Davey exhaled, shaking his head. "Wasn't fast enough."

"It was fast enough for him to still be breathing."

That shut him up.

Rowan let the silence sit between them for a beat before nudging him again. "And just for the record? You're an insufferable bastard when you're stewing like this."

Davey huffed a quiet laugh, the tension in his shoulders loosening just *slightly*.

"I need to figure out who did this," he murmured.

"You will."

He finally looked at her, something dark and determined in his eyes. "And when I do—"

She held his stare. "We burn them down."

A muscle ticked in his jaw. Then, slowly, he nodded.

Rowan let the moment settle before tipping her head toward the rooftop door. "Come on. Sabin's probably already causing problems."

Davey sighed, rolling his shoulders before pushing off the ledge. "God help us all."

twenty

THE MEETING WAS ALREADY in full swing when they walked in.

Sabin, arms crossed, was glaring at Liam. "I never should've brought her into this."

His sister. Vivianna.

Sabin wasn't prone to guilt, but Davey knew he worried about those he cared about. And right now, he was spiraling.

"She's not a kid, Sabin," Rowan pointed out, dropping onto the couch.

"She's not a soldier, either," he shot back.

"Sabin." Davey waited until the man's angry blue eyes met his. "Look, I know you're pissed off and worried. We all are. But Vivi's okay. She was never at the safe house, and Frost has no reason to go after her."

251

"You don't know that for sure. Frost is unpredictable, and he's already proven he'll go after anyone associated with us."

Rowan let out a sharp breath. "You mean like Rue?"

Silence.

Sabin shifted uncomfortably, but Brody was the one who finally said it. "You have to face the facts, Bristow. She's working with Frost, which makes her an enemy."

Rowan's jaw clenched, her hands curling into fists against her thighs. "No. He's using her. He's funding her upcoming expedition to Antarctica. Why, I don't know, but it has nothing to do with the contract on Davey's head."

Davey exhaled. "Ro—"

"No," she repeated, cutting him off. She leaned forward and rested her elbows on her knees as she met his gaze. "Rue's not in this, Davey. She's a pawn in some other game he's playing, and I'll figure out what that is, but I guarantee it has nothing to do with what's happening here now."

He studied her face, searching for any sign of doubt. But all he saw was fierce determination. He knew that look well—it was the same one she'd worn every time she'd slipped away from him these last few weeks. If he didn't tread carefully here, she was going to run again.

"All right," he said, holding up his hands in a placating gesture. "We'll operate under that assumption for now. But we need to be prepared for any possibility. If she's involved—"

Rowan's eyes flashed with anger. "She's not."

Sabin cleared his throat. "We were talking about *my* sister. How do you plan to protect *her*?"

Davey rubbed at the tension in his temples. "I'll assign her protection until this is over. Or," he added when Sabin just scowled at the suggestion, "have her visit your parents. Frost isn't going all the way to Louisiana for someone who knows nothing about our operations. Plus, your dad is one of the deadliest guys I've ever met."

"He's retired."

"What, so he won't keep his daughter safe?"

Sabin's scowl deepened, but after a stubborn moment, he nodded. "*Mais*, yeah. I'll talk to her about going to New Orleans for a few days."

"Good," Davey said, turning his attention to the rest of the team. "Now, we need to focus on our next move. Without Elliot—"

"How is Elliot?"

The question landed like a punch and rocked him back on his heels. He glanced around, taking in the tight expressions, the worry etched into every face. But it was Brody's that he settled on since he asked the question.

"He's okay. He's awake and breathing on his own."

"And surly as hell," Dom added.

"If anyone has a right to be grumpy tonight, it's him," Sullivan muttered.

Brody exhaled a shaky breath and dropped his head into his hands. His shoulders curled inward, hands clasped together like he was bracing for impact. "I'm just so fucking glad he's alive. I don't know what I would've done—" His voice cracked.

Sullivan, ever the steady one, put a comforting hand on his twin's shoulder. "We tried to get in to see him, but the hospital wouldn't let us."

Brody and Elliot had been through the shit together in the military. They'd always had each other's six, no matter how bad things got. And judging by the slump of Brody's shoulders, he was drowning in the same guilt Davey felt.

Davey rubbed a hand over his jaw, suddenly exhausted. "Shit, man, I'm sorry about that. I told the hospital nobody but family until we can figure out where the threat's coming from."

Brody's head snapped up, and just like that, the raw grief was gone. In its place was cold fury. "And what if the threat's coming from the family?"

Davey's denial was instant. "No."

But even as it left his tongue, he knew it might not be true. He shot a look at Liam. His cousin stared back, his stern face even more grim than usual. Of Uncle Greer's two sons, Liam looked the most like his father, and the similarities had a knot of dread tightening in Davey's gut. He respected Greer more than any other man alive, and Greer had trusted him with this company, this family. They all had—his uncles, his dad. They believed in him.

"Something's happened to our family over the last few years. We're splintering, and that's a problem because we Wildes work better as a team."

That was what Dad had said to him after they signed the company over at Christmas.

"Greer has faith in you, but I know you. You're worried you're not good enough and will let everyone down. You're terrified of failing, which is how I know you won't fail. I know you're the only man for this job, and you will not rest until you've solved all of the family's problems."

But he'd only been in charge for a little over a week, and look what happened. Maybe their belief in him had been misplaced.

"No," he finally said with more certainty. "It's not someone in the family."

"We have to consider all possibilities," Liam said quietly. "We know Cade wanted the company, and he was pissed when they gave it to you."

But, still, it didn't fit the Cade he used to know, the one he'd once seen as not only a cousin but his best friend. Was Cade really so different now? And would he risk going to prison, leaving his baby daughter an orphan, just to get his hands on the company?

Davey shook his head. "Cade's ambitions don't

make him a murderer. We've had our differences, sure, but killing for power? And with poison? That's not his style."

Dom winced. "Normally, I'd agree, but I keep thinking about what Elliot said at Christmas. Cade doesn't *get over* things. He gets revenge."

"But he's family. You really think he'd poison a family member?"

Dom lifted a shoulder. "We all know Elliot never eats when he's on an op. It was a fluke he did this time. Maybe Cade thought he'd be safe."

"If he hurt Elliot, I don't give a fuck what his last name is," Brody said softly. The cold had thawed, and his anger now boiled like magma preparing for an eruption.

Davey held up his hands. "Okay, okay. Let me talk to him. If we all go in guns blazing, we'll only escalate things. I'll bring Cade in for a conversation, try to get a feel for where his head's at."

"You know exactly where his head's at," Brody muttered.

"Maybe, but I'm not throwing a grenade into my family on a hunch."

"Davey," Rowan said softly, voice laced with concern as she stood and crossed to him. She laid a hand on his chest, over his heart, and lifted her gaze to his. "You can't face him alone. I know you don't want to think it, but if Cade *is* involved in all this—"

"I know." He sighed, pinching the bridge of his nose. "But if I appear weak or panicked, it'll only give him more power over me. I don't want to be at war with him, and finding out we have a common enemy, attacking the company he wants, might be the catalyst we need for a truce."

"Assuming he's even willing to cooperate," Sabin added, his skepticism evident.

"That's my problem to figure out." He met each of their gazes in turn, willing them to see his perspective. Cade had made himself an adversary, yes, but the last thing any of them wanted was him as an enemy.

Brody's anger still simmered, but he finally nodded in agreement, as did Sullivan.

Sabin threw up his arms. "If you think you can talk Cade Wilde down, be my guest, *mon ami*. But it'll be a first."

"You know I'm always with you, brother," Dom said after a beat of silence.

Liam exhaled hard, but he also nodded. "Dad chose you over the rest of us for a reason, so I'm with you. I'll back your play no matter what."

Davey met Liam's gaze, and, for the first time, he wondered what all of his other cousins thought about him getting the company. He knew his brothers hadn't wanted it, and Cade had made his feelings about it damn clear at the family Christmas party. But what about Liam or Bridger? They were Greer's sons, and although all five of the original Wilde brothers had an equal share in the company, everyone knew it was really Greer's baby. He'd created Wilde Security thirty-five years ago, setting up an office in a rundown strip mall in D.C. to protect his younger brothers and make sure they all had a safe place to land when they left the military.

Davey faced his cousin and switched to sign language: *"Did you ever want it?"*

Liam's eyes widened in surprise, then the first genuine smile Davey had seen from him in a long time spread across his face. He signed back, *"Hell no. I love this company, but running it? That's all you, cuz. Dad made the right call, giving it to you."*

"What about your brother?"

"Same deal. Bridger is happy working undercover." He dropped his hands and said out loud, "We have your back."

Some of the tension eased out of Davey's shoulders. "All right, so we're agreed," he said out loud and turned his attention back to the group. "I'll reach out to Cade, see if I can get him to come in tomorrow for a talk. In the meantime, we need to keep digging into Frost."

"Speaking of which," Sullivan cut in, ever pragmatic. "Without Benji and with Elliot out of commission, we need someone to handle the tech side of things."

"We'll figure it out."

Liam arched a brow. "We *have* someone. Daphne."

"No. After what happened to Elliot, I don't want to bring any more cousins into this. Especially ones without combat training."

"You think she's not already in this? I bet my next paycheck she's already poking around, probably hacking into things as we speak. If we don't bring her in, she'll just *insert herself*—and we both know she's capable."

Davey glanced at Rowan to get her take, and she shrugged. "Gotta admit, Daphne is scary good. We could use her help."

Fuck, they were right. Daphne would've taken the attack personally, and she'd fight back the best way she knew how—with her computers. Knowing her, she probably already had information for them. "All right, yeah. Liam, Sabin, go talk to Daphne. Tomorrow," he added after a glance at the clock on the wall. It was late, and they were all exhausted. "Take the rest of tonight to recharge. Brody and Sullivan, I want you to dig around in the mud and see if anything pops on Frost or the contract on me."

Sullivan gave a smile that was more than a little mean. "I do love getting dirty."

"Which is why I'm sending you. Check all the usual haunts, see if anyone's talking."

"On it, boss," Sullivan replied, already heading for the door with Brody close behind.

"Tomorrow," he called after them. "Catch a few

hours of sleep first." Sullivan waved a hand over his head in acknowledgment without looking back, but Brody didn't reply. He doubted they'd listen. Brody was too angry to take the night off.

Sabin and Liam followed them out.

"We'll wait until morning to talk to Daphne," Liam confirmed from the door.

"She's probably awake," Sabin protested. "Hell, I'm betting she's still holed up in that computer lab, tapping away like she got the devil at her heels. Ain't no such thing as quittin' time for that one."

Yeah, he was most likely right. Daphne was a workaholic like that. But as much as Davey wanted answers *now*, he shook his head.

"I want you both to get some rest. If shit hits the fan like I think it's going to, it might be the last quiet night we have for a while." When the door closed behind them, he turned to Dom. "I don't want you going home. The brownstone might not be secure. Go sit with Elliot at the hospital. Keep him safe and keep him from doing anything stupid."

Dom grinned. "So, basically, be his babysitter? He'll love that."

"Tough shit. He'll get over it. Just keep an eye on him and keep me updated on his condition."

"Will do." Dom headed toward the door but paused beside Davey, resting a hand on his shoulder. "Take your own advice tonight. Get some rest, brother. You look like hell."

Davey nodded, but the weariness in his bones told him sleep wouldn't come easy. As the door closed behind Dom, he turned to find Rowan had returned to the couch, her hazel eyes fixed on him with an intensity that made his skin prickle.

"What?" he asked, suddenly self-conscious.

"You're not planning on getting any rest tonight, are you?"

He scrubbed both hands over his face and sighed. "There's too much to do. I need to—"

"What you need," she said, cutting him off and rising from the couch, stepping closer, "is to take care of yourself."

Her proximity was intoxicating, stirring up memories of heated nights and whispered promises. "I appreciate the concern, but I'm fine."

Her eyes narrowed. "You're exhausted, stressed, and carrying the weight of the world on your shoulders. Let me help."

"How?" The word came out harsher than he intended, laced with frustration and fatigue.

She didn't flinch. Instead, she reached out, her fingers ghosting along his jaw. "Let's go to bed."

Jesus, he wanted to. Wanted to lose himself in her warmth, her scent, the silky slide of her skin against his. For a moment, he let himself imagine it— tangling his fingers in her dark hair, tasting the salt on her neck, hearing those little gasps she made when he hit just the right spot.

"Ro, I can't. I need to—"

She pressed a finger to his lips, silencing him. "Shut up, Davey. You need to rest. Your mind needs a break. You won't be any good to anyone if you're running on empty."

He caught her wrist, gently pulling her hand away from his face. "And how exactly is sex going to help me rest?"

A wicked smile curved her lips. "Who said anything about sex? I'm talking about actual sleep."

He blinked, taken aback. "Oh."

Rowan laughed, a rich, throaty sound that sent a shiver down his spine. "You look so disappointed." She cupped his face in her hands and rose onto her toes to press a surprisingly chaste kiss on his lips.

Physical contact between them had always been electric— a sizzle that burned fast and hot and always left them both a little singed. But this kiss was different. Soft. Tender. It made his chest ache in a way he wasn't prepared for.

When she pulled back, her eyes were serious. "Sex isn't off the table, but it's 5 a.m., and you've been going non-stop for over twenty-four hours. Longer, really, because the night before, as amazing as it was, we didn't do much sleeping. You're not a robot. You need sleep, Wilde. Real, restful sleep. And I'm going to make sure you get it."

Davey hesitated, torn between the mountain of work waiting for him and the allure of rest—and

Rowan. Her hands were still on his face, warm and grounding. He leaned into her touch, letting out a shaky breath.

"Come on," she said softly and trailed a hand down his arm to entwine their fingers. "You know I'm right."

twenty-one

ROWAN HAD BEEN RIGHT, damn her.

He had needed sleep. As soon as his head hit the pillow, he was out like a light. No tossing and turning, no nightmares. Just blissful oblivion.

When Davey woke, weak sunlight filtered through the blinds over the two narrow windows on the wall opposite the bed. He blinked, disoriented. This wasn't his apartment, wasn't his bed. Then he felt Rowan's warm body pressed against his side, her arm draped across his chest and the tension leaked out of him.

The safe house.

He turned his head, drinking in the sight of her. Her dark hair was tousled, fanned out on the pillow. Her lips were slightly parted, her expression peaceful.

Jesus, she was beautiful. Fierce and deadly, yes, but in this moment, she looked almost angelic. He trailed his fingers lightly along her arm, savoring the softness of her skin. His pulse hammered against his ribs, his skin prickling with awareness as she shifted closer. Every nerve in his body seemed attuned to the heat radiating from her, to the whisper of her breath against his jaw.

Rowan's eyes fluttered open, instantly alert. A slow, seductive smile curved her lips as she met his gaze. "Good morning," she purred, pressing herself more firmly against him.

Without a word, Davey cupped her face and kissed her deeply. Rowan responded instantly, pressing her body against his as she returned the kiss with equal fervor. Her hand slid down his chest, fingertips tracing the defined muscles of his abdomen before dipping lower.

Davey groaned into her mouth as she wrapped her fingers around his cock and gave him a long, slow stroke from root to tip.

"Someone woke up happy," she teased.

"You have no idea," he growled, nipping at her lower lip, then he rolled, pinning her underneath him. He kissed a trail down her neck, reveling in her breathy sighs as he laved attention on her sensitive skin.

His hands roamed her curves, caressing and teasing as he mapped every dip and swell. He cupped her breast, thumb flicking over the peaked nipple. Rowan arched into his touch, a needy whimper escaping her throat. The sound sent a bolt of lust straight to his groin.

Davey took his time worshipping her body, determined to bring her pleasure. He traced the tip of his tongue along the valley between her breasts before drawing one straining nipple into his mouth. She buried her fingers in his hair, holding him to her as he suckled and nipped. A shudder rattled through her.

"Davey, please..."

He released her nipple and kissed his way down her taut stomach, swirling his tongue around her navel. Her breath hitched as he nudged her thighs apart and settled between them. He could smell her arousal, musky and intoxicating. Reverently, he trailed his fingers along her inner thighs, savoring the way her muscles quivered under his touch. She watched him through heavy-lidded eyes, her cheeks flushed and lips parted.

"Show me where you want my mouth, Hellcat."

She slid a hand down between her legs and parted her folds with her fingers, exposing her slick, swollen flesh to his hungry gaze.

"Here," she breathed, tracing a finger around her clit. "I want your mouth here."

He licked his lips, then lowered his head and dragged the flat of his tongue along her slit, from her entrance to her clit. He groaned at the taste of her, sweet and tangy on his tongue.

Rowan let out a sharp cry, her hips jerking upward. He gripped her thighs, holding her steady as he explored her with long, slow licks, savoring her taste, her texture.

"Oh. Oh, fuck, Davey..." She fisted her hands in the sheets as he slid one finger inside her slick heat. She was so tight and wet, and he shook with the need to bury his cock deep inside her, but he held back. He wanted her to come first. He wanted to watch her unravel as he teased and stroked and sucked. Curling his finger, he found that always made her lost her mind, stroking it in time with the flicks of his tongue against her clit.

Rowan writhed beneath him, reduced to incoherent whimpers and pleas and gasps as he worked her higher. Her legs trembled against his shoulders.

"That's it, Hellcat." A second finger joined the first, stretching her, preparing her to take all of him. The wet sounds of his ministrations filled the room, obscene and arousing. He reveled in every hitched breath and choked off moan he drew from her lips.

"You're so fucking beautiful like this. Spread out for me, lost in pleasure. I could feast on your sweet little pussy for hours." He punctuated his words with deep, deliberate strokes of his tongue, lashing against her clit in rapid flicks that had her hips bucking off the bed.

Rowan's back arched off the bed, her body drawn bowstring tight. "Davey, Davey please...I need..."

"Tell me what you need, Hellcat," he growled against her flesh. "I want to hear you say it."

She let out a strangled moan, her hips undulating against his face. "I need you inside me. I need your cock. Please, Davey..."

"Not yet. You're going to come for me first like a good girl." He hummed against her, the vibrations making her cry out sharply. "I want to feel you come apart on my tongue. I want to taste your pleasure." He closed his lips around her clit and sucked, curling his fingers inside her to rub mercilessly against that sensitive spot, driving her towards the precipice. He kept her teetering on the knife's edge of release, backing off every time he felt her start to clench around his fingers.

She made a desperate sound that was something between a sob and a groan of frustration. Her hands fisted in his hair, tugging insistently. "Damn you, Davey Wilde. I swear, if you don't let me come right now, I'll..."

Davey grinned against her slick flesh, savoring her desperation, the way she trembled and writhed beneath his touch. He loved reducing her to this quivering, needy mess. This powerful, deadly woman, utterly at his mercy, begging for release. "You'll what, my little hellcat?"

Her threats dissolved into a wail as he lashed his tongue against her clit in rapid strokes. He pumped his fingers faster, grinding the heel of his palm against her mound. Her inner muscles fluttered around his fingers, and her back bowed off the bed as the orgasm crashed over her. He worked her through it, lapping at her hungrily, fingers stroking in time with the pulsing of her walls, prolonging her ecstasy until she collapsed back against the mattress, spent and trembling.

He gentled his touch, easing her down from the high with soft, open-mouthed kisses along her inner thighs.

When the last aftershocks had faded, he crawled up her body and claimed her lips in a searing kiss.

Rowan reached between them and slipped her hand under the band of his sleep pants, wrapping her fingers around his aching cock.

"Need you," she murmured against his lips. "Now."

Davey didn't need to be told twice. He was shaking as he positioned himself at her entrance. With a flex of his hips, he pushed inside her welcoming heat, sheathing himself to the hilt in one smooth thrust, groaning at the incredible way her body gripped him.

She was perfect, every inch of her. And she was *his*.

She wrapped her legs around his hips and dug her nails into his shoulders, urging him to move. He obliged, setting a deep, steady rhythm that had them both gasping for breath.

They rocked together, lost in the slide of sweat-slicked skin and the pleasure building between them. Rowan wrapped her legs around his waist, changing the angle so he hit that perfect spot inside her with every thrust. Davey braced his forearms on either side of her head, his hips snapping forward with increasing urgency. He wasn't going to last as long as he wanted to. Heat coalesced at the base of his spine.

"I'm too close, Hellcat," he rasped, his face buried in the crook of her neck. "I'm not going to last."

The sensation built until it was almost unbearable, a tightly coiled spring threatening to snap at any moment. Rowan clenched around him, her nails raking down his back as she let out a keening cry. The sharp sting only heightened his pleasure, pushing him closer to the edge.

"Then come for me," she panted and nipped at his earlobe. She locked her ankles at the small of his back, pulling him impossibly deeper. "I want you so deep inside me I don't know where you end and I start."

Her words were his undoing. With a hoarse cry, he buried his face against her neck and let go. The release roared through him like a wildfire, consuming his every thought, frying all of his nerve endings, his entire body shuddering as he spilled himself deep inside her. Rowan held him tight, her body milking every last drop as she tumbled over the edge with him, gasping his name like a prayer.

They clung to each other as the aftershocks rolled through them, trading soft, lazy kisses as their racing hearts gradually slowed.

Finally, he lifted his head and looked down at her. Her hair was a wild, tangled mess against the pillow, her lips swollen from his kisses. But it was her eyes that captivated him—those fascinating tiger eyes filled with satisfaction and so much love it made his throat tighten.

"My hellcat." He brushed her hair back from her face and kissed her softly. "I love you."

Rowan smiled up at him, her expression soft and open in a way he rarely saw outside of these stolen moments. She traced her fingertips along his jaw, her touch feather-light. "I love you, too, so whatever happens today, you better stay safe. I can't lose you."

Davey's heart clenched at the undercurrent of worry in her voice. He turned his head and pressed a kiss to her palm, his heart so full it felt like it might burst. He'd never imagined he could have this—a love like his parents have, so deep and true it defied all logic. She was his match in every way, and he knew with bone-deep certainty that he would spend the rest of his life by her side, come what may. "You're not going to lose me. I'm not going anywhere, Rowan. I promise you that."

She let out a shaky breath and wrapped her arms around him, holding him tight. "You better keep that promise, Wilde. Or I swear, I'll track you down in the afterlife and kick your ass back to the land of the living."

Of course she would. His deadly, vicious hellcat would fight the devil himself to keep the people she loved safe. He laughed and kissed the tip of her nose. "Noted."

They stayed like that for a long moment, foreheads pressed together, just breathing each other in. Finally, with a sigh of regret, Davey eased out of her and rolled onto his back, pulling her with him so she was draped across his chest.

Rowan pillowed her head on his shoulder, absently tracing patterns on his sweat-dampened skin. "I could get used to waking up like this every morning."

He tightened his arm around her, his heart clenching at the wistful note in her voice. He wanted that too, more than anything. Waking up with her in his arms, making love to her first thing, starting every day just like this. But with the threats hanging over their heads...

He pressed a gentle kiss to her forehead. "I know we've got a hell of a fight ahead of us. But I want you to know that when this is all over, when we've dealt with the threats and put all this behind us, I'm going to ask you to marry me."

A soft gasp escaped her lips. For a long moment, she was utterly still, staring at him with an unreadable expression in her eyes.

He'd surprised her. Hell, he'd surprised himself. He hadn't meant to blurt that out, but now that he had, he realized how desperately he wanted it.

She pushed herself up on one elbow and searched his face, her eyes wide with a mixture of wonder and vulnerability that made Davey's heart ache. "Are you serious?"

"Dead serious." He cupped her cheeks in his hands, stroking his thumbs along her cheekbones. "I love you, Rowan Bristow. I love your strength, your fire, your fierce loyalty. I love the way you challenge me, the way you see through all my bullshit and call me on it. I love your courage, your intelligence, your wicked sense of humor. I love every beautiful, maddening, incredible inch of you. I want to wake up with you in my arms every day. I want to make love to you as the sun rises and fall asleep with you curled against my side every night. I want to build a life with you. You're it for me, Hellcat. You're my forever."

Rowan's eyes glistened with unshed tears. She opened her mouth to respond, but before she could speak, the sound of the front door slamming open startled them both.

A sharp knock at the door cut her off mid-sentence. Davey's head snapped toward the sound, his body instantly tensing. Rowan was already moving, rolling off him and reaching for the gun on the nightstand.

From the other side of the door, Sabin's voice called out, thick with amusement and his unmistakable Cajun drawl.

"Y'all best be decent in there, 'cause I ain't got the stomach for seein' Wilde's bare ass before breakfast."

A beat of silence.

Then, with even more mischief, he added,

"Though Rowan, cher, if you're the one who's naked, feel free to invite me in."

Davey growled, already reaching for his pants. "I'm going to kill him."

Rowan rolled her eyes and tossed Davey's shirt at him. "Ignore him. He's just trying to get a rise out of you."

"Well, it's working," Davey muttered, yanking on his clothes.

Rowan dressed quickly, efficiently. As she reached for the doorknob, Davey caught her wrist. He pulled her close, claiming her lips in a fierce, possessive kiss that left them both breathless.

"We're not done with this conversation," he murmured against her lips.

She gave him a soft smile and stroked his stubbled cheek. "I know. Later."

<h1 style="text-align:center">twenty-two</h1>

WHEN THEY EMERGED from the bedroom, they found Sabin lounging against the kitchen counter, a shit-eating grin on his face.

Liam stood beside him, far more composed, though the tick in his jaw suggested he wasn't entirely thrilled about Sabin's antics. Across the room, Daphne was already seated at the dining table, her laptop open in front of her, fingers flying over the keyboard. The glow of the screen cast eerie shadows across her face, making her hazel eyes gleam with sharp intensity.

Sabin pushed off the counter, arms spread wide. "Well, look at y'all. Hair a mess, lips all swollen—hell, Davey, you ain't even got your damn shirt on. Must've been real nice, sleepin' in, tangled up all cozy while some of us were bustin' our asses all night."

"Hey, I told you to go home and get some sleep."

Davey grabbed a shirt from the duffle bag on the floor, yanking it on as he crossed to the coffee maker that Liam already had going.

"Couldn't," Liam said and handed him an empty mug. He hooked a thumb over his shoulder at Daphne. "Sabin suggested we check the lab before going home and, surprise, surprise, that one was there, and she was already working on our problem." He yawned and grabbed another mug, filling it with coffee. "We were there all night."

"I didn't need you to stay." Daphne didn't look up from her screen as she responded. Unlike the two men, she didn't look the least bit tired. Her dark hair was pulled back in a messy bun, and her gaze was laser-focused on her computer. She'd work in this hyper-focused state until her body would eventually demand rest, and she crashed. Until then, her blood was at least ninety percent caffeine.

Liam yawned again and leaned against the counter. "And I told you we weren't leaving you alone in that lab when we have no idea who tried to take out Davey and almost took out Elliot."

Davey poured a cup of coffee and offered it to Rowan.

She waved it away.

He frowned, lingering a second too long as she turned back to whatever thoughts had taken her hostage. Rowan didn't turn down coffee—not unless something was eating at her. He wanted to press, wanted to tell her to sit down and take a damn breath, but she wouldn't listen. So, instead, he kept the coffee for himself and leaned against the counter, glancing from Liam to Sabin. "Either of you hear from Brody or Sullivan?"

Liam shook his head. "Not yet. But you know how they are. If they found something, we'll know when they're ready."

Sabin smirked. "Or when one of 'em gets arrested for excessive enthusiasm. My money's on Sullivan."

Davey grunted, but the tension in his gut didn't ease. He'd told them to catch a few hours of sleep first, but he doubted either had listened—especially not Brody. The man had been pissed when he left, and angry men didn't sleep. They hunted.

That was either good news or very, very bad news.

He exhaled sharply and took a sip of his coffee. Instant regret. It was like someone boiled asphalt, then dared to call it coffee. His throat burned as he swallowed, the bitterness clawing its way down like it had a personal vendetta. He coughed and scowled at Liam as tears leaked from his eyes. "The hell is this?"

"Coffee," Liam said, genuinely confused, and took a long drink from his mug.

Sabin made a face. "*Mon frère*, I think we need to talk about what coffee actually is, 'cause whatever you brewed up in there? That ain't it."

Davey had to agree. He moved to the fridge for some creamer and dumped a large amount in. It helped. Marginally. He stirred the so-called coffee as he walked over to Daphne. "Have you found anything?"

Her fingers stilled on the keyboard. She looked up, her expression grim. "You're not going to like it. Our systems were compromised, alright. We've got multiple security breaches. Someone's been poking around in WSW's network, and I mean deep. Not just scraping the surface. This was coordinated, precise, and meant to go unnoticed."

"For how long?"

"Best I can tell? Over a month, just before you took control of the company," she said, finally glancing up at him. "I started digging after the attack on Elliot, looking for anything that didn't sit right. And I found something." She turned the laptop toward them.

Rows of code and access logs filled the screen. Daphne tapped the trackpad, and a highlighted string of credentials appeared.

Cade's credentials.

The tension in the room turned electric.

Sabin cursed in Cajun French.

Liam's expression remained unreadable, but his shoulders stiffened.

Rowan exhaled hard and lifted her gaze to his. She didn't need to say anything. He could see the worry and sadness all over her face.

A cold weight settled in his gut. He turned back to Daphne. "That can't be right."

"I triple-checked." She tapped the screen again. "Every one of these breaches ties back to Cade's login. Every. Single. One."

Silence stretched, thick and suffocating.

Sabin broke it first, pushing off the counter with a grim smile. "Well, *mon frère*, hate to say I told you so, but—"

Davey leveled him with a glare. "Don't."

Sabin held up his hands. "Just sayin'. You went to bat for the guy. Put your rep on the line." He shrugged. "And now it looks like he might've used that trust to stab you in the back."

Daphne sat back in her seat and worried her lip through her teeth. "It's not just a breach, Davey. Whoever did this had access to everything—mission reports, security protocols, financials. Everything. And if Cade really did hire that hit on you..." She trailed off, letting the implication hang in the air.

Davey clenched his jaw. He didn't want to believe it. He refused to believe it. But the evidence was staring him in the face.

And then his phone vibrated in his pocket.

Everyone went still.

Slowly, Davey pulled it out, glancing at the screen. Cade.

His stomach twisted. "It's him."

"Shit," Liam said softly. "Don't answer it."

"I have to. If he's behind this... I have to." He exhaled sharply before answering. "What do you want, Cade?"

Silence stretched between them for a beat before Cade spoke. "We need to talk."

"So talk."

"Not over the phone," Cade said. "Meet me."

Davey's grip on the phone tightened. "My office. Thirty minutes."

"No." The response was immediate. "Neutral ground. My choice."

"Why?"

"If you don't trust me, don't come."

A sharp, bitter laugh escaped before he could stop it. "Not exactly reassuring."

Cade sighed. "Look, you want answers or not?"

More silence.

Then, he finally relented. "Okay. Where?"

Cade gave an address that he committed to memory before muttering, "I'll be there."

The line went dead.

When he lowered the phone, everyone was watching him.

"Absolutely not," Rowan said immediately.

Davey pocketed the phone. "It's happening."

"He refuses to meet at WSW, demands his own location—and you're just going to walk into that? Alone? It's suicide."

Sabin whistled softly. "Yeah, I gotta say, sounds

like a pretty shit plan, *mon ami*. If Cade's innocent, why all the cloak-and-dagger bullshit?"

Liam, quiet until now, finally spoke. He nodded toward Daphne's laptop. "I don't doubt Cade is capable of all this, but..."

"But what?" Davey demanded when he trailed off. "Yesterday, you all but accused Cade of mutiny."

"Yeah, and after thinking it over, I changed my mind." Liam met his gaze steadily. "Whatever else Cade is, he's a father first, and he would never do anything to put Nova at risk. You said you don't want to throw a grenade into our family over a grudge? Well, neither would he. If he put a hit out on you and succeeded, Uncle Cam and Aunt Eva would disown him. Tessa and Weston would never forgive him. He'd lose his entire immediate family, including Nova, because no way would his parents let him keep custody after he goes to prison for solicitation of murder. You really think he'd risk all that for a *chance* at getting the company when there's no guarantee he's next in line?"

Silence descended on the room.

"All valid points," Daphne said finally and motioned to her computer. "But those credentials don't lie. Someone accessed our systems using Cade's login. Whether it was him or not, he's compromised somehow."

Davey ran a hand through his hair, frustration and uncertainty warring inside him.

Liam had a point. Cade adored his daughter. Would he really jeopardize her future just to get back at him?

But Daphne was right, too. Cade's company login wasn't something he would just share with anyone, so if it wasn't him accessing secure files he had no business being in, then who? And how did they get his information?

"All the more reason I have to go talk to him." Davey kept his voice firm, cutting off any further debate. "If there's even a chance this is all some misunderstanding, I need to hear him out."

Rowan took a step closer, her eyes dark with worry, and for a second, he nearly reached for her. But she crossed her arms, tucking her hands under her elbows like she was physically holding herself back—from him, from this fight, from the fear neither of them wanted to name.

Her voice was quieter now but no less sharp. "And what if it's a trap?"

His pulse ticked up. Yeah, there was no denying it could be a trap. But he forced himself to hold her gaze, tried to convey with his eyes that he wasn't worried. "Then I'll handle it."

Frustration tightened her features. "Fine." Her fingers curled against her arms, knuckles going white, and she exhaled in a rush. "If you're doing this, we go in with a plan."

Davey shook his head. "*We* are not going

anywhere. I go in alone."

"Like hell you do!"

He knew that mulish expression, and he heard the warning bells clanging in the back of his mind: *Danger! Danger!* But he still stepped closer and lowered his voice for her ears alone. "You're a target, Ro."

"So are you."

She finally touched him, her fingers curling around his forearms, holding on tight as if she could physically anchor him in place. The anger in her eyes still burned, but it was the fear barely veiled behind it that nearly undid him.

She was terrified of losing him.

He exhaled slowly to ease the sudden tightness in his chest. "I know." He covered her hand with his. "But if I show up with an entourage, Cade will take one look and vanish. He won't talk if he thinks it's an ambush."

Liam nodded slowly. "Cade's a ghost when he wants to be. If he vanishes, we won't find him."

Rowan's breath hitched—subtle, but he caught it. She knew he was right. But that didn't mean she had to like it. "I hate this plan."

"Me too," Sabin said. "But if Davey's dead set on bein' a stubborn bastard, best we work around it."

Rowan's nails bit into his skin briefly before she let go. "If *anything* feels off, you run. No heroics."

Before he could respond, she grabbed the front of his shirt and yanked him down into a kiss—fierce, desperate, laced with everything she couldn't say out loud.

Davey wrapped an arm around her waist, pulling her in tight, stealing every ounce of warmth she pressed against him. His fingers slid into her hair, holding her there, needing this, needing her, needing to remind himself what he was fighting for.

When she pulled back, she didn't step away. She fisted her hands in his shirt like she wasn't ready to let go, and her gaze searched his, raw and unguarded. "When this is over, I'll say yes."

The word was so quiet, so full of something fragile and fierce all at once, that for a second, he thought he'd imagined it.

His breath caught.

A thousand things rushed to the tip of his tongue —a promise, a vow, a fierce declaration that he'd get them through this, no matter what. But he couldn't speak past the knot in his throat, so instead, he framed her face in his hands, brushing his thumbs over her cheekbones.

"Damn right you will." His voice was rough, filled with everything he couldn't put into words.

She let out a shaky breath, her lips quirking just slightly. "Then come back to me, Wilde."

His heart twisted painfully. He wanted to promise her. Wanted to say nothing in the world could keep him from her.

Instead, he kissed her one last time, slow and deep,

lingering like he could sear this moment into his memory.

And then Sabin cleared his throat. "If y'all are gonna start makin' babies right here, I'd rather know so I can make a graceful exit. I like to watch, but you're like a brother, and that's just nasty."

Rowan sighed and dropped her head to his shoulder, closing her eyes briefly before muttering, "I really hate him."

Sabin grinned. "Now, *cher*. Given how much you hated Davey just a few weeks ago, I'll take that as the highest of compliments."

Davey shook his head, pressing one last quick kiss to Rowan's temple before stepping back.

A quiet snort drew his attention, and his eyes flicked over to Daphne, still half-hidden behind her laptop. She didn't look up, but there was no missing the way her lips curved—not into a smirk, not into a sneer, but into something dangerously close to a smile.

Huh. Weird.

Daphne wasn't exactly the smiling type. His cousin was about as goth as a person could get without literally haunting a graveyard. She was black clothes, sharp eyes, and had that dry, deadpan voice that made people second-guess whether she was joking or planning something vaguely illegal.

And yet, here she was, clearly amused.

She noticed him watching and casually dragged her sleeve across her mouth like she could wipe away the expression before anyone called her on it. "I'll keep digging. If Cade's being framed, I'll find proof."

Davey nodded. "Do that."

Sabin stretched, then cracked his knuckles. "And me? I'll go make some coffee that don't taste like swamp water boiled with battery acid."

Liam bristled. "My coffee is perfectly fine."

Sabin scoffed. "Yeah, if you like sufferin'."

"It's coffee, not a damn dessert."

Sabin gestured toward Davey's untouched cup. "It's a hate crime against taste buds, is what it is."

Rowan arched a brow. "He's not wrong. I knew from just the color it was deadly."

Liam muttered something under his breath and took a sip of his toxic brew just to prove a point.

Davey barely registered the argument, the words turning into background noise as his gaze drifted back to Rowan. She was watching him—not the way she had a moment ago, with fire and fight in her eyes, but quietly, cautiously. Her arms were crossed, her weight shifting slightly from foot to foot. Her fingers flexed restlessly against her arms as if she didn't know what to do with her hands.

For just a second, the worry bled through. The part she tried so hard to swallow down. The part that had been there since the moment he refused to let her run, refused to let her fight this alone—the moment he jumped headfirst into the fire with her.

The banter around them kept rolling, but the weight in his chest didn't lift.

The coffee was the least of their concerns.

His gut churned, tension settling low in his spine as he braced himself for what came next.

One way or another, by the end of the day, he'd have his answers.

Even if he didn't like them.

twenty-three

DAVEY EXPECTED a lot of things when he walked into the café.

He expected Cade to be pissed. Expected the conversation to turn into a fight, maybe even come to blows.

What he didn't expect was Cade Wilde, six-foot-three of tactical menace, bouncing a drooling baby on his knee while feeding her pieces of toast like it was a delicate military operation.

The Glock concealed under his jacket was standard Cade. The pink sippy cup? That was new.

He sure as hell didn't expect Nova Wilde—small, chubby, dressed in a onesie that said "Daddy's Boss" —to look up at him with wide, delighted blue eyes and immediately fling her slobbery teething ring straight at his chest.

Davey caught it, reflexes sharp as ever, but he was

stunned enough that he nearly dropped the damn thing.

Cade, for his part, didn't even blink. Just wiped drool off Nova's chin with one hand while lifting his coffee to his lips with the other, scanning the room like he expected a sniper to take the shot the second he let his guard down.

The guy was holding a baby like a pro but looking at his surroundings like a battle-hardened operative. The sheer contrast made Davey's brain short-circuit for a second.

"The hell is this?" Davey finally muttered, lowering the teething ring.

Cade barely glanced at him. "It's called breakfast." He tore another piece off the croissant and held it up for Nova. She grabbed it with a tiny fist, immediately stuffing it into her mouth.

Davey didn't sit. He didn't want to get comfortable. He wanted to get to the point. "You could've picked anywhere. Why here?"

"Because I don't trust you enough to meet without witnesses."

That shouldn't have stung. But it did. "When have I ever given you cause not to trust me?"

Nova gurgled happily, but Cade didn't answer.

Not that Davey actually expected the guy to. He pulled out the thick folder from inside his jacket and dropped it onto the table. It landed between them with a heavy thunk.

Cade didn't even look at it. "If you came here to accuse me of poisoning Elliot, just fucking say it."

"Did you?"

Cade finally looked up. His navy blue eyes were like a sheet of glacial ice with something dark and dangerous swimming beneath the surface. He never showed his temper the way others in their family did. No sharp words, no raised voice. Just that cold stillness. "No."

Davey shoved the folder closer. "Then explain this."

Cade still didn't touch it. Didn't even glance down. Just stared like he was waiting for the punchline to an unfunny joke he already knew.

"Your credentials were used to breach our system. Either you're the mole, or you're so sloppy you let someone waltz through your firewalls with your access codes."

"Watch your tone."

"I vouched for you, Cade. Told them you wouldn't betray us."

"And yet, here we are."

Davey's temper snapped, and he slammed his palm on the table. Nova startled, making a small squeak of alarm, and Cade instantly, automatically soothed her. He rubbed gentle circles on her back, but his eyes had gone downright arctic. "Scare her again. I dare you."

Fuck.

He looked at the baby, who had burrowed into her dad's side. Her dark blue eyes—Cade's eyes—watched him warily as she stuck her thumb in her mouth.

Jesus. He needed to get a hold of himself.

He wasn't usually the kind of guy to lose control like that. Especially not around a baby. "Sorry," he said, feeling awkward as hell. "I used to be good with kids."

Cade huffed. "Yeah. Back before you turned into an uptight hardass."

It wasn't sharp. It wasn't even sarcastic.

It was just true.

For a moment—just a flicker of a second—it almost felt like old times. Like they were two dumbass kids sneaking beers on the fire escape, arguing over which pizza place was the best in the city, knowing damn well they'd end up at the same hole-in-the-wall they always did. Like summers spent weaving their bikes through Central Park at full speed, trying to see who could cut the sharpest corners without wiping out. Like that one year they both had black eyes at the same time—Cade's from a fight, Davey's from an ill-advised attempt to do a backflip off the playground swings.

Like before.

And then it was gone.

Cade's expression smoothed over, his posture locking back into cold, unreadable calculation. Nova gave a soft whimper, still watching Davey with those same blue eyes he and Cade had both inherited from their grandfather.

Davey pulled out a chair and took a seat, inhaling deeply before he spoke again. "I have a hit out on me," he said finally, keeping his voice low, controlled. "Elliot nearly died. My team—our family—is compromised. And if you're involved, I swear to God—"

Cade's eyes flashed dangerously. "You'll do what, exactly? Take me out? Arrest me?"

"If I have to."

"You'd try."

Davey gritted his teeth. "Just tell me I didn't make a mistake vouching for you."

Nova whimpered softly.

Cade immediately softened, pressing a gentle kiss to her forehead. "Shh, it's okay, sweetheart. Daddy's got you."

Davey watched the transformation, torn between disbelief and a grudging admiration. The cold, ruthless operative melting into a tender, protective father in an instant. It was jarring to witness.

Cade reached into the diaper bag at his feet, pulling out a small stuffed elephant. Nova grabbed it eagerly, immediately shoving one of its ears into her mouth.

Only then did Cade's gaze snap up, ice-cold once more.

"You think I'd put my daughter in danger?" His voice was quiet. Flat. Deadly. "You think I'd sit here, feeding her fucking toast, if I had anything to do with this?"

"I don't know, Cade." Davey's voice was quiet now, too. But it was just as dangerous. "You've made it clear how much you resent me."

That got a reaction.

"Resentment doesn't make me a traitor. If it did, I would've betrayed you a long time ago." Cade laughed once, sharp and bitter. "You never trusted me after Belgrade, did you?"

And just like that, they weren't talking about security breaches anymore.

They were talking about the mission. The one that broke them.

Davey exhaled sharply, his pulse spiking at the mention of it. He had spent the last ten years trying to bury that day, but Cade's words yanked it right back to the surface. His SEAL team had been called in after US intelligence indicated WSW was preparing to extract a high-value defector without full operational clearance. The mission had been Cade's for six months—his contacts, his planning, his team. And then, at the last second, the U.S. government stepped in, overriding WSW and sending in Davey's team to "assist" with an operation Cade already had under control.

Only it hadn't been under control.

Davey had seen the warning signs the second he landed. The extraction point was too exposed, the Serbian paramilitaries too quiet. The whole thing smelled like a setup. He tried to warn Cade. Told him to pull back, reassess, abort if necessary.

But Cade hadn't listened.

And people had died because of it.

"You ignored my warning," Davey said evenly.

Cade scoffed. "Your warning? You were barely on the ground a week before that op. You got to walk in at the last second with your orders and your authority, while I was the one who had spent six months laying the groundwork, earning trust, building something real. And then, just like always, you got to be the one they listened to."

"And I saw what you didn't," Davey snapped. "It was a setup."

Cade shook his head, jaw flexing. "I had reliable intel. It only became a clusterfuck when you and your SEAL buddies stormed in, acting like you were the only ones who knew what the hell you were doing."

Davey barked out a laugh, sharp and humorless. "That *reliable intel* got one of my guys killed."

"And I lost two of mine. *Ours.* WSW employees that you never knew before that op because you were never here." He thumped a finger down on the table for emphasis. "I was. I've always been here—working in the trenches, putting in the time, proving myself to a company that never once looked at me the way they looked at you. You were their golden boy, their perfect leader, and I was just the guy who kept the machine running in the background, waiting for a shot I was never going to get."

Silence stretched between them, thick with old wounds and unspoken accusations. Nova squirmed slightly in Cade's lap, and he adjusted her without missing a beat, his touch instinctively gentle despite the tension rolling off him.

Davey swallowed back the sharp words sitting on the tip of his tongue. He hadn't come here to rehash the past, but it was clawing its way up between them anyway.

"You made a bad call," Davey finally said, his voice quieter now, rougher. "And the uncles stopped trusting you after that."

Cade's gaze flickered. "No. *You* stopped trusting me."

Davey didn't deny it. Couldn't.

Cade exhaled, his expression unreadable. Then, without a word, he reached into Nova's diaper bag.

Davey's muscles coiled. He knew Cade wouldn't be stupid enough to pull a weapon here, but instinct still had him preparing for a fight. Instead, Cade pulled out another folder and dropped it onto the table. "A few weeks ago, I noticed my credentials were being used when I wasn't in the building and started investigating. Thought maybe you were the problem."

Davey's gut clenched as he flipped the file open. His blood turned to ice. Cade wasn't the mole. But someone inside Wilde Security was.

Cade took a slow sip of coffee, his expression unreadable. "You got the wrong fucking cousin."

"Liam?" he breathed in disbelief. The man who told him earlier today, *I'll back your play no matter what.*

Davey felt physically ill. He forced himself to look up, heart hammering. He flipped through the file, scanning the supposed evidence: access logs showing Liam's credentials used to enter secure areas at odd hours, suspicious bank deposits, and snippets of intercepted messages—out of context but damning enough.

He pushed the file away. "No. No way. Liam wouldn't—"

But the words tasted like a lie.

And then—

Davey felt something ripple along his senses. That tiny, almost imperceptible shift in the air. That instinctual prickle at the back of his neck.

"Get down!" He shoved Cade just as the window shattered. A bullet tore past his shoulder and embedded itself in the wall behind them with a dull thud. Nova let out a piercing wail as Cade turned sharply, tucking her against his chest, his entire body a shield between her and the threat.

Screams filled the café. Patrons scrambled for safety, chairs clattering to the floor. The barista behind the counter ducked out of sight, and a family near the window yanked their children beneath the table.

"Shit. Adrenaline surged through his veins as he rolled behind an overturned table, drawing his weapon in one fluid motion. But a Glock was no good against a fucking long-range rifle. The sniper—he *refused* to think it was Liam—could still be out there, waiting for people to run out so he could pick them off. "Everyone, stay down! NYPD will be here soon. Stay calm, and don't move!"

"You better fucking find Liam before I do," Cade hissed, then he moved low and fast toward the kitchen at the back of the café. Nova was tucked against his chest, her tiny form completely shielded by his bulk.

Davey exhaled hard, relief hitting him in a sharp wave.

Cade and Nova were out of the sniper's line of sight. That was the only thing that mattered.

For half a second, his shoulders threatened to uncoil. He could feel his pulse pounding in his ears, his body thrumming with the raw adrenaline of knowing they'd made it to cover. The worst of the danger was past—

Except it wasn't.

The relief curdled into ice.

The back door let out into an alley.

A dead end.

Unless Cade planned to break through a solid brick wall, the only way out was right back into the sniper's line of fire.

Shit.

Davey's stomach clenched. They weren't safe. The sniper was still watching, still waiting. If Cade made a move—if *anyone* made a move—the next shot would be clean.

The civilians in the café were still huddled under tables, their terror thick in the air. Trapped.

Rowan's voice echoed in his head. *"No heroics."*

He almost laughed.

That ship had sailed.

His gut already knew what his brain was trying to catch up to.

He was the target.

Not Cade. Not Nova. Not the barista cowering behind the counter or the young couple whispering prayers beneath an overturned table.

Him.

And if he ran, if he made himself a moving target—he could buy them time.

"Fuck," he muttered under his breath.

This was going to hurt.

twenty-four

ROWAN HAD A BAD FEELING.

It had settled in the moment Davey announced he was going to meet Cade alone, and it hadn't gone away since.

She paced the length of the apartment, arms crossed tight over her chest, trying to ignore the two men keeping watch over her like a pair of sentinels.

Liam hovered near the door, arms folded, watching her like he knew exactly what she was thinking. Which, unfortunately, he did.

But if she left, she wasn't going to make a run for the door. No, she'd use the fire escape. Without her climbing equipment, it was her only option as she wasn't too keen on free-soloing down the side of the building.

The problem was Sabin.

He sat sprawled in the armchair, one ankle resting on his knee, flipping a coin between his fingers like he hadn't a care in the world. But his lazy grin was deceptive. Jean-Sabin Cavalier never missed a thing, and as a former thief, he knew the fire escape was her only option.

Which was why he'd positioned himself at just the right angle to see the window.

Not directly, not obviously—but enough that if she so much as touched the latch, he'd clock it.

Rowan narrowed her eyes at him, wondering if he was actually watching her or just playing some elaborate game of psychological warfare.

Sabin caught her look and smirked. "Problem, princess?"

Damn him.

"No."

"Uh-huh," he drawled. "You're fidgeting. I suspect that means you fixin' to do something reckless."

Rowan stopped pacing long enough to glare at him. "I don't fidget."

Liam arched a brow.

Shit. She was definitely fidgeting.

Damn them both.

She exhaled sharply. "You don't have to hover. I'm not going to vanish into thin air. I'm not a magician."

Sabin grinned like he'd already won the argument. "Mm. Now, cher, that's exactly what a magician would say."

Liam snorted.

Rowan rolled her eyes and turned toward the window, but before she could start pacing again, Daphne closed her laptop and pushed up from the table. "I gotta go back to my lab."

Rowan turned to her. She's almost forgotten the other woman was there. "Why does she get to leave?"

"Maybe because she wasn't stabbed a few days ago," Sabin suggested.

Daphne pushed her glasses up her nose. "And unlike the rest of you people, I have actual work to do."

Liam unfolded his arms. "I'll drive you."

Rowan whirled toward him, seizing on the opportunity to get out of his apartment. "I'll go with—"

"No." Liam shot her a look. "Not a debate." Then he softened the blow with a faint smile. "You gotta be hungry. I'll grab some food on the way back."

Sabin stretched, still looking thoroughly unbothered. "*Mais*, yeah, I'm hungry. Get me fries."

Liam didn't dignify that with a response.

Daphne, already halfway to the door, smirked over her shoulder. "He means extra fries."

Sabin grinned.

Rowan crossed her arms. "And what about you?" she asked Sabin. "Shouldn't you be Liam's backup?"

Sabin gave her an exaggerated yawn. "Nah. You're my priority. Plus, it takes a very special kind of idiot to go after Liam. He'll be fine."

Rowan's unease didn't just settle—it sank, deep and heavy, like a storm rolling in.

The longer she stood there, the worse it got, tightening low in her ribs like a warning she couldn't shake. She turned back to the window, scanning the street below. "I don't like this."

Sabin flipped his coin, caught it, and flicked it into the air again. "You don't like anything."

She shot him a glare. "I mean it. Something feels wrong."

Sabin sighed. "Rowan. Davey's not stupid."

"You sure about that?"

He smirked. "Okay, fine, he's stupid, but not the suicidal kind. And if Cade was going to put a bullet in him, he'd have done it years ago."

"That's not what I'm worried about," she muttered.

Sabin arched a brow. "Then what?"

She hesitated, half afraid that if she put it into words, and it would become reality.

She exhaled sharply, rubbing a hand down her face. "He's out in the open. In a public place. With people watching."

Sabin flipped his coin lazily. "Yeah, that was kind of the point. Neutral ground, witnesses. Harder for Cade to try anything."

Rowan's jaw tightened. "And easier for someone else to take a shot."

Now she had his attention.

Sabin caught the coin mid-flip, his long fingers closing around the metal. "You think this is a setup?"

"I think Davey's has more enemies than friends right now. So, yeah, I think if someone wanted to take him out, this would be a damn good opportunity."

Sabin considered that. "So why let him go?"

Rowan exhaled sharply, forcing herself to unclench her fists. "Because we're all working off scraps right now. We don't know who's pulling the strings. We don't even know if we're playing the same game. Talking to Cade was our only option."

Sabin's eyes narrowed. "So what do you want to do about it?"

She wanted to call Davey, but if something had already gone sideways, she didn't want to distract him. She wanted to run straight to him, but if she was wrong, she'd just make herself a target.

She turned back toward the window, gaze flicking down to the street again. The light was different now. Time had passed.

More time than she'd realized.

She'd spent the last hour pacing this fucking apartment like a caged cat, obsessing over Davey's meeting, and she hadn't even noticed how long it had been since Liam walked out that door.

A sharp prickle of unease ran down her spine. She glanced over at the door, frown deepening. "How long ago did Liam leave?"

Sabin didn't answer immediately. He was still

watching her, reading her, and that only made the unease in her stomach twist tighter.

Finally, he shrugged. "Dunno. Maybe an hour? Hour and a half?"

Too long.

WSW wasn't far. Neither was a damn burger joint.

So where the hell was he?

Her pulse kicked up.

Had something already happened at the meeting? Was that why Liam hadn't come back?

But no—Sabin would know if something had gone wrong. Wouldn't he?

Unless—

Unless there hadn't been time to call.

Her stomach dropped.

Her mind started ticking through every possibility, every terrible fucking scenario.

What if Liam never made it to WSW? What if someone had been waiting for him?

What if *he'd* walked into a trap?

She turned back to Sabin, heartbeat too loud in her ears.

"He should be back."

Sabin's smirk faded completely. His posture shifted, subtle but noticeable. "You worried about Liam now?"

Rowan clenched her jaw. "He should be back," she repeated, sharper this time.

But saying it out loud didn't make it true.

The uneasy weight in her chest solidified into something colder, heavier.

This wasn't just paranoia.

Something was wrong.

She could feel it, crawling up her spine, pressing against the back of her skull like a warning too loud to ignore.

Rowan glanced back at the window one last time, like she'd see Liam or Davey walking down the street —like she'd been wrong.

But the street was empty.

Enough.

She spun away from the window, pulse thrumming in her throat. "I'm taking a shower."

Sabin's grin returned instantly. "So this is the part where we pretend you're not about to do something incredibly reckless, yeah?"

Rowan didn't answer, just headed for the bedroom. Slow. Controlled. Like she wasn't already halfway out the door.

"Don't you go closing that bedroom door," Sabin warned idly.

"Yeah, you'd like to see me naked, wouldn't you?"

"As appealing as you are, cher, I'd like to keep my balls intact more and Davey'll have them for earrings if he thinks I saw anything."

Rowan shot him a sidelong glance before shutting

the door. She could hear his chuckle on the other side. "We both know what you're gonna do. You get a five minute head start, then I'm comin' after you."

She didn't bother turning on the shower. Sabin already knew it was a ruse, so why waste the water? She grabbed her Glock from the nightstand, checked the mag, and slid it into the holster at the small of her back. A blade followed—a slim, wickedly sharp karambit, strapped to her thigh.

Prepared, not paranoid. That had been drilled into her since she was a kid.

Only now, it didn't feel like paranoia.

It felt like survival.

Her boots barely made a sound as she slipped to the window, pried it open, and climbed out onto the fire escape.

By the time her feet hit the pavement, she was already running toward the café thirteen blocks away.

Because she *knew*.

She didn't know how she knew. Maybe it was gut instinct. Maybe it was a lifetime of training. Maybe it was the simple, unshakable fact that Davey Wilde attracted trouble like a damn magnet.

And right now, something wasn't right.

Then—the first gunshot cracked through the afternoon air.

Rowan froze.

Then she ran.

Another shot.

Her pulse hammered as she reached the café, barely processing the chaos—patrons screaming, tables overturned, the sharp crack of glass as a bullet shattered another window.

Then—movement.

Davey.

He was running into the street.

What the hell was he doing?

And then she saw it.

He was drawing fire away from the civilians.

The sniper was hunting him.

Rowan's stomach twisted, her fingers already reaching for the gun at the small of her back.

A shadow moved at her side, and she didn't have to turn to know Sabin had caught up to her.

He was watching, his usual easy grin gone. His expression was sharp now, calculating.

"Is he out of his fucking mind?" he murmured.

Rowan's grip tightened around her weapon. "Always."

Davey kept moving, deliberately making himself a target.

The sniper didn't fire.

Rowan didn't trust that silence.

"Come on." She was already in motion, but Sabin grabbed her wrist.

"Wait."

Her pulse jumped. "What—"

"The cops."

Red and blue lights flickered down the street.

Rowan cursed.

The sniper was gone.

And now, the cops were here.

Davey had stopped moving. He stood at the center of the chaos, gun still in his hand, breathing hard. He looked wired—adrenaline still riding him hard—but his eyes found hers immediately.

She didn't know what he was expecting.

Relief? Praise?

Too bad.

She stalked toward him.

"What the hell was that?" she snapped.

Davey dragged a hand through his hair. "Buying you time."

She swore. "You—"

"I need to know where Liam is."

That stopped her.

She blinked. "What?"

Davey turned to Sabin, his expression sharp. "Tell me you were with him. Tell me you know exactly where he is."

Silence.

Sabin hesitated. "No. He—uh—went to take Daphne back to her lab and get food."

"When?" Davey's voice came out too sharp, too fast. A single, deadly demand.

Rowan's stomach dropped. It wasn't just urgency. It was fear.

Sabin rubbed a hand across the back of his neck. "He said he'd be back in an hour. I figure he's at the safe house wondering where the hell we are."

Davey's jaw clenched. "Then let's go."

Rowan didn't argue.

Because suddenly, her gut was screaming again.

twenty-five

DAVEY SHOVED the door open first, gun in hand, clearing the entry before stepping inside.

The apartment was silent.

Too silent.

His stomach twisted.

"Liam?" Rowan called, already moving toward the back rooms.

Nothing.

Sabin checked the kitchen, the bathroom—every possible place Liam could be. He reappeared a moment later, his face unreadable, as he grabbed his phone and tapped out a text message, probably to Daphne.

Rowan stepped out of the bedroom doorway, arms crossed, tension in every line of her body. "So maybe he ran into traffic. Or a delay getting food. Or he hung out at the office for a bit before—"

"Daphne says he never went inside. He dropped her off and left." Sabin's voice was too flat. Too controlled. His gaze flicked up from his phone, narrowing on Davey. "What aren't you telling us?"

Davey swallowed the knot in his throat.

Fuck.

No easy way to say it.

He met their gazes head-on. "Cade thinks Liam is the mole."

Sabin exploded.

A sharp string of French and English curses filled the space as he paced the room, his long legs eating up the floor in a few short strides before he hit a wall and had to pivot.

"No. It's not Liam."

"Sabin—"

"No." His hands curled into fists. "Not Liam. No fucking way in hell it's Liam."

"Cade noticed his credentials were being used when he wasn't in the building," Davey said, forcing his voice to stay calm, level. "So he started investigating himself and Liam—"

Sabin laughed. Sharp. Humorless. "*Mais*, if Cade says so, we should just believe him, yeah?" His voice dripped with sarcasm and barely restrained fury. "'Cause no way he'd lie, tryin' to cover his own ass."

"He's right," Rowan said after a beat of heavy silence. "I don't trust Cade. I don't think you should either."

Davey exhaled hard, dragging a hand through his hair. "I don't. Not fully."

Sabin stopped moving. "Then why the hell are you telling us this?"

"Because whether it's bullshit or not, Liam is still missing."

"He didn't shoot up that cafe. Liam wouldn't. I can promise you that." Sabin started pacing again, his jaw tight.

Rowan folded her arms over her chest. "We need more information."

Davey checked his watch. Sullivan and Brody were probably asleep, but he needed them to come back in. Without another word, he pulled out his phone and dialed Sullivan.

The line rang once. Twice.

Then—

"Yeah, boss, I'm not coming in."

Davey's grip tightened on the phone. "Sully—"

"But I do have a gift for you."

That made all of the hair prickle in warning along the back of his neck. "What kind of *gift*?"

Sabin went rigid, color draining from his face. His hands curled into fists at his sides, his usual easy smirk wiped clean off his face. He turned in a slow circle, muttering a long string of curses in French, one hand dragging through his hair.

"Merde," he finally muttered. His eyes snapped to

Davey, wide and full of something dangerously close to panic. "He didn't."

Davey's gaze snapped to Sabin, his gut clenching like it used to before he jumped out of a plane. "Didn't what? Sabin, what the hell are you talking about?"

Sabin ran a hand through his hair, mussing the blond strands into chaotic spikes. "It was just a joke, yeah? A stupid, off-hand comment after not enough sleep. We were talking about how frustrating it was, always being one step behind Frost. And I said, half-kidding, 'Maybe we should just grab the bastard and make him talk.' Sully got this look in his eye, like when he's about to do something spectacularly reckless, and he..." Sabin trailed off and shrugged helplessly. "I didn't think he'd actually go do it."

Oh, fuck. That feeling—the sharp, gut-twisting realization that he was already mid-air, no parachute, no backup—hit fast and hard. The split-second before a mission went to hell. The moment before a detonation. The kind of second that stretched endlessly, when you knew you couldn't stop what was coming, only brace for impact.

He'd seen it before—seen it in ops that turned into disasters. Seen it in soldiers' eyes right before they realized they weren't going home. And now?

Now he was watching it unfold in real-time, and he didn't have a goddamn parachute.

He put the phone on speaker so Sabin and Rowan

could hear the conversation. "Sullivan, tell me you didn't kidnap Atlas fucking Frost."

"For the record, Brody was against this. But we need answers," Sullivan said, voice calm, level, like he didn't just drop a fucking bomb on them. "And this fucker has answers."

Davey pinched the bridge of his nose. "Jesus Christ."

"Again, for the record," Sully repeated, "Brody was very against this. This is all me."

Davey exhaled through his teeth, already feeling the massive headache forming. "Where the fuck are you, Sully?"

"Went off grid. Don't trust the safe houses anymore," he said, sounding annoyingly pleased with himself. "Really, I thought you'd be thanking me, boss. You wanted answers, didn't you?"

Davey shut his eyes. Breathed in. Out. Failed to find his calm.

"Sullivan." His voice was dangerously even. "You kidnapped a billionaire with connections to every major criminal organization on the planet. What the fuck were you thinking?"

"I was thinking we needed answers," Sullivan replied, his tone unapologetic. "And who better to give them than the man pulling all the strings?"

Davey exchanged a look with Rowan and saw his own frustration and disbelief reflected in her eyes. But under that—concern.

For Elliot. For Brody. For Liam. For how completely fucked this had just become.

"Where's Brody now?" she asked, her voice tight with concern.

Silence.

A long one.

Too long.

Rowan straightened. Sabin stopped pacing. Davey's grip on the phone tightened.

Finally, Sullivan muttered, "He, uh... he wasn't too happy about the plan. We had words. He stormed out."

Another complication they didn't need. "And he hasn't checked in since?"

"No," Sullivan admitted. "Look, boss. I know this wasn't exactly protocol—"

"Understatement of the fucking century." Davey shut his eyes for half a second. Liam was missing. Brody was missing. Cade was possibly lying. And Atlas Frost was now his hostage.

One problem at a time.

He wanted to tear into Sullivan for this idiotic, potentially catastrophic move, but there wasn't time. "Send me directions to your location. We're on our way. Don't touch him. Don't interrogate him. Don't—"

"Yeah, yeah," Sully cut in. "Relax, boss." A beat of silence. Then, with pure exasperation, he added, "Sure I can't punch him? This asshole's been smirking at me for two hours."

Davey inhaled. Exhaled. "I don't have the time or patience to dig a grave for you today, Sullivan. Tomorrow, though? You keep pressing my buttons, and I'll clear my schedule."

Sully snorted. "Roger that, boss man."

Davey ended the call and just... stood there.

One problem at a time, he reminded himself. *One fucking problem at a time.*

His temples throbbed. He needed two Advil, a nap, and a time machine to undo the last ten minutes. Instead, he got Rowan staring at the floor like she was already blaming herself and Sabin muttering in French like he was debating murder.

Yeah. That felt about right.

Rowan sighed. "I knew today was going to be shit, but even I underestimated."

"Yeah." And to think he'd woken up feeling rested. He dragged a hand down his face. "Let's go."

twenty-six

THE PENTHOUSE WAS HALF-FINISHED, half-forgotten.

Cold concrete floors, exposed steel beams, and floor-to-ceiling windows that overlooked a skyline Frost probably owned half of. No furniture, just a single flickering work light in the corner and a few crates that served as a makeshift table.

The elevator had been shut off. One way up. One way down.

Which meant Sully wasn't expecting company.

Atlas Frost sat in the middle of the room, tied to a chair, looking entirely too comfortable for a man in his position.

He grinned as they entered, all ease and amusement.

"Ah, the cavalry."

Sullivan was leaning against the far wall, arms

crossed, looking bored as hell. But Davey didn't miss the tension in his stance.

Not relaxed. Coiled. Waiting.

He ignored it for now, stepping closer to loom over Frost. "You're gonna start talking."

Frost tilted his head, all lazy amusement. "Well, that depends. Are you actually going to ask me something interesting?"

Davey opened his mouth, but Rowan beat him to it. "Rue. Why was she at your gala?"

Frost's gaze flicked to her, smirk widening into something slow and knowing. "Ah. The professional."

Davey caught the smallest twitch of Rowan's fingers at her sides.

Frost chuckled. "Or do you prefer Vesper? That's the name on the contract, isn't it?" His gaze slid toward Davey, and his smile became wolfish. "The one you accepted to kill him."

Rowan didn't blink. Didn't flinch. "Nice try, but he already knows. Now answer the question."

Frost's smirk didn't falter. "Your sister is a brilliant, fascinating, gorgeous woman. Why wouldn't I invite her?"

Rowan's jaw tightened. "You funded her expedition."

Frost sighed dramatically, shaking his head. "You make it sound so nefarious."

"Because it is."

A thoughtful tilt of his head. "Believe it or not, I

have a vested interest in keeping this planet habitable. I subsidize a lot of scientific endeavors."

Rowan crossed her arms. "So, what? That's just your little charity project?"

Frost's eyes glinted with amusement. "Oh, I wouldn't call it little. But yes, philanthropy is important to me."

Davey cut in now, his patience thinning. "Cut the bullshit, Frost. Is Liam working for you?"

Laughter. The sound bounced off the bare walls, grating. "Liam Wilde? Please. That boy scout wouldn't know how to be corrupt if I handed him an instruction manual."

Davey studied him. Searching for any crack in that polished, infuriatingly pleasant mask.

Nothing.

"Cade, then."

Frost exhaled, almost *disappointed*. "Oh, come on, Davey. Do you really not know your family at all?" A shake of his head. "If Cade Wilde wanted you dead, he wouldn't have hired someone else to do it. He certainly wouldn't have hired me to broker the deal and he definitely wouldn't have hired her"—his gaze flicked to Rowan again—"given that you two eye-fuck each other every time you're in a room together."

The muscle in Davey's jaw twitched. He ignored it. "So who hired you to hire her? Who wants me dead?"

Frost's smile sharpened. "Now that's a much more interesting question, isn't it?" He leaned forward in the chair as much as his restraints would allow. "But I'm afraid I can't answer it. Client confidentiality and all that."

Davey's fist clenched at his side. "Cut the shit, Frost. You're not exactly in a position to negotiate here."

Frost's amusement didn't waver. "Aren't I?" His eyes glittered, calculating. "You can't touch me, Davey. Not really. And we both know it."

A shift to Davey's right. Sabin, usually the easiest one in the room, moved forward. At that moment, he looked less like the snarky prankster and more like the deadly operative Davey knew him to be. "Want to bet on that, Frost? We could make you talk."

Another laugh. "Oh, please. You're not going to torture me. That's not your style."

Then he turned, eyes landing on Sullivan. And Davey knew—knew—before he even spoke.

"Well, maybe it's his. Tell me, Sullivan. Do you know where your brother is?"

The air turned razor-sharp.

Every muscle in Sullivan's body went rigid.

Rowan stepped forward. "What do you mean?"

Frost didn't even look at her. Didn't have to. His attention was still locked onto Sully, like a predator watching for the first sign of weakness.

"You're all so worried about Liam or Cade." The mockery faded from his voice, leaving something colder behind. "But you should be worried about Brody."

Sullivan went very, very still.

Sabin's coin slipped from his fingers, the soft *clink* against the floor barely registering. "What?"

"You heard me," Frost said.

Davey had never wanted to put a bullet between a man's eyes more.

Sullivan pushed off the wall. His face was blank, but Davey knew him well enough to see what was underneath.

"You're lying," Sully said, voice low and dangerous.

Frost tilted his head. "Am I?"

Another beat of silence. Then Sullivan grabbed him.

Frost chuckled. "Now, now. Let's not get emotional."

Sullivan's grip tightened. His voice wasn't calm anymore. "Where is he?"

Frost just kept grinning that Cheshire Cat smile.

Shit. Sully was about to do something stupid.

Davey moved, but not fast enough. In a blink, Sullivan had Frost by the collar and yanked him forward so violently into the punch, the chair screeched against the concrete.

Frost only laughed, all teeth and blood.

Davey reached them in two strides, shoving a hand against Sullivan's chest before this turned into something messier. "Back off."

Sullivan didn't move.

"Sully."

Nothing. His grip was locked, his jaw tight, his whole body wired.

Dangerous. That was the only word for what this moment was turning into.

Davey dug his fingers dug into Sullivan's shoulder and dropped his voice to a low growl. "Stand down. Now."

For a heartbeat, Sullivan didn't move. His eyes were locked on Frost, something feral and desperate in his gaze. Then, with agonizing slowness, he released his grip on Frost's collar. The chair settled back onto all four legs with a dull thud.

Frost's grin widened, blood pearling at the corner of his mouth. "Ah," he said, voice just this side of taunting. "I see it now. It could have so easily been you if they'd touched the right nerve, but you're too unpredictable. Brody was the safer bet."

Sullivan lunged forward again, but Davey was ready this time. He caught him around the chest, shoving him back. "I said stand down!" Then, softer: "Let me handle this. You're too close."

When Sullivan turned, Davey was struck by the raw fear and turmoil in the man's eyes. Then, as quickly as it came, the moment passed. Sullivan's jaw clenched and he pulled back, lifting his hands in a silent surrender.

Davey kept his gaze on Sullivan for a beat longer,

making sure he wouldn't lunge again. When he was satisfied, he turned back to Frost, who was watching the exchange with undisguised glee.

"You're enjoying this."

Frost's smile was all bloody teeth. "Immensely."

Davey kicked at his chair, tipping it onto its back. "Enough. You have exactly ten seconds to start talking before I decide whether to take you apart piece by piece. Or I can let Sully finish what he started."

"Fine." The amusement was still there, but underneath was the sharp, assessing eyes of a predator. "Fine. I'll be generous. Consider this a freebie." He smiled over at Sullivan. "Broderick O'Connell is your mole."

The silence that followed was a black hole—sucking all the air, all the sound, all the sense out of the room.

For a full five seconds, no one moved.

"Bullshit," Sullivan snarled and yanked the chair upright hard enough to give anyone whiplash.

Frost grunted in pain, but then just shrugged. "I know. Hard to hear, but your twin is a traitor. He's been working against you this whole time." He tilted his head toward Davey, lazy, like this wasn't about to end in blood. "But he sees it, don't you, Wilde?"

His stomach turned to stone. There it was. The thing he hadn't wanted to name, hadn't let himself believe.

And yet...

The second Frost had said it, something deep in his gut had twisted because it made too much sense.

Brody was the mole.

This whole time, he'd been the one pushing the hardest to go after Cade. He knew the evidence would back him up because he'd fucking planted it.

"You son of a bitch," Davey growled, advancing on Frost. "How long has he been working for you?"

Frost's smirk widened. "Oh, Brody doesn't work for me. I'm just the messenger."

"You're lying," Sullivan repeated, but this time his voice was quieter. More desperate.

Frost sighed, shaking his head. "No, Sully. You just don't want it to be true."

"Prove it."

Frost's smile stretched wider. "Ah. Now you're thinking."

Davey had never wanted to hit someone more in his life.

Frost licked the blood from his lip and settled back, in control now. "Here's the deal. I give you what you need. Brody's last location. His contacts. His leverage. And in return?" He spread his fingers as best he could against his restraints, like he was about to make the most reasonable offer in the world. "You let me walk."

Sullivan went still again.

Davey exhaled through his nose in a sound that was almost a laugh of disbelief. "You're out of your goddamn mind."

Frost grinned. "Oh, come on, Davey. You know I'm good for it. Otherwise, you'll spend weeks chasing the ghost of the twin who doesn't want to be found. By the time you catch up? Liam's going to be a corpse and everything will point to him as the mole. It'll break your Uncle Greer's heart to lose his first born that way. How is the old man's heart? Can it handle that?"

Davey's fists clenched at his sides, every muscle coiled tight with the effort not to lash out. Frost's words burrowed under his skin like shards of glass, each one a calculated jab designed to provoke a reaction.

Frost leaned forward, the ropes digging into his wrists, leaving his hands a waxy white color. "Tick-tock, Wilde. This is a limited time deal. What's it going to be?"

Davey's fingers curled into fists. He could feel the weight of every eye in the room on him.

Sullivan wanted vengeance.

Sabin wanted answers.

Rowan was waiting, watching, calculating.

And Davey fucking hated this. He hated that it was his decision, and hated the fact there was really only one option here that didn't tear his family apart...

But that same option tore Sully's family apart. The twins only had each other. But the cold, tactical part of his brain knew Frost was right. They needed the fucker. He knew too much.

"I'm sorry, Sully." His voice came out hoarse and

he cleared his throat before nodding to Sabin. "Cut him loose."

The sound of Sullivan's breath leaving his lungs was like a gunshot. He didn't say a word as Sabin pulled out a knife and sliced through the ropes. Didn't move at first, barely appeared to be breathing. Then he turned and stalked toward the stairs, the metal door slamming against the wall with the force of him yanking it open. His boots hit the concrete stairs with hard, measured steps.

Rowan made to follow, but Davey caught her arm. "Let him go."

Sabin yanked Frost to his feet. The bastard brushed off his suit and rolled his shoulders like he was getting up from a relaxing spa day.

Then, just for a second, his smirk slipped as the door swung back closed with a resounding clank. It wasn't much. Just a fraction of hesitation. A crack in the polished mask. "Should probably keep an eye on him. This is going to hurt him more than either of us."

"What do you care?"

Frost rubbed at his wrists where the rope had cut into them. "I don't, but if he does something reckless, it could jeopardize our new partnership."

"This is not a partnership," Davey said. "Now get out."

Frost gave an exaggerated bow. "A pleasure, as always." He turned toward the door, but before he could step away, Davey caught his arm. Frost looked down at his hand, then back up, raising a brow. "If you wanted to hold hands, you could've just asked."

"You might've brought yourself some time." Davey tightened his grip. "But we're not finished here."

The smirk didn't drop completely, but something behind it shifted. The sharp edge of it dulled, replaced with something softer. Something real.

"No," Frost said, voice quiet but certain. "We're not."

Frost pulled his arm free and looked at Sabin, then Rowan. His gaze finally returned to Davey. "Something big is coming, Wilde." His voice wasn't mocking now. It was low, even. "And when it does, you're going to want me as an ally."

Rowan shifted beside him, eyes narrowing. "Allies are people you can trust."

"Mostly." Sabin stopped flipping his damn coin. "But allies can also be secured through mutually assured destruction."

Frost pointed at him. "He gets it."

"We're nothing alike, Frost."

The smile returned, as quick and sharp as ever. "You only wish that to be true, Cavalier." He switched to French and said something that had Sabin's eyes narrowing dangerously.

Jesus. Frost just couldn't help himself, could he? He had to push everyone's buttons until he got a reaction.

Davey stepped between them before a fight could

break out. He held Frost's gaze, searching for any hint of deception, but the man's expression was unreadable. "What's coming?"

Frost's lips curved, but the humor was gone. "That would be telling." He scooped his black hair away from his face, then straightened his jacket, composure firmly back in place. "Let's just say the world is about to change. And not everyone will survive the shift."

"Cut the cryptic bullshit," Rowan snapped. "If you know something—"

"I know many things, Ms. Bristow," Frost interrupted smoothly. "But knowledge is power, and I'm not in the habit of giving that away for free." He glanced at his watch like he was late for a pressing engagement, but when he looked up again, the smug mask slipped completely, revealing something almost... human underneath. "But I will tell you this— there are some things in this world even I wouldn't sell. And if Praetorian has their way, one of those things will be auctioned very soon. That's why they want to destabilize Wilde Security. You can stop them. I'm *counting on you* to stop them because I can't."

"Can't or won't?" Sabin demanded.

Frost's eyes flickered to him, a hint of amusement returning. "Can't. Won't. Does it matter? The result is the same." He turned back to Davey, expression serious now, and with a flick of his wrist, a small data drive appeared between his fingers. "All the data I have on Brody O'Connell. Use it wisely. And now I expect a favor in return." He tossed the drive, and Davey caught it reflexively.

"That wasn't part of the deal."

"It is now."

"And you just happened to have exactly what we needed on you when Sully captured you?" Davey turned the drive over in his hand, then swore softly. "This was your plan all along, wasn't it?"

Frost drew a handkerchief from his pocket. "I didn't expect Sullivan to be quite so..." He winced as he dabbed at his bleeding lip. "*Enthusiastic* with his fists, but yes, this was always the plan."

"You're a manipulative fuck."

Frost pocketed the handkerchief and tipped his head in a slight bow. "Thank you."

He turned to leave, but Rowan's voice cut through the air like a whip.

"Wait."

Frost paused, eyebrow raised.

Her stance was rigid, but Davey caught the desperation in her eyes—the raw, unguarded fear she rarely let slip. It twisted something deep in his chest. He stepped closer, creating a silent barrier between her and Frost. He wanted to pull her in and shield her from that sharp, knowing gaze that always cut too deep, always found the places that hurt.

"Please," she said softly. "Just tell me. Rue. Is she safe?"

Something like genuine regret flickered across Frost's face. "Define safe."

Rowan took a step forward, fists clenched.

Davey caught her arm before she could get any nearer to Frost, pulling her back against his chest, keeping her from making a mistake she couldn't take back. She was shaking, not with fear, but with fury.

"Easy," he murmured. "I know you want to put a few holes in him, but we might still need him." He looked at Frost again. "Rue is innocent. She's not an operative. She has nothing to do with any of this."

He felt Rowan tense under his grip. He could tell she wanted to argue, wanted to say Rue wasn't helpless. But this wasn't about whether Rue could handle herself.

It was about whether Frost had decided she was disposable.

Davey's voice dropped, lethal now. "If she dies because of your manipulations, I'll give your name to her father. I know you know who Gabe Bristow is." He took a step closer, forcing Frost to actually meet his gaze. "Do you want *him* coming after you?"

For the first time, Frost hesitated. His gaze flicked —just briefly—somewhere past Davey's shoulder like he was actually calculating the risk.

And that told him more than Frost ever would.

"Okay." Finally, the bastard sighed, rolling his shoulders like he didn't like the weight of the moment.

"You might want to send an operative to Antarctica with her." That smirk—slow and sharp—slid back into place. "And now, you owe me two favors."

twenty-seven

DAVEY STEPPED through the doors of Wilde Security Worldwide's headquarters, the weight of responsibility pressing down on his shoulders. The familiar hum of activity filled the space—agents moving purposefully, voices crackling over comms, the low murmur of strategists dissecting mission details. But today, the tension in the air was different. Tighter. Sharper.

Rowan and Sabin flanked him as they moved toward the tech room, their expressions mirroring his own urgency. They didn't need to speak; the stakes were clear. Brody O'Connell's betrayal had left them scrambling for answers, and if there was one person who could break through the layers of deceit, it was Daphne.

Daphne was already at her workstation, multiple screens casting a cold glow over her face as her fingers flew across the keyboard. She barely glanced up as they entered.

"You're late," she muttered, not breaking her rhythm.

"Traffic," Davey deadpanned. "What do you have?"

Daphne exhaled sharply, tilting her head as if debating how much to say before settling on the truth. "Brody didn't even try to hide some of this. It's like he wanted someone to find it. Just... not until it was too late."

Davey frowned, stepping closer to watch the lines of code and decrypted files flashing across the monitors. "Explain."

Daphne tapped a few more keys, pulling up a folder labeled Red Hook Operations. "Some of this data was buried under layers of encryption, but other files? Practically sitting out in the open, like breadcrumbs left behind. He had kill orders, personnel tracking data, even a few financial transfers that scream 'black ops.'"

Rowan crossed her arms. "That doesn't make sense. If he's been a successful mole for all these years, why would he suddenly get so sloppy?"

"Because he knew we'd come looking," Daphne said, her voice tight with frustration. "And if we found it, that meant we were already playing the game on his terms. But here's the kicker—he wasn't just setting Cade up as a distraction. Everything in here is pointed straight at Liam. If you didn't believe him about Cade, then he had it all set up for Liam to take the fall."

"So when I met with Cade to hear him out, he knew his first plan had failed and grabbed Liam—"

"His backup plan." Rowan nodded. "But he hadn't expected Sully to grab Atlas Frost."

"And he knew Frost would give him up." Sabin let out a low whistle. "So now he has Liam—a witness he needs to get rid of before he can disappear."

"You have to prepare yourselves for the possibility he already killed Liam," Rowan said gently. Davey's vision blurred for half a second, but then Rowan was there, gripping his arm, grounding him. "I know what you're thinking, but we don't *know* that yet. Until we do, we keep moving. Liam needs us."

Davey nodded stiffly, forcing himself to push past the doubt clawing at his mind. His chest tightened, the burn of frustration settling into something heavier—fear. He dragged in a slow breath, steadying himself as the thought of Liam already being gone twisted like a knife in his gut. The idea of losing another brother, another member of his family, was a weight he didn't know how to carry. He didn't like playing by someone else's rules. Especially not someone who had been under his command. Brody had been one of theirs—a trusted asset, a man who knew how Wilde Security operated from the inside. That made him dangerous. Potentially desperate.

And desperate men made the most reckless choices.

That was what scared him the most.

"We need to find—"

The door opened, and Davey broke off, turning to tell whoever it was that this was a private meeting, but the reprimand died on his tongue.

Elliot.

He looked like hell. He was still pale, and he was moving more slowly than usual, but the glint in his blue eyes was pure defiance.

Dom followed him in and gave a helpless shrug. "Sorry, Davey, I tried to stop him. But you know how stubborn he is. I figured it was either let him walk in here or tackle him, and I'm not in the mood to wrestle a stubborn jackass today."

Elliot smirked. "Please, Dom. You couldn't take me on my worst day, let alone now."

Dom scoffed. "Yeah? Keep talking, and I'll put that theory to the test."

Sabin snorted. "I'd pay to see that, honestly."

Davey sighed. "Are you done?"

Elliot lifted his chin, his usual smirk flickering for just a second before hardening into something more serious. "Not even close. But for now, yeah. So, fill me in."

Davey hesitated, studying his brother. The stubborn determination in Elliot's face didn't quite mask the exhaustion underneath. He shook his head. "You need to go home and—"

"If you say rest, I will punch something. All I've done is rest while this whole shitshow is my fault."

"Ah, *mon ami*," Sabin started, his tone softer now, but Elliot held up a hand, stopping him before he could say more.

"No, it is. I brought Brody into our lives, into our company. I vouched for him, so he's my responsibility. I'm not sitting on the sidelines for this, so fill me in. Or..." He started toward one of the computer stations. "We can waste time while I fill myself in."

Davey exhaled through his nose. He could argue—should argue—but it was a fight he wasn't going to win. And so he filled Elliot in on what they knew.

Elliot nodded as he listened. "And Sully's in the wind?

"Yeah, Sullivan took off as soon as Frost dropped Brody's name as the mole."

"That makes Sully a problem for Brody and for us," Elliot said. "Sullivan knows him like nobody else. If he leaves Sully alive, that's like exposing his jugular for an attack."

Davey stilled, the pieces clicking together. Brody had run out of moves. He had no exit strategy, no contingency plan. Sully, knowing the truth, meant Brody couldn't just disappear—he'd be hunted. Which meant he was more desperate than ever. A dangerous, cornered man.

Before Davey could respond, Daphne let out a frustrated growl. The entire room stilled as she shoved away from her desk and turned to scowl at them.

"What is it?" Davey asked.

"I need quiet to work. You all hovering isn't helping."

Rowan arched a brow. "You're kicking us out?"

"Yes. Leave. Now." Daphne pointed to the door. "Give me space, and I'll have something real for you. Until then, go breathe or eat or fuck or whatever it is you do when you're not making my job harder."

Silence stretched between them, thick with unspoken questions. Then, Rowan cracked her knuckles, and Sabin let out an exaggerated sigh. "Well, I don't have a choice on breathing, but I could eat or fuck or both." He smirked, casting a glance around the room. "Any volunteers?"

"No, thanks," Dom said. "You're pretty and all, Cavalier, but I prefer females."

Sabin spread his hands, utterly unbothered. "Me, too. But we're short on time, and Daphne told us to fuck. I'm nothing if not efficient."

Daphne groaned and rubbed at her temples. "Get. Out. Seriously. Before I throw something at one of you."

Sabin headed for the door but stopped and glanced over his shoulder. "This isn't your fault, Elliot." He grinned again, but this one was not from the playful, joking Sabin. This was the predator's grin, and it was all sharp edges. "And Brody's not going to like what's coming next. I can promise you that."

Elliot scoffed lightly, but there was no humor in it. "Yeah, well, that doesn't change the fact that I handed him the keys and welcomed him in."

Davey knew the weight of that guilt, had carried it before. "You can beat yourself up about it after we get Liam back."

Elliot didn't answer right away, but the tension in his jaw loosened slightly. He gave a short nod, then gestured toward the door. "Let's let Daph do her job so we find this son of a bitch."

Everyone followed him out, but Davey hesitated.

Daphne glanced over at him. "That means you, too, Davey. I can't work with you looming like the world's most stressed-out gargoyle." Her gaze slid to Rowan before returning to him. "I wasn't joking earlier with the breathe, eat, fuck comment. This might take a while, and you need to relax."

Breathe. Eat. Fuck.

Right.

The last two weren't happening, but he could manage the first.

He exhaled, but the unease still coiled tight in his chest. The feeling of helplessness gnawed at him, an itch beneath his skin that no amount of planning or strategizing could soothe. Stepping back went against every instinct, but right now, he had no choice. He reminded himself that waiting—letting Daphne work —was action in itself.

"All right. I'll be in my office. Let me know the moment anything pops."

As they left, Rowan weaved her fingers through his, giving his hand a gentle squeeze. The warmth of the gesture anchored him, a quiet reassurance that he wasn't carrying this alone. He didn't acknowledge it, but he didn't pull away either. And for the first time since the sniper attack at the cafe, he let himself take a deep breath.

<h1 style="text-align:center">twenty-eight</h1>

ROWAN FOLLOWED Davey down the hall, her heartbeat steady but purposeful. As soon as they stepped into his office, she reached past him, closed the door, and turned the lock with a decisive click.

Davey arched a brow. "What are you doing?"

"Distracting you," she said, stepping into his space. "Daphne had a point."

His hands found her hips instinctively, but there was hesitation in his touch. "Which point exactly?"

She slid her hands up his chest, feeling the tension coiled beneath the surface. "Breathe, eat, fuck." She leaned in, her lips brushing his as she whispered, "And we both know which one we need right now."

Davey let out a rough exhale, his grip tightening, his forehead pressing against hers. "Rowan..."

She kissed him. Hard. She felt his resistance, the constant weight he carried, but as her fingers wove into his hair and she pressed closer, his walls began to crack. His lips fused with hers, each kiss increasing in urgency as her touch shattered his self-control. She playfully tugged at his lower lip, drawing a deep, primal growl from his chest.

"Jesus, Ro. You're trouble."

"The best kind," she shot back, her voice breathless as she slid her hands under his shirt, her nails scraping against the hard planes of his abs. She pushed the fabric up impatiently, breaking away just long enough to yank it over his head and toss it to the floor. God, he was a fucking master-piece—broad shoulders, a chest carved from gran-ite, and a trail of dark hair leading down to the waistband of his pants that made her mouth water.

Her fingers danced down his torso, tracing every dip and curve of muscle with deliberate slowness. She lingered just below his navel, her touch feather-light, and he jerked away with a strangled laugh.

"That's right." A wicked grin spread across her face. "You're ticklish."

His eyes narrowed, but the corners of his mouth twitched. "Don't even think about it, Hellcat."

"Too late." She dug in, skittering her fingertips across his skin in a flurry of feather-light touches. Davey jerked, a strangled laugh escaping as he tried to twist away from her merciless assault.

"Rowan, I swear to God——" His threat dissolved

into another burst of laughter as she found a new weak spot along his ribs near his tattoo.

His hands shot out, capturing her wrists in a firm grip. With a swift, fluid motion, he spun her around, pinning her back against his chest. "You're playing with fire, Hellcat," he growled, his breath hot against her ear as he ground his hips into her ass.

Her pulse raced, desire pooling low in her belly. She arched back, grinding against the ridge of his arousal. "Maybe I like the heat."

A low, rumbling chuckle vibrated through his chest. "Careful what you wish for." His hands slid down her arms, leaving a trail of goosebumps in their wake. When he reached her hips, he gripped them tightly, pulling her flush against him so she could feel every inch of his hard cock straining against his pants.

She bit back a moan, her head falling back against his shoulder as his lips found the sensitive spot just below her ear. His teeth grazed her pulse point, sending a jolt of electricity straight to her core. She reached back, threading her fingers through his hair and holding him close as he nipped and sucked at her neck, marking her in a way that made her thighs clench.

Davey's hand slipped under her shirt, calloused fingers brushing against the swell of her breast before finding her nipple already hard and aching. He rolled it between his fingers, giving it a firm tug that shot straight down the center of her body to pool between her legs.

"I want to fuck you," she hissed, spinning in his arms and crashing her mouth against his in a searing kiss. She dug her fingers into his shoulders, nails biting into flesh as she pulled him impossibly closer.

He groaned into her mouth, the sound raw and needy as his hands slid down to cup her ass, squeezing roughly as he ground his hips against hers. The friction sent jolts of pleasure ricocheting through her body, stoking the flames higher.

"Do you, Hellcat? Right here where anyone could walk by and hear you screaming my name?"

"Yes, right here." Rowan tore her mouth away, gasping for air, her pulse a wild drumbeat in her ears. "Right now. Only you'll be the one screaming." She shoved him back, step by step, until his legs hit the desk—then pressed forward, palms flat against his shoulders, and forced him down onto the polished wood with a wicked grin. Papers scattered across the surface, a pen clattered to the floor, and a half-full glass of water teetered dangerously at the edge.

Davey let out a sharp breath, his head tipping back to eye the glass for half a second before his gaze snapped to hers—dark, heated, full of challenge.

She slid off her pants and climbed onto his lap, straddling the solid strength of his thighs. The heat of him burned through the thin fabric of her underwear.

She rolled her hips, grinding against the thick ridge of his erection.

"Fuck, Rowan," he groaned, hands gripping her ass, pulling her closer as he thrust up to meet the motion of her hips.

"I already told you, that's the plan." She leaned down, capturing his mouth in another searing kiss as she fumbled with the button of his pants. She needed him inside her, needed to feel his skin against hers, to lose herself in the heat and passion that always consumed them. Finally the button slipped free and she pulled down the zipper of his fly.

He was bare underneath. Of course. She had yet to see him in any kind of underwear. His erection sprung free, thick and hard against her palm.

"What should I do with this?"

"Whatever you want, Hellcat," he said between clenched teeth, his fingers digging almost painfully into the globes of her ass.

"*Anything* I want?"

She kept her touch light as she stroked him from base to tip, her fingernails grazing the sensitive skin. Davey let out a hiss, his hips jerking up into her hand seeking more friction.

"Rowan…" Her name fell from his lips, half warning, half plea.

She tightened her grip, pumping him in a steady rhythm that had him panting and cursing under his breath. Satisfaction curled through her, heady and intoxicating, at seeing him rapidly unraveling beneath her touch.

Leaning down, she flicked her tongue across the broad head of his cock, tasting the salty tang of pre-cum. Davey groaned, low and guttural, his hands fisting in her hair. She took him into her mouth, swirling her tongue, hollowing her cheeks as she slid down his impressive length.

"Jesus, your mouth," he ground out, his grip on her hair tightening to the edge of pain as she bobbed up and down. She loved seeing him like this— stripped bare, desperate, completely at her mercy.

Rowan released him with a wet pop, crawling back up his body to claim his mouth in a filthy kiss.

Davey groaned into it, one hand roaming from her ass to slide beneath the scrap of lace between her thighs. He growled low in his throat when he found her already slick and swollen for him.

"So fucking wet," he rasped, pressing two fingers inside her. "You liked having my cock in your mouth."

"Yes." She cried out, head falling back as he pumped them in and out, his thumb circling her clit with devastating precision. Pleasure crashed through her in dizzying waves and she rocked against his hand, chasing the delicious friction.

"Where else do you like my cock?"

"Here." She reached between them and pulled aside the gusset of her panties, giving him access.

He repositioned himself under her, gripping the

base of his cock so that the broad head brushed against her slick folds. "You want me deep inside you, filling you up."

"Yes."

"Then ride me, Hellcat." His voice was gravel, his blue eyes darkening with primal need as he watched her.

Slowly, torturously, she sank down, taking him inch by delicious inch. They both groaned as he plunged so deep she swore she could feel him in her soul.

And his desk phone rang.

Davey cursed, pulling back just enough to glare at the offending device.

She started to move, undulating her hips. "Ignore it."

"Fuck," he groaned and caught her hips in his hands, stilling her. He was trembling, his breath sawing in and out of his lungs like he'd run a marathon. "As much as I want to, I can't."

No, of course, he couldn't. Not with everything going on. How could she forget? Her goal had been to distract him from his fears and worry, but she'd distracted herself, too.

That always happened with him.

A flicker of irritation sparked in her chest. At herself, for letting him pull her under so easily. At him, for being so damn impossible to resist. For making her want so completely, so recklessly, that she lost sight of the dangers closing in around them.

She clenched her jaw, forcing down the sharp edge of frustration before it could spill over. This wasn't his fault. Not really. But it didn't change the fact that every time she got too close, every time she let herself sink into his heat, she forgot.

Forgetting could get them both killed.

Or get others killed, like Liam.

And yet, disappointment curled low in her stomach, stubborn and insistent.

She leaned over to kiss his lips—lightly and more controlled this time, more for herself than for him—before climbing off him to perch on the edge of his desk. "To be continued."

"Abso-fucking-lutely. I won't be able to sit at this desk now without thinking of you riding me on it." He stood and fastened his pants, adjusting his very obvious erection before grabbing his shirt from the floor. Circling around the desk, he tugged the shirt over his head, rolled his shoulders, and dropped into the big leather executive chair. He drew a deep, measured breath and let it out slowly, then reached for the phone, and just like that, he became the name on the polished brass plate outside his door.

David G. E. Wilde, CEO.

It was hot as fuck.

"Mia, I'm going to need you to hold all my calls," he said, voice still a little rough. Not rough enough that anyone else would notice, but just enough that Rowan wanted to tease him, see how long that cool CEO composure would last with her hands sliding down his abs, wrapping around his cock.

"We have a situation and I need to..." He trailed off, and whatever his secretary said had his expression shifting, sharpening. "No. Yeah, you're right. I can't keep putting him off. Send him through. I'll talk to him, but no more calls today." He hit the hold button for the line and then looked at her—really looked at her.

Not with the heat that had burned between them moments ago.

Not with the teasing challenge that always made her want to push all his buttons.

This was different.

Heavier.

Dread curdled in her gut—it was that slow, sinking weight of inevitability, the moment before the other shoe dropped, and she wished she could rewind. Go back to the heat of his body under hers, back to the wicked grin on his lips and the rasp of his voice when he told her to ride him.

But there was no going back now.

She wrapped her arms around herself, suddenly cold. "What's wrong?"

He looked at the phone for a beat too long, then lifted his gaze back to hers. "It's your father."

twenty-nine

"WHAT?" The word came out strangled as she launched herself off the desk.

Oh, God.

She was half-dressed, her panties soaked, the taste of Davey's cock still on her lips, need still thrumming through her veins.

She searched the floor for her pants. She needed clothes. She need to—focus. Relax. It wasn't a video call. Dad couldn't see her, didn't even know she was there.

She dragged her hands through her hair, trying to smooth away the evidence of just how sex-mussed she was. "Why's he calling you?"

"He wants an update on my progress tracking you down." Davey leaned back in his seat, completely at ease despite his erection still standing at half-mast.

Cool. Calm. Unbothered. "What do you want me to say?"

She stared at the phone in his hand, at a complete loss. Her mind went blank, her pulse hammered in her ears. For months, she had avoided this conversation, convinced that keeping her distance was the only way to protect her family.

And now?

Now, her father was waiting on the other end of that call, thinking she was still lost, still a ghost he hadn't been able to track down.

"Ro. Look at me." Davey set the phone down and rose to his feet, crossing to her in long, quick strides. He caught her chin between his fingers and turned her head until their eyes met. "I'll tell him to fuck off if you want me to. He doesn't need to know you're here. He doesn't need to know anything about what's happening or why. Just tell me what to say, and I'll say it."

The temptation was there—to let Davey tell her father off, to put off dealing with the truth for just a little longer. But... she couldn't hide forever. And now that she knew staying away hadn't kept Rue from falling into Atlas Frost's orbit, it was time to face this head-on.

She held Davey's gaze, drawing strength from the steadiness in his eyes. Then, she inhaled slowly. "I'll talk to him."

Davey studied her, like he was checking for any

last hesitation, then gave a slow nod. "Do you need me to step out?"

"No." It came out a little too quickly, and she reached for his hand. "Please stay."

"Come here." He hooked an arm around her waist and guided her back toward the chair, pulling her down with him as he sat.

No hesitation. No second-guessing.

She settled against him, and there was nothing sexual about it this time. Just warmth. Just solid, steady reassurance.

Davey reached for the phone and held it out. "You sure you want to do this now?"

She wrapped her fingers around his, took another steadying breath, and nodded. "Take the line off hold."

He hit the button.

She raised the receiver to her ear. "Dad."

There was a beat of silence. Then, a quick, sharp inhale of surprise followed by a gruff exhale. "Well, I'll be damned. You do still know how to pick up a phone."

Rowan swallowed. She had prepared herself for anger, for disappointment—but not for this. Not for the rough-edged relief in his voice, like he'd been waiting half a year for this exact moment.

"I'm sorry, Dad." Rowan closed her eyes, focusing on the feel of Davey's arms around her, steadying her. "I should have called sooner. I should have..." Her throat tightened, the words sticking.

"You're damn right you should have." Gabe Bristow's voice was gruff, as usual, but there was no real heat behind it. Just an aching weariness that made her chest constrict. "Do you have any idea what it's been like, not knowing where the hell you were or if you were even alive?"

"I'm sorry," she whispered again, though she knew the words were too small, too inadequate to make up for the months of heartache she'd caused her parents. "I had to leave. If I stayed, you'd have all been in danger because of me. And you had just had surgery and— I thought leaving was the only way to keep you safe."

Gabe made a sound—something between a snort and a scoff. "Safe from what? You think a missing leg makes me any less capable of protecting my daughter?"

Rowan swallowed. "You couldn't protect me from this, Dad. Or from the things I've done."

There was a pause, a slight hesitation before he spoke again, softer this time. "Tell me, then. Help me understand, Rowan. Please."

God, that *please* nearly broke her. Her father was a brusque, sarcastic, hard man. He didn't say please, much to her mother's constant annoyance.

She hesitated, but she owed him the truth. "I was hired to kill Davey. I took the contract to protect him and figure out who wanted him dead, but I haven't always been that noble in the past. I have taken other contracts, and I have carried them out."

Dead silence.

Then, Gabe let out a long, slow breath. "Huh."

Rowan winced. "That's... all you've got to say?"

"I mean, I'd yell, but it sounds like you're already doing a good job of punishing yourself."

She almost laughed. Almost.

"Jesus, Ro," he added softly after another beat of silence. "You always did take after me in the worst ways."

"No." The protest all but jumped from her lips. "You're a hero. You save people. I've only ever been good at killing them."

Gabe let out a low, humorless laugh. "I was a SEAL, Rowan, and I fought in a long, bloody, unwinnable war. And when I left, I built a team that pulled people out of hellholes. I'm good at killing, too, baby girl. I got paid to pick up a weapon, same as you."

Silence. A long, painful silence.

Rowan wanted to argue with him, to insist that it was different, that her father had killed to protect people while she had killed for money. But the words wouldn't come. Because deep down, she knew he was right. They were more alike than she wanted to admit.

Finally, Gabe exhaled heavily on the other end of the line. "I've always known who and what you are, Rowan. There is nothing in this world—nothing you could do or say or be—that could make me love you less."

Rowan clenched the phone tighter, turning her

face away so Davey wouldn't see the rush of tears in her eyes. But he did anyway, and he gently brushed one from her cheek when it slipped out.

God, she loved him.

And her dad.

And she'd been so wrong to shut them both out for as long as she had.

She tried to form words, wanted to tell them both what they meant to her, but her throat was too tight, her chest too full.

"You hear me, baby girl?" Gabe pressed. "*Nothing.*"

She managed to nod before realizing he couldn't see her. Her dad was old school and almost never called with video. "I hear you," she rasped. "But I don't deserve that."

"That's not your call to make, baby girl. You're family. And family doesn't just walk away because you screwed up. You should know that by now—after all the shit you've seen my men pull. Hell, after all the shit your sister's pulled. And I've kept them all around."

A laugh caught in her throat—rough, brittle. She wasn't sure if it was amusement or something closer to grief. Maybe both. "I do know it, Dad."

"Good. So you can come home now, and we'll figure out the rest later." A pause. A breath. And when he spoke again, his voice had lost some of its gruffness. "Just come home, Rowan. Your mother misses you."

Translation: *I miss you.*

She closed her eyes and pressed her fingers against her lids to hold back the tears. How easy he made it sound. As if stepping back into the life she'd left behind was as simple as walking through the front door.

But it wasn't that easy. It never had been.

She wanted to tell him that. Wanted to say that she wasn't ready, that there were still things she needed to do, that she wasn't the same little girl he imagined her to be.

Instead, all she managed was a whisper. "I don't know if I can."

Silence stretched between them, heavy and knowing.

Then, after a beat, he made a sound that was half grumble, half sigh. "Don't make me hire Davey again, for fuck's sake. The man charges too much."

Rowan huffed out something that was almost a laugh. She tipped her head down, resting her forehead briefly against Davey's shoulder before turning her face into his neck and breathing him in. "If it's any consolation, I think he'd do it for free now."

Davey let out a quiet chuckle, shifting beneath her as he lifted their joined hands. He mouthed, "Damn right," before pressing a kiss to her palm.

A choking sound crackled through the receiver. "Who the hell was that?"

"Davey." She let herself sink into him, her body molding against his as she matched the slow, steady rise and fall of his breathing. "If you used video like a normal person, you'd know he's right here with me."

There was a beat of dead air, thick with suspicion.

"*With* you?" Gabe finally said, his voice dropping into that dangerous, measured tone she knew too well. "Rowan Kendra Bristow, you better not be telling me what I think you're telling me."

Why did she suddenly feel like a teenager caught making out on the couch?

She curled into Davey's chest a little more, and his arms tightened around her in a silent show of support. "If you think I'm telling you that Davey and I are together, then yes. I love him."

Silence.

Then—a sharp inhale, followed by the kind of explosive sound a volcano might make before it obliterated an entire coastline.

"Oh, fuck, no. Not a Wilde. Not Jude-fucking-Wilde's son."

Rowan could practically see it—the way his granite face darkened, his skin turning a dangerous shade of red, a vein in his temple about to burst. A beer bottle was definitely being squeezed within an inch of its life.

Yep.

This was a full Dad detonation.

She pinched the bridge of her nose. "After everything I just told you, *that's* what you're mad about?"

"I paid him to find you—not to put his damn

hands all over my baby girl like he owns her! Like he —" A sharp inhale, followed by a muttered curse. "No. Fuck, no. I forbid it."

She grinned, and even though her dad couldn't see her, she slid a hand under Davey's shirt, fingers gliding over the hard ridges of his abs.

Davey sucked in a sharp breath, his whole body going rigid beneath her.

Oh, she knew that reaction. Knew exactly how ticklish he was.

Her grin widened as she dragged her nails lightly across his skin.

A strangled sound caught in his throat as he barely stopped himself from flinching. His hand snapped around her wrist in a firm grip, his glare searing into her, half warning, half plea.

She bit her lip to keep from laughing. "Maybe I have my hands all over him."

"Jesus Christ. Why the hell would you say that to me?" The sheer horror in her dad's voice was palpable before he launched into a string of colorful curses that did his sailor heritage proud. "I should have known. The way he dropped every-fucking-thing to find you, the urgency in his voice whenever we talked about you—"

A sharp crack, followed by the unmistakable shatter of glass.

Rowan blinked. "Did you just break your after-dinner beer?"

He grumbled like an unhappy bear. "I need another drink."

"Mom won't let you. You only get one."

"She'll make an exception when I tell her who our girl's been fu—" He broke off and made a deeply pained sound, something between a groan and a strangled whimper.

Rowan rolled her eyes, but the fondness crept in anyway.

For all his gruffness, all his over-the-top reactions, he was still her dad. The man who had taught her how to ride a bike, how to shoot a gun, how to throw a punch. The man who had always, always shown up—whether it was for scraped knees or a broken heart.

And now, here he was, freaking the hell out because she had fallen for someone he never saw coming.

She pressed her forehead against Davey's shoulder, letting the warmth of his body ground her.

"Goodbye, Dad," she said softly. "I can't come home yet, but I promise I'll talk to you again soon."

Gabe didn't respond right away, and for a second, she thought he might capitulate. Maybe he'd let go of the fight just this once, tell her to be safe, that he loved her, that he just wanted her to be happy.

Ha.

His breath left him sharp and agitated, thick with disapproval. "Yeah, yeah. We're gonna talk, all right.

After I fly there and test my new metal leg on Davey's ass."

Rowan groaned. "Dad, no."

"Decision made. Audrey!" he called away from the receiver. "Book us a damn flight to New York! We're going to get our daughter."

The call ended.

She didn't move right away. Didn't turn. Just sat there, staring at the dead receiver until Davey plucked it from her hand and placed it in the cradle. Then he pulled her tight against his chest and just held her.

She curled against him, exhaling slowly. "He's going to kick your ass."

Davey sucked in a breath through his teeth and dropped his head against the back of the chair. "Yeah, I did hear that part."

She huffed a quiet laugh. "Specifically, he said he was going to test his new metal leg on it."

"Well, joke's on him." He tapped his thigh, right over the scar she knew too well, where the metal rod reinforced his femur. "I'm half metal, too. We'll clash like a couple of pissed-off cyborgs. Think we'll make sparks?"

Rowan let out a breathy, startled laugh and pressed a hand to her face. "Jesus, Davey."

He smirked, but there was a glint of something else in his eyes. "Look, your dad scares the hell out of me, and I fully expect to suffer for this. But I'd still take the hit."

Her damn heart went warm and liquid, melting away all her usual defenses. But she refused to let him see it. Instead, she rolled her eyes, aiming for exasperation. "Great. You and my dad are going to fight over me like I'm a goddamn prize goat."

Davey dragged his fingers down her spine, slow and deliberate, just to feel her shiver. "Pretty sure I already won, Hellcat."

She scowled at him, but it held no real heat. "You're impossible."

"And yet, here you are, still curled up in my lap."

She sighed, shaking her head, the last of her tension slipping from her shoulders like a loosened knot.

He watched her for a beat, then reached out, gripping her chin gently, tilting her head up until their gazes met. She should hate when he did that. It was so goddamn controlling.

So why did she melt every time?

He studied her expression, and the worry she saw in his eyes faded. He stroked his thumb across her cheekbone. "But the rest of it went okay?"

"Better than I expected." The words felt strange on her tongue, and she didn't quite believe them yet. She'd braced for anger, for blame. Instead, her taciturn, hardass father had just... accepted her. Forgiven her. "I mean, Dad didn't disown me or threaten to murder you—"

"Only kick my ass."

"Right. That's basically a hug from him. So we're already ahead of my worst-case scenario."

"That's a pretty low bar, Hellcat," he murmured, his voice warm with amusement as his lips brushed the shell of her ear.

She sighed. It was. But it was also just... the way things had always been.

She'd been raised in a compound full of mercenaries, where bedtime stories were replaced with field tactics, and instead of lullabies, she'd fallen asleep to the sound of her dad cleaning his sidearm. She had an ex-SEAL father who loved her but struggled to express it—a man who could dismantle an assault rifle blindfolded but never quite knew what to do when his daughters cried.

And then there was her mother—warm and wild and full of love but as untethered as the wind. She adored her children with everything she had. But she was an artist first, a dreamer who painted in broad, sweeping strokes, sometimes forgetting that life didn't always fit neatly onto a canvas.

And Rue. Sweet, reckless Rue, who could charm her way out of anything, lived life like a runaway train and somehow still believed in love and fairy-tale endings.

They had grown up surrounded by gruff, scarred men who gave hugs like they were taking enemy fire and spoke in military lingo instead of heart-to-hearts. Their world had never been quiet. Never easy. It had been built on chaos and adrenaline, stitched together with gunpowder, oil paint, and the steady hum of a life lived on the edge.

Rowan wasn't sure she knew how to exist any other way. How could she? She wasn't built for anything else.

"This is my life, Davey." She tightened her hand in his and drew back far enough to meet his gaze. "I don't know how to have a normal one."

"Then don't. Normal is overrated. Messy, dangerous, chaotic—I don't give a damn what kind of life you have." His voice was quiet but sure, the weight of a promise in every word. He lifted their joined hands, pressing a kiss to her knuckles, lingering over her ring finger. "As long as it's one with me."

Her breath hitched. She was already there, already his in ways that terrified her. The warmth of his body, the steady strength of his arms wrapped around her, the quiet certainty in his touch—it unraveled something inside her, something reckless and raw.

That was all it took.

She surged forward, gripping his face as she kissed him. It was hungry, reckless, all heat and need. He met her with a growl, his lips crushing against hers, devouring her like he'd been starving for this. His fingers dug into her hips, pulling her closer like he could keep her there forever if he just held tight enough. One hand tangled in her hair, the other fisting the back of her shirt as if letting go wasn't an option.

A sharp knock sounded, followed by the doorknob rattling and Sabin's unmistakable drawl. "Y'all done in there, or I gotta hose you down? 'Cause our Daphne's about to pin down Brody's exact location, so you ain't got time for no post-lovin' cuddles. We have a Liam to rescue."

Davey pulled back just enough to rest his forehead against hers. "Guess that's our cue."

Rowan let out a breathless laugh, shaking her head. "His timing's impeccable as always."

Sabin knocked again, louder. "I swear, I'm gettin' the hose! In three... two..."

"Jesus, we're coming!" Davey groaned and stole one last firm kiss before lifting her off his lap. "Thank you for the distraction. I needed it. You ready?"

Rowan nodded and stood, rolling her shoulders back, letting the weight of the moment settle. "Let's finish this."

thirty

LIAM CAME to with a sharp inhale, a gasp that cut through the thick, suffocating darkness. White-hot pain lanced through his skull, sharp and immediate, like a live wire sparking behind his eyes. His vision blurred at the edges, swimming between flickering light and shadow. The scent of mildew and rust curled in his nostrils, damp and cloying. Cold metal bit into his wrists.

Cuffed. Trapped. Fucked.

He forced his breath to even out, shoving past the disorientation. His body still felt sluggish, like his brain was half a step behind the rest of him. But the last thing he remembered surged back into place—

Brody.

The pieces snapped together with brutal clarity. Dropping Daphne at HQ. The gut feeling he couldn't explain, the certainty that had sent him straight to the café to warn Cade and Davey.

And Brody—waiting for him.

The pain in his head.

A vague memory of gunfire.

And then... nothing.

A few feet away, Brody stood, arms crossed, watching him with a casual detachment that set Liam's teeth on edge. Too calm. Too at ease for someone who had just betrayed everyone.

Liam swallowed against the nausea rolling through him, blinking hard to clear his vision. His head throbbed, but something else was wrong. His ears—

Silence.

No breathing. No footsteps. No quiet hum of the city vibrating around him. Just an eerie, static-filled void where sound should be. The wrongness of it sent a cold spike of adrenaline through him. His implant—fucked.

But then—

"...ghost station."

The words cut through the static, distant but there, muffled like he was hearing them from the other side of thick glass. The smaller noises—shifts in Brody's stance, the click of his boot against concrete— were missing. Gone. But voices, louder sounds, those still bled through the distortion, warping at the edges.

He clenched his jaw, keeping his expression

neutral. He couldn't let Brody see how much he couldn't hear.

"Did you know the city's got plenty of these?" Brody's voice echoed through the vast emptiness, bouncing off the tiles, its cadence sharper than the words themselves. "'Course you did. You grew up here. You and all of your fucking cousins probably used them like your own personal playground."

Liam watched him pace, hands in his pockets, posture lazy but calculated. He should have heard the subtle shifts in weight, the scrape of fabric against fabric as Brody moved—but there was nothing. Just the vacuum, swallowing everything that wasn't sharp enough to punch through the interference.

Brody scoffed. "There are so fucking many of you Wildes—" He broke off. Looked up. "Huh. Think that's them coming for you?" he asked, eyes tracking something Liam couldn't hear.

Liam didn't blink. Didn't shift. Let the words settle. Then he fired back, low and steady—

"I think it's Sullivan coming for *you*."

The flinch was small, but Liam saw it. A hesitation —just a fraction too long. "You leave my brother's name out of your mouth. He's not involved."

"You involved him when you betrayed us."

Brody's expression tightened, something raw flashing across his face before he snapped, "He's not one of you!" The words came out sharp, clipped—too fast and too certain. Like he needed them to be true. "He'll see reason soon enough."

But the way his jaw tensed, the way his fingers curled just a little too tightly at his sides—Liam wasn't sure which of them Brody was trying to convince more.

"Then you don't know your twin at all." He flexed his fingers against the cuffs, testing. Too tight. Circulation cut off, fingers numb. *Fuck.* "Sullivan doesn't follow. He never has. And he will absolutely not see your reasoning for turning traitor, no matter what it is."

Brody's jaw flexed, a muscle jumping near his temple.

"So you can spin it however you want. Tell yourself you're playing the long game. That you had no choice. But when this is over?" Liam held his gaze, let his voice go quiet, deliberate. "Sully's never gonna see you as anything other than exactly what you are."

For the first time, Brody's smirk slipped completely. He exhaled, short and sharp, nostrils flaring. Resentment, frustration—raw anger—flashed across his face before he locked it down again.

Liam let the silence stretch. It was the only weapon available to him, and he was going to wield it to his full advantage. Luckily, he and silence were old friends.

He waited. Watched. Made Brody stew in it.

Then, when it was heavy enough, when it pressed just the right way—

"Why?" Quiet. Steel-edged. A scalpel of a question.

"They pay me more." The answer was flat, unapologetic. But something shifted beneath the surface. A flicker of justification. Like he thought the numbers alone made it make sense. Like he had to believe they did.

Liam gave a low, humorless laugh. Shook his head. "You're gonna die for a paycheck."

The smirk barely held. Just a fraction too tight. "You think this is just about money?"

"Isn't it?"

His jaw flexed. A flicker of something there—anger? Doubt? Resentment?

"I got here first," he muttered, more to himself than to Liam. His gaze flicked aside, as if remembering. "Elliot brought me in. I got Sully a job. Me. And somehow, I ended up the afterthought."

Liam stilled. "Sullivan." Not a question. A statement. "This is all about Sully?"

The laugh that followed was sharp, bitter. Not even a denial.

"I was the one here first. I put in the time. And somehow, he became the one you all trusted. The one who fucking mattered. You sent him overseas, into battles, and you regulated me to the glorified babysitting jobs."

Liam didn't blink. Didn't move. *Let him keep talking.* Brody was on a roll now, pacing and agitated.

"Sullivan has rules. A code. He pretends that makes him better than me." A scoff. "But tell me, Liam—what's the difference between us, really? He kills for the job. I just stopped pretending I needed a reason."

There it was.

Not just money. Bitterness. Resentment. Maybe something even deeper than that.

Liam couldn't stop the laugh of disbelief. "All this is because you couldn't stand being second to your own twin?"

The pause was just a beat too long.

Which meant Liam was right.

"It doesn't matter," Brody muttered and stopped pacing. Again, he seemed to be listening to something.

Liam felt it this time. A faint vibration beneath his boots, the kind he might have ignored if his implant wasn't fried.

A train? Or something else?

"Sounds like I need to shift to Plan C." He tapped his ear.

Liam went still. Shit. How had he missed the earpiece? Brody was in contact with someone else, someone who was feeding him information.

Atlas Frost?

Another Praetorian operative?

Brody exhaled, rolling his shoulders like he was resetting. His smirk returned, but this time, it was sharper. "Your cousins have found us and they're armed for war. So..." He grabbed a duffle bag and dragged it over. "I am sorry for this, Liam. Believe it or not, I did like you."

Liam kept his expression blank, but his pulse kicked hard. "Plan C?"

"Yeah, Plan A was to frame Cade. I figured with his and Davey's history, it was a done deal, but Davey had to be all fucking noble and go hear him out. Plan B was to frame you, which I've been laying the groundwork for, just in case. I even mentioned my suspicions about you to Cade a few months ago. Just an offhand comment, a gentle push in your direction. It was brilliant. Should've worked, but after that whole thing with Elliot—"

"You *poisoned* Elliot. Your best friend."

Brody shrugged. "And I hate my twin brother. So what?"

The words hung between them.

"Yeah, okay, fine. If you want to point fingers, I poisoned him. It was meant only for Benji. Not my fault Elliot ate a slice."

"That's fucking cold."

Brody's smirk faltered—not in guilt, but in genuine confusion.

"Cold?" His brows drew together, his head tilting slightly, as if he were struggling to translate a foreign language. "Benji was a threat. Elliot was collateral damage. That happens in war."

His tone was so flat, so eerily reasonable, it made Liam's skin crawl.

"Why is it cold when I do it, but not when someone like Davey—a SEAL—does it under a flag?"

Jesus. He wasn't playing dumb. He really didn't get it.

Silence stretched between them.

Brody blinked, waiting like he expected an answer. When none came, he sighed. "Is that why you got suspicious of me?"

Liam didn't respond. Couldn't. There was no way to explain the difference to someone whose moral compass was that broken.

Finally Brody shrugged it off. "Well, no matter what tipped you off, I knew you couldn't have you hanging around. So I followed you to the office, waited until you dropped Daphne off, and grabbed you. Took a few shots at Davey and Cade at the cafe to make it look like your doing—"

He snorted. "*I* wouldn't have missed."

"Even with your own cousins in the crosshairs?" Brody gave a low whistle that he couldn't hear. "And you say I'm cold? Even I know that's sub-zero, man."

Jesus, this was bad.

Liam yanked on his cuffs, but there was no give at all. He could move his legs, but that wasn't going to do him any good as long as his arms were trapped around the back of this fucking bench, which was bolted to the concrete floor.

He had to keep Brody talking. It was his only chance. "So why isn't Plan B working?"

"Because my fucking brother grabbed Atlas Frost without telling me."

"And Frost knows your identity," Liam concluded. "You couldn't guarantee he wouldn't spill it for the right price."

Brody unzipped the duffle. "I wanted to wait and see if my cover held, if the evidence I'd planted to make you the mole was compelling enough, if Frost kept his mouth shut. Judging by the amount of firepower headed this way, it didn't and he didn't. So. Meet Plan C." He pulled out a tactical vest lined with explosives.

Liam wasn't surprised, but the sight of it still settled like lead in his stomach. "Bit dramatic, don't you think?"

"I don't do half measures." Brody crouched in front of him, draping the vest around his shoulders like a man helping a friend into a jacket.

Liam exploded into motion.

He drove his knee up, fast and brutal, aiming for Brody's face, but Brody twisted at the last second. The blow glanced off his shoulder instead of breaking his nose.

Brody swore, but Liam wasn't done. He lunged, teeth bared, and sank them deep into Brody's forearm.

Brody yelled in pain. Real pain.

Liam bit down harder. He tasted blood. Coppery, hot, a victory he didn't have time to savor.

Brody slammed his elbow into Liam's jaw. A sharp, bone-jarring impact that rattled his teeth and snapped his head back. Stars burst in his vision, and for a second, everything tilted.

Brody yanked his arm free, blood dripping from the fresh wound. He staggered back, shaking out his arm, eyes wild with something between fury and admiration.

"Jesus, Liam." Brody wiped at the blood on his forearm with an almost amused shake of his head. "Don't fight me on this. It won't change a damn thing.

Liam panted through the pain, the metallic taste still on his tongue. He smirked and felt blood drip down his chin. His or Brody's was anyone's guess, but his money was on Brody's.

Brody let out a breathless laugh, but it wasn't quite steady now. "Damn shame this had to end like this. You'd have made one hell of a Praetorian."

Liam braced himself for another fight, even as his vision swam, even with his hands useless behind his back—but Brody was done playing.

He moved fast, too fast.

Liam twisted, trying to throw his weight, kick out, anything—

But Brody got the vest on him.

Straps snapped into place. Metal buckles locked

down. The weight of the explosives settled across his chest like a death sentence.

"I really did like you." Brody's voice was almost gentle now, like a man regretting the inevitable. "But WSW won't leave you behind. Even if they think you're the mole, they'll still try to save you. That's the Wilde family's biggest weakness. You're too loyal to each other."

Liam controlled his breath, forcing himself not to hyperventilate. Slow in, slow out. "Want to know your biggest weakness?"

"I don't have any." Brody pulled a small detonator module from the bag and slotted it into the vest's wiring. The LED screen blinked to life with a countdown. Six minutes.

Six minutes until his team found him.

Six minutes until they had to decide if they could disarm the vest in time.

Six minutes until Brody was gone.

Brody tightened the last strap and patted the vest like it was a job well done. Then he stood, brushing imaginary dust off his pants, and exhaled. "But before this all kicks off, I really just gotta know. How did you figure it out? Nobody else had any goddamn clue, but you did."

"You flinched," Liam said. "After we found Benji dead and Elliot on death's door, you flinched. I saw genuine regret as the medics carried Elliot out and I knew. That's your weakness, O'Connell. You're not as cold as you want to be."

Brody stared at him for a long moment, before tapping his earpiece, listening. Then he moved.

Liam lunged before he could think better of it, using every ounce of strength he had left, but Brody was already pivoting, already a step ahead. He dodged, grabbed the duffle, and leapt onto the platform edge.

Brody's smirk returned, but this time, it was almost pitying. "Tough break, Wilde. Looks like you're out of time."

Then he was gone.

thirty-one

DAPHNE WAS A GENIUS.

Davey found her and the rest of the team—Elliot, Dom, and Sabin—in the computer lab.

Sullivan was still missing.

Davey could only hope that wherever he was, he wasn't doing something stupid.

Sabin sprawled in one of the empty computer chairs, his long legs stretched out, his hands folded over his stomach. He looked like he didn't have a care in the world, but Davey knew better. Sabin's relaxed posture was a front, a carefully crafted facade masking the sharp intelligence and constant vigilance that made him such a valuable asset to the team. His eyes were sharp, darting between the multiple screens Daphne was furiously typing on.

Elliot still looked pale and slightly nauseous as he sipped from a bottle of water, and Dom prowled the room in restless loops, muscles tight with unused energy. He wasn't pacing like a man waiting for a fight —he was pacing like a man who needed to move, or he'd explode. Davey could practically feel his frustration crackling off him like static.

And he wasn't the only one wrestling with frustration.

Around the room, the rest of their family waited, tense and ready.

Fiona, WSW's lead counsel, sat primly at one of the empty workstations, her legs crossed, her black hair pulled back in a sharp ponytail, her business suit still as tidy as the moment she took it off the hanger that morning. Her dagger-sharp red nails clicked as she typed on a tablet, no doubt already working to legally cover their asses from the fallout of Brody's betrayal.

Cade was there, too, hanging back by the door with his siblings, Tessa and Weston, flanking either side.

Daphne's twin, Celeste, had pulled up a chair beside her sister. Where Daphne was a perpetual storm cloud, Celeste was a rainbow. She rolled a lollypop around in her mouth as she nodded at whatever Daphne was doing on the screen. "Oh, that's good, sis."

Liam's younger brother, Bridger, stood with his arms crossed, jaw clenched like he was grinding down a molar. He was as tall as Liam but leaner, built more like their dancer mother than their tank of a father. His dark hair, usually kept so neat, was a mess, and stubble darkened his jaw. His gaze was fixed on the screen like sheer focus could bring Liam home.

It was like a damn family reunion. The only ones missing were Fiona's brother, Griffin, who was on an op in France, and, of course, Liam. And they were all kitted up, ready for war—primed like a loaded gun, waiting for Daphne to aim them in the right direction. A stack of weapons sat on one of the long conference tables.

"… really thought he could make us believe *Liam* is a traitor?" Bridger was saying as Davey and Rowan stepped through the door. His voice was as calm and measured as always, but the fury in his eyes betrayed him.

"Brody mistook quiet for suspicious," Daphne said, glancing over her shoulder. She did a double-take when she spotted Davey and Rowan, and a smile tipped up the corner of her mouth. "Someone took my advice literally."

"Hey, I ate," Sabin drawled, stretching like a cat full up on gumbo, lazy and content. "And I'm breathing just fine, thank you. I even tried fucking, but wouldn't you know—some folks got no appreciation for my generosity." He tipped a smirk toward Fiona, who didn't so much as glance up from her tablet. "Ain't that right, cher? Shot me down so cold, I damn near caught frostbite."

Fiona didn't even blink. "You'd have a better chance arguing a contract clause with me than getting me in your bed, Cavalier. And we both know how that would go."

Sabin let out a low whistle. "Oof. Y'all hear that? Brutal. She's got a mean streak, that one."

Fiona flicked him a cool glance. "Not mean, Sabin. Efficient."

Sabin grinned, unbothered. "Efficiently breakin' my heart, sugar. But I like a challenge." His grin turned wicked as he eyed Davey and Rowan. "Glad at least someone got to relax."

Rowan's cheeks flushed. She cleared her throat, glancing anywhere but at Sabin as she smoothed a hand over her hair. "So, uh—Brody. You found him?"

"Actually, I'm looking for Liam, but Brody is definitely with him." Daphne turned back to her computer, typing rapidly. Several of the wall screens filled with data, maps, and an overlay of a city grid.

Davey walked forward to stand beside Bridger. He settled a hand on his cousin's shoulder, squeezing once in a silent show of support before shifting his gaze back to the screens. "How?"

Celeste popped the lollipop from her mouth. "Liam's cochlear implant," she said, twirling the stick between her fingers. "He had us add some fun upgrades to it last year because he was struggling to wear an earpiece during missions, so we integrated BlueLink."

Davey's pulse spiked. "GPS?"

Daphne scowled. "No, but you can bet I'm gonna patch that in as soon as we have him back. I'm slapping hardcode GPS on all of you."

Sabin raised his hand. "Uh, question. Is that mandatory?"

"Yeah, no," Dom said and finally stopped pacing. "Definitely passing on that."

Weston spoke up. "Wholeheartedly seconding that no."

"Third," Cade said.

Daphne grumbled something about pain-in-the-ass cousins under her breath.

Celeste patted her shoulder in sympathy and then turned toward the group. "BlueLink is our internal encrypted short-range communication system. It's what connects all of your earpieces when we're on an op, and we rigged Liam's implant to connect directly to the system, his gear, and any nearby WSW devices. No earpieces, no lag, no jamming. Unhackable. Well..." She stuck her lollipop back into her mouth and grinned at her sister. "Unless we're hacking it."

"You *hacked his implant?*" Bridger asked, enunciating each word in disbelief.

"That's like hyper-blackhat bullshit," Weston muttered, rubbing his jaw. "I mean, I'm impressed but also mildly concerned that you can hack medical equipment implanted in someone's skull."

"You should be," Celeste said sweetly. "Nothing is completely safe."

"*Mon Dieu*. You're cute, but you are utterly terrifying," Sabin said with a shake of his head.

Celeste curtsied. "Thank you."

"Okay, but how does this help us find him?" Davey asked to get everyone back on track and scanned the maps on screen.

Daphne barely spared him a glance as she typed at lightning speed, the screens shifting to display a new data overlay. "It helps because I can hear what he hears," she said like it was obvious. "BlueLink isn't just a comm tool—it's integrated into his implant's audio processing. Even damaged, it still transmits, which means—"

She hit a key.

A wave of static-filled audio crackled through the speakers.

For a second, nothing but distortion. Then, through the garbled noise—a voice.

"*Plan A was to frame Cade. I figured with his and Davey's history, it was a done deal, but Davey had to be all fucking noble and go hear him out.*"

The room went still.

Bridger exhaled sharply.

Dom stopped pacing.

Elliot leaned forward, eyes sharp.

Cade growled.

"Is that—?" Rowan started.

"That's live," Daphne confirmed. "That's happening right now."

Another voice, clearer this time.

Liam. Alive.

"You poisoned Elliot. Your best friend."

Davey's stomach tightened.

"And I hate my twin brother. So what?" Brody's voice was light, almost amused.

"I don't get that," Celeste whispered and looked at her sister with her heart in her eyes. "How could you hate your twin?"

Daphne shook her head. "I don't know."

Fiona lifted her gaze from her tablet for the first time. Her tone was all business. "I need a recording of this. It's a confession. I can file charges the moment you bring Brody in."

Cade let out a quiet laugh, but there was no humor in it. "We're not bringing him in alive."

Fiona glowered at him. "You did *not* say that, Cade Wilde. I did *not* hear that. *Nobody* heard that, understood?"

"Heard what?" Sabin asked innocently.

"Exactly."

Davey ignored them all. "Do we have Liam's location?"

"Nearly there. A few more seconds..." Daphne's fingers flew over the keyboard. "I pulled the last five minutes of Liam's audio logs and ran a location scan alongside them. The implant still has a weak BlueLink signal—it's not transmitting at full range, but it's giving me pings from nearby devices."

She tapped another key, and a red marker blinked on the city map.

"And there he is."

Bridger took a sharp breath. "That's underground."

"Yep." Daphne pulled up a schematic of old subway tunnels. "That's why it took me a minute—his implant was glitch-looping off old network infrastructure before I could isolate the core signal."

Celeste popped her lollipop back into her mouth and mumbled around it. "That's a real pain in the code."

"Tell me about it," Daphne muttered. "But—" She zoomed in. "That is an abandoned subway station."

Cade let out a sharp breath. "Fuck."

Sabin rocked forward, all lazy charm gone. "That where we're goin'?"

Daphne nodded. "That's where you're going."

The room snapped into action.

Bridger turned on his heel, already reaching for his rifle. "I'll drive."

"Finally." Dom grabbed extra mags from the table, practically vibrating with energy. "Let's move."

Sabin grabbed his rifle, grinning. "Gonna be a real shame if Brody's face accidentally meets my fist."

Celeste popped the lollipop from her mouth and grinned. "Better make sure it happens at least twice."

Mags snapped into place, the metallic clicks crisp and certain.

Velcro ripped as vests were tightened.

Weapons slid from their holsters, checked, loaded, secured.

Boots scuffed against the floor as the team shifted, tension crackling like a live wire.

Daphne met Davey's gaze. "Go. I'll keep the audio live."

He grabbed her in a quick hug, pressing a kiss to the top of her head. "You're a genius." He did the same to Celeste. "You both are."

Celeste crunched down on her lollipop. "I know. But I never get tired of hearing it." She bumped her shoulder against Daphne's. "Now go raise some hell."

"Copy that." He turned, locking eyes with Bridger, Dom, Elliot, Sabin, Cade, and finally, Rowan. He took the rifle she held out to him, chambered a round, and nodded once. "Let's bring our cousin home."

thirty-two

THE TUNNELS SMELLED LIKE ROT, metal, and old piss—a stench that clung to the back of Davey's throat, acrid and suffocating. The air was thick with damp decay, the kind that settled in places forgotten by time. He adjusted his grip on his rifle, sweeping the darkness ahead as he led the team down the crumbling maintenance stairwell and onto the narrow concrete walkway running parallel to the rusted tracks below.

Every step sent tiny puffs of dust spiraling into the air, settling in his lungs like cement. Rats scattered at their approach, claws skittering against stone, their sleek bodies vanishing into the cracks and debris.

Somewhere overhead, the distant, muffled rumble of a train vibrated through the steel and stone, making the walls shudder slightly. A reminder that even down here, buried beneath the city, the world kept moving.

They moved in tight formation, weapons up, eyes scanning. The space was pitch-black, the only illumination coming from their night vision glasses, casting the world in crisp, high-contrast green and gray. No grain, no distortion. The enhanced optics rendered every detail with sharp precision.

Davey took point.

Rowan was just behind him. He didn't have to turn around to know exactly where she was. Her footfalls were measured, deliberate, perfectly in sync with his own. Never too far, never too exposed.

A quiet presence at his back, steady as a heartbeat.

It should've reassured him.

Instead, it made something in his chest tighten.

She shouldn't be here.

He knew better than to think that. Rowan was more than capable. She was fast, lethal, trained for this, just like the rest of them. But knowing it didn't change the way his gut twisted at the thought of something going wrong, of turning around and—

He cut the thought off before it could settle.

She was here. And there wasn't a damn thing he could do about it except trust her to watch his back the same way he watched hers.

Even if he did want to swaddle her in bubble wrap and send her back to HQ where she'd be safe.

Sabin moved smoothly behind them, spraying ultraviolet markers along the tunnel walls—tags invisible to the naked eye but glowing faintly in their

NVG filters. Breadcrumbs leading home. Not that it would matter if things went to hell.

Tessa followed in the middle of the group, exactly where she should be. She kept one hand tight on Bridger's shoulder, using him as a guide, her other hand clutching the strap of her med bag, ready to move the second she was needed. She wasn't slow—she knew how to keep pace, how to stay small and out of the way—but she wasn't a fighter.

That's why Bridger stayed close, his head on a swivel, eyes tracking every shadow. And why Weston was right behind her, moving like a man expecting a fight. His rifle was steady in his hands, his steps light and controlled, but there was a sharpness to him—coiled tension beneath all that calm. Every few strides, he adjusted his grip, fingers flexing around the weapon, already measuring distance, angles, preparing for whatever was waiting for them in the dark.

Cade and Dominic held the rear, silent and steady. Davey couldn't see their faces without turning, but he could hear them—the controlled rhythm of their footfalls, the soft shuffle of movement as they adjusted their positions, always covering the gaps.

They didn't need orders.

They knew their job.

And on comms—Elliot was in the van at the maintenance tunnel's entrance. He was their eyes in the sky, piloting their drone, monitoring every possible angle aboveground. Daphne was back at HQ, watching their movements in real time and feeding them intel.

It should've felt like a full force. A team with every gap covered, every angle secured.

So why did Davey's gut keep twisting?

Because tonight had the makings of something bad.

His earpiece crackled, and Elliot's voice came through, clipped and annoyed: "Talk to me."

"You still in the van?"

"Where else would I be? Oh right. In there, where all the action is—except you benched me."

Davey exhaled sharply, already regretting this conversation. "You were poisoned two days ago."

"Yeah, and yet here I am, still capable of basic motor function."

"We need someone running point," he said, cutting off any argument. "You're it. And we need eyes —get the drone in the air."

A pause. Then Elliot let out a dry, unimpressed laugh. "You realize you're underground, right? Or did the smell of piss and despair down there get to your brain?"

Davey sighed. "If Brody gets aboveground, I want to know about it before he ghosts us."

Silence. Then a grudging, "Yeah, okay."

Elliot was pissed, but he also understood the necessity of strategy. Someone had to monitor surveillance, track movement, and coordinate reinforcements on the ground. They were already operating with one hand tied behind their backs and couldn't afford to go in blind.

Davey immediately lifted a hand, signaling for everyone to hold. The team froze, instinct taking over, shifting into firing positions.

The tunnel stretched behind them, wide enough to fit an old subway track—one that hadn't seen a train in decades. Through the grainy green glow of his NVGs, the space was all jagged stone, crumbling walls, and rusted steel. The air was thick with damp and dust, every inhale laced with the scent of rot and stagnant water.

Then—movement.

A figure moving fast.

Sullivan.

Davey's chest tightened. "Stand down. It's Sully."

Fucking Sullivan.

He wasn't supposed to be here alone.

Hell, he wasn't supposed to be here at all.

But of course he was.

Sullivan was on them in a matter of heartbeats, moving too fast, rifle slung across his chest, his gaze locked straight ahead. He wasn't even looking at them as he powered down the tracks, his strides unshaken, his focus fixed on whatever was waiting ahead.

Davey jumped down onto the track, boots hitting steel and gravel with a muted thud. He moved fast, planting himself directly in Sullivan's path.

"Sully."

Sullivan didn't slow.

Davey's pulse ticked higher. The guy wasn't hesitating. Wasn't even acknowledging them.

Shit.

He reached out and grabbed Sully's shoulder, fingers digging into the fabric of his jacket, forcing him to stop. "Damn it, look at me."

Sullivan finally stopped.

But when he turned, his face was set like stone—cold, detached.

Davey had seen that look before. He'd seen it on men about to do something they couldn't take back.

The kind of men who had already made up their minds.

Sullivan wasn't thinking anymore. He was acting.

And if Davey didn't stop him now, he wasn't sure anyone could.

"You're too close to this," he said, voice low, steady. "You know it. I know it. Get out of here. Go home. You don't need to see this if it goes south."

No reaction. Not even a flicker. "If my brother has to die tonight, I'm the one pulling the trigger."

Davey's stomach turned. "Sully, no."

He wasn't sure if it was a plea or a warning.

Maybe both.

For the first time since Davey had stepped in his way, Sullivan looked at him.

The enhanced optics of their next-gen NVGs made

the world crystal clear even in total darkness—no grainy static, no distortion. Just sharp, high-contrast detail, every feature rendered in eerie shades of green.

And what Davey saw unsettled him.

There was nothing behind those eyes—just a calculated, empty stillness.

Not rage.

Not grief.

Nothing.

Like he'd already made his peace with what was coming.

Davey's stomach twisted.

That wasn't Sullivan.

That was a man who'd already decided someone wasn't walking out of this tunnel alive.

Sullivan's voice was flat. "Would you sit this out? If it was one of your brothers?"

The question hit like a punch to the ribs—sharp, direct, and impossible to ignore. His grip tightened on Sullivan's jacket, but he had no answer.

Instead, his gaze flicked up to the walkway.

Through the ghostly green glow of his NVGs, he picked out Dominic from the group. His brother was holding position near Cade, rifle steady, expression unreadable. But Davey didn't need to see his face to know the truth.

If Dom was the one standing in Brody's place, Davey wouldn't stop either.

His stomach clenched.

Sullivan wasn't just chasing a traitor. He was hunting his twin.

His other half.

And if it was Elliot or Dominic on the other side of this?

Davey would be the one marching down that tunnel, too.

The others were watching, waiting to see how this would play out. He could order Sullivan to stand down, but that wouldn't do shit. If he forced the issue, Sullivan would go completely rogue.

And Davey couldn't afford to lose both of the O'Connell twins in one night.

He exhaled, tension coiled tight in his chest. "Fine. But you follow my lead."

Sullivan didn't answer.

Didn't need to.

Because if it came down to it, they both knew he wouldn't.

But at least, for now, he fell into line with the rest of the team.

They moved forward, leaving the cramped tunnel behind as the space ahead opened up into something larger. The walls widened, the air shifting—less suffocating, but colder.

The ghost station.

A cavernous expanse of crumbling tile and rusted steel, forgotten beneath the city.

The station's platform stretched out beside them,

half-swallowed by darkness. The remains of old signage clung to the walls—letters half-faded, warped with time and water damage. Stagnant puddles lined the cracked concrete floor, their surfaces rippling as rats scurried through them, disturbed by their approach.

Somewhere above, the distant vibration of a train rumbled through the infrastructure, a ghost of movement in a place meant for the dead.

Davey kept his weapon raised, scanning the space ahead, every muscle tight.

Then—he saw him.

Liam.

Cuffed to a rusting bench.

A bomb vest strapped to his chest.

The world narrowed.

His vision tunneled, everything zeroing in on the blinking red countdown.

Five minutes.

Someone inhaled sharply.

Bridger went still.

A long string of Cajun French flowed from Sabin.

"Shit," Weston breathed.

thirty-three

LIAM'S HEAD ROSE, slow and sluggish. His face was bloodied, bruised, and his eyes were glazed. "Took you long enough." His voice was little more than a harsh whisper.

"Jesus," Bridger said and hurried to his brother's side, crouching down. "You okay?"

"Be better when you get this thing off me."

Davey crouched at his other side and drew a steadying breath as he studied the vest—wires, explosives, a small LED screen blinking way too fast.

Four and a half minutes.

He knew bombs. Not like Weston did, but enough to know this wasn't a quick and dirty setup to facilitate an escape.

This was calculated. Cruel. Meant to kill as many as possible and bring down the tunnel, burying the evidence.

His pulse pounded against his skull as memories of other bomb vests tried to claw out of the lockbox in his head.

A vest strapped to a kid, too young, wide-eyed, shaking —his hands trembling over the trigger.

Fuck. Not now. No time for that.

He shoved the memories down. Locked them tight.

Rowan brushed her fingers against his arm. A fleeting touch, barely there, just a silent, *I'm here*. But it was enough. He wanted to lean into her, let her anchor him. But he couldn't. They didn't have time.

He had to think. Lead. Assess, not react.

"Where's Brody?" he forced out.

"Set the timer and left. Knew you were coming." Liam's skin was ghost-white beneath the grime and blood. "He's working with someone else. Someone who knows our movements."

Another fucking mole in WSW?

Jesus.

Maybe his uncles had been right to pass the torch to him. Old age had made them sloppy if they'd let that many double agents onto the payroll.

Davey tapped his earpiece. "Elliot, I need to know our nearest exfil routes."

"Give me thirty seconds," Elliot responded.

Davey eyed the clock on the vest. "We don't have thirty seconds."

"Yeah, we do," Weston said, already dropping to his knees in front of Liam, ripping open his bag. His hands were steady, his voice clipped. He was fully in bomb tech mode. "Sabin, get those cuffs off—"

"Already on it, *mon ami*." Sabin circled to the back of the bench, pulling out a well-used leather roll of lock picks. He bent over the handcuffs and got to work, fingers moving with the kind of smooth confidence that came from breaking into far too many things. "Ooo-wee, *cher*. Bet ya can't even feel them fingers no more, huh? They white as a gator's belly in the moonlight."

Liam exhaled a rough chuckle. "'S okay. The headache makes up for it." His words slurred. He'd sounded weak when Daphne tapped into his implant's audio back at HQ, but now he was fading. His eyelids fluttered for half a second before he forced them open again. "And fucking—the static..."

Tessa crouched next to him and checked his ear. "Your processor's cracked."

Liam muttered a curse under his breath. "Figured. Feels like a damn wasp nest in my skull, and you sound miles away."

Bridger hadn't moved.

Still crouched beside Liam, still holding his shoulder like an anchor.

Still too still.

Bridger thrived in high-stress situations. He didn't panic. Didn't break.... but the tremble in his hand betrayed him. He was feeling the stress now.

They all were.

Still, his voice was even when he said, "You're always turning the damn thing off anyway. Thought you liked silence."

Liam's mouth pulled into something that might have been a smirk if he weren't so pale. "Not when it's permanent. If I die, there's nothing after. Just... eternity in silence."

That wasn't a joke.

Liam said it like he'd thought about it before. Maybe not exactly like this, not with a bomb strapped to his chest and minutes on the clock, but Davey knew the sound of someone trying to make peace with the inevitable.

For a beat, no one spoke.

Tessa went into medic mode. "Okay, well, you're not going to die at all. Davey won't let you."

She meant it as reassurance, but something about it settled wrong in Davey's chest.

Davey won't let you.

As if it was that simple. As if he could just will this into not being a worst-case scenario.

As if someone hadn't already died on his watch.

As if Elliot hadn't nearly died two days ago.

He shoved the thought down. He could do this later—process it, feel it.

Right now, Weston needed light to do his job.

"Did anyone pack an NVG-friendly light?" He wished he'd thought of it, but he hadn't expected to find Liam strapped to a fucking bomb.

Bridger finally moved, letting go of his brother long enough to reach into his pack. He pulled out a low-intensity red LED headlamp—dim enough to keep them from being blinded but enough for Weston to see the wiring clearly.

"West," Davey said, forcing himself to stay level.

Weston didn't look up. "Yeah, I know."

Then, he got to work.

Tessa dropped her med kit and started digging through it. "Everyone except West needs to back up. Give Liam some breathing room." She ducked so Liam could see her without turning his head. "I need to check your head wound. Is that okay? No, don't nod."

"Yeah. Hurts like a motherfucker."

"I know." She flicked on a penlight set to its dimmest setting, the small amber glow NVG-compatible to avoid blinding anyone. She tilted Liam's head toward the meager beam, parting his blood-matted hair with careful fingers. The cut was ugly, skin split deep, already swelling.

"You're concussed," she said grimly, running the tiny beam over his pupils. "Slow dilation. Disorientation."

She looked up at Davey. "I think he has a skull fracture. We need to get him to a hospital."

Liam let out a breathy laugh. "Preferably before I blow up."

Tessa rolled her eyes and ripped open a packet of gauze. "Preferably."

Weston cursed softly, his fingers still working over the tangle of wires and triggers. "This setup is nasty."

"How nasty?" Davey asked.

"Nasty enough that I'm about to have a real bad time."

Liam exhaled through his nose. "I think I'd still rather be you right now." His voice was dry, edged with exhaustion. "You screw up, you break a sweat, but I break into a thousand fucking pieces. So tell me again—who's really having a bad time here?"

Weston muttered something about punching Liam when this was over, but his fingers never stopped moving on the wires. "Sabin, how are those cuffs coming?"

Sabin stood up with a flourish, the cuffs dangling from his middle finger.

Liam exhaled heavily, flexing his stiff fingers. "Finally."

"Don't move yet," Weston said. "I need to make sure this isn't motion-act— Jesus Christ, he's got you padlocked into it. Sabin—"

"Yep." Without hesitation, the former thief dropped to his knees again and started working on the line of locks along the side of the vest.

"Form a perimeter," Davey ordered. "Let's make sure nobody sneaks up on our ass while they get him out of that torture device."

The team moved, shifting into a loose defensive circle around Liam, Tessa, Sabin, and Weston. Bridger squeezed his brother's shoulder once, then let go and palmed his gun, shifting his stance slightly—protecting Liam without stepping away.

Every tick of the countdown was a hammer to Davey's skull.

"Don't like this," Dominic said, bouncing back and forth on his feet. "We're sitting ducks here with a bomb at our backs."

"*Stay cool, Dom,*" Elliot said over the comms. "*Focus.*"

"Hate when you say that," Dom grumbled, but he stopped bouncing.

Davey scanned the tunnel and then checked their progress over his shoulder. "How we doing?"

Weston worked fast, hands steady as he traced the wires, his expression unreadable. "There's a secondary trigger. The fucker has a remote. Even if I get the vest off, he could still detonate it while we're in range and bring this whole tunnel down on us."

"Brody's an asshole," Liam muttered, thick and slurring as his head started to droop.

Tessa was on him in an instant.

"No, no, no—stay with me, Liam." Her hands cupped his face, not gentle, but firm—demanding. She lifted his chin, forcing his glazed eyes to meet hers. "I don't care if your head feels like it's splitting in two. You do not pass out on me."

Bridger swore under his breath, holstering his gun in a single sharp motion before grabbing Liam again, his grip tighter this time. "You hear her? You drop, you're making West's job a hell of a lot harder. Don't do that to us."

Liam's eyelids fluttered, his breath shallow. "Yeah..." But he sagged again.

Tessa gave his face a quick slap—not hard, but sharp enough to make his head jolt upright.

"Eyes open," she snapped. "You check out now, and I swear to God, I will find a way to bring you back just to kill you myself."

Liam sucked in a breath, his voice weak but dry. "You sure slapping a guy with a head injury is in the medical handbook?"

Tessa huffed a laugh—half exasperated, half relieved. "Worked, didn't it? You're welcome."

The countdown on the vest ticked lower, a relentless reminder that time was running out.

This wasn't just any bomb.

Brody had set it up to screw with them, to force them into a situation where even winning felt like losing.

"How much time left on the clock?" Davey asked.

Weston's jaw clenched. "Ninety seconds."

Davey's stomach turned, and sweat dripped down the side of his neck despite the cool temperature. "Elliot, tell me you've got something for a fast exfil."

Elliot's voice was sharp in his ear. *"Exfil options are limited. Nearest clear tunnel is behind you, but if Brody really left a remote trigger, you're still in blast range."*

Weston let out a low curse. "This is a bastard of a setup. The wrong cut trips the secondary trigger. I need more fucking time."

Elliot's voice was tense. *"Daphne and I are working on it. We think we can disrupt the countdown for an extra minute—maybe two."*

"Make it happen," Davey said.

"I'm not a miracle worker, asshole, I—"

"But I am." Daphne's voice cut in, cool and confident. *"Shut up and give me ten seconds."*

Davey exhaled, blowing out a breath that did nothing to settle the tightness in his chest. His mind ran the numbers, the contingencies, every possible outcome. Even if Daphne bought them an extra minute, it still wasn't enough. But leaving Liam to his death wasn't an option either.

Weston stayed calm and cool as he worked. Sabin swore in a constant stream of French as his long fingers popped one lock after the next. Bridger gripped Liam like he could hold him together through sheer will alone.

This was a fucking coin toss.

And if it landed wrong?

Liam wouldn't be the only one who didn't walk out of here.

Davey's gaze flicked to Rowan.

She was exactly where he'd told her to be—holding the perimeter, scanning for threats, her back to him.

And that made it worse.

He couldn't see her face, couldn't read her expression. Couldn't tell if she was afraid.

He was fucking terrified, because he knew what came next if Weston ran out of time. Not from stories. Not from training videos. From experience.

He remembered the blast wasn't a sound—it was a force. A violent, consuming thing that crushed the air from his lungs and sent him weightless for half a second before he hit the ground.

He remembered the pressure wave slamming into his chest like a freight train, his ribs creaking, his ears ringing so loud it felt like his brain was trying to escape his skull.

He remembered the heat. The shrapnel. The smell of burning fuel, burning flesh.

The way everything fractured in an instant—steel, bone, bodies.

The way his Humvee had turned into a coffin.

The way he'd clawed his way out of it, feeling pain but not understanding where it came from, knowing something was wrong, but not knowing what.

The way his teammates hadn't crawled out at all.

And if Weston ran out of time now, Rowan would die. Just like his teammates did. Broken, burning.

He wanted to grab her, shove her out of the blast zone, force her to run, but she'd never go. She'd fight him every step of the way.

So, instead, he just gritted his teeth and forced the thought down.

No time for this.

Not now.

"West, you're getting more time. Not much, but enough."

Weston gave a short nod, his concentration never breaking. "I'll make it work."

"Got it!" Daphne said. *"You have two extra minutes, West. Three at most. Work your magic."*

Jesus, it still wasn't enough. Weston was good under pressure, but this was a goddamn pressure cooker.

Elliot's voice came over the comms, sharp and tactical, all business. *"Drone's got movement on a railway bridge almost directly above your position. Nearest access is an old service stairwell—should be about forty meters to your right, near the west end of the platform. It'll put you out near the base of the bridge."*

"Brody?" Davey asked.

"Confirmed. It's him."

Sullivan was already moving. "I'm going."

"Fuck." Davey looked back to where Weston and Sabin were still working methodically on the vest. The clock had stopped at forty-five seconds, but how long could Daphne hold it there?

Rowan's fingers brushed his arm again, and, yet again, it was enough to drag him out of his own head, out of the spiraling what-ifs.

She met his gaze. Steady. Unshaken.

"Go," she said. "I've got their six."

Christ, she was perfect.

Davey's hand found the back of her neck before he could stop himself.

The kiss was fast, desperate, full of things he didn't have time to say right now.

Be safe.

Don't die.

Come back to me.

"Shoot to kill, Hellcat," he murmured when he pulled away.

"Always do." She grinned, and fuck, did he love her for that casual deadliness. She gave his shoulder a shove. "Now, go."

"Dom. Cade. With me." He turned away from his heart and didn't look back. Didn't hesitate.

He just ran.

thirty-four

DAVEY'S FOOTFALLS echoed against the worn concrete of the service stairwell as he took the steps two at a time.

Sullivan was ahead, moving fast.

Too fast.

That was the problem with adrenaline. It made men reckless. Made them forget what they were trained to do. And Sullivan wasn't thinking anymore. He was reacting—raw, unfiltered emotion taking the wheel.

Davey hit the last step and burst out onto solid ground. The winter night slammed into his lungs, a shock after the stagnant, metallic rot of the tunnels.

Scan. Process. Control.

They were at the base of the bridge. The massive steel structure spanned the river, its main deck lined with parallel railway tracks, flanked by thick metal beams and cross-braces.

Above, dim industrial floodlights cast weak patches of yellow light onto the steel framework, flickering against the night. A narrow strip of grated steel ran alongside the bridge—some kind of walkway for maintenance workers. It had a single guardrail on the outer edge, and the inner side was open to the rail lines.

No room to run. No room for mistakes.

His gaze tracked upward.

There. The access point.

A rusted metal ladder ran straight up from the support column to the walkway. And halfway up...

Brody.

He was moving fast, not trying for stealth. He didn't know they were on his heels. He reached the top and hauled himself through a hatch onto the walkway.

Davey's grip tightened around his rifle. They had the upper hand, the element of surprise. But that only meant something if they used it right.

If Sullivan went in half-cocked, they'd lose that advantage in a heartbeat. Worse, Brody could force a fight on the walkway—a fight where one misstep meant a hundred-foot drop into the icy river.

Not an option.

"Brody!" Sullivan's voice ripped through the night, sharp as a gunshot.

Davey snapped toward him, heart lurching.

Fuck.

Brody froze and then, slowly, turned. A smirk curled at the edges of his mouth.

The element of surprise was gone.

Davey moved, instinct kicking in. "Sully, hold—"

But Sullivan wasn't listening. He was already on the ladder, hauling himself upward in quick, furious movements, his boots clanging against the metal rungs. His rifle was slung across his back, forgotten in his single-minded focus.

Brody watched from above, completely still.

Not running.

Not reaching for a weapon.

Just... watching. Waiting for his brother.

Davey's gut twisted.

This wasn't a chase anymore.

This was a confrontation.

Cade swore under his breath. "He's not even trying to get away."

"Maybe he thinks he can talk his way out of it?" Dom suggested, ever the optimist, trying to find some hope to hold onto. Trying to believe there was a way this didn't end with a bullet.

"This is fucked," Cade said.

Dom exhaled. "Okay, so what's the plan—tackle Sully, shoot Brody, or just stay here and pray neither of them falls?"

Davey's jaw tightened. "Brody has a detonator."

Dom blinked. "Right. Forgot about that."

Cade gave a short nod. "Let's move."

Dom huffed out a breath. "Awesome. Climbing. Love that." But he followed.

Davey moved swiftly, grabbing the cold metal rungs of the ladder, eyes locked on Sullivan's back above him as he climbed. The wind whipped around them, carrying the distant sounds of the city.

"Sully!" he called out, but the wind snatched his voice. "Don't do anything stupid!"

But Sullivan showed no sign of slowing. He reached the top of the ladder, hauling himself onto the narrow walkway with a grunt. Davey cursed under his breath, pushing himself faster. His leg ached, but he ignored it.

As he neared the top, he heard Sullivan's voice, raw with anger and pain. "You selfish fuck. How could you?"

Davey emerged onto the walkway just in time to see Sullivan lunge at Brody. The two men grappled, teetering dangerously close to the edge. The steel grating creaked ominously beneath their feet.

"Sully, stand down!" Davey barked, raising his rifle. But in the tangle of limbs, he couldn't get a clear shot.

The night wind whipped through the steel beams, rattling the bridge like bones shaking against one another. The train tracks were silent. No engines, no movement. Just the five of them on that narrow walkway, the river stretching out below.

A fight that had been a long time coming.

Davey's eyes darted between Sullivan and Brody, his finger hovering near the trigger of his rifle. His muscles tensed, ready to spring into action at a moment's notice.

Then, out of the corner of his eye, he caught a flash of movement. Dom.

His younger brother had jumped onto the train tracks and was edging around the fight, his lean frame hugging the inner edge of the walkway. Dom's bright blue eyes were narrowed in concentration, his dark hair whipping around his face in the gusting wind.

Davey's heart rate spiked. "Dom, stop!"

If Dom heard—which he probably had—he ignored the command. He kept moving until he popped up onto the walkway behind Brody and Sullivan.

"Fuck," he said, voice perfectly clear in Davey's earpiece despite the wind. "Still no shot."

Yeah, he'd definitely heard and ignored that command. "Hold your position." He didn't want to have to worry about Dom falling, too.

Sullivan's fist connected with Brody's jaw, the impact echoing across the bridge. Brody stumbled, his heel catching on the edge of the grating. For a heart-stopping moment, he teetered on the brink, but Sully grabbed a fistful of his jacket, holding him tipped over the low railing.

Davey's finger tightened on the trigger, ready to take the shot if Brody made a move. But Sullivan was still too close, his body partially shielding Brody from a clean line of fire.

"Don't have a shot," Cade said, deadly calm.

"Same," Dom said.

"Sully, get clear!" Davey commanded, trying to find an opening.

But Sullivan was beyond hearing. His face was a mask of rage as he slammed Brody against the railing. The metal groaned under the impact.

"Why?" Sullivan growled. "Why'd you do it?"

Brody's teeth flashed in a bloody smile. "You know why."

His voice wasn't cocky. Wasn't mocking. Just calm. Matter-of-fact.

Sullivan's breath came in sharp and uneven pants. His grip on Brody's jacket was ironclad, his whole body trembling with the force of holding himself back.

The railing creaked beneath Brody's weight.

The wind whipped through the steel beams, rattling the bridge.

Even with blood smeared across his mouth, his body half-dangling over the drop, Brody looked at Sullivan like he'd already won.

Like he wanted this.

"I had to pick a side." His gaze flicked briefly to

Davey, to Cade, to Dominic. Then, back to Sullivan. "And you weren't on it."

Sullivan flinched. Barely. Just a fraction of a movement, but Brody saw it and laughed. Low. Rough. A little breathless from the fight but still simmering with something ugly underneath.

"Christ, you still don't get it, do you?"

Sullivan's hands shook. "You—" His voice caught. He swallowed hard. "You betrayed us."

Brody's smile widened, but his eyes were flat, empty. "Yeah."

"Our friends. Our team. *Me*. For what? Money?"

Brody barked a laugh. "That's the excuse, isn't it?" He licked the blood from the corner of his mouth and tilted his head. "But, really, I just stopped pretending I care." He leaned in, voice low enough that only Sullivan would be able to hear it if not for their open comm line. "You were always the golden boy, Sully. The one everyone respected. The one everyone trusted. Didn't matter what I did. Didn't matter how hard I tried. You were always the first choice. Mom's. Even our fucking dad's. Everyone's."

Sullivan inhaled like the words had cut deeper than any knife.

Brody laughed again, but this time, it wasn't sharp or cruel. This time, it sounded almost... broken. Like he hated himself for meaning it. "I tried to be charming, funny, likable, but I was always just... there. In your shadow."

Sullivan's grip loosened. Confusion and hurt warred across his face as he backed up a step. "That's not—"

"Don't." Brody's voice hardened again, the vulnerability vanishing as quickly as it had appeared. "Don't try to tell me it wasn't true. We both know it was." He fumbled something out of his pocket.

The detonator.

The air froze in Davey's lungs as Brody looked right at him and grinned. "But at least now I'll have their fear."

Dom lunged, going straight for Brody's wrist. His fingers locked around the detonator, yanking it away in one clean, fluid motion.

Brody's eyes widened—the first time his composure cracked. Then he moved. Not to throw a desperate punch. Not to escape. Instead, he went straight for Dom's sidearm in a clean, calculated play for the kill.

Sullivan saw it, too, raised his weapon, and squeezed the trigger. The shot cracked through the night like a thunderclap.

Brody jerked. His feet slipped against the slick grating. For a second, he hung there, his weight tilting toward the edge, his hands reaching for nothing—

Then he was gone.

Falling.

His body hit the water below with a sickening splash, the darkness swallowing him whole.

Silence.

The four of them stood frozen, staring over the railing, waiting... but nothing broke the surface.

No movement.

No body.

Davey exhaled sharply, chest heaving, his hands tight on his rifle, but his mind was already somewhere else.

Rowan.

His fingers flew to his earpiece. "Hellcat, talk to me."

Nothing.

"Rowan. Status."

Still nothing.

Jesus.

The bomb.

Liam.

Had they made it? Had Weston gotten the vest off in time?

"Rowan, answer me."

Still nothing.

His breath came faster now, pulse thudding against his skull as he switched channels. "Elliot, report."

The response was immediate. "Liam gave us a scare, but he's back with us now. He's stable. Tessa, Bridger, and I are en route to the hospital with him."

Davey exhaled sharply, some of the tension uncoiling from his spine.

Liam was safe.

But Rowan—

"Where the hell is Rowan?" His voice came out sharper than intended, but he didn't care.

A slight pause. "They went back in."

His heart kicked hard against his ribs. "What do you mean, *back in*?"

"They thought they could get to you faster through the tunnels. You know her, man. She wasn't gonna stay on the sidelines if she thought you were still in danger."

"How long ago?"

"A few minutes, maybe?" Static crackled, proof that Elliot was getting farther away by the second. "They should've reached you by now."

"Fuck," Davey growled, his grip tightening on his rifle. He spun to face Dom and Cade. "We need to move. Now."

Cade was unreadable, but his gaze flicked toward Sullivan's back. Sully was still staring at the water below, barely breathing.

"You two go," Cade murmured. "I'll stay with him."

In case he decides to follow his twin over the edge.

That second part went unspoken, but the subtext was clear.

Davey nodded sharply, already turning to race back to the ladder.

Dom fell in step behind him. "We'll find her."

Davey didn't point out what happened the last

time Dom was optimistic. Just as he reached the ladder, a muffled thump echoed from somewhere beneath the bridge, and he froze.

Listened.

That wasn't…

Another sound. Sharper this time, faster. Unmistakable.

Automatic gunfire.

His hand flew to his radio. "Rowan!"

Nothing.

"Rowan, do you copy?"

Silence.

A cold weight settled in his chest and wound around his lungs, thick and suffocating. "Weston. Sabin. Somebody fucking answer me!"

Static.

Another gunshot.

Louder. Closer.

Behind him, something shifted. Not movement. Not footsteps. A change in the air itself, and the hair on the back of his neck prickled. He spun, half-raising his weapon, expecting to see a threat, but it was just Sullivan. He wasn't staring at the water anymore. The grief was gone. The rage was sealed shut. His breathing had steadied, his stance locked. His hands, still gripping his rifle, were now perfectly still.

When he lifted his head and met Davey's gaze, his eyes were cold.

Not blank.

Not broken.

Just ice fucking cold.

A man who had done what needed to be done and had nothing left.

A soldier who knew he still had a job to do.

Sullivan had snapped back because their team was in danger, and that was what they were trained to do no matter the loss, no matter the cost. They kept moving. Kept fighting.

Saved who they could.

But could they save Rowan?

Jesus.

He needed to move. *Now.* But his body wouldn't obey. His boots seemed to weigh a thousand pounds each. His lungs stuttered, and his vision blurred at the edges.

Heat. Shrapnel. Fire. The blistering shockwave hit like a fist to the chest, tearing the air from his lungs. The Humvee rocking from the blast—no, not rocking—flipping. His body wrenched sideways, everything tilting, spinning, weightless for a breathless second before metal screamed and the roof slammed into the sand.

His ears rang. Too loud. Too sharp. The sound of war pressed into his skull, but beneath it—beneath the chaos—was something worse.

Silence.

Louder than the explosion. Louder than anything.

Because silence meant someone wasn't screaming anymore.

Silence meant someone hadn't made it.

And Rowan was silent.

His chest seized. His lungs locked.

Oh, fuck, no.

A hand clamped down on his shoulder. Steady. Firm. Grounding. He blinked and focused on Sullivan's hard, cold eyes.

"We gotta move, boss." Despite the ice in his eyes, his voice was shockingly gentle. "We gotta go save your woman."

The words hit like a sledgehammer.

Davey's pulse slammed against his ribs. The gunfire. The silence. The fucking static. His vision blurred at the edges, his mind lagging behind his body. It was still stuck in the Humvee halfway across the world with a dead team and a busted-up leg.

He couldn't lose Rowan.

Not like that.

Not like *them*.

Sullivan shoved him. Not gently. A sharp, jolting push. "Davey."

Adrenaline slammed through him like a goddamn freight train, and his mind finally caught up. He turned to Dom, who was all but vibrating with the need to kick ass. So Davey cut his leash.

"Go. We're right behind you."

Dom moved with startling speed, swinging his rifle to his shoulder and taking the ladder so fast he might as well have jumped.

Davey followed. No hesitation. No thought. Just action. Just movement. His boots hit the concrete in time with the pulse hammering in his ears.

Rowan was down there.

And he wasn't losing her.

Hold on, Hellcat. I'm coming.

thirty-five

BREATHE.

Rowan inhaled. The subway air was thick—rust, sweat, something stale.

Just breathe.

She exhaled slowly, shifting her weight.

Stay loose. Stay ready.

Despite the pulse thundering in her ears. Despite the bomb at her back. Despite the near-irresistible need to chase after Davey and make sure he was safe.

And breathe again. In for four. Hold for four. Out for four.

She forced the rhythm, grounding herself against the fear. Scanning the dark tunnels. Watching. Waiting.

No movement. Just the occasional rat scurrying along the tracks. No threats. Yet.

Behind her, Weston worked fast, his hands moving

with precision as he traced the wires along Liam's bomb vest. Sabin was crouched beside them, working the last of the locks, his fingers nimble despite the sweat beading along his brow.

Almost there.

Bridger hovered just behind them, silent but watchful, his rifle steady in his hands. He wasn't pacing—Bridger never paced—but there was something in the tightness of his stance, the way his fingers flexed against his weapon, that told Rowan exactly how much he wanted to.

Liam gritted his teeth as Tessa held pressure to the gash on his head. He was swaying, barely upright, but still holding on.

"We're still clear," Rowan murmured. "No movement."

Sabin hissed through his teeth and paused long enough to swipe at the sweat dripping down the side of his face. "*Merde, cher*, why don't you just ask the universe to smite us while you're at it?"

A hiccup of a laugh burst out of her with her next exhale. "The universe obviously wants us smited."

"Isn't it smote?" Bridger asked.

Liam, voice hoarse, offered, "Smitten?"

"Oh my God," Tessa said with a nervous laugh.

"Whatever it is, we're gonna be it soon," Weston muttered, his attention locked on the final sequence of wires. "This thing has more failsafes than I like."

"I'd like *zero* failsafes," Liam rasped. "If that's an option."

"You and me both, *mon ami*." Sabin twisted the last lock, the metal clicking softly as the hasp popped free. A heartbeat later, the final restraint keeping the vest in place loosened. "Well, Liam, good news—you are now free from your fashionable straightjacket of death." He flicked the now-useless padlock onto the ground with a dramatic flourish. "Bad news—it's still trying to kill you."

Bridger shot him a flat look. "You're not funny."

Sabin placed a hand over his heart like he was mortally wounded. "*Mon ami*, that is simply untrue."

"Sabin, shut up," Tessa said and looked at Weston. "Can we just take it off him and run?"

Bridger shifted, glancing at the vest like he was considering ripping it off his brother. Weston's hands never stopped moving, but he didn't answer immediately.

"What if it has a pressure trigger?" Rowan asked the obvious question since nobody else seemed to want to.

Weston didn't hesitate. "It doesn't. I checked."

"And if you're wrong?" Sabin asked.

"Then we won't have to worry about it for long."

Tessa made a strangled sound. "Oh my God, West."

Liam huffed out a pained laugh. "Yeah, not comforting, man."

"Can we take it off him or not?" Rowan asked.

Weston finally looked up, but instead of looking at the rest of them, he met Liam's exhausted gaze. "I don't think we should take the time. I only have minutes. If we waste them trying to get it off you, we won't have time to get clear of the blast zone. But it's your call, Liam. Either way, I'm here with you until the end."

Liam swallowed hard. "Diffuse it."

Weston nodded, his jaw clenched tight as he refocused on the tangle of wires. "The rest of you should leave."

"Fuck that." Rowan's fingers flexed around her weapon. She hated this waiting, but she wasn't running. "We're staying."

"But..." Liam lifted his head sluggishly, his gaze locking onto his brother with quiet determination. "Bridger has to go."

Bridger crossed his arms. "I think Rowan said it best: Fuck that."

"Bridge—"

"I'm not leaving." He signed as he spoke, as if making damn sure his brother understood him. "Stop asking."

"Stop being stubborn."

"Stop being an ass."

Liam exhaled hard, his bloodied face set like stone. "Mom and Dad are *not* losing both of us tonight."

Bridger flinched. The words had landed like a physical blow, just as Liam had calculated.

Bridger held his ground, shaking his head. "No."

"Please," Liam rasped. "If you stay and we die, it'll break Mom's heart. And Dad... I don't think he'll survive it. Then she'll lose all of us."

A muscle in Bridger's cheek jumped. His throat bobbed in a hard swallow, his hands flexing at his sides like he was fighting an internal war. Then, finally, his shoulders dropped, and he nodded, once, stiff and reluctant. "Fine."

His hand came down on Liam's shoulder, solid, firm, the kind of grip that meant more than words. More than a goodbye. A promise.

Then he turned and walked away.

Rowan saw his face as he passed. His expression was a mask of stone, but his eyes... God, his eyes. They held a raw, desperate pain that made her chest ache. She wanted to say something, offer some kind of comfort, but the words stuck in her throat. There was nothing to say that could ease this moment.

Bridger disappeared into the darkness, his footsteps fading into silence.

A distant rumble echoed through the tunnel, and Rowan's muscles tensed. Her eyes narrowed at the ceiling, tracking the source of the sound as dust rained down on them.

A train, passing somewhere close.

She relaxed, but only marginally. "How are we doing on time?"

"Uh," Sabin said and audibly gulped. "West, it's tickin' again. Thirty seconds."

"Go," Liam whispered. "Leave me."

Rowan glanced back, her heart in her throat. "No. We're all walking out of here."

"Yes, we are. Hang on..." Weston's fingers moved faster, methodically clipping wires, then moving to the next.

Time slowed to a crawl.

Sabin crossed himself.

Liam closed his eyes.

Rowan held her breath, gripping her rifle tighter, her muscles coiled.

Tessa was frozen—not watching the bomb but watching Weston. Not her patient. Not the danger. Just her little brother.

Weston didn't look at her. Didn't do anything but work, his hands steady as ever.

"Tess," Sabin muttered, side-eyeing her. "Don't pass out on us."

She blinked and sucked in a startled breath like she'd forgotten how to breathe. Her fingers curled into a white-knuckled fist on Liam's shoulder, like she was trying to keep herself from reaching out and yanking Weston away from the bomb.

Rowan felt it, too. The helpless ache of knowing

someone you love was doing something impossibly dangerous, and all you could do was stand there and watch.

Like Davey.

The thought struck sharp and sudden, burrowing deep.

He was out there right now, running toward danger because that's what he did. That's what they did.

Had he made it to Brody yet? Had he caught up? Was he fighting? Bleeding?

Her chest tightened.

Because if she could feel this—this helpless, desperate ache watching Weston work—then what the hell was Davey feeling right now?

Wherever he was, whatever he was facing, he'd be thinking of her.

And she hated knowing that, just like she couldn't help Weston now, she couldn't help Davey either.

Weston exhaled sharply. "Final wire." His wire cutters hovered for half a second, just long enough for Rowan's pulse to spike, for her breath to catch—

He snapped the wire in half just as the timer hit zero.

A heartbeat of silence.

Nothing.

No explosion.

No flash of heat.

Weston let out a shaky breath. "We're clear."

Sabin and Weston moved as one, grabbing the vest and hauling it away from Liam's chest like it might still go off.

Liam's breath shuddered out of him, somewhere between a laugh and a groan. "Holy shit. I'm not dead."

Tessa choked out something halfway between a sob and a curse. She didn't let go of Liam, which was probably a good thing as the guy was white as toothpaste and looked about ready to pass out.

Sabin sat back on his knees and let his head drop back, breathing out a low, shaky laugh. "*Bon Dieu, mon ami...* I think I just lost fifteen years off my life."

"It was bound to be a short one anyway," Liam muttered.

"This is the thanks I get? I just helped save your miserable ass."

"You want a medal?"

Sabin smirked. "*Non.* Just a stiff drink and a woman who appreciates my sacrifices."

Weston snorted, wiping sweat from his brow. "Yeah, good luck with that. You praying back there didn't help your odds."

Sabin narrowed his eyes. "What?"

"The whole crossing yourself thing," Weston said, and quirked an eyebrow. "Since when are you Catholic?"

Sabin spread his arms wide. "When explosives are involved, I get real religious."

Rowan huffed out a breath, finally forcing herself to breathe again. "Right. And when they're not?"

Sabin grinned. "Then I sin."

Tessa, still clutching Liam's arm, shot them all an exasperated look. "Can we go? He's about to pass out, and I'd rather not have to drag him out of here."

"I'm fine," Liam muttered, but his knees wobbled as he tried to push upright.

Tessa caught him before he could list sideways. "Yeah, tell that to the blood dripping down your face, dumbass."

"Don't listen to her," Sabin chirped. "You look amazing, *mon ami*."

Liam let out a weak laugh. "Oh yeah?"

"*Bien sûr*." Sabin grinned. "Very edgy. All the ladies love a man who survived an explosion."

"Shut up and move," Tessa snapped, practically hauling Liam toward the exit.

Rowan tapped her comms. "Elliot, bomb's disarmed. We're on our way to you with Liam."

A pause—then a sharp exhale. "Jesus Christ. Copy that. Get his ass out of there."

Sabin pushed to his feet, stretching dramatically. "We all deserve hazard pay."

Weston grunted as he ducked under Liam's other arm and took most of his weight. "We don't have time for your bullshit, Cavalier."

"There's always time for bullshit," Sabin said. "That's the secret to survival."

Liam groaned. "I think I'd rather be unconscious."

"Oh, hell no, you are not checking out now," Weston said, tightening his grip on Liam as they made their way off the old subway platform. "I didn't risk my very valuable life and pull off some bomb-diffusing magic just for you to do some dramatic fade-to-black bullshit. Walk it off, cousin."

"Walking it off might not be the best plan." Tessa kept a sharp eye on Liam, her grip firm on his waist. "He's favoring his right side, and his legs are barely keeping up. If he goes down, we're carrying him."

Rowan took point, weapon raised, scanning every inch of the tunnels as they made their retreat. Her pulse was still too fast, her nerves still too sharp.

They didn't stop. Didn't breathe easy until the first gust of cold night air hit them.

The moment they reached the van, Bridger yanked the back doors open, already reaching for Liam. "Jesus, about time."

Tessa didn't even slow down. "Help me get him inside."

Bridger caught Liam under the arms, hauling him into the van. Tessa climbed in right after him, already tearing open medical supplies.

Elliot paced the sidewalk, rubbing a hand over his face. When he looked up, his relief was evident—but so was his barely restrained frustration.

Rowan grabbed his arm. "Where's Davey?"

"They're on the bridge. Last I saw, Sullivan and Brody were throwing punches."

She exhaled. He wasn't safe, but he wasn't in immediate danger. He was okay.

"I'm going back in," she said.

"Nah, *cher*," Sabin said and cocked a hip, shouldering his rifle with a grin. "*We* are going back in."

"Damn straight," Weston said.

Elliot's eyes snapped from one of them to the next, his expression darkening. "Like hell you are."

Rowan met his glare, unflinching. "We're not leaving Davey without backup."

"Hey!" Tessa's sharp voice cut through the argument from the back of the van as she poked a needle into Liam's arm, starting an IV. "Liam just lost consciousness. We need to get him to the hospital now! You need to drive, El. I want Bridger back here with me in case his crashes on us."

Elliot swore under his breath, raking a hand through his hair. He leveled one last glare at the three of them, then turned on his heel and climbed into the van. "Fine. Go. But don't get yourselves killed. Be smart."

Sabin grinned, slinging his rifle back into position. "Smart is my middle name."

Weston shoved his shoulder. "Thought it was Henri."

Rowan rolled her eyes but couldn't entirely suppress the smile tugging at her lips. She waited until the van peeled away, then turned back to the tunnel and pulled her NVGs back into place. "Let's move."

She rolled her shoulders, gripping her rifle tighter, as she stepped back into the tunnel. The darkness swallowed them whole, NVGs shifting the world to an eerie green and black. The air stank of rust and damp concrete, and the old tracks running parallel to them were slick with condensation.

The air felt different down here now—heavier, wrong. The kind of quiet that didn't just mean an absence of sound. It meant something was waiting.

Her skin prickled.

Her gut twisted.

"Heads on a swivel," she murmured. "Something—"

Crack.

The first shot ripped through the tunnel.

Weston slammed into Rowan, driving her sideways. The impact was bone-jarring, the concrete biting into her shoulder as she hit the ground.

A second shot followed. A third. Too many. Too fast.

Sabin fired back, his face grim. "Merde. Where they comin' from?"

Rowan rolled onto her knees, rifle raised, scanning—

Figures flickered into view, bleeding out of the shadows like ghosts. No glow of NVGs, no telltale rustle of movement. Just shifting air, like heat rippling over pavement, and...

Solid forms materialized from the darkness. No, they weren't appearing from the dark. They were already here.

Soldiers dressed in black with rifles. Trained, polished, precise. They moved in sync, their weapons held with a comfort and familiarity that spoke of countless hours of training.

"What the fuck," she breathed. Either they were magic, or they had access to cloaking technology she'd never seen before.

Weston spun, bringing up his weapon, but then froze as one of the bigger shadows peeled off from the pack and advanced.

Rowan caught the flicker of confusion in his expression, like something wasn't adding up. His whole body locked up, muscles going rigid, breath catching like he'd just taken a gut punch.

"No, that's—"

The shadow attacked. Fast. Precise. Brutal. No hesitation. No pause. Just a blur of motion.

The rifle butt smashed into Weston's skull with a sickening crack. His head snapped sideways, his knees buckling before his body followed.

Rowan lunged for him, but another shot rang out, forcing her back.

Weston hit the ground hard, blood spattering across the concrete when he landed.

He didn't move again.

"No! Weston!" His name ripped from her throat as she twisted, trying to get to him—

A fist crashed into her jaw, rattling her skull. White-hot pain exploded behind her eyes, but sheer willpower kept her upright. She staggered, clenched her teeth, and twisted—

Another shadow pounced.

God, there were so many of them.

She spun with lightning speed, her arm snapping up in a fierce strike. Her elbow cracked against bone, the impact jarring her down to her teeth. Her attacker barely stumbled.

Not enough.

For every one she fought off, another materialized to take his place.

An arm clamped around her throat from behind like a vise, dragging her against a body made of pure muscle. She bucked wildly, driving her heel down with all her strength, but the hold only tightened. Her boots scraped against the grimy tunnel floor as she tried to find leverage.

Five feet ahead, Sabin moved like a ghost.

One second, he was pivoting, feet braced wide on the uneven track bed, rifle raised—the next, he fired.

The gunshot cracked through the tunnel. A round slammed into the first attacker's thigh, dropping them hard onto the gravel.

Another figure surged from the dark behind him. Fast. Silent.

Sabin pivoted, but he was too late. A hard strike to his wrist sent his rifle skidding across the tunnel floor, clattering into the shadows.

But he didn't slow. His hand snapped to his belt, and a knife unsheathed in a blur of silver. He snarled, the sound feral, and brought his blade up in a vicious arc.

Blood sprayed.

His opponent staggered back just as another attacker crashed into them from the side, slamming them both into a steel support column with a sickening clang. Sabin twisted, ripping his knife free, swinging again—

A rifle butt slammed into his ribs.

Hard.

He grunted, but instead of falling, he used the momentum. Turned into it. Drove his shoulder into his attacker.

The impact sent both of them stumbling—but Sabin stayed on his feet.

Another shadow dropped in behind him.

Rowan saw it before he did.

She twisted violently, trying to scream a warning, but the vise around her throat crushed her airway, turning her warning into a choked rasp. Blood pooled in her mouth.

A boot crashed into the back of Sabin's knee, and

he buckled. The two men moved in on him, fast, efficient, their strikes brutal and precise.

Sabin roared, twisting, his knife still clutched in his hand—

A rifle butt smashed into his temple.

His whole body jerked.

His knife slipped from his fingers.

He stayed on his knees for a heartbeat longer, his face swelling with each blow, blood flying. He met her gaze, his eyes filled with pain and fury and a flicker of defiance even as they swelled shut.

Then his body sagged.

His breath hitched—like his lungs had just given up.

He pitched forward. The impact was ugly. Final.

Now both Weston and Sabin lay motionless on the grimy tunnel floor. So still. Too still.

And Rowan couldn't fucking get to them.

Rage and desperation surged through her. She thrashed against her captor, every muscle straining. Her vision started to gray at the edges from lack of oxygen, but she refused to give in, even when a fist slammed into her ribs. She twisted, throwing her weight backward, trying to break the hold on her throat. Her attacker—the same one who had so brutally attacked Weston—didn't budge. He might as well be made of stone. He tightened his arm across her windpipe, cutting off her air.

She couldn't breathe.

Couldn't think.

Dark spots danced in front of her eyes.

The world tilted.

No!

She clawed at his mask. If she was going to go down, she wanted to see this fucker's face so she knew who to haunt.

Her lungs burned. The pressure in her skull was unbearable. Dark spots exploded in her vision. Her limbs went lead-heavy.

No.

No.

She willed her body to stay upright, to breathe, to move—

Then something slammed into the side of her head.

A sharp, concussive crack. A brutal, final blow.

Her knees buckled.

The tunnel tilted.

Warped.

She was falling.

The last thing she saw before darkness enveloped her was the tunnel ahead.

The path to Davey.

He needed to know it was a trap. He needed— needed...

Her thoughts grew disjointed, sluggish, slipping away. She fought against it. Tried to move. Her body betrayed her.

Davey.

He needed to know.

He needed—

A warning. A chance. A fighting shot.

She couldn't give it to him.

Her fingers twitched, reaching for the tunnel... for him...

Then the darkness swallowed her whole.

thirty-six

THE GUNFIRE HAD STOPPED.

In its wake, only silence.

Rowan.

He couldn't raise her on the radio.

Or Weston.

Or Sabin.

Davey's boots slammed against the cold concrete as he hit the tunnel at the bottom of the service stairwell. He wanted to run, wanted to scream Rowan's name, but he forced himself to bite his tongue and fall in line behind Dom, who was WSW's best at close-quarters combat. Cade was right behind him, methodical, sharp-eyed, ready for anything. Sullivan—silent, locked-down, and unreadable—brought up the rear, moving with a deadly efficiency.

Dom turned a corner and hesitated, lowering his

weapon. Just for a second. And that alone made Davey's stomach lurch. Because if Dom, who could find a silver lining in the middle of a firefight, was shaken, it was bad.

Davey followed, every step a painful eternity until he rounded the corner. Adrenaline buzzed in his veins, but it wasn't enough to drown out the sheer, visceral panic clawing at his throat.

The tunnel was a war zone.

Davey didn't care about the black-clad bodies on the ground. He didn't care about the blood smeared across the concrete. His gaze locked on Weston, who was on his knees, barely staying upright, and Sabin, sprawled on the ground beside him.

Sabin's face was a mess of bruises and blood, one eye swollen shut, his usually easy-going smirk nowhere to be found. Weston was in only slightly better shape, swaying on his feet, blood pouring from a deep gash on his forehead. He was trying—and failing—to keep Sabin from slipping into uncon-sciousness.

But Rowan—

Rowan wasn't here.

His brain refused to process it. She had to be here. She had to be close. Maybe—maybe she was just out of sight. Maybe—

His stomach bottomed out, the walls pressing in, the air thinning. He turned in a slow circle, looking, searching—like if he just looked hard enough, she'd be there.

"Where is she?"

Weston's eyes struggled to focus. "The... the shadows," he mumbled. "They came out of nowhere." He swayed, and Cade's hand shot out to keep him upright.

Davey's breath was sharp and uneven, his heart hammering against his ribs. He yanked his radio off his vest. "Daphne, where's Rowan?"

A crackle, then her voice, sharp and focused. "Still tracking. No signal yet. Backup en route. Elliot and Tessa left Liam and Bridger at the hospital— ETA eight minutes. Rest of the team, thirteen to fifteen."

Davey swallowed down the panic and turned back to Weston. "What the hell happened?"

"He doesn't need an interrogation right now." Cade's jaw ticked as he took in the full extent of his little brother's injuries. Blood matted Weston's dark hair, trickling down his temple and staining the collar of his tactical gear. His skin was ashen, eyes glassy.

"West," Cade said, his voice low and urgent. "Sit down."

That unfocused gaze went to the ground. "But Sabin..."

"We'll help him now."

"I got him," Dom said, shouldering his rifle and kneeling beside Sabin. He pulled the compact First Aid kit off his vest. His hands moved quickly, efficiently, as he assessed Sabin's injuries and tried to staunch the bleeding from the worst of his head wounds. "He's okay, West. It looks bad, but his pulse is steady, and he's a stubborn bastard. He'll live."

Apparently satisfied, Weston collapsed back on his butt and exhaled a ragged breath. Tears streaked from his eyes, leaving rivulets through the blood on his face. He probably didn't even realize he was crying. The guy was deep in shock.

Davey crouched in front of him and made his voice as gentle as possible despite the fear and rage crashing through his system with the adrenaline. "Hey, West. What happened?"

Weston blinked slowly like he didn't understand the question. "They... they weren't there. And then they were. Like ghosts. Like— No, not ghosts. He was... is... was... a—" He cut off, squeezing his temple like he could press the memory into place. "Fuck. My head."

Davey clenched his jaw. "West. Focus. Who took Rowan?"

"A shadow. But not... He was real. Solid. Like he stepped out of thin air. Moved like... like nothing I've ever seen. But I felt like I had seen him somewhere before. Like I knew—" He winced and touched the gash at his temple, hissing in pain. But his eyes cleared. "We didn't stand a chance. They had some kind of cloaking tech. We didn't see them coming."

"Waiting for us," Sabin muttered, voice hoarse. They all whipped toward him as he tried to push to his hands and feet. "Knew we were coming back. Had to be watching."

Dom put a hand on his back, keeping him still. "Stay down, buddy. You took a hell of a beating."

"*Oui*, okay, if you insist." He sank back to the ground with a groan. "I'll just lay here and get some beauty sleep, yeah?"

Dom huffed out a laugh. "You need it. That pretty face isn't so pretty right now, but you need to stay awake until we can get you professional help."

"My ma always says no help for me," Sabin muttered, his eyes fluttering closed.

Cade scoffed. "Jesus. The man's half-conscious and still cracking jokes."

Davey ignored them, his focus still on Weston. His chest burned. He couldn't seem to draw a full breath. "Who was it? West, you see where they took her? Any clue at all?"

Weston wiped blood from his mouth. "I don't know. I thought—" He stopped and a flicker of confusion crossed his face. Then, he winced hard, squeezing his eyes shut. "Ah, fuck. My head's splitting."

"I'm sure it is. It looks like someone tried to cleave it open," Cade said, his usually gruff voice gentle like he was soothing his daughter rather than his badass younger brother. "Lucky for you, you have a notoriously hard head."

"Yeah, lucky. The bastard was big. And fucking strong. He could've killed me easily." Weston's breath hitched. His fingers clenched the fabric of his blood-stained pants. For half a second, it looked like he might break completely.

Then Cade's grip tightened reassuringly on his shoulder and he exhaled. Blinked hard and looked at Davey. When he spoke, his voice was whisper. "I'm so sorry we couldn't stop them from taking her."

Davey's world tilted on its axis.

Jesus. Rowan was gone.

Someone had taken her.

The walls felt like they were closing in, his pulse a hammer, his breath coming sharp and uneven. He had to move. Had to do something. But there was no one left to hit. No one to shoot. No one to punish.

"Fuck!" He spun away, his body coiled so tight he could snap. His fists ached to smash something—anything—but he restrained himself. The only thing that mattered was getting her back in one piece and that would be much harder to do with a broken hand.

"It's Praetorian," Sullivan said, breaking his icy silence, and nudged one of the dead men with the toe of his boot. "Brody—" His voice cracked. He cleared his throat and continued, "Liam said he was in contact with someone. It had to be a Praetorian team."

Davey's stomach turned to stone. His hands curled into fists. The thought tried to unmoor him—but he couldn't afford that. Not now. He locked it down, forced the rage into something cold. Something sharp. Something lethal.

She was gone. Someone had taken her.

And whoever it was, they were about to learn exactly what it meant to steal from a Wilde.

"We're going after them." His voice was steel, cold and sharp and absolute. "We're bringing her back, and we're burning them to the ground."

"No." Cade's voice cut through the tunnel, firm and controlled. "Think, Davey. You can't go after Praetorian without proof."

Davey turned on him, rage thrumming under his skin. "Rowan is gone. She could be—"

He couldn't say it. Couldn't even think it.

Silence stretched between them, thick with tension. His breath came hard and fast, his body vibrating with the need to act, to do something. But Cade wasn't wrong.

That didn't make it any easier to accept.

Daphne's voice suddenly came back, sharp and urgent. "Davey."

He pressed his earpiece. "Go. Did you find her?"

"No, but Sully's right. It's Praetorian, and they just sent a message."

Ice slid down his spine. "What do they want?"

Daphne hesitated. Then, carefully, "You."

His pulse didn't spike. It did the opposite—it slowed. His breathing evened out, his muscles coiled tight. A predator locking onto its prey.

"They want you to meet them at The Echelon."

Cade grabbed his arm, his fingers digging in. "If

you charge into The Eschelon and start a war, we'll have every major power player in the world hunting us down. You want to get her back?" His voice dropped low. "You need to do this their way."

Davey's teeth ground together. "And what's that?"

Cade's jaw tightened. "Negotiate."

Negotiate.

The word slammed against the walls of his skull, jagged and impossible. He flinched like Cade had just put a knife in his gut.

"I'm not negotiating with the fuckers who stole her."

"And if you go in hot, they'll kill her before you even get close."

The tunnel seemed to shrink around him.

Fuck.

Cade was right.

They wanted him.

They wanted a war.

They had Rowan.

And they thought they had control.

His nails dug into his palms. One more second, and he might've shattered. But he exhaled instead, forcing the rage into something he could use. "I'm going."

Cade swore.

Silence from Daphne. Then, carefully, "You sure about that?"

Davey's hand curled into a fist, his knuckles aching. "I'm sure."

Because if Praetorian wanted to play games, they were about to find out just how badly they'd underestimated him.

If they wanted him?

They were getting him.

And they'd regret it.

thirty-seven

PAIN ARROWED through Rowan's skull, dragging her from the dark. It pulsed behind her eyes, a relentless, throbbing beat. Her body was slow to follow, limbs weighted and uncooperative.

There was a sound. A faint whirr, the soft vibration of an electric motor beneath her. The thrum of wheels on pavement. Moving. A vehicle.

Where was she going?

Where was—

The tunnel. The shadows. Weston bleeding. Sabin down.

Panic ignited, spreading through her limbs like fire.

Oh, God. Davey.

Was he alive? Had he been hurt? Or... worse?

No. No, she couldn't think like that. If anyone could fight his way through hell, it was Davey Wilde.

Her pulse kicked against her ribs, her breath coming short and sharp as she tried to remember more.

Chaos. Gunfire. The sickening crack of fists against flesh.

And the shadow with the cold, ink-black eyes....

She forced her eyes open.

And there he was.

The one who had held her back while Sabin was beaten into the ground. The one who had hurt Weston.

He sat across from her, his flat, dark gaze watching through the holes of the black balaclava he still wore.

Her muscles screamed in protest as she fought to sit up. Thick restraints dug into her wrists. Zip ties. She twisted, testing them, but they held firm. She turned her head, swallowing against the nausea rising in her throat, and saw the looming silhouette of a building through the window.

The Echelon.

Atlas Frost's luxury hotel. A sanctuary for the world's most powerful, where billion-dollar deals were sealed over whiskey. And now, it seemed, where captives were delivered like gifts.

She needed to get out of here.

Across from her, the icy bastard sat motionless, his dark gaze fixed straight ahead. Lights on, nobody home. It was weird. Unnervingly weird.

If she hadn't seen his buddies bleed out back in the

tunnel, she might've wondered if they were all machines.

But maybe he was distracted. Maybe—

She sucked in a breath and threw her weight toward the door in a last-ditch effort to escape.

She didn't have any real hope of it working. But she had to try.

Before she even registered his movement, he was already there, blocking her. One brutal hand wrapped around her throat.

Not squeezing.

Just there.

Just a reminder that she was his prey.

She froze.

He didn't even glance at her. Didn't react like he'd stopped an escape attempt. He just... adjusted to the situation. Like she was nothing more than a variable in an equation.

God. Maybe he really was a machine.

Her pulse fluttered under his fingertips as she glared at him, breathing hard.

"If I kick you, do you reboot?"

Nothing. No flicker of irritation, no hint of anger. He simply released her, shoved her back in the seat, and turned his head toward the window as the SUV slowed.

Her throat burned where his fingers had pressed. She wanted to lunge at him again. Wanted to fight, to make him feel something.

"Seriously, I've seen mannequins with more personality."

Still nothing.

She huffed out a laugh, shifting against her restraints, testing the zip ties again—not that it would do her any good.

"What are you, some kind of experiment?"

His fingers twitched, and he finally looked straight at her.

A cold ripple skated down her spine.

She'd hit something.

Not just a nerve. A fault line.

Slowly, she wet her lips. "Oh. Did I find a crack in your armor?"

For a second—a fraction of a second—a spark of life flickered behind those dead eyes. His fingers flexed and then curled into a fist.

And just like that, the spark went out.

Rowan got the sinking feeling she had just seen something he wasn't supposed to show. Something he wasn't supposed to have. A glitch in his programing.

Or maybe... something fighting to break free?

The vehicle rolled to a smooth stop.

The doors unlocked with a soft click and opened. Two more masked operatives stood there, weapons in hand.

The cold bastard stepped out first. He didn't offer a word or a glance in her direction. Just exited and waited.

The message was clear: *Move or be moved.*

Grinding her teeth, Rowan swung her legs out and stepped onto the pavement. The cold winter air bit at her overheated skin, a welcome contrast to the bruises blooming beneath her clothes.

Valets, dressed in sleek black uniforms, stood discreetly at their posts, eyes forward, trained to ignore anything that wasn't their business. The driveway gleamed under the glow of soft, recessed lighting, casting long shadows that stretched toward her like reaching hands.

She held her head high, matching her captors' pace, refusing to let them drag her like cargo.

The lobby was a cathedral of wealth and power.

Gilded chandeliers dripped from the high ceiling, giving the plush velvet seating and elegant sculptures a warm golden glow. Conversations murmured beneath the clink of crystal glasses. The air was thick with expensive perfume and the kind of arrogance that came with absolute control and disgusting wealth.

Nobody paid them any attention.

Nobody but Atlas Frost.

He was at the lobby bar, swirling a glass of something dark and expensive. His posture was relaxed, but his gaze was sharp. Watching. Calculating.

Their eyes met.

Emotion flickered across Frost's face—guilt, regret, hesitation. His tawny skin went pale, his blue eyes widening slightly before narrowing again, locking down whatever war was raging beneath the surface. He pushed away from the bar, and his lips parted as if he might actually say something, but then he caught himself.

Instead, almost imperceptibly, he mouthed, "Sorry."

Rowan's stomach twisted.

Just as quickly as the emotion appeared, it was gone, buried beneath a carefully constructed mask of indifference. He settled casually back into his seat and focused on a woman dripping in diamonds, smiling indulgently at whatever she said.

Bastard.

He knew exactly what was happening. He could stop it.

But he wouldn't.

Because doing so would cost him something— power, alliances, control—and she wasn't worth tipping the balance. She was just another expendable pawn on the board, another problem too inconvenient to solve.

A hand landed on her shoulder, guiding her forward. Not the icy bastard with the ink-black eyes this time, but someone else. Still, the touch made her skin crawl and Black Eyes was so close on her ass, she felt like he should at least buy her dinner first.

Her mind raced, cataloging every exit, every potential weapon, every face that turned their way.

But there was no opening, no weakness to exploit. The security was too tight, and the players were too powerful. She was outnumbered and outgunned.

As they approached the elevators, Rowan's heart rose into her throat. Once those doors closed, she'd be trapped. Cut off from any hope of rescue.

From Davey.

The thought of him sent a fresh wave of panic through her. Was he looking for her? Did he even know she was gone?

Yes and yes.

She knew those answers with absolute certainty. He knew she was gone by now, and he would tear the city apart to find her.

The elevator dinged softly, and the doors slid open with a whisper. Inside, the walls were mirrored, reflecting her captors and their prize infinitely as the numbers ticked higher. She looked like hell. Bruised, dirty, blood-streaked.

How had every person in the lobby just... looked away?

The ride was smooth and silent. She watched the numbers climb and couldn't help but feel like each passing floor brought her another second closer to death.

Time slipping. Options dwindling.

This was her last chance. If she was going to act, it had to be now.

The two men at her sides would be easy.

The one on her right stood stiff, tense. He was uncomfortable. Maybe he was the new guy, not yet jaded by the work.

The other was bulkier, but he was too comfortable. His stance was lazy. He didn't see her as a threat.

She could take them.

Black Eyes was the problem.

She knew he was fast. She'd barely seen him move before he'd had a hand around her throat. And he was almost supernaturally strong. Down in the tunnel, she'd thrown everything she had at him, and he'd held her back like it was nothing.

But even he wasn't immune to a bullet. If she got hold of one of the other guys' weapons, she could take him, too.

She tensed, preparing to make her move—

"I wouldn't," Black Eyes murmured, his voice low and cold. "You won't like the consequences."

Fuck.

She swallowed down her frustration and tried to keep her voice light. "Look at that. It does speak."

"Only when necessary."

She scoffed. "Go to hell, Terminator."

Again, that spark flared in his gaze, and a twist of a smile touched his lips. She swore she heard him murmur, "Already there," as the doors slid open on the 60th floor, revealing a corridor lined with dark wood paneling and soft, ambient lighting.

Another glitch.

Something she could exploit?

But as he shoved her out of the elevator car, that flicker of personality vanished. He was the black-eyed machine again.

He marched her to a set of huge double doors at the end of the hallway, removed his gloves, and pressed his thumb against a scanner. The doors unlocked with a muted click, and the other two men hung back as Black Eyes pushed her inside.

The penthouse was massive, filled with lush leather furniture, marble accents, and the kind of art that was more about price than appreciation. Floor-to-ceiling windows stretched over the glittering city below.

Then the doors closed, sealing her in with Black Eyes, who took up a parade rest stance behind her, blocking her escape.

"You've caused a lot of problems for us, Rowan Bristow."

Her gaze snapped toward the new voice. He was a brute wrapped in a tailored suit, his shoulders broad enough to block the light. His face was all sharp angles and cruel lines, a scar cutting through the stubble along his jaw.

This guy was the muscle, not the big boss in charge.

"Good," she said. "I hope I was a royal pain in your ass."

He chuckled, but there was no warmth in the sound. "I did hear you're a fighter. You like to win."

"Untie me, and I'll show you how much."

Cold, assessing eyes raked over her—a man appraising the durability of his new toy before deciding how hard he could break it. He tsked, obviously finding her lacking in some way. "Gabe Bristow's prodigal daughter. Tell me, does Daddy Dearest know about your... extracurricular activities?"

She remained silent, her gaze tracking his movement.

"Revenant One, you're dismissed," he ordered, without taking his eyes from her.

The black-eyed bastard—Revenant One—didn't hesitate. He was gone without a sound, the door clicking shut behind him.

Rowan's hands curled into fists behind her back. The fucking zipties were cutting off her circulation and her fingers tingled painfully.

He stopped in front of her, towering over her smaller frame. Not for the first time in her life, she wished she'd inherited her father's height as well as his bullheadedness.

"Not feeling chatty?" the brute said and lightly trailed his fingers over her shoulder. "That's all right. I have ways of making you talk."

She curled her lip in disgust. "I've dealt with men like you before. You're nothing special. You don't scare me."

"I doubt that very much." He leaned in close, his breath hot and moist against her ear. "You have no idea what I'm capable of. But you will learn. And by the time we're done, you'll beg to lose."

Her skin crawled, but she forced herself to remain still. She refused to give him the satisfaction of seeing her flinch.

The backhand came so fast she didn't see it coming. Pain exploded across her cheek as she stumbled sideways, vision blurring, blood filling her mouth. He seized her by the throat and slammed her against the wall, cutting off her air. Just as darkness started to creep in at the edges of her vision, he released her. She crumpled to the floor, gasping and coughing.

He loomed over her, a twisted smile on his face. "That's better. On your knees where you belong."

Rage and humiliation burned through Rowan. She glared up at him, hatred blazing in her eyes. "Fuck you," she spat, blood and saliva spraying from her lips.

His boot connected with her ribs. Pain exploded through her side as she curled in on herself, struggling to breathe.

He drew a knife from under his suit jacket and crouched down, laying the flat of the blade under her jaw, forcing her to look up at him.

"You know, I've always been fascinated by the human body." His voice was deceptively soft, but his eyes glittered with cruel anticipation as he traced the knife along her collarbone, leaving a thin red line in its wake. "The way muscles and tendons work together, the intricate network of nerves…" He pressed the tip against her shoulder, just hard enough to dimple the skin and draw a pinprick of blood. "I've always wondered just how much you can cut off a person before they break. Physically. Mentally." The knife danced along her collarbone, then traced her arm down to her bound hands.

She curled her fingers into tight fists, but he drove his thumb into a pressure point, forcing her fingers open. The tip of the blade pressed into the skin at the base of her index finger.

"How do you think Daddy would react if he received your trigger finger in the mail?"

Rowan's stomach churned with revulsion and fear, but she forced herself to meet the brute's gaze defiantly. "He'd hunt you down and tear you apart piece by piece."

He chuckled, and he sounded genuinely amused. "Maybe thirty years ago. Now he sends the likes of Davey Wilde to do his dirty work."

Then the door opened again.

Revenant One stepped in again, gave the room one quick, assessing scan, then moved aside and held the door open. The air itself seemed to still, tension stretching taut as if the very room was recalibrating in response to this new man's presence. Even the brute went still like an animal that had just realized it wasn't the apex predator in the room anymore.

This man wore power like a pristine suit, tailored just for him.

And, suddenly, Rowan knew without a shadow of a doubt that he was the man behind everything.

His gaze settled on her. A heartbeat passed. Then, those eyes shifted to the brute, and there was the briefest flicker of disgust. "Enough."

One word, nothing more.

But it was absolute.

The brute straightened and hauled her back to her feet, his grip bruising her arm. "I was questioning her."

Revenant One shut the door and again took up an alert, military-rigid stance beside it, hands folded in front of him, eyes forward.

"I didn't tell you to question her, Raines." The man stepped closer, his movements fluid and precise. He was older than Raines, perhaps in his early fifties, with salt-and-pepper hair and a face that might have been handsome if not for the utter lack of warmth in his eyes. They were the color of flint. "I believe I made myself clear that Ms. Bristow is not to be harmed."

Raines's jaw tightened, but he didn't argue. "Yes, sir. My apologies."

"Leave us," he commanded, his voice smooth and cold as polished marble.

Raines hesitated for a fraction of a second, his

fingers digging into Rowan's bicep. But then he released her with a curt nod. "Yes, sir."

As Raines exited the room, Revenant One stepped forward and efficiently cut the zip ties binding her wrists. She rubbed at the angry red marks, eyeing both men warily.

"That will be all, One," the man said without looking at his subordinate.

Revenant One inclined his head and departed without a word.

The door clicked shut, leaving Rowan alone with the man who had so effortlessly brought Raines to heel. She held her aching wrists close to her body, her muscles coiled tight, ready to fight or run at the first opening.

But the man simply moved to the bar, poured two glasses of amber liquid, and turned to offer one to Rowan.

"Drink," he said. It wasn't a request.

"I'll pass."

The man's lips curved into a cold smile. "It's not poisoned, Ms. Bristow. If I truly wanted you dead for your disobedience, I'd have sent Revenant One months ago." He held out the glass again. "It'll help the headache."

Her head *was* thundering, and she hated that he knew that. She took the glass, if only to have something to throw at his head. The whiskey burned as it slid down her throat, warming her from the inside out.

He took a sip from his own glass, then set it on the bar. "I apologize for Malcolm's... enthusiasm. He can be overzealous at times." He gestured to one of the plush leather armchairs. "Please, sit."

She didn't move. "Who are you?"

"Alexander Stirling." He walked over to the wall of windows, gazing out over the glittering city. It had started snowing, and the flakes swirled against the glass, obscuring the skyline. "I lead the Praetorian Group."

Stirling.

It was a name whispered in dark corners, the boogeyman of the intelligence world, the puppet master pulling strings from the shadows. He was rarely ever seen, but he'd crawled out of whatever luxurious cave he'd holed up in to... what?

Kill her?

Kill Davey?

She clenched her hand around her glass, fighting the urge to lunge at him. "What do you want?"

Stirling turned from the window but didn't answer right away. He simply studied her like a man appraising a chess game. Then he smiled like he'd already figured out checkmate.

"Oh, Ms. Bristow," he said, voice smooth as the whiskey in his glass. "I want everything."

thirty-eight

DAVEY STEPPED out of the sleek black car that had been sent to WSW headquarters for him and eyed The Echelon's entrance. He rolled his shoulders, exhaling slow and controlled. Unarmed. Outnumbered. Walking straight into a den of vipers.

Every instinct in his body told him to turn back.

He ignored it.

Because Rowan was in there.

The lobby was exactly what he expected—power wrapped in a velvet chokehold. There were more black-clad soldiers, like the ones from the tunnel, stationed at key points. A force meant to be invisible, but he knew exactly what they were. He didn't recognize any of them, but one caught his eye. Broad frame, dark eyes, standing too still.

Something nagged at him, but he pushed it aside as Malcolm Raines stepped forward. From what

Daphne had managed to dig up on Praetorian, he knew Raines was Alexander Stirling's right-hand man. He also knew the guy was a twisted fuck. If Rowan had spent any time alone with the man, she might not be in good shape.

"This way," Raines said, voice clipped, and held out an arm toward the elevators. There was a small spatter of blood on the edge of his sleeve. Fresh, but it didn't appear to be his.

It took everything in Davey not to react. His stomach clenched, but he forced himself to keep walking, keep breathing.

She was alive.

She had to be.

Across the room, Atlas Frost lounged at the bar, but he ignored the woman all but throwing herself into his lap and instead stared at the closed elevator doors with narrow-eyed intensity. When Davey and Raines reached the elevator, he met Davey's gaze and nodded.

A greeting or a warning? It was anyone's guess.

The ride up was suffocating. The mirrored walls reflected Raines's smug sneer. Bastard was enjoying this.

The doors slid open, and Raines led him to a penthouse guarded by two more of the black-clad soldiers. One of them opened the door and motioned Davey inside.

Rowan.

She was sitting in a high-backed leather chair, clenching an empty glass in her hand. Bruised, her lip bleeding, but very much alive.

Thank God.

Their gazes locked, and relief slammed into him so hard it almost knocked him off balance.

Her posture was stiff, wary—but not broken. Anger burned in her gaze, and that alone let him breathe again.

"Mr. Wilde." The voice was calm, almost pleasant. "Thanks for joining us."

"You didn't give much choice, Stirling." Davey tore his gaze away from Rowan and turned to the man standing near the windows, dressed in a perfectly tailored suit, silver-streaked hair neatly combed back.

"No, I didn't," Stirling said smoothly. "Sit. It's time we talked."

Davey didn't move. "You could've tried that before resorting to violence."

"Violence hadn't been my original plan."

"You put a hit on me and strapped a bomb to my cousin."

"Hm, yes. Things escalated." Stirling crossed to the bar and refilled his own glass before pouring another and holding it out. "Let's get to the point, shall we?"

Davey didn't reach for the drink and instead crossed his arms. "Yeah, let's. I want you to stop attacking me, my friends, and my family. What do you want?"

Stirling set the drink on the coffee table as he sat across from Rowan. He leaned back and sipped his drink, watching Davey with an almost clinical detachment. "Not you." His gaze shifted to Rowan before turning dismissively away again. "And not even her. I'll let you both walk out of here if you agree to my terms."

Davey frowned. This wasn't what he expected. "What terms?"

"Give me Cade Wilde."

Cade?

The demand didn't make sense.

Davey's gut twisted, his instincts screaming that there was a larger play in motion, one he couldn't see yet.

He inhaled slowly. "No. My family is off the table."

"You misunderstand, Mr. Wilde. This is not a negotiation. It's a transaction. Cade for Ms. Bristow."

"Then you're leaving empty-handed," Davey shot back.

Stirling's expression remained calm, but there was something darker lurking beneath. He flicked his fingers, and Raines moved to stand behind Rowan with a gun in hand. He pressed the barrel against Rowan's temple.

Davey's heart slammed against his ribs.

"I wonder," Raines mused, "just how stubborn you'll be with her brains splattered on your shirt."

Rowan went utterly still, her jaw tight, but her eyes locked on his. "Don't, Davey. I'm not worth it."

How could she think that? How could she not know by now that she was worth everything to him? He'd give up Cade for her in a heartbeat. He'd give up WSW. Hell, he'd burn down the world for her if she asked him, too.

He forced his attention back to Stirling. "Why do you want Cade?"

"That's for me to know." Stirling sipped his drink and smiled like this was amusing to him. "This is mercy, Mr. Wilde. Take it while it's still on the table."

Davey let out a slow breath. His grip on control was desperate and razor-thin, and he felt like he might snap at any second. His pulse was a hammer in his ears, and his muscles coiled so tight they ached. His gaze flicked from Stirling to Raines and back to Rowan, measuring every angle, every risk. He needed an opening, a weakness. But there was nothing.

He could take Raines, but not before the bastard pulled the trigger. He could go for Stirling, but that wouldn't stop the dozen black-clad operatives stationed throughout the building.

No clear exits.

No easy outs.

Just a line he had to walk without slipping, and backing down wasn't an option. If he let them see weakness now, they'd exploit it the next time.

Because there would be a next time.

His skin prickled with sweat beneath his shirt, and his muscles ached from holding tension too long, from fighting the raw, animal urge to lunge. To do something.

But he couldn't win this through physical force. He had to talk his way out, and he suddenly wished Elliot was in his ear. He could use his brother's calm logic right now, but it was just him, and he couldn't afford to fuck this up.

What would Elliot tell him?

Don't panic. Think, Davey. Outplay them. Trust your gut.

All his instincts told him the same thing: Stirling was bluffing.

"You call this mercy?" His voice was low, lethal. "You put a gun to her head and make demands, and now you expect me to thank you for sparing her?"

Stirling laughed softly. "I expect you to understand the reality of your situation and that this is the best offer you're going to get."

Davey held the man's gaze, hate boiling up to fill every inch of him. "Let's be real. You need this just as much as I do. Otherwise, you wouldn't still be talking. So, yes, this *is* a negotiation. Call off your rabid attack dog, and then we can talk like civilized men."

Stirling's expression didn't change, but Davey caught the slight pause before he nodded to Raines. He hadn't liked being called out like that.

Scowling, Raines backed up a step. He removed the

gun from Rowan's temple but still kept it trained on her.

Stirling smoothly regained his composure. "All right. Let's negotiate. My offer remains the same. Give me Cade, and you and Rowan walk out of here unharmed."

"What about the contract on my head?"

"I'll remove it."

"And Rowan's family will be safe?"

Stirling exhaled like this was all a big annoyance to him and waved a dismissive hand. "I have no interest in them."

Davey uncrossed his arms, trying to look casual despite the adrenaline roaring through him. "You're not getting Cade. What else do you want?"

Stirling leaned forward, his eyes narrowing. "Your bravado is impressive, but since we're being 'real' with each other, at least admit you don't trust him. You want him gone. It'll make your life easier."

"Maybe, I'm not giving him to you like a goddamn Christmas gift."

"Okay, then fire him." Stirling spread his hands. " It's win-win. You get rid of him, and it gives me the opportunity to recruit him."

Davey forced himself to stay loose, tilting his head slightly as if considering the offer, like he might actually be weighing it. But he wasn't. He was watching, waiting, searching for cracks in Stirling's carefully constructed mask, all while keeping Raines's gun in his periphery.

One wrong move, one miscalculation, and Raines would pull the trigger just to prove a point. The bastard was itching for an excuse.

"You really want Cade that bad?"

No reaction.

"You could've gone after him years ago, but you didn't. Why now? What changed?"

It was subtle, but Davey caught the barest flicker in Stirling's expression. A shift in his posture. An almost imperceptible glance toward the black-clad soldiers stationed by the door.

Gotcha.

Davey laughed, genuinely amused. "If you think you can turn Cade into one of your mindless drones, you don't know him. He doesn't do orders. Or rules."

Stirling's smile simmered with irritation. "As I said before, my reasons are inconsequential. What matters is your answer."

Davey let the silence stretch, enjoying the way Stirling's mask slipped by degrees as each second ticked by. Then, finally, he inclined his head. "I could agree to your terms, but Cade is family. To betray family, I'm going to need more from you."

Stirling's eyebrows rose. "More than your lives?"

Davey didn't blink. "Yes. Because we both know Rowan and I are already walking out of here alive. Killing us in your suite would start a war with Praetorian on one side and WSW and HORNET on the other. Don't need to be a psychic to figure out how badly that would end for you. It's why you haven't done it already. So, yeah, I want more. I want a full list of Praetorian's moles inside WSW. And if you have any in HORNET, I want their names, too. Every last one. Names, locations, and confirmation they've been pulled out. And I want proof that no further action will be taken against us or our families."

"That's ambitious."

"It's non-negotiable. You want Cade? Then I want to know I'm not getting another knife in the back next week like I got tonight."

Stirling tapped his fingers against his glass again, considering, then set the drink down with a loud thunk. "You already have Broderick O'Connell."

Davey leaned forward, his voice low. "Brody is dead. And if you don't pull the rest of your operatives, I'll make sure you lose every fucking one of them."

Raines stiffened, his grip on the gun tightening as if waiting for a signal.

Stirling raised a hand, stilling him. "What do you think, Rowan?" He turned his attention to her, ignoring Davey's threat. "You think we'll go to war over you?"

"Not over me." Rowan rose from her seat to stand beside Davey, and he felt her hand brush his. It steadied him, reminded him that they were in this together.

Hatred burned in her eyes when she refocused on Stirling, but her smile was ice cold. "But I do think you're lying when you say you don't care about my family. They scare you, and they should."

Stirling sat back, his fingers steepled in thought. "Your terms will take time."

"You have twenty-four hours," Davey said.

"And Cade?"

"Cade stays with us until I get what I want."

"You're in no position to impose such demands."

"Then shoot us," Davey challenged. "See what happens."

Stirling's eyes narrowed to calculating slits. "You're asking me to trust you," he said slowly, testing the words like they were foreign.

"Yep."

"And in return, I get nothing but your word."

"Yep."

Stirling's jaw tightened, and Davey thought the man might actually snap. But then he stood and straightened his suit before holding out a hand. "We have an agreement. I'll remove my operatives in the next twenty-four hours, and you'll remove Cade from your payroll."

"And you'll remove the contract on me?"

"It's already done."

"Then we agree." Davey accepted the handshake, but he didn't relax. Not yet. Not until they were out of this place.

He took Rowan's hand the moment he released Stirling's, and they turned toward the door.

And Stirling took his final shot: "You think you won something today, Wilde. But trust me—one day, you'll realize what you lost."

Davey didn't break stride. Didn't turn. Didn't give Stirling the satisfaction of seeing his reaction. "The only thing I lost today is my patience with you."

The elevator doors slid shut, sealing them away from Stirling and his men, and Rowan exhaled in a rush.

Davey turned to her, pulling her into his chest, locking his arms tightly around her. She tensed for half a second, then melted into him, pressing her forehead against his shoulder. He felt her breath hitch, the tension she'd been holding finally cracking just a little.

"Are you okay?" he murmured, voice rough.

Her fingers curled into his shirt. "Not yet. But I will be."

His grip tightened. "You scared me, Hellcat."

She pulled back just enough to look at him. "I knew you'd come."

Jesus, she was beautiful, even covered in bruises. She was stubborn and fierce and everything he'd ever wanted.

"Always." He cupped the side of her face gently, brushing his thumb over a fresh cut on her cheekbone, then leaned down to kiss her. He couldn't take it as deep as he wanted, couldn't brand himself on her like he wanted, but for these few stolen moments as the elevator descended, he poured everything he had into that kiss—relief, fear, desperation, and love. So much love it threatened to overwhelm him.

For just a moment, the chaos faded, and all that mattered was that she was here. Safe. Alive.

He broke the kiss and pressed his forehead to hers. "I never want to see a gun to your head again."

A ghost of a smirk tugged at her bruised lips. "Next time, you'll have to look away."

It was such a perfectly Rowan response, and even as much as he hated the way she plowed into danger, it was also why he loved her.

Still, he groaned. "Next time?"

"There will always be a next time."

"Because my hellcat doesn't know how to live a danger-free life."

She exhaled shakily and drew back, searching his gaze. "I told you I didn't. I told you a normal, white picket fence life is not for me. You said you didn't care. You said—"

He stopped her with another short, hard kiss. "I know what I said. And I meant it. If I have to fight through hell, I'd rather do it with you. I want you by my side. Always. Forever. Through sickness and health and megalomaniacs."

Rowan gave him a tired smirk, resting her head against his chest. "I love you."

He let out a slow breath, his hand sliding up her back, fingers tangling in her hair as he held her close. "I love you too, Hellcat. More than you'll ever know."

She tipped her head back to look at him, something softer flickering in her bruised eyes. "Even if I drive you insane?"

His lips brushed against her temple. "Especially because you drive me insane."

Rowan huffed a quiet laugh, her grip tightening on his jacket. "Good. Because you're stuck with me."

"Exactly where I want to be." He leaned in to kiss her again, but the elevator dinged, and he reluctantly released her as the doors slid open. They stepped out into the opulent lobby, and he was hyper-aware of the eyes on them. The black-clad soldiers hadn't moved, including the one that had set off his warning bells on the way up.

Rowan leaned into his side and whispered, "Stirling called that guy Revenant One. He led the ambush in the tunnel, and he's ice cold." She hesitated, then added, "He took Weston down without blinking like it was nothing—almost like he was programmed for it. And when he grabbed me..." She swallowed. "He's impossibly strong, Davey. He held me there and made me watch as his men beat Sabin to death."

"Sabin's very much alive and still cracking jokes. Weston, too. They'll be okay."

"Oh, thank God."

He glanced back at the soldier, at the broad frame, the dark, dead eyes behind the black mask, the way he stood too still. Something familiar there. Something that itched in the back of his mind.

Revenant One was trouble.

His hand found the small of Rowan's back, a protective gesture as much as a reassuring one. He guided her across the gleaming marble floor of the lobby. If anyone noticed her bruises or split lip, they quickly turned away and minded their own business.

Just another night at The Echelon.

Atlas Frost was still at the bar, swirling the same glass of whiskey. His eyes tracked their movement, a knowing smirk playing at his lips. He raised his glass in a silent toast as they passed.

Yeah, Fuck Frost.

Whatever game he was playing, now wasn't the time to confront it.

But as they stepped into the night, Stirling's words whispered back through his mind.

One day, you'll realize what you lost.

He had a sinking feeling that day was already here.

thirty-nine

DAVEY STOOD at the rooftop door, the handle cold beneath his fingers. Cade was already out there, back turned, shoulders rigid, the bitterly cold wind snapping at his shirt like it was trying to rip him away.

The sunrise reflected off the glass towers of the city like fire.

Somehow, it was morning.

The last time they'd stood on a rooftop together watching the sunrise, it had been after a late night of drunken escapades, not... whatever the hell this was now. Not standing on opposite sides of a fault line, waiting for it to crack wide open.

Jesus, he wasn't ready for this. He wasn't sure if he'd ever be ready.

He stepped forward, his boots scuffing against the concrete. Cade didn't turn, but Davey knew he'd heard him. Cade always had a way of knowing when someone was there—one of the things that had made him so good at his job. One of the things Davey used to admire.

"I figured you'd come up here," Davey said, keeping his voice low. Neutral. "We both like to brood on rooftops."

Cade snorted but didn't respond, his gaze still fixed on the skyline.

Silence stretched between them. Davey forced himself to breathe through it as he searched for the right words. None came. He'd never been good at this — at talking when it mattered.

"Cade, about what happened—"

"Don't." Cade cut him off, finally turning to face him. His blue eyes burned with anger, but there was something else there, too. Something that looked like betrayal. Maybe sorrow. And a touch of hate. "Don't do the whole 'let's talk it out' thing. I know you don't mean it."

God save him from stubborn Wildes. They were all the same—proud, reckless, and incapable of giving an inch, even when it cost them everything.

He bit back a curse and tried to keep his voice level. "That's not fair."

Cade let out a sharp breath, his fists clenching at his sides. "Yeah? Well, neither is getting sold out by my own goddamn family."

"I didn't—" Davey caught himself on the edge of the explosion. That was what Cade wanted. He wanted anger and punches because that was easier than talking. "Look, I'm here, aren't I? If I didn't really want to work this out, would I be up here, freezing my ass off, when I just got my woman back?"

"Yeah, you would," Cade snapped. "Guilt has always been your best motivator."

Davey exhaled his frustration in a low, slow breath that clouded in the air. "Of course I feel guilty. I accused you of being the mole. I didn't want to believe it, but the evidence—"

"The evidence was bullshit, and you knew it. But you still looked at me like I was the enemy. And now you're firing me?"

Still trying to ignite that explosion. Well, he wasn't going to get it. "I was—and still am—only trying to protect the company. The family. You think I wanted to suspect you? To fire you? You think I've enjoyed any of this?"

"You didn't hesitate." His voice was louder now, rough and frayed at the edges, barely held back. "Not for a second. Either time. You just decided I was guilty. End of story."

"We had evidence—"

"Bullshit evidence."

"Maybe, but what was I supposed to do? Ignore it?"

"You could've trusted me," Cade said, his voice quieter now but no less cutting. "That's what you were supposed to do."

Davey exhaled sharply, dragging a hand through his hair. "You punched me at Christmas when you found out the uncles were giving me the company."

"And now you're taking WSW and throwing me out with the trash. Hell of a full-circle moment."

The words hit harder than Davey expected, knocking the wind out of him for a beat. He looked away, his gaze drifting to the city below, to the faint glow of dawn bleeding into the skyline. "You're right. I never should have accused you. I fucked up. I let my doubts get in the way, and I'm sorry. But, Jesus, Cade, do you think I wanted to fire you? I didn't have a choice. They had a fucking gun to Rowan's head, and it was the only way to make the deal work. I never wanted any of this. I never wanted us to—" He stopped, swallowing hard. "I miss the way things used to be with us."

Cade scoffed. His hands curled into fists, knuckles whitening. "You miss it? Really?" He let out a humorless exhale, his breath shaking with the force of everything he wasn't saying. "You're the one who came back from the military, the conquering hero with the busted-up leg, and took everything I've spent my life working for."

"That's not true," Davey snapped, anger flaring despite the lead weight of guilt in his gut. "I didn't want to take anything from you."

Cade's eyes burned into him, searing with something deeper than anger. Resentment. Betrayal. Hurt.

"Yeah? Well, you did." His voice cracked, but he steam-rolled past it. "You think I don't know how people look at me now? I'm the fuck-up. The problem. The guy the uncles didn't trust. The guy barely keeping his shit together. But you?" He let out a sharp laugh, shaking his head. "You get handed the company, the loyalty, the legacy—like it was always supposed to be yours because you were born first. Like all the work I've done for this fucking company—this family—never even mattered. Like I never even mattered."

Davey's breath came sharper now, the fight in him clawing to be let loose. "You know I never wanted WSW. I never wanted to be in charge, but I did it because the uncles asked me to."

Cade let out another bitter, humorless laugh. "You could've said no."

"Yeah, I could've, but I didn't. If I could go back…" Davey exhaled hard, dragging a hand through his hair. "No, I won't lie to you. I would've still signed those papers. I love you, Cade. You're family, but—"

Cade's head snapped toward him, his eyes flashing. "Family," he repeated, voice rough. "Family didn't stop Brody from betraying Sullivan. Didn't stop Sullivan from pulling the trigger and putting a bullet in his brother."

Davey's stomach twisted. The fractures between Brody and Sullivan led them to that bridge over the river. And now, staring at Cade, Davey wondered if they could heal this fracture between them or if they were headed toward another bridge somewhere down the road.

"Cade—"

"No. I don't need your pity, and I don't need your apology. What I need—" He stopped short, exhaling through his nose. "What I needed was for you to let me do my job without treating me like a liability."

Davey's throat tightened. "You've never been a liability."

"And yet you all but handled me to Praetorian on a silver platter."

Silence.

Davey felt it like a fist to the ribs—sharp, unrelenting, and deserved. Because he had. He had. He'd sat in that goddamn penthouse and let Stirling name his price. He'd agreed to cut Cade loose to save Rowan, to end the threat, to walk away from that table with his people still breathing.

And it didn't matter that he'd had no other choice. Cade was still the one who paid the price.

Guilt churned in his gut, but fuck if he could afford to drown in it now. "We'll figure out a way to keep you on the payroll."

Cade let out a sharp, humorless laugh, shaking his head like he couldn't believe what he was hearing. "Keep me on the payroll? Jesus, Davey."

His voice was quieter now, but that only made it worse. "You think this is about a paycheck? That you can write a number on a check and make this go away?" His lips curled into something almost like a smirk, but there was no amusement in it. Just something hollow. "You didn't just fire me. You traded me."

The word hit like a punch to the ribs, and he couldn't control his sharp intake of breath. "Cade—"

"You let Stirling put my name on the table like it was a fucking bargaining chip. Like I was something to be leveraged. And now you want to throw me a bone? Like that'll fix it?" He pushed away from the railing and turned, his eyes burning. "You can't fix this, Davey. You got what you wanted. The company, the trust, the team. You don't need me. And honestly? I don't think I need you anymore, either. So let me save you the trouble of firing me. I quit."

The words cut deeper than Davey cared to admit. He opened his mouth to argue, to plead, but Cade didn't give him the chance. He brushed past him, his shoulder bumping Davey's, and walked toward the stairwell door.

"Cade—" Davey tried again, but the door slammed shut.

Davey stood frozen, staring at the spot where Cade had been. The weight in his chest felt unbearable as if something had cracked wide open, and he wasn't sure it could ever be put back together.

The door behind him creaked open, and he thought—hoped—it might be Cade coming back. He turned, but it was Rowan who stepped out, her silhouette backlit by the warm glow of the stairwell.

She hesitated, her hand resting on the doorframe. "Hey."

"Hey." His voice was rougher than he wanted it to be, the weight of everything pressing down on him. He turned back to the skyline, his shoulders tight. He didn't want her to see how much Cade's departure had gutted him.

But then, this was Rowan—she probably already knew.

She crossed the rooftop, the click of her boots soft against the concrete. She stopped beside him, so close that her shoulder brushed his arm, warm even through the chill of the early morning air. She didn't say anything, just stood there, her gaze on the horizon where streaks of gold and violet bled into the city skyline.

"Hell of a night."

His laugh was rough, nearly a scoff. "Understatement, Hellcat."

She reached for his arm, fingers curling around his bicep as she leaned her head against his shoulder. "I saw him on the stairs. He looked pissed. You okay?"

Davey let out a slow breath and turned toward her, dragging her into his arms, needing her warmth, her presence. He buried his face in her hair and repeated her words from the elevator: "Not really."

She smiled, but worry filled her eyes as she pulled back to study his face. She brushed a wayward lock of hair from his forehead. "He'll cool off and come around."

He wanted to believe that, but...

He shook his head. "You didn't see the look in his eyes, Ro. I offered to keep him in the company, off the books, but he quit. And he meant it. He's done."

"Maybe for now," she said. "But people don't stay angry forever."

"Have you met Cade?"

She huffed a small laugh. "I have, and I stand by what I said. Even he won't stay angry forever. He cares too much. About you, this company, this insane family of yours."

His throat tightened. "It's not just anger. He doesn't trust me anymore. And maybe he's right not to. I fucked this all up."

Rowan tilted her head up to meet his gaze, her touch achingly gentle as she cupped his face, her thumbs brushing over the tension at his jaw. He closed his eyes for half a second, just long enough to absorb the warmth of her hands, to hold onto the moment before reality crashed back down on him.

"Don't do that," she murmured. "Don't carry all of this on yourself. What happened wasn't all on you."

He stared down at her. "Feels like it is."

She stepped closer until there was nothing between them but the press of her body and the steady thrum of his heartbeat against her own. Her fingers traced the edge of his jaw before sliding down his arms, linking their hands together. "You're not perfect, Davey. You're human. You make mistakes. But you're also the most loyal, protective person I've ever met. Cade knows that. He just needs time."

He searched her face, looking for cracks, for hesitation. But she believed in him. Even now. Even after everything. The weight of that belief—of her love—settled deep in his chest. Humbling. Terrifying.

"What did I do to deserve you?"

Rowan's lips curved. "Probably something fantastic in a past life. Maybe you saved the world."

Despite himself, he chuckled, the sound low and rough, but God, he felt like she was the world. And maybe he hadn't saved it before, but he'd spend the rest of his life trying to keep her safe, keep her standing, keep her here.

The tension in his chest loosened just a little as he took a slow, steadying breath.

Rowan's gaze softened, her hazel eyes catching the sunrise, making them glow with something almost too bright, too good, too much. "For real, though, I'll tell you exactly what you did," she murmured, her fingers brushing over his like an anchor. "You've fought for me, Davey. Even when I made it impossible."

"I'll fight for you forever."

Her eyebrows lifted. "Forever, huh?"

"Yeah." His voice was rough, steady, an oath, a promise, a truth written into his damn bones. "I'm serious, Ro. If I have to spend the rest of my life proving how much you mean to me, I'll do it. Every damn day."

Her lips parted, something unreadable, raw, and beautiful passing through her expression—like maybe she felt the weight of his words settle somewhere deep.

Davey couldn't resist the invitation of her parted lips. He bent his head, closing the space between them, his lips brushing over hers—soft at first, almost reverent. But when she sighed against him, he deepened it, one hand sliding to cup the back of her neck, the other gripping her waist like he needed to anchor himself to her, to this moment. To something real.

She melted into him, her fingers curling into his shirt, holding him like she wasn't planning to let go. And, Jesus, he never wanted her to. He kissed her slow and steady, pouring everything into it—his relief, his devotion, the aching gratitude that she was here, safe, his.

Forever.

Then she made a small sound—a sweet, soft hum in the back of her throat—and it sent heat curling low in his gut. His mind flickered back to yesterday, to the feel of his back against his desk, her knees clamped around his hips as she rode him, the way she moaned as she sank onto him. He was suddenly very aware of how close they were, of how easy it would be to take her downstairs, lock the office door, and finish what they started.

But just as he started to pull her closer, Rowan let out a quiet laugh and pulled back, pressing a single finger against his lips. "Hold that thought."

Davey blinked through the haze of lust, his brain taking a moment to catch up to the sudden change. "What?"

"There's someone you need to meet first." The spark of mischief returned to her eyes, but this time, it didn't quite hide the softness beneath it. "My parents are downstairs, and my dad has questions. *Lots* of questions."

Davey's stomach dropped. "Your dad."

"Yep." She patted his chest, her grin widening. "And my mom. Don't worry— they're mostly harmless. Dad's only brought, like, three knives."

"Not funny," he muttered.

"Come on." Rowan squeezed his hand reassuringly as she tugged him toward the door. "You'll survive. Probably."

forty

DAVEY FOLLOWED Rowan down the sleek staircase from the rooftop, the sound of her boots a steady rhythm against the polished steel steps. Each step felt heavier than the last as the weight of what lay ahead settled on his chest. Meeting Rowan's father wasn't something he'd prepared for—especially not when that father was Gabe Bristow, a man who could make Navy SEALs quake in their boots with a single glare.

"Relax," Rowan said over her shoulder, her tone light but laced with amusement. "He doesn't bite."

Davey let out a dry chuckle. "That's not exactly comforting, considering I've heard what he does do."

She paused at the bottom of the stairs, turning to face him with a smirk that was both infuriating and endearing. "You'll be fine. Just don't say anything stupid."

"Great advice," he deadpanned. "Anything else? Like how to dodge flying knives?"

Her eyes sparkled with mischief. "Oh, he doesn't throw knives. He just uses them to... make a point. Usually in soft, sensitive parts of the anatomy."

Davey's stomach dropped, and he barely resisted the urge to shield his balls. "Oh, fuck."

Rowan laughed, the sound soft and teasing. She reached out, brushing her fingers over his arm. "I'm kidding. Mostly."

"Mostly?" he muttered under his breath.

Before he could talk himself out of it, she grabbed his hand and gave it a reassuring squeeze. "Relax, Davey. It's just my dad."

"Yeah? Then why do I feel like I'm walking into my execution?"

She just laughed, pushed open the door to his office, and stepped aside, letting him walk in first.

Davey froze.

Oh, shit.

He'd been preparing himself for Gabe Bristow's infamous death glare. He had not been preparing for this meeting to take place in his damn office.

Or for Gabe Bristow to be standing in front of the same desk Davey had very recently—

Jesus Christ.

His face went scorching hot before he could stop it.

Rowan knew. He could tell by the way her lips

twitched, by the barely concealed amusement in her hazel eyes. She was enjoying this.

Meanwhile, Gabe was staring at him. Arms crossed, stance deceptively casual but radiating authority. His gold eyes locked onto Davey, sizing him up in a single glance.

Behind him, Audrey sat perched on the edge of the desk—*the desk*—her gray hair streaked with wild shades of teal and purple, her smile warm.

Next to her sat Rue, who was a carbon copy of their mother.

And then there was Gabe. Still staring.

Davey resisted the urge to gulp. He'd faced down armed enemies, infiltrated hostile territories, and survived things most men couldn't fathom—

But the steely gaze of Rowan's father? That was something else entirely.

Gabe didn't say anything. He just kept looking at him. Like he was trying to decide how many different ways he could kill him.

Audrey tilted her head, watching Davey's sudden shift in color. Then her gaze flicked to the desk.

Something clicked.

Her lips twitched.

Oh, fuck no.

"Everything all right, Davey?" she asked sweetly.

Rue's gaze followed hers. She looked at the desk. Then at Rowan. Then back at Davey.

And then she grinned like the little menace she was.

"Oh my God. Did you two—" she pointed at the desk, then back at them, "—on the desk?"

Davey choked on air.

Gabe's expression turned lethal. "What."

Audrey smacked her husband. Not on the arm or shoulder. No, she slapped his ass. "Oh, c'mon, sailor. Like we've never done it on your desk at home. In fact, yesterday…"

"Oh, no!" Rue clamped her hands over her ears. "No, no, no. We're resetting this conversation right now." She dropped her hands from her ears with an exaggerated shudder and pretended to jab a button. "Reset. I came here for an interrogation, maybe some bloodshed, not psychological trauma."

"You started it," Rowan pointed out, smirking.

Rue ignored her, turning to her father. "Aren't you supposed to be threatening him or something?"

Gabe, who had been glaring at the desk like it had personally wronged him, exhaled through his nose and dragged his death stare back to Davey.

"Right," he muttered, straightening to his full, imposing height. "Where were we?"

Davey braced himself.

Gabe held out a hand. "I never thought my daughter would end up with a Wilde."

Davey's hand was engulfed in an iron grip, the older

man's palm callused from years of hard work and combat. He exhaled and met Gabe's gaze steadily, refusing to flinch even though his face still felt like it was on fire.

"Sir," he said, proud that his voice was calm. "It's an honor to meet you."

Gabe's eyes narrowed slightly, searching his face for any sign of weakness. "Is it now? And why's that?"

He could feel Rowan's eyes on him and knew she was waiting to see how he'd handle her father's interrogation. He took a deep breath, choosing his words carefully. "Because you raised an incredible daughter."

"Yeah, I did." Gabe's grip turned painful, grinding the bones in his hand together. "And if you hurt her—"

"Let me stop you right there," he said, cutting off the threat. "I have no intention of ever hurting Rowan. I love your daughter, sir, and I'm going to marry her. My only goal is to make sure she's safe, happy, and never forgets how much I love her. If I ever fail at that, if I ever cause her a moment's heartache, then I will personally hand you the dull knife so you can castrate me."

Gabe held his stare for a stony moment, then a slow smile spread across his stern face. And suddenly, Davey knew exactly who Rowan inherited her smile from.

"I believe you mean that." Gabe finally released his hand to sling an arm around his shoulders. "But it's not me you'll hand the knife to." He nodded toward his daughter. "She's more than capable of doing it herself. And then, after you bleed out, I'll make sure nobody ever finds your body."

Davey resisted the urge to gulp. "Understood, sir."

"Sailor, you better not be threatening him." Audrey strolled over with an arm looped with each of her daughters and gave her husband a sharp look. Her voice was a whip-crack of authority that had Gabe snapping to attention. "I won't have you scaring him away when I like him, and he's clearly head over heels in love with our girl."

Gabe held up his hands in surrender, his rough features melting into the semblance of innocent amusement. "Only making sure the boy knows what he's getting into. And that it's not me he needs to be afraid of."

Davey smiled at Audrey and held out an arm for Rowan. "Nothing could scare me away."

She slid into his arms like she'd always belonged there, her slim, muscular body fitting perfectly against his. Hazel eyes met his with a warmth that always softened the heart he'd tried so hard to harden against her.

She traced the line of his jaw with one finger. "Is that so?"

"Yeah. I'd walk through hell for you, Rowan."

Her eyes clouded. "You already have."

"I'd do it again in a heartbeat." He bent his head and pressed his lips against hers in a kiss that was sweet, full of promise. Everything else faded into the background, and it was just them…

Until Gabe cleared his throat.

Davey looked up and found Gabe scowling. Audrey beamed with approval and reached for Gabe's hand. The man let out a gruff sound but didn't pull away from his wife, holding her hand like he never wanted to let it go.

Davey knew how that felt.

"Aww." Rue clasped her hands in front of her, her eyes welling with tears. She rushed forward, enveloping them both in a hug. "I always knew you two were meant for each other!"

Davey chuckled as Rue pulled back. "Thanks for the vote of confidence. Glad someone saw it before I did."

Rowan laughed, the sound light and free, and leaned into his side. He wrapped an arm around her waist, holding her close. For the first time in what felt like forever, the weight on his chest lifted.

Audrey's smile—so much like Rue's—was bright as she clasped her hands in front of her. "Well, I, for one, am thrilled. And I hope this means we'll be seeing more of you, Davey."

"Absolutely. You'll have a hard time keeping me away."

"Good answer." Audrey's gaze shifted to Rowan, her expression turning serious. "And you, my fierce girl. Are you happy?"

Rowan hesitated. Just for a heartbeat. But it was long enough for Davey's stomach to drop. His brain took that second's hesitation and ran with it. *Why was she hesitating? Was she not sure? Was she second-guessing them?*

Then, her fingers curled tighter around his.

"Yeah, Mom." Her voice was steady. Sure. "I am. Very."

Relief crashed through him so hard he nearly swayed. Jesus Christ. He'd survived combat, near-death experiences, and some of the most brutal missions imaginable—

But that single pause had almost taken him out.

"Good," Audrey said, her voice a little rough. She stepped forward and kissed Rowan's forehead, then squeezed his arm as she turned to face him. "You keep her that way, mister."

"I plan to, ma'am."

"Well, this has been touching and all," Gabe grumbled, breaking the moment, and strode for the door. He still moved like a SEAL with only the slightest hitch in his step from his prosthetic leg. "But we've got a long drive ahead, and I'm not getting any younger. Let's wrap it up."

Audrey shot him a half-amused, half-exasperated look. It was the same look Davey's mother often gave his father. "Sailor, we're flying back."

"We've still got a drive to the airport, and there's traffic."

"Not until tomorrow morning. I told you we're staying the night, and we're taking our girl and her man out of dinner."

"I hate this city," Gabe grumbled.

Audrey rolled her eyes at her husband's back. "Sorry. He's cranky."

"He's *always* cranky," Rue added.

"I heard that," Gabe called over his shoulder, not bothering to turn around. "And I'm not cranky. Toddlers are cranky."

Rue snorted. "And old men."

"Yeah? Come over here and say that to my face, brat."

Rue grinned and bounded over to her father, wrapping her arms around his waist from behind. "You're a cranky old man," she said, her voice muffled against his back. "But we love you anyway."

Gabe's scowl softened slightly as he patted Rue's hands. "Yeah, yeah. Love you too, kid."

Despite his gruff exterior, it was clear there was a deep well of love beneath the surface.

"So, dinner?" Audrey looped her arm through Davey's and steered him toward the door. "I'm thinking that little Italian place down on Fifth. The one with the homemade pasta. What do you say, Davey? Up for some carbs and more interrogation? Oh, and you can invite your parents! I haven't seen Jude and Libby in—"

"No," Gabe growled. "Not fucking Jude. Cam and

Vaughn, fine. Reece, sure. Greer, great. But not Jude. The man is a goddamn menace. I'd rather chew glass than have dinner with him."

Audrey cleared her throat pointedly and tilted her head in Davey's direction. "Jude is Davey's father," she reminded in sing-song.

Gabe's glare softened marginally. "I mean... he's all right."

Davey smothered a smile and decided to let Gabe off the hook. "If he was anything like my brother Dom is now, 'goddamn menace' is a good description."

That got a faint smirk out of Gabe as he turned back to the door. "All right. If we're doing this dinner shit, let's move. I'm hungry. And, yeah, invite your parents."

As the group walked toward the elevator, Davey hung back to text his parents. He had planned to anyway. He wanted to see them, and he wanted his dog back. He missed Luka.

Dinner tonight? Italian place on Fifth with Rowan and me. Thought you might want to come and meet the woman I plan to marry. Gabe and Audrey will be there, too.

Mom: WHAT?!

Dad: Oh, hell yes. I never miss an opportunity to annoy Gabe Bristow.

Davey huffed out a laugh, shaking his head. Of

course. Mom was already hyperventilating, and Dad was gearing up for chaos. Gabe was definitely going to regret inviting them, and he wouldn't have it any other way.

See you soon. I'll pick up Luka after dinner.

He pocketed his phone and ran to catch up with the Bristows, only to find Rowan and Rue right there in the hall by his office door, murmuring to each other.

"We good?" Rue's voice.

He paused. The conversation seemed intense, and he didn't want to interrupt.

Rowan bumped her shoulder against Rue's. "We're good."

A flicker of something crossed Rue's face—relief, maybe. But she didn't say anything, just nodded.

Rowan's voice softened. "You know I'm always here for you, right? Even if I'm not physically with you. Just call, and I'll be there in a heartbeat."

Rue exhaled, then gave Rowan a quick hug before sprinting ahead to catch up to their parents.

Davey walked over to Rowan. "What was that about?"

Her hand slipped into his. "Sister stuff."

That was vague as hell, but he wasn't about to push. She'd tell him about it when she was ready.

She squeezed his hand and nodded toward her family. "See? That wasn't so bad."

"Easy for you to say. You weren't the one getting your hand crushed." He flexed his hand and swore he could still feel her father's punishing grip.

Rowan smirked. "Consider it a rite of passage. You survived the Gabe Bristow handshake. That's more than most can say." She tilted her head up, hazel eyes gleaming with mischief. "And, by the way... you told Dad you were going to marry me."

"Yeah, I did. Just told my parents, too."

She scoffed. "And when were you planning on telling *me*?"

"I already did. I told you I want forever."

Rowan's lips parted slightly, her steps slowing as she searched his face. "You meant it?"

He turned to her fully, lifting his free hand to tuck a stray strand of dark hair behind her ear. His thumb lingered, brushing over the delicate curve of her cheek. "I don't say things I don't mean, Hellcat."

Her breath caught.

And for once, she didn't have a snarky reply.

Instead, she curled her fingers into his shirt, fisting the fabric and dragging him closer. "Seems to me you missed a crucial step. You're supposed to ask me, Wilde."

Something in his chest snapped, unraveled, and reformed into more than he knew how to hold.

He thought of his parents and Gabe and Audrey. He wanted what they had. Thirty years from now, he still wanted Rowan pushing his buttons, driving him insane, making his life better in every single way.

And just like that, he knew.

Knew it wasn't a question of when.

Knew it wasn't about finding the right moment.

Because *this* was the moment.

Before he could second-guess himself, before he could stop to wonder if he should wait—

He dropped to one knee right there in the middle of the WSW hallway with Rowan's entire family standing at the elevator doors.

Rowan's eyes widened in shock. "Davey—"

"Marry me."

She sucked in a sharp breath, her fingers trembling where they still fisted his shirt. "That's not asking. And you don't even have a ring."

"Will you marry me?" He grinned up at her, unapologetic, reckless, and madly in love. "I'll get you a hundred rings later if you want, but I'm not waiting another damn second to make this official. You could run away from me again."

She shook her head once like she couldn't believe this was happening.

For half a second, Davey braced. This was the moment—the one where she could run, where she could push him away again.

But she didn't.

"Not this time. I'm done running."

The final piece clicked into place. Every chase,

every fight, every damn mile between them had led to this. And now she was right here, choosing him. Choosing forever.

Davey reached for her hand, pressing a kiss to her knuckles before holding it between both of his. "I love you, Rowan. I want every fight, every challenge, every stubborn second of every single day for the rest of our lives. And if you say yes, I promise—" His voice caught in his throat, and he exhaled. "You'll never have to doubt how much I love you. Not for one goddamn second."

Her lips parted, her eyes glistened, and she looked at him like he was the only thing in her world.

"Yes." She huffed out a laugh. "Like there was ever another answer."

A grin split his face just as she dropped down to him, her knees hitting the floor, her hands cupping his jaw. She kissed him like she wanted to steal the very air from his lungs.

And just as his hands slid around her waist—

"Hell, yeah!"

They jerked apart, startled, to see the entire Bristow family still standing at the elevator doors.

Rue bounced on the balls of her feet, grinning.

Gabe looked half-pained and half-amused.

Audrey sniffled and swiped her hand under her suspiciously bright eyes.

And every single one of them had just witnessed the whole damn thing.

Rowan let out a horrified groan, burying her face in Davey's chest. "Oh my God."

Davey just laughed, tightening his grip around her waist.

And then Rue plowed into them, wrapping her arms around them and nearly knocking them to the floor. "Welcome to the family, Wilde!"

epilogue

THE SCOTCH SAT untouched on the edge of the desk, the amber liquid catching the glow from the desk lamp. Elliot Wilde didn't reach for it.

Not yet. Not when his head was still a hurricane of thoughts, each one slamming into the next with the weight of everything that had happened.

Brody O'Connell.

The name alone soured his stomach, sent a sharp twist of regret cutting through his ribs.

He should have seen it.

Elliot prided himself on being the guy who noticed things. The cracks before they widened, the lies before they unraveled. He was the one with the instinct for deception, for danger lurking beneath the surface.

And yet, Brody had fooled him.

Not just fooled him. Broke him.

Hell, he'd considered him a brother. The kind of friend you take into your confidence, into your family.

Elliot had brought him into WSW.

That was the part that sat like a rock in his chest. Elliot had vouched for him. When they'd both left the military, when WSW was growing and Davey needed more trusted operatives, it had been Elliot who convinced his brother to bring Brody in.

Brody had been his guy.

Smart, sharp, loyal—or so Elliot had thought.

How many times had they worked side by side? Trained together. Covered each other's six. Laughed over beers after long missions.

And all the while, Brody had been betraying them.

A Praetorian mole, embedded inside Wilde Security Worldwide.

Feeding intel to their enemies. Sabotaging operations. Putting his people in danger.

Putting Elliot's people in danger.

And worst of all?

He'd done it with a smile.

Elliot clenched his jaw, forcing himself to stare at the tablet in front of him, files scrolling past in a blur. Daphne had decrypted everything. The extent of Brody's treachery was all laid out in black and white, cold and damning.

And now Brody was gone.

Dead.

At least, that's what they were telling themselves.

It should have made him feel better. More in control.

It didn't.

No body, no confirmation.

Which meant Elliot couldn't shake the feeling that Brody wasn't finished with them yet.

The sharp buzz of his phone cut through the silence. Elliot blinked, dragging himself back to the present as he glanced at the screen.

Rue Bristow.

He hesitated—just for a second.

The last time they talked, she'd been running her mouth about how she didn't need a babysitter in Antarctica. How Rowan and Davey were overreacting.

Elliot knew that tone. Knew her.

Knew the way she deflected with humor when she didn't want people worrying about her.

He exhaled and swiped to answer. "Rue."

The second he answered, her face filled the screen —framed in dim hotel lighting, honey-gold hair still damp from a shower, an energy drink in her hand. She looked tired. But knowing Rue, she'd never admit it.

"Hey," she said, too casual.

She wasn't pacing—yet—but he could see it in the restless twitch of her fingers against the can, like she was debating something.

That alone set him on edge.

"What's going on?"

A pause. "Rowan and Davey are nagging the hell out of me about taking an operative to Antarctica," she admitted, her voice somewhere between amusement and exasperation. "They even had Frost back them up, which feels deeply unfair. But if I have to drag someone along, it's going to be you."

Elliot's brows lifted. That, he hadn't expected. "...Me."

"Yes, you," she said like it was obvious. "Problem is, your boss-slash-brother is being a real pain in the ass about it."

"Yeah," Elliot muttered, rubbing a hand over his jaw. "He would."

Davey had been treating him like a fragile glass egg ever since the poisoned pizza incident. And when he'd reminded his brother that Davey, himself, had hated being treated like that after he returned from his last deployment with more metal than bone in his leg, it had only caused a fight.

"So, talk to him!" Rue insisted. "Tell him you're fine and want to take the job."

"Do I *want* to take the job?"

"Of course you do. You'd get to spend three whole weeks with me!"

"In Antarctica."

"I'm *extremely* good company."

"In Antarctica."

"Look, I know it's not the ideal location, but I promise to make it worth your while."

Elliot leaned back in his chair. "That right?"

"Obviously."

He could hear the grin in her voice before she even said the next part.

"I'll keep you warm."

His fingers curled around the armrest. Jesus.

She did this on purpose. Threw out lines just to watch him react, just to push that one extra inch until he gave in.

"You'll keep me warm," he repeated dryly.

"Well, sure. Body heat and all that." A pause. "Are you going to make me beg? 'Cause I don't beg."

I could make you beg.

The thought came out of nowhere, hot and sudden, and he shoved it down immediately. Jesus. Not going there. Not with Rue.

Not when she was halfway across the world, about to drop herself into one of the most isolated, dangerous places on the planet. Not when he was supposed to be thinking tactically, not about her mouth and what she'd sound like if—

Nope. Not doing this.

She huffed out a breath. "If you don't come with me, I'll just pick someone *really* incompetent. Maybe that guy who almost shot himself in the foot during training?"

Jesus Christ, she was impossible.

"Unless you want to volunteer..." she said sweetly and let the suggestion dangle.

"You mean unless Davey lets me volunteer," he corrected.

"Ugh. I know." She sighed. "Your brother is so overprotective. So are you, for that matter." She made a face. "Maybe I don't want you to come after all."

Elliot smirked. "Yeah, well, you don't exactly make it easy to look after you."

Rue gasped, offended in the way only Rue Bristow could be. "I am *very* easy to look after."

Elliot huffed a laugh. "Right. That's why your file is flagged as a flight risk."

She scoffed. "Okay, *first of all*, WSW has a file on me? Can I see it?"

"No."

"Fine." She pouted. "And, secondly, that was one time—"

Elliot arched a brow. "Four times."

"Semantics." She waved it off. "What can I say? I'm the fun Bristow sister. Rowan's the scary one."

Elliot huffed a quiet laugh. Not wrong. "Can't argue with that. Your sister once looked me in the eye and told me she could kill me with a hairpin."

Rue snorted. "She wasn't bluffing."

"Yeah, I figured."

She grinned. "But *I* would never say something like that."

"No, you'd just wing it and hope for the best."

"Because I'm the fun one," she insisted.

"You're a catastrophe in the making."

Rue gasped again, this time with dramatic flair. "Excuse you—I am a *delight*."

Elliot exhaled, rubbing a hand down his face. "A menace."

"A delightful menace," she corrected. "Anyway, since you're considering signing up for three weeks of my company, I figured you should know something important."

Elliot frowned. "That sounds ominous."

Rue tilted her head, a slow, syrupy grin spreading across her face. "Well, I hate to break it to you, El..." She leaned in slightly, those golden eyes filled with unholy amusement. "...but once Rowan and Davey get hitched? You and I are family."

Elliot froze.

She cackled, the sound bright and wicked like she was savoring every second of torturing him. "Ooooh, that look on your face. You just realized, didn't you?"

"That's not how that works," he said immediately.

"Sure it is." She took a sip of her energy drink and looked smug as hell. "I'll be your adorable, charming, favorite sister-in-law. So all those naughty thoughts you've been having about me are a big, taboo no-no."

This woman.

Elliot closed his eyes. "Rue..."

But even with his eyes closed, he could hear the grin in her voice.

"Hey, I saw your face when I made that beg comment. You were considering it. All the ways you could make me beg." She clucked her tongue. "Such naughty thoughts for a *good boy* like you."

"I don't have—" He cut himself off, jaw tightening. No way in hell he was finishing that sentence.

A beat.

"Oh, come on, El." Her voice dripped with mock innocence. "That pause was incriminating."

"I did not pause."

"You totally did."

"I was choosing my words."

She let out a low, delighted laugh. "Mmm. And yet, somehow, that only makes it worse."

"Jesus Christ." He exhaled sharply, pinching the bridge of his nose. He didn't dare open his eyes and look at her. Not when he felt heat crawling up the back of his neck. Not when he knew she was watching him, waiting, thriving off the reaction she'd just pried out of him.

"Relax." The warm, throaty sound of her laughter slid under his skin and burned like a slow fuse. "I'm flattered, really. I'd be concerned if you *weren't* thinking about me like that. I'm gorgeous, and, as we've already established, I'm a delight."

He couldn't avoid looking at her forever, so he steeled himself and opened his eyes. "I'm *not* thinking about you like that."

Her golden-brown eyes sparkled. "But now you're thinking about *not* thinking about me like that."

He rested his head back against the chair and stared up at the ceiling.

This was hell.

This was actual hell.

And if he gave in and went to Antarctica, there was a very real chance he wouldn't survive three weeks alone with her.

He could fight this. Pretend he had a choice. But that was a joke, because the second she called, he was already going.

The silence stretched for several beats, and the laughter faded from her expression. "Listen, if you really don't want to do it, just say so," she said breezily, like it didn't matter. Like he didn't already know her well enough to hear the weight under it.

He dropped his gaze back to his desk. Scowled at the untouched scotch, at the files laying out Brody's betrayal, the puzzle pieces of Pratorian's game.

A game in which Rue was an unwitting player. Frost had all but confirmed it.

And if she was in danger, there was no goddamn way Elliot was letting her go to the most isolated place on Earth alone.

He sighed. "Text me the details. I'll be there."

There was a pause, then—

"Yeah?"

"Yeah."

Rue let out a breath, quiet and quick, like she didn't want him to hear she'd been holding it. For all her bravado, she still wanted someone in her corner.

He had a feeling she didn't get that nearly as often as she should.

"You're the best, El."

The line disconnected, leaving him in silence.

Elliot sat there for a long moment, staring at his phone. Then, finally, he reached for the scotch. Instead of drinking it, he poured it back into the decanter. He wasn't getting blindsided.

Not again.

Not with her safety on the line.

And definitely not by her.

He'd need a clear head for whatever was coming.

And with Rue Bristow? Something was always coming.

The Wilde Security Worldwide adventure continues with **Wilde & Untamed**!

Elliot Wilde is a man of control. Rue Bristow is chaos incarnate. Their flirtation was always harmless—an easy game of sharp words and slow smiles. Until Antarctica traps them in a deadly mission with no rules, no backup, and only each other to rely on.

Her latest expedition isn't just about adventure. It's

about survival. And to stay one step ahead, she needs a cover story. A fake fiancé. A man she can trust.

Elliot should have said no. But when it comes to Rue, walking away has never been his strong suit.

Now, with enemies lurking in the ice and nowhere to run, the most dangerous thing between them isn't the cold.

It's the heat.